James H. Pope

# The State

The Rudiments of New Zealand Sociology for the use of Beginners

James H. Pope

**The State**
*The Rudiments of New Zealand Sociology for the use of Beginners*

ISBN/EAN: 9783337387594

Printed in Europe, USA, Canada, Australia, Japan

Cover: Foto ©Andreas Hilbeck / pixelio.de

More available books at **www.hansebooks.com**

# THE RUDIMENTS OF NEW ZEALAND SOCIOLOGY

## FOR THE USE OF BEGINNERS

# JAMES H. POPE,

*Inspector of Native Schools.*

NEW ZEALAND:
BY AUTHORITY: GEORGE DIDSBURY, GOVERNMENT PRINTER, WELLINGTON.

1887.

# PREFACE.

THE original intention with regard to this book was that it should be used by young Maoris able to understand easy English, and that the purpose of the book should be to give them clear ideas with regard to the institutions existing around them. Some progress had been made in this direction, when it became evident that, if such subjects as *rent* and *value* were to be dealt with, the original extreme simplicity of matter and of language could not be maintained throughout; and it was equally clear that unless these subjects and many others of equal difficulty were dealt with the book would be of but small utility. Accordingly the standard of difficulty was raised, and made such that young men educated at Native boarding-schools might be expected to find the new chapters just within their grasp. But then it seemed plain that if the book could thus be made suitable for this class of readers it would also be easy, by somewhat extending the scope, to make it serve the purpose of a general introduction to sociological subjects for European beginners of any age. With this object in view, therefore, fully one-half of the book was written. A few chapters of a somewhat more advanced character were added to make the work fairly complete within certain limits.

The book, then, is expected to serve three purposes: (1) The easier chapters (about one-third of the whole)* will give Maoris acquainted with the English language elementary ideas about such matters as wealth, production, money and exchange, and law and

---

* Chapters I., VI.–XI., XIV.–XVI., XX., XXIX., XXXIV.

liberty; (2) these chapters, in connection with twenty others, will serve for all beginners as an easy introduction to the social sciences; and (3) the remaining chapters* may be interesting to those who have already made some little progress in the study of sociology.

There is another purpose for which the book may possibly be of use. It covers the whole (and much more than the whole) of the ground taken up by the social science prescribed for the Sixth Standard of the public schools. As all the chapters in the book have been constructed on *skeletons*, it is very likely that most of them are in a convenient form for use as *notes of lessons* on social-science subjects. Probably a perusal of Chapters XIII.–XVI., for instance, would give a teacher who had never made such subjects a study the framework for a series of suitable lessons on exchange, money, banks, and business. Similarly, a brief study of Chapters XXIX.–XXXII. would yield a teacher a series of easily manageable lessons on the government of New Zealand.

The material used in the construction of the book has been obtained from various sources, and not without much labour. A list of the principal books that have been found useful is given on page vi. In no case has the author endeavoured to hide the source from which ideas or facts have been derived; what was found quite ready for use has been used. But only a very small portion of the book, certainly not one-twentieth of the whole, has been adopted from other writers without very considerable modifications. A good deal of the matter is altogether new, and it is so necessarily, seeing that there is no work from which established views on the subjects treated of can be obtained. It is hoped that much of this matter will be found to be true as well as new.

The author has to express his thanks for much very useful help received from the Rev. W. J. Habens, B.A., in the shape of criticism of both matter and

---

* Chapters V., XVIII., XIX., XXI., XXVI., XXVII., and XL.

style, and for many valuable hints and suggestions leading to the incorporation of new matter. While the book has been going through the press Mr. Habens has sacrificed a great deal of what ought to have been his leisure time in order to render this assistance. It should be added that the writer alone is ultimately responsible for the views stated in the book, and for the manner in which they are expressed. Thanks are due also to Sir E. O. Gibbes, of the Education Department, who has kindly read all the final revises.

The chapters on law were undertaken with considerable diffidence, but it seemed probable to the author that a short sketch of the law written by a layman having no technical proclivities might be more interesting to beginners than one written by a professional lawyer with even fifty times the author's practical knowledge of the subject. The chapters referred to have been examined and criticized by a high legal authority, who, however, is in no way responsible for the final form in which they now appear.

Although the author has been fortunate in getting so much valuable assistance, he cannot hope that mistakes have been entirely avoided. No doubt errors, perhaps grave ones, will be discovered. It is not impossible, however, that a second edition may be called for, seeing that, whatever may be the faults in the execution of the book, few critics, probably, will doubt that the general design of it is good. At all events, it is the author's intention to make the best use of such criticisms as he may be favoured with, and to prepare himself for the work of excluding from the second edition the faults that will no doubt be discovered in the first. It is hoped, however, that even in its present form the book will be found useful, and will serve the purpose intended, which is to give those who approach such subjects for the first time a good general idea of the State and its workings, and to fit them for reading with profit more advanced works on sociology.

It may be said, in conclusion, that the publication

of " The State " has no kind of political significance. The author does not know even how far its contents are in accord with the views held by the Government, or how far they disagree with those views; and he has to thank the Government for allowing him to publish the book without any restrictions of a political character.

---

List of Works from which important aid in the writing of this book has been obtained.

| | |
|---|---|
| Harmonies of Political Economy .. .. .. | F. Bastiat.* |
| Principles of Political Economy .. .. .. | J. S. Mill. |
| Progress and Poverty .. .. .. .. | H. George.* |
| Political Economy Primer .. .. .. .. | Prof. S. Jevons.* |
| Political Economy .. .. .. .. | N. W. Senior. |
| Political Economy (Art. Enc. Brit.) .. .. | J. K. Ingram. |
| Gilbart on Banking. | |
| Principles of Sociology .. .. .. .. | H. Spencer.* |
| On Prisons .. .. .. .. .. | Dr. Wines. |
| On the Care and Cure of the Insane .. .. | Dr. Glanville. |
| A Short History of the English People .. | J. R. Green. |
| The English Constitution .. .. .. | W. Bagehot. |
| Stephen's Commentaries. | |
| The Science of Law .. .. .. .. | Prof. Sheldon Amos.* |
| The Basis of Ethics .. .. .. .. | Prof. W. R. Sorley. |

The following writers also have been frequently consulted with advantage: Prof. T. Rogers, A. Mongrédien, Prof. Hearn, A. R. Wallace, A. H. Dick, Mr. and Mrs. Fawcett, Archbishop Whately, Adam Smith, Broom, G. H. Lewes, Hallam, and Sir E. Creasy. On special points much valuable information has been obtained from various articles in the Encyclopædia Britannica.

---

* Other works by those authors have also been used.

# TABLE OF CONTENTS.

---

### ERRATA.

The reader is requested to make the following corrections; most of them are, however, of trifling importance :—

Page   6. Read " State," for " tree," in the 13th line from the bottom.
  „   33. Delete " it may," in the 11th line from the top.
  „   51. Read " water-carts," for " water-cart," in the 15th line from the top.
  „  106. Read " perhaps seventy-five," for " ninety-five," in the 6th line from
          the bottom.
  „  115. Read " that may," for " who may," in the 2nd line from the
          bottom.
  „  199. Read " advantage," for " advantages," in the 14th line from the
          bottom.
  „  201. Read " Chapter XXII.," for " Chapter XXIV.," in the 4th line from
          the bottom.
  „  251. Read " the peculiar work of each," for " its peculiar work," in the
          11th line from the top.
  „  267. Insert " do," after " may," in the 17th line from the top.

# THE STATE.

## PART I.—GENERAL.

## CHAPTER I.

### INTRODUCTORY.

IF we were told that near at hand there was a great machine, working night and day with very wonderful results, many of us would gladly take the trouble to go and see this machine, to examine the work done by it, and to try, if possible, to understand all about it.

If we were told that the machine was alive; that each of its parts was made up of living creatures; that, though each of these creatures had a will of its own, and could not be actually forced to labour at all, yet, somehow, almost every one really performed its own special duty; that when one of these creatures died its work was taken up by another; that, as time went on, the whole machine actually grew and adapted itself to the kind of work it had to perform; that the moment it ceased to do this it would begin to grow weak and decay;—if we were told all this, we should probably no longer take much interest in the matter. We should begin to perceive that this wonderful machine was nothing more than the society in which we live, and about which we are prone to think that we already know everything that is really worth knowing.

The great machine here alluded to is called the State;*

* As used in this book, the word *State* means a society united for the common good under one system of law and government; but not necessarily an inde-

1

you are now invited to examine it carefully, to notice the
different parts of which it is composed, to endeavour to find out
how it was formed, to learn the nature of the powers that keep
it working, to see how its work is regulated, and to try to discover how it may most easily be preserved from danger and
decay. It is hoped that you will find your examination of this
machine more interesting than you now expect, and that in the
end you will confess that you have learnt many things about the
State that are well worth knowing.

There is a great deal of what is constantly taking place
around us that we think we could thoroughly explain without
very much trouble, but which, when we make the attempt, we find
that we cannot explain at all : the answer that we are ready to
give to a seemingly simple question we discover to be merely a
starting-point for a string of questions, each one of which is more
difficult to answer than that which preceded it. Let us take a
simple example, to show that this is true. If you were asked
to explain fully how it has come to pass that you are able to
have a cup of tea at breakfast-time, your reply would perhaps
be that tea is supplied by the grocer in exchange for money.
This would lead to these two questions : Why is a grocer
willing to receive money in exchange for his tea, and where does
he get the tea from ? You would perhaps reply that the grocer
knows that he can exchange money for anything of equal value
that he may happen to want; and that his tea was obtained from
a general merchant, who bought it from a tea-dealer in China,
who bought it from a tea-farmer, who grew it in order that he
might thereby obtain rice and clothing for himself and his
family, and be able to pay his taxes to the Chinese Government.
But, then, if you are to explain this matter fully, you may now
fairly be asked two other questions; one is this : Seeing that
hardly any one uses money itself for any other purpose or work
than that of buying and selling with it, how is it that everybody
seems so willing to take it in exchange for more useful goods or
for labour ? You have told us that every one is willing to take

pendent, sovereign, political society. The large measure of self-government
granted to this colony by the Mother-country makes it possible to use the word
State in the sense explained without practical inconvenience and without offence.
No other word would answer the purpose.

money in exchange for other things, but we wish to know how this has come about. The other question may be put thus: You say that, among other things, the tea-farmer has to pay taxes. Yes, but why do the Chinese, or any other people, pay taxes, and what right has a government to make people pay taxes? We have not nearly got to the bottom of this simple matter yet; but perhaps you see that you have already met with questions that you would find it hard to answer without thinking very carefully about them.

Let us take another case: No doubt there are in New Zealand people who would, if they could, steal whatever they happened to take a fancy to; and yet every one is able without much difficulty to keep what belongs to him. If you were asked to explain this you would probably say that the law and the police protect us from robbery; perhaps you would add that, as long as this is done for us, it does not matter much how it is done. But it does matter very much indeed: we shall find as we go on that nations that have allowed themselves to be governed without ever asking how or why their laws were made or enforced, and who have permitted a power to grow up amongst them which they could not control, have always sunk into decay and ruin. Unless, then, you really mean to neglect your country and, as far as you are concerned, let it go to ruin if it will, you should learn to answer such questions as these: What is the law, and who made it? What are the police, and what is their work? How has the law come to be just what it is? Is it well that the laws, or some of them, should be altered now and again, and, if so, how can the changes be made? Probably you would find these questions very much harder to answer than you think; but, at any rate, you should do your best with them. Even though you may not be able to learn very much about the actual practice of the law, you will find that it is a good thing to understand some of its simpler principles, which are perhaps also the most interesting and important. When you have mastered these you will not think much of the little trouble it may have cost you to do so.

Again, if you were asked to say how it has come about that a man can now travel by land from Dunedin to Christchurch in a few hours, while twenty years ago the same journey would have taken a week, and you replied that a railway has been made between the two places, you would have merely begun to answer the question. Before you could think that you had thoroughly answered it, you would have to say who made the railway, who paid for it, and how the money was obtained. When you had said that the Government made the railway, and paid for it with borrowed money, you might at once be asked this string of questions : What do you mean by the Government? Who gave them the power to make the railway ? Who lent the Government the money that the railway cost ? What do the lenders receive for the use of it ? Who has to pay this ? How and when will the debt incurred on account of the railway be paid ? Who will pay it? Will all the people receive benefit from the railway ? If not, which class of them will not ? Is there any possible way by which every one may get his proper share of the benefit? It is not likely that you could answer all—perhaps you could answer none—of these questions properly ; but it is very desirable that you should learn to answer some of them.

If you are asked how it has come about that every child in New Zealand, whether European or Maori, may obtain a good education, and you reply that the Government provides schools and teachers without charging the parents anything for them, you again only just begin to answer the question put; and in part you answer it wrongly, for most parents really do pay the whole, or nearly the whole, cost of their children's education, as will be shown further on. You might next be fairly asked, Why should the State interfere with children's school-education at all? Why should it say who is fit to teach and who is not ? Why should the State decide what children are to learn, any more than it should decide what kinds of hats and boots they are to wear ? Do you think you could answer these questions ?

Then there is the case of those who are feeble, or sick, or suffering from accident, and are without the means of supporting themselves in their trouble ; and there are those who are insane or who are criminals. All these are taken charge of by the State under certain circumstances, and provided for in one way or another for longer or shorter periods. All sorts of simple looking questions might be asked about the State's treatment of these people, and it would generally be found that the replies to those questions would at once lead us to put new questions that would be much harder to answer.

You will easily understand that many of the questions that may arise in this way about society, law, and government are so extremely difficult to deal with, that learned men, judges, and statesmen have not yet been able to determine what the proper answers to them are. These questions we shall have to leave carefully alone ; but our being unable to master difficult questions is no reason why we should not do our best with easier ones. In this book we are going to try to answer a good many of those that appear to be within our reach ; and it is hoped that the effort will prove to be both useful and pleasant.

It will not do, however, for us to be satisfied with finding answers to single questions : if we are, our work will not do us the greatest possible amount of good. We must try to find out, if we can, general rules and laws that will serve to explain a number of particular cases. For instance, after learning that some nations have been poor and others rich; that some have been strong and others weak, some industrious and others lazy, some humane and noble and others cruel and mean ; that some have sprung up very suddenly, but have soon decayed, while others have grown very slowly, have endured for many centuries, and even now show no signs of weakness ; we shall next have to consider the relations between the characters and the fates of these nations. When this has been done we shall perhaps be able to say, "All nations that act in such-and-such a way may become strong, wealthy, and happy ; those that act otherwise will surely become weak and die out."

But there is an excellent way of studying such a subject as this—a way that should not be neglected. We may try to trace the growth of the State. An illustration will show what is meant.

Suppose that three Polynesian visitors come to New Zealand at different times of the year—one in the month of June, another in September or October, and the third in February. Suppose that the attention of each of these visitors is directed to a certain peach-tree by its owner, who has planted and grown it, and that the owner explains to his visitors that the peach is one of the principal fruit-bearing trees of the colony. What different impressions the three visitors would have of the same tree! One would think of it as a bare, withered object, hardly worth a passing glance; the second would remember only the beautiful pink flowers; the third, only the delicious fruit. Even the combined knowledge of the three will would amount to very little. The owner of the tree, on the contrary, would understand the peach very thoroughly. He grew the stock, and grafted the scion on it; he watched the tree in summer and in winter, and learnt how it was affected by storm and rain, by frost and sunshine. He could tell you its whole history—how at one period it was a tender little thing that could be easily crushed or torn out of the ground; how it grew very rapidly for a time, and then more slowly; how it sometimes needed pruning and sometimes did better without it; how the blight came, what effect it had, and how it was got rid of; how one year the young fruit was so abundant that it had to be thinned out, while the previous year the crop had been very small and poor. Perhaps he could tell you, too, that manuring did not always suit the tree, and that he often found it his best plan to do next to nothing himself and let Nature do everything.

Now, the State is in many respects like a tree: at the beginning it is very small and weak; it grows up gradually, passing from one condition to another; it is subject to diseases which are often hard to cure; what suits it well at one time is hurtful at another; and its growth depends mainly on the powers of Nature, but partly also on the way in which the tree is managed by those who have the care of it. If, then, we wish to fairly understand the State we must not be content with noticing what things are going on around us now, or we shall be like the Polynesians with regard to the peach-tree; but rather we must try to find out how the State seed was planted, and what kind of soil it was placed in; we must also consider how it was affected by different kinds of treatment, and why this branch grew and flourished and why that had to be cut off. If we do this kind of work carefully we may hope that in the end we shall understand something about our great tree—the State. Perhaps one of the most important things that we shall thus learn is, that though something can be done by a Government, yet very much must be left to be done by the slowly-acting but mighty powers of Nature ever working in the minds and hearts of the people, and preparing them for changes that always take place when the proper time has arrived.

It is not necessary to say much about the importance of the subjects we are going to study : a knowledge of the laws, government, and institutions of New Zealand must be useful to all young New Zealanders, whether of European or of Maori race. You young people will soon step into the places now held by the older colonists and by the Maori chiefs that have seen Te Aotearoa change into New Zealand ; you will have to form judgments on these subjects, and to act upon them while managing the noble estate that your fathers are soon going to leave you ; and you may do very much either to make or to spoil the great nation that is being founded here in this Southern Sea. You must try to understand these things, and the sooner you do so the better. If you wait till by-and-by the chances are that you will never understand them, that you will be in a muddle about them till the very end of your lives, and that, instead of being able to manage your own affairs and to secure liberty and equal rights for yourselves and the generations that will come after you, you will have to commit yourselves to the guidance of others who will perhaps be far less mindful of your needs than of their own advancement.

# CHAPTER II.

## WHAT IT IS THAT HAS FITTED MAN FOR PROGRESS.

MAN is related to lifeless matter, to plants, and to the brute creation. Our bodies are composed of such things as those we see around us, or as may easily be brought under the observation of our senses. It has been said that a man is made of a small quantity of ashes, a few pounds of charcoal, and two or three buckets of water. In one sense this is very nearly true. As far as we know, too, this matter of which our bodies is made up is quite like other matter. If we take some common salt, dissolve it in water, boil it until a great deal of the water has gone away in steam, and then let the liquor cool, we shall find that the particles of the salt—which we know must be exceedingly small—will join themselves together so as to form crystals each bounded by six equal squares. If we did the same thing with salt got from human remains we should find that exactly the same thing would happen. So it is also with all the other materials of which the body is made up. The oxygen that is in the body does not differ from the oxygen of the air. It is true that in the body it is combined with other substances to form flesh, blood, and bone; but there is no real change in the oxygen itself. It could be separated, and it would then be found to be just what it was before it was taken into the body. "Dust thou art, and unto dust thou shalt return."

But, though we are related to matter in this way, we know that the difference between a living, thinking man and a mass of lifeless matter is enormous. In mere matter there is not even the beginning of anything like feeling or consciousness; and, though matter and mind are so closely connected, we cannot even think of them as being in any respect forms of the same thing, any more than we can think that the lightning-flash is, in another shape, the black cloud from which it seems to spring.

Man's likeness to the vegetable world is somewhat greater— that is, it would be a little less absurd to say that man is like a tree than to compare him to a rock : plants have life and growth, and in some cases something that seems very like a kind of feeling. When, however, we come to the brute creation, we find much greater resemblances. If we begin even at the bottom of the scale of animal life and gradually ascend, careful observation will show us that many of the lower animals have habits and feelings very much like our own ; indeed, we shall often be startled at the strong family likeness the lower animals bear to ourselves.

Mark the bee, and see how industrious and careful it is ; how it unites with others to promote the common good ; how bravely it will attack an enemy ; how helpful it is to its weaker brethren. Watch the ant, which does quite as much as the bee, and even more. Very likely you have read how it keeps "cattle," and how it goes to war and makes slaves, just as human beings do. Notice the little Zosterops, or wax-eye, and see how playful it is, and how much it enjoys the society of its fellows. You have learnt at school about the beaver, and the patience and skill he brings to bear upon the *public work* of constructing a safe dam. Many of us have noticed the steady perseverance of a horse on a long journey, when, though quite tired out, he has still pushed on fast, of his own accord, in order to reach a well-known stopping-place, thus encountering present pain for the sake of future rest. Who has not observed the affection and constancy of two pigeons engaged in bringing up their little family, or the valour of the game-cock, and his desire always to excel and be above others ? Have you not often read of the sagacity of the elephant, of his bravery, and of his tenderness towards the weak and the helpless ; of the grizzly bear, and his enduring desire for revenge when he considers that he has been insulted ; of the tigress, the fiercest of all wild animals, and her tender affection for her offspring, and of her contempt for danger and death while defending them. You know how faithful the dog is to his master, and how much men might learn from him in this respect. Have you not seen, too, how readily one dog will quarrel with another about the merest trifle, and how cold and distant a sleek well-fed dog is to a cur of low degree? You must have noticed the jealousy of a dog whose master has patted a stranger. And no doubt you have seen a dog thoroughly ashamed of himself after he has been beaten in a fight, or has stolen something and has been found out, or has felt himself in some way disgraced; you could hardly see a better example of the effects of the feeling of shame than that afforded by a dog with his tail between his legs, sneaking away from his offended master.

You will thus see that many of the feelings and affections, of the virtues and vices of human beings are to be found in the brute creation—some of them, indeed, in a more striking form than they ever take in the case of human beings. Nevertheless, there is a very great difference—an immense difference—between a man and a brute, even between an exceedingly stupid man and a very clever dog. It must be most important to find out exactly what the nature of this difference is. Most probably several elements combine to cause man's superiority over the brutes, but the only element on which we need insist at present is his power of making progress in the arts of providing for his own comfort and well-being and of developing social institutions.

It is remarkable that so many animals are like man in one respect or another, and yet that so few of them have hit upon the plan of living a social life, while those that have, such as the beaver, the ant, and the bee, have never got beyond doing what is necessary to secure food, shelter, and protection. Men, on the contrary, combine for all sorts of purposes that have little or nothing to do with the mere procuring of food and protection. But the really important difference is that, while brutes remain as they are, man makes progress—that when one difficulty has been overcome by him another is immediately attacked. Thus, in New Zealand we find first the bush-track, then the bridle-path, then the mud-road, then metal, and last the railway, coming fast one after the other. The lower animals— even the cleverest of them—go only so far and no further. We have no reason to think that a hive of wild bees of the present day differs from a hive of two thousand years ago. There is no reason to believe that ants are making any kind of progress. But compare what we have here in New Zealand, our railways, public buildings, libraries, schools, churches, and home comforts, with what existed in Britain two thousand years ago, or with what was to be found in New Zealand fifty years ago, and you will not doubt that man moves on.

It is plain, then, that man has some faculty that fits him not only for complex social life, but also for progress in that life. What is this faculty? It cannot be the mere power of joining with others for a certain object : ants and bees excel him in this. It cannot be valour, or fidelity, or steadiness of purpose, or strong affections. He is surpassed in each of these respects by one or more of the lower animals. Can it be that there is something altogether new in man? Can it be that, just as life when applied to matter produces quite a new thing, with entirely new powers, so an entirely new faculty bestowed on man has made him leave the brute far behind? Can it be that if man's great gifts are rightly used they in the end place him as far ahead of the mere animal as the animal is in advance of mere senseless matter?

Brutes are the slaves of the conditions by which they are surrounded to a much greater extent than men are. If animals can find enough food to support them they live; if they cannot they die. None of them have found out how to grow food. If the weather suits them they live and thrive; if not they die. It is so throughout. It may be said, as a general rule, that if the lower animals are by nature suited to the circumstances in which they are placed, they live, and if not they perish. Man, on the contrary, can alter his surroundings and make them suit him. If he is likely to want food he grows it; if the rain is troublesome the sheep or the india-rubber tree supplies him with a great-coat; if he is cold he makes a fire; and so on. Thus it comes about that in the heat of the tropics or in the cold of the polar regions, in the fertile valley or the sandy desert, on the sea or on the land, man can make himself a home, and live and do well. It is plain that man's power of altering things so that they may suit him is a very important one, and that it must be one of the things that make progress possible; but it cannot be the only one, seeing that ants, and bees, and some other animals have it to a degree that enables them to construct dwellings and store up food. By itself, this power of making his circumstances suit himself would only cause man to be very clever in securing food and avoiding death. The real advantage possessed by man is this: Brutes cannot store up their knowledge and experience, and hand them down to those that come after them; man, being endowed with a faculty of speech which enables him to form and hand down general ideas, has this power. Thus, it is easy to see, the knowledge gained by one generation of the brute creation must die with them, the next generation having to go over the same ground again; there can therefore be no increase of knowledge for them, though there may be a very slow improvement of their natural powers. But the knowledge possessed by one generation of men is passed on to the next; and these, instead of having to begin where their fathers did, can start where they left off. That is to say that, as soon as children have by practice got their powers of thought into full working order, they are ready to make use of all that has been thought and done by their fathers, and to add to it the results of their own thought and observation. It seems, then, that men differ from the brutes in having a faculty of which speech is the sign and the instrument, and that it is this that has made them capable of progress.

As the store of knowledge grows larger the pleasure and use of adding to it become better known, and men work harder to increase it. Every faculty, too, becomes stronger the more it is used, and as time goes on men become better able to make use of their knowledge and to add to it. Now, as parents have a tendency to hand down their mental as well as their bodily powers to their offspring, it is plain that, when man, possessing as he does the faculty of speech, no longer has to struggle for his life with wild beasts, he can hardly help advancing, though perhaps he moves very slowly at first; and it seems certain also that there can be no limit to man's progress in the future if he will only make a proper use of the grand gifts that have been bestowed upon him. He must go on, and gain strength by going.

It all amounts to this, then; what fits man for progress is

his power of storing up and using the knowledge of others, and he has gained this power through being able to hear and understand speech. If he wishes to add in the future to the progress that he has made in the past, he must continue by careful observation and thought to increase his store of knowledge; he must also increase his wisdom by training himself to make proper use of his knowledge.

# CHAPTER III.

## HOW A STATE IS FORMED.

More than two thousand years ago a very clever Greek fell into serious trouble by declaring that he thought the sun might be larger than Greece. Men had settled in their own minds that the sun, or Helios, as he was called, was a divine person, and that to talk about him in any such way was very wicked indeed. We now know for certain that the sun is not a person, but an enormous globe of matter, like that of which the earth is composed, but exceedingly hot, and that its bulk is nearly thirteen hundred thousand times that of the earth. The sun shines down upon us just as it did upon the Greeks; for us, as it was for them, it is the supporter of life and the provider of nearly every comfort that we possess; only, we know a great deal more about the sun than the Greeks did.

The relation of people of the present day to the history of the men of the most ancient times is not exactly the same as that of the Greeks to questions concerning the nature of the sun, but there are so many differences of opinion with regard to the subject, and so little is as yet proved and known about it, that we may fairly consider it as being one of the things that are too difficult for us to deal with, and we therefore leave the history of the earliest men untouched. It is certain, however, that man does not always remain exactly the same : nations rise from the savage to the civilised condition ; nations also fall from a lofty to a lowly position. It is certain also that at the present day there are still many tribes, and even peoples, in an extremely barbarous and uncultured condition. Discoveries have been made of late years which render it possible to understand how a tribe or a people in this condition may gradually rise till they become perfectly civilised. It has even been thought possible to sketch the history of peoples supposed to have thus risen.

It may be asked how it can be possible to construct a probable history of a savage tribe that knew nothing about books or writing. In the first place, it may be answered, careful observation of trifling circumstances may often yield most important information. If while taking a walk through the bush we came to what had evidently been an old cooking-place, and if, on turning up the ground with a stick or a knife, we saw one or two stone axes, a great number of cockle-shells, some bones, and a greenstone ear-ornament, what should we think? We should feel almost certain that Maoris had been there, and also that they had probably lived in the neighbourhood.

Conclusions arrived at in this way may possibly be false ; but perhaps other knowledge possessed by the observer may afford him the means of making necessary corrections. If we entered a cave and found moa-bones mixed with human bones, what ought we to think — that Maoris and moas had lived at the same time, and had gone into the cave to die? We might think this at first, but a little reflection would show us that it was more probable that the moas had died in the cave a very long time ago, and that the human bones had been placed there much more recently : first, because we have no reason to think that the Maoris ever knew anything about the moa, seeing that it was an Englishman—Professor Owen—who first found out that its bones were those of a bird ; and, in the second place, because we know that it is the practice of the Maoris to take up dead bodies of chiefs after they have been buried for a year or two, to scrape the bones carefully, and then to send them away in charge of one or two of the oldest men of the tribe to be hidden away by them in the most secret places they can find.

Careful reasoning about observed facts may even render it possible to say whether events of which neither history nor tradition is preserved took place a long or a short time ago ; for instance—if you lived near a river that overflowed its banks once every year, and you found that after every flood there was left behind a very thin layer of mud—say, of about the thickness of a threepenny-piece—you might believe that in time the ground would rise to some extent; but would you not think that it would take a very long time for it to rise fifty feet? If you were afterwards told that on the banks of another great river, the Nile, wells had been sunk to a great depth; that it seemed certain that the soil had been formed in much the same way as it was on the banks of the river with which you were acquainted; and yet that the men who had dug these wells had found pieces of bricks and broken pottery at the very bottom of them,—would you not say that the people who used those bricks and pots must have lived a very long time ago?

We have given these illustrations and explanations in order that you may see how things that happened in times long gone by are found out and reasoned about. We may now state an important result arrived at by similar means, but we must not stop to go into particulars. Sharpened flints, stone axes, tools and weapons of many different kinds, and skeletons of men and bones of animals that have evidently been killed and eaten by men, have been found in such places as to show that, even long before the Nile mud began to be laid down in its valley, men in a backward stage of civilisation lived and worked, and suffered and died.

Let us now endeavour to trace the steps by which an utterly rude and uncivilised race of men might gradually become fit to form a State. In doing this, we shall make what use we can of the facts that have been brought to light by careful study of the traces that ancient man has left behind him.

Men of science tell us that there is a very wide gap between the lowest man and the very highest ape. No skull has yet been found about which there could be a doubt as to whether it belonged to a man or to an ape; for, while the smallest full-grown human skull yet found could, if all the holes in it were stopped with clay, contain 62 cubic inches of water, the skull of the largest ape would hold but $34\frac{1}{2}$. There can therefore be no sound reason for saying that any kind of man we know about is the near relation of any kind of ape that we have seen or heard about.

Judging from skulls and skeletons found, we may say that the very rudest savage seems to have been a man, every inch of him—he had his hand, his brain, and his erect gait; but for all that he must have led a very poor kind of life. He lived on wild berries and fruits, and, probably, such small animals as he was strong enough to catch and destroy with his hands, feet, and teeth. When he lived near the sea-shore his chief food was cockles and shell-fish. No doubt he would, along with his fellows, engage in fights with larger animals, perhaps of species that have long been extinct. In these fights he would sometimes come off second-best. His cunning and his hand would by-and-by enable him to use sticks and stones in his contests. He would be sure to find out that a sharp stone fastened to a stick with some kind of fibre would make a useful weapon. He would next hit upon the plan of sharpening one stone by rubbing it upon another. He could now hardly fail to discover that his stone axe might be used for many purposes—amongst others, for cutting wood and shaping other weapons that he might wish to make.

Then, perhaps he would, on some very hot day, learn how to make a fire by rubbing two pieces of wood together; and soon the plan of using fire to hollow out a tree for a canoe would occur to him. In the summer, instead of being constantly in his cave, he would live out in the open air, making a rough shelter of boughs to sleep under at night, just as the Australians do to this day. He would soon find that with the aid of a fire he could manage to live thus during spring and autumn. Then he would perhaps discover that by digging a square hole in the side of a slope, making a framework with the timber that his axes would enable him to cut, and covering the whole with rushes and mud, he would be able to do almost entirely without his miserable cave. All this time his skill in fighting and con-quering wild beasts would be increasing. He would surely have learnt that advantages could be gained by two or more working together—that they could thus get more to eat, with less work. A sort of rude friendship might thus have been formed, especially among those that had been neighbours from childhood; groups would gradually become distinct : certain men, women, and children would move about together, just as the Victorian blacks used to do thirty years ago, and these would by-and-by look upon themselves as a group or tribe separated from all others.

2

Generally, there seem to be three well-marked stages of savage life. It is the custom to call these periods Ages, though the term stages would be much more correct. The first of these is called the Stone Age. During this period all tools and weapons were made of stone. At first these were very rudely shaped, but as time went on improvement took place. Men soon learnt to make canoes, and at the end of the Stone Age they had even learnt how to make a coarse kind of pottery. Then came the Bronze Age. It had now been found out how to work some of the softer metals, to construct fairly comfortable dwellings on piles, to build pretty large boats, and to make shields and swords of bronze, which contained nine parts of copper to one of tin. At last the Iron Age arrived. When men had got on so far as to be able to deal with iron, they were well on their way towards civilisation. Iron is so difficult to smelt that people who can manage to smelt it are almost sure to be able to do a great many other things. It should be mentioned, however, that the Fan, a people in Western Africa, who are in many respects still very savage, are able to work iron; this shows that too much stress must not be laid on the method of measuring the progress of peoples by finding what metals they can work. A further proof of the uncertainty attached to this means of estimating human progress may be stated. In very ancient times there were men living on the Swiss Lakes who built large wooden platforms on piles driven into the water; on these platforms, which were sometimes more than an acre in extent, they erected houses of considerable size. These people made canoes and fish-hooks, and made and burnt pots and pans; they also kept horses and cattle, and grew wheat and apples. Yet the men that lived on these platforms knew nothing of either bronze or iron, all their weapons and tools being made of either wood, bone, or stone. But, although they were still in the Stone Age, they must already have been somewhat advanced in civilisation and in comfort.

During the earlier periods of the Stone Age it is likely that men were exceedingly wild and savage; for but little gentleness or culture could be expected among people whose whole lives were passed in fighting with wild animals and their fellow-men. Still, even in very early times men were much more clever and took far more pains to amuse themselves than we should have expected. In some of the caves containing the remains of Stone-Age men of very early times, carvings in bone and horn, very well done, have been found. Like the uncivilised Eskimo of the present day, the earliest men of the Stone Age did not bury their dead; but long before the end of that age much attention was paid to this matter.

It may occur to those who have read English history that when the Europeans arrived in this country the Maoris had not yet found out the use of iron, and were still in the "Stone Age;" and that, although they seem to have been as far advanced in most respects as the Britons were when Julius Cæsar visited them nearly two thousand years ago, yet the Britons then knew the use of iron, seeing that they had iron scythes fastened to the axles of their war-chariots. The explanation is that, though the Britons were very. rude and barbarous themselves, they had long been within reach of more civilised nations; for the Romans and the Phœnicians had long traded with some of them for tin and other things. Thus the Britons had had the chance of learning certain arts which they were not yet far advanced enough to discover for themselves. The Maoris, on the other hand, had been for long ages cut off from the outer world, and had had to find out for themselves everything that they knew.

We shall here merely suggest how family ties somewhat resembling our own might grow up amongst the members of a savage tribe living in mere groups. No doubt the institution of the true family in such a group would generally (perhaps always) be caused by some impulse from outside the group, perhaps by contact with a thoroughly civilised nation. Still, it has been thought possible to show that many of the family relationships known to us might gradually grow up among a people entirely without them—among.a people having customs like those of the Tibetans, or the Nairs of Malabar—that among a group of human beings that had long lived without any true family ties, the family—consisting of a man, his wife, and children—might by-and-by be recognised. If some powerful man were to establish his claim to be master of a family by fighting and overcoming those who disputed it, afterwards, perhaps, the same sort of arrangement would be made throughout the whole group or tribe.

Then, if the people in the district were few in number, it would most likely come about that the families would be scattered for a time; that each family would live apart from the rest; that each man would rule his wife—or, perhaps, his wives—and his children, and would be their sole master and lawgiver. In the course of time these families would be much enlarged: marriages would take place, and other events might cause outside people to become members of the family. Then, though the character of the family would be much altered, the father would still hold the supreme power, and would now, perhaps, be known by such a name as chief, headman, *eorl*, or *ariki*, and would rule the whole family just as he had been accustomed to rule his wives and children. In such cases as these, perhaps, the bond between the members of a household would hardly be stronger than that between any individual and the whole of the family. For if any wrong was done to any member it would be the business of the whole family to have that wrong set right. The same kind of obligation exists among the Maoris to this day.

Family ties once formed, we may be sure that, as time went on, various other improvements would take place. Gradually the arts of growing food by planting seeds, and of taming the young of wild animals, would be found out. Then people would learn to fence in their cultivations, and other arts would spring up: progress would lead to progress—perhaps to more rapid progress. At first everything that a tribe possessed, including their land, would be used by everybody, but there would soon be rough ideas about ownership; for it would be found convenient that a man who tilled a piece of ground and planted seed should get the fruit, and that he who tamed a beast should have the best right to its milk and flesh. Still, for a long time everything would be in common to a certain extent, and it would be only after a vast number of quarrels and disputes that it would be found to be a convenient custom for every man to have as his own all that he had worked for. Gradually other useful customs would grow up, and at last we should probably find people, all observing the same customs, scattered over the district and living in little groups wherever the land was good, or on the sea-coast where fish could be procured, or in places that were easy to defend against an enemy. This is just what Europeans found when they came to New Zealand.

Let us suppose, now, that the people of a country have got so far on that they have already made some progress in the arts of tilling the ground, of building fairly comfortable dwellings, and of making clothing ; that they live in families or groups, and are ready to band themselves together to defend any one or more of their number from injury ; that certain customs have grown up among them (such as *tapu* amongst the Maoris) which are respected by everybody ; and that there is a certain amount of agreement among them as to a man's right to enjoy what he has worked for.  In a society of this kind there is always a strong tendency for the family, consisting of father, mother, and children, or, for larger groups like the hapus of the Maoris, to unite with other families or groups, in order that the safety of all may be secured, along with other advantages that separate families or small groups can hardly hope to possess.  If it were not for tribal jealousy and hatred—generally the results of acts of violence committed by individuals of one tribe on those of another, and leading on, of course, to revengeful deeds—union would always very soon follow the formation of numerous families or groups.  Causes of many sorts may at last bring about a union that will lead to the formation of a real State.

We have now reached the point at which we begin to emerge from the region of probability, and to come among certainties.  Hitherto we have had no guide except our power of inferring from a few—sometimes a very few—observed facts a possible or probable explanation of them.  Now, however, we can begin to make use of the lights of real history.  These lights burn dimly at times, but on the whole they enable us to see our way instead of guessing it.  We have no longer to do with what may have been, we have come on that which has been or is.  With the aid of history, then, let us see how the union that leads to the formation of a real State may be caused.

About a thousand years ago numerous bands of men in small vessels used to set out from Norway and Denmark to rob and plunder people that could not defend themselves.  A great many of these vessels went to Normandy ; and the pirates, finding it a pleasant country, much better than their own, determined to settle there.  They soon got families around them ; but, being intruders, they knew that they were not safe unless they stood firmly by one another. This they did, and so a great State came into being.

The descendants of these people, under William the Conqueror, attacked and subdued England. All the races of people in England were made to obey the Norman laws for a long period, and, as time went on, English, Normans, Danes, and Celts gradually became bound together and formed a great compact State, which took the place of the weaker Anglo-Saxon State that had preceded it.

In Arabia some twelve hundred years ago the people were divided into tribes or very large family groups, with very little union amongst them. A great lawgiver, statesman, and general, the false prophet Mahomet, brought forward a new religion, and, after many hard struggles and much fighting, at last succeeded in banding the people together for the purpose of spreading the new faith. Here, again, a mighty and long-enduring State was brought into being.

Sometimes a number of small States combine to form one large State. Bismarck, now Chancellor of the Empire of Germany, perceiving the desire of the Germans for union, made the best use of an opportunity that occurred, and united them. The result was that a very powerful State, the great German Empire, was formed through the union of many weaker ones.

Our own little State has come into being somewhat differently; it may be compared to a layer from a mulberry-tree, planted in a new soil, and grafted with shoots from other mulberry-trees. But here, as elsewhere, it is union of the various peoples in the colony—English, Maoris, French, Germans, and others—that is the basis of our State. The Maoris by themselves were never able to form anything resembling a State; their tribal jealousies were far too strong to allow any considerable number of them to unite for any purpose whatever.

If, then, you are asked to say how a State is formed, you may reply that when a large number of families, groups, or small tribes are scattered over a country, and some cause has made them unite for a common purpose, the formation of a State has been begun. When the groups or tribes have ceased to aim only at getting as much good for themselves as they can, even if it be at the expense of the other groups, and have learnt to consider themselves as part of a great whole, for whose interests they must be prepared, if necessary, to suffer some hardship when their turn comes; and, above all, when they have learnt to connect the future with the present, and to look forward with pleasure and with pride to the coming greatness of their nation;—then the formation of the State is complete.

It may be that in the far future it will become plain that there should be only one State, and that all peoples ought to combine for the good of all; but the day when this will take place must be very far off, and till it comes men may well believe that one of the noblest works in which they can engage is the promotion of the welfare of the State to which they belong.

# CHAPTER IV.

## THE PROPER WORK OF THE STATE AS A WHOLE.

So far we have spoken of a State only in a general way. We have shown that it is one of the results of man's progress. You have seen that when once men are ready to become members of a large society they may be brought into union by various causes. A common danger may unite them and form them into a State, or a new religion may do it. Foreign laws may, if strictly enforced, unite peoples of different race and language, and in time form them into a real State. A colony may be sent out from a State, and, after uniting with or conquering the original inhabitants of the new country, and having its numbers increased by colonists from other States, may form a new State not unlike that from which it sprang. You have seen, also, that through the spread of some grand idea, such as that all the people of one race should form a single nation, many small nations may combine and form one great State. There are many other causes that may determine when and how a State may be formed; but we have mentioned enough for our purpose.

You must not think that people always know when they are combining to form a State, or that a State is perfect the moment the union has taken place. When a large number of people have been made to feel strongly the need for union they unite; but often they are not in the least aware that they are forming a State: they have combined for this purpose or for that, and the consequence is that they are bound together as one nation, but perhaps they hardly know it. Sometimes, too, long ages will pass by before all the old barbarism is got rid of. The people belonging to a real State may not all be free—the rich may oppress the poor ; there may be a ruling caste, and all the others may be little better than slaves—but, when once real union has taken place, a State has been born, though it has yet to grow up.

You may now go on to learn what purposes a State should always have in view, and what kind of work it should try to perform. To begin with, you may safely take it for granted that the chief object aimed at by a State should be to secure the greatest possible amount of safety, comfort, and general well-being for all the people that compose it. In order to secure this object, the first and the principal thing to be settled is that all shall combine to secure the good of all, and that each must therefore give up the habit of acting quite independently, of doing things without considering what their effect will be on others : that is, every member of the State must be prepared to sacrifice his own freedom of action when such a sacrifice is necessary in order to promote the general welfare. Then, law and government are needed. It is plain that some person or persons must have the power to decide what duties must be performed or what conduct must be refrained from by the members of the community. In modern times and in free States it is believed that this power is best used when it is in the hands of the majority of the people. Further on in this book it is explained how this matter is dealt with in New Zealand. It will suffice to say here that the people of New Zealand manage their own affairs almost entirely, and that our own State is probably as well governed as any that is to be found in the world.

You may now consider what particular kinds of work a State should undertake. In most societies, whether large or small, some of the members give trouble to the others. The ruder the society the more trouble of this kind there is. In a community not yet formed into a State there are always many men who, in fits of anger or from mere wantonness, are ready to assault or to kill any one whom they may dislike or who may have offended them ; and there are others who will not respect the rights of owners, but will take what does not belong to them whenever they can. Now, unless there is some power that can put this kind of thing down, every one feels himself very unsafe. A man whose neighbour was robbed or killed yesterday cannot be sure that his own turn will not come to-day. It soon gets to be felt that this state of matters must be put an end to, that they who act thus must be restrained, and that it is not right that all should be made uncomfortable and unhappy through the conduct of some. Steps must be taken to make violent and dishonest people behave properly, and to punish them if they will not do so. All must combine to restrain those who are really the enemies of all. One of the first duties, then, that a State undertakes is to provide protection for all its members.

As time goes on people learn to submit to these needful restraints, and even to take pride in doing so. Acts of violence become very rare. People learn to keep their wild and savage tendencies under control, and to get their pleasure and happiness in such ways as do not bring trouble or unhappiness to others. If this process goes on it must in the end result that every one will find himself able to do just what pleases him without annoying others. To bring this about is to render a service of the highest order, and the State could hardly have a nobler aim than to arrange things so that every one shall be safe from all kinds of violence, and shall be free to do whatever pleases him, provided that what so pleases him does not prevent others from enjoying the same freedom.

Another duty of the State—on the performance of which its very existence depends — is to protect itself and its members from injury by a foreign State. In extreme cases it may be necessary for the State to gather all its forces together and fight with the utmost bravery in order to save itself from destruction. Unfortunately, most nations, as far as regards their relations with other nations, are still quite uncivilised, and choose to settle their disputes by brute strength and acts of violence instead of bringing them before Courts of Arbitration. While nations remain in this brutal condition it is to be feared that even the best and wisest States will sometimes have to go to war in their own defence.

All writers on the subject agree in thinking that it is the duty of the State to protect itself and all its members from violence and robbery ; but many of them stop just there, and say that this is all that a State should do—that, having given men freedom to go their own way, it should let them go that way. One of the first of living writers appears to hold this view very strongly. When speaking of education he says, "Conceding for a moment that the Government is bound to educate a man's children, then what kind of logic will demonstrate that it is not bound to feed and clothe them?" But, as this writer believes that the State should afford protection, some one might ask him this question : "Conceding for a moment that the Government is bound to protect a man's children, then what kind of logic will demonstrate that it is not bound to feed and clothe them?" The fact is that the State is not bound either to educate or to protect a man's children, but it does both because the members of the State believe that both of these works may be done better by the people as a whole than by private individuals. Consider what hardship would be inflicted on us as individuals if as a State we said, "Well, we are going to take this writer's advice, and do nothing but protect people. We are not going to carry their letters any more ; this work must be left to private individuals." At first the expense of sending letters would, of course, be enormous ; but, by-and-by, perhaps a company would take the matter in hand ; then there would be opposition, other companies would be formed, and a great many more people would be employed in the work than there are now. These would have to be paid with part of the wealth of New Zealand, as the Post Office people are ; but there would be many more workers to keep, and so the cost of letter-carriage would be higher, and there would be a great waste of labour. Besides, the work would not be very well done. Those people that live in out-of-the-way places would hardly ever get letters at all without paying heavily for the carriage of them. One of the effects of this would be that people would be less willing than they are now to settle in and open up places of this description, because they would feel that they were shutting themselves out from communication with the rest of the world. Thus we see that if the State, instead of undertaking the carriage of letters, let every man get his own letters carried, the work would cost a great deal more and would not be so well done. Nothing has been said about money-orders, savings-banks, parcels, and other things that it has been found possible for the Post Office to deal with ; but a very long chapter might be written about this extra Post-Office work and the inconvenience that would result from leaving it to private individuals.

A great many rather foolish notions about what the State should and should not do have been handed down to us from the evil times when there was no such thing as the kind of State that New Zealanders know. These notions belong to times when the people might have been divided into the rulers and the idle classes on the one hand, and, on the other, those who might fairly be called slaves, seeing that their function was to work for the other class and be governed by them. In some countries it has been even worse than this, for a certain French king was able to say, "The State! I am the State!"

Now, in New Zealand the people can say, "The State! We are the State." Everything is in our own hands. We appoint this man to do this work, and that man to do that work; and if we find that the work is well done we honour and respect the men that do it. It will be shown further on that New Zealand is one of many States that together form the British Empire and are subject to the British Crown; but practically, in our relations to the State and to one another, we New Zealanders know of no power outside of ourselves. In many countries, even at the present day, through the ignorance or cowardice of the people, who are still willing to be slaves, there is a power in which the people have no share; but in this country the highest officers of the Government have no more power than the poorest Maori has, apart from that conferred upon them by the people of New Zealand. Well, then, seeing that there is no State outside of ourselves— that we are indeed the State—is it not rather ridiculous to look upon the State as an enemy that will do us harm if it can, and whose help we must do without if possible? Why should we say that the State must not do this, and must not do that? Why should we not make full use of our freedom to do what we think best? What is to hinder us from combining to do what we believe will be done better by the whole of us together than it will if it be left to private individuals? It must be remembered that even protection of life *might* be left as a matter for private persons to manage. As a State we *might* say, "We will carry people's letters for them; but for the future every man must take care of himself—it will make men hardier and more self-reliant." The reason why we do not say this is that we know, through our forefathers having tried this plan, that it answers very badly. This leads us to the conclusion that it is impossible to lay down any fixed rule as to what the State, acting as a whole, should or should not do, and that each case must be dealt with as it arises. If experience has shown us that any work that most of the members of the State want done is badly done by individuals, there is and can be no reason why the State should not take it in hand, and try to manage it better.

And now let us attempt to state exactly what we mean by a State—that is to say, a State in its perfect form. A State is a considerable society of persons who live under one particular system of law and government, and who combine to do the following work for the whole society and for each member of it in every case in which they consider united action necessary : (a) To protect each and all from being injured by the actions or through the negligence of any individual or class in the society, and to defend the whole community from injury by any individual or class, or by a foreign State ; (b) to perform services for the whole people (or for individual persons in it), which, in the opinion of the State judging as a whole, are likely to promote the general welfare, and which cannot be as well performed in any other way ; and (c) to make it possible for every one to do whatever pleases him, so long as what pleases him does not interfere with the freedom of others to do what pleases them, and does not hinder the efforts of the community to reach a higher stage of progress.

To this we may add that, natural hindrances being equal, the State will do its work well or badly accordingly as the motives of the people are high or low, and are regulated by wisdom and right feeling based on sound knowledge, or are governed by folly based on ignorance. For the wiser and better the people of a State are, the more likely are the rulers chosen by the people to be wise and good also, and the greater is the chance that the rules made by them will secure the general welfare with the least possible loss of freedom on the part of the individual members of the State.

Your chief aim in your enquiries about the State should be to discover when, where, and how these conditions have been most nearly approached, and to find out how they may best be reached now.

# CHAPTER V.

## WORK OF THE STATE AS A WHOLE.—APPLICATION OF PRINCIPLES.

It is well for a man to have noble aims, and to be able to say in clear and precise terms what these aims are. The State also ought to know what line of conduct it intends to follow, and ought to set before itself well-marked rules and principles. But such rules must always be general; that is, they cannot be made to suit every possible case unless what is called common-sense—the faculty that enables practical men to form wise judgments about ordinary matters—is also brought into play. Let us see whether the rules stated at the end of the last chapter, along with this common-sense, will help us to deal properly with some of the questions that are raised with regard to the work that the State does or refuses to do.

In New Zealand a large proportion of the people have some knowledge of the laws of health, they wish to act in accordance with this knowledge, and they are very willing to bear the burden of the trouble and expense of keeping their premises clean and wholesome. Others, again, know very little about these laws of health, and care even less : if disease and death come, such persons are troubled by them as other people are, but they would never of themselves think of doing what doctors say will prevent disease. Now, the question is, Why should these people be meddled with in any way ? If they like to live without fresh air, and to have filthy outhouses and· no drains, why should the State interfere with them ? Those who break Nature's rules must suffer for it, and man is taught by suffering; if a householder gets an attack of typhoid fever through sleeping near a cesspool he will learn, perhaps, that cesspools are bad things to have near a dwelling, and will get his removed.

It may be right to try to persuade people to keep their houses clean, but it is another thing to force them to do so. Can it be that people do not know what suits them best, or that those who think they are wise should force the ignorant to do what it is thought will keep them in good health? The answer to all this is that there is, perhaps, no reason why people should not live filthily if they are determined to do so, if only they will go and live in the bush or in some place where they can do no harm to others ; that it has been proved beyond all doubt that diseases caused by want of cleanliness spread from those who are dirty to those who are clean ; and that people who wish to live with other people must observe the rules that have been made for the good of all. The first duty of the State is to protect each and all from being injured by the action or the negligence of any individual or class in the society.

There are many persons who see hardly any good in education. They have had little or no schooling, they say, and they have got on pretty well without it; their children too will most probably always be labouring people, and it would be useless to fill their heads with such stuff as is taught in schools. There are others, again, who think education rather a good thing, but find their boys and girls so useful that they prefer to keep them at home, or, at all events, they try to withdraw them from school at an early age. Many of these people think that the law that compels them to keep their children at school till they have been fairly educated is a very hard law, and that it interferes with people's freedom. This idea of freedom seems to be something like that of the American who said that " freedom " meant the right of every man to thrash his own nigger. But, after all, what right has the State to interfere between parents and children ? Why should a man be compelled to educate his children if he thinks it better not to do so ? Why should he be forced to do without the help they can give him in order that they may be made to conform to the State model, of which perhaps he does not approve ? The answer to these questions depends greatly upon the meaning of the word " his " in the second of them. If it means that the children belong to their father in the same way as a slave belongs to his master, perhaps it is rather difficult to answer these questions. But even then it may be said that the time will come when the child will cease to *belong* to his father, and will become a member of the State; and that, looking forward to that time, the State is bound to do its best to have the child properly trained to take his place in the State and to do his share of the State's work. It might be added that experience has shown that as a rule educated men and women are far more desirable members of society than those who are not educated; that it is quite plain that the progress of a nation depends very largely on the degree to which the people are educated; and that, while the State tries to make it possible for every man to do whatever pleases him, it is on the condition that his doing what pleases him must not hinder the efforts of the community to reach a higher stage of progress.

If, on the other hand, you use your common-sense, and refuse to consider a man's children *his* in the way in which his dog, his pig, and his gun are his; and if you look upon children as members of the State from the moment of their birth, and as *persons* having rights and privileges just as the other members of the State have; you will be compelled to say that the State is bound to see that a child suffers no injury from the action or the negligence of his parents, and, especially, to have him educated in such a way as is likely both to promote his own welfare and to enable him when he is grown up to manhood to discharge his duties to the State effectively. The parent has a parent's rights, but the child has his rights too: one of these is that he shall be saved from growing up a fool through the neglect of an ignorant, greedy, or careless parent. The State must enforce this right, if necessary, seeing that the child cannot do it for himself. The State must protect each and all of its members from being injured by the action or through the negligence of any individual in the society.

In England all the great railways, extending over many thousands of miles, have been made by private companies, and not through the action of the State as a whole. Would it not be well if all States left railway-making to companies? It is true that States might sometimes have to wait a few years longer for their railways; but would not the work be better done, would not better routes be chosen, and would not the lines be in every way better managed by private companies than by a State?

Private companies, looking out only for profit, will make a line
only where it is certain or almost certain to pay, and will not be
induced to make one where it is certain that it will not pay;
the work, instead of being done according to a fixed plan that
may suit one district, but not another, will be adapted to circumstances; large bridges will not be put up where smaller ones
will do; carriages suitable to the particular trade will be used;
and so on. Then, seeing that the railway has to be made to
pay, things will be so managed that the convenience of the people
rather than that of the railway officers will be kept in view, in
order that as many people as possible may be induced to it may
travel. Now, even if we suppose State management to be defective,
it may still be better that railways should be in the hands of the
State—that is, of the whole people—for this reason : Any fault,
anything that may at any time be wrong, in the management
of State railways can be righted. If anything does go wrong
how soon complaints are made in the newspapers and in Parliament ! These complaints are considered by the Government, and
if they are well founded the cause of them can soon be removed.
Really the only cases in which mistakes that cannot be immediately set right are made are those in which railways are given
to districts that do not yet require them; and time itself will
most likely correct most of these mistakes, for if the railways do
not pay at once they probably will in a few years' time. But,
on the contrary, in the case of railways made by great private
companies, many evils may arise that never can be set right. The
great danger arising from these, and perhaps from all other very
large companies, is that in time they may form a power within
the State that will be able to set the State itself at defiance. If
the railways of a country belonged to one huge company, that
company, by its wealth and the number of people depending
upon it, would be able to interfere very much with the freedom
of the people. Very great wealth nearly always gives very great
power. In the case of a State that is still young and not very
rich, if all the railways within its borders were owned by one
great company, that company would possess no small part of
the whole wealth of the State, and there would surely be a sort
of State within the State. Of course the company would be
able to use its power far more readily than the State could,

3

because companies are so compact; and when this power was used the State would find it very difficult indeed to resist it. If the railways were held by numerous separate companies the danger would be much less; but, still, when any question affecting railways or the land near them was being dealt with in Parliament, these companies could quite easily combine and use their influence to have things arranged in accordance with their own interests. This is what is occurring in the United States of America. Very large tracts of land have been given to companies to induce them to make railways, and it is said that some of these companies now both own and rule the districts through which the railways pass, and that companies, and not the State, really control the Governments. It seems plain that this is a great evil, and that it would be difficult, if not impossible, to cure it. Taking all things into consideration, then, and bearing in mind that it is most important that a State should always be at perfect liberty to do what it considers best for all its members, we may fairly say that it is not a bad thing for a country when the State owns and works the railways in it, seeing that by so doing it performs services for the people that, on the whole, cannot be so well performed in any other way.

It is certain that the abuse of strong drink works dreadful mischief in a country, that in thousands of cases it destroys men's health and makes them poor, that hundreds of deaths are caused by it every year, that many women are made widows and children orphans by its use, that it costs a country an immense sum annually, and that it is doubtful whether it ever does much real good to anybody. Would it not, therefore, be well for a State to do away with the use of strong drink, and to make the sale or the use of it a crime punishable with imprisonment? This drink question is a very important one, and it is forcing itself on people's attention more and more year by year, as the effects produced by drunkenness, the waste and ruin that it brings about, are more clearly understood. At first sight it would seem that strong drink is one of the things "that hinder the efforts of the community to reach a higher stage of progress;" but it is not really so. It is not strong drink, but drunkenness, that does the mischief. Many a man uses drink without any apparent injury, and it seems certain that if it were used in very great moderation few evil effects would be brought about by it. It appears, therefore, that to make a law altogether forbidding the use of strong drink would be to no longer allow " every one to do whatever pleases him provided that what pleases him does not interfere with the freedom of others." But, if this is the case with drink, it is otherwise with drunkenness. Every one of the rules laid down in the last chapter directs the State to put this down, and to punish those who get drunk and those who assist them in doing so ; for a drunken man is a source of danger to every one he comes in contact with, and there is no knowing what he' may do or when he may do it. To lessen the amount of drunkenness is a real service to the community ; and it is right to prevent a man from wasting his substance and neglecting his family, and from thus adding to the misery and poverty that hinder the State from advancing.

Many of us, no doubt, often think that it is useless to wait for the time when the evil effects of strong drink will be understood by everybody, and when all will treat rum and beer as they do arsenic and other poisons ; but that time seems to be coming. Temperance societies of various kinds are slowly but surely doing good work, and in time public opinion on the subject will be so strong that the habit of using strong drink will gradually die out of itself without our having had to interfere with the freedom of those who do not in any way interfere with the freedom of others. The State should always try to avoid interfering with the liberty even of the few when a desired end can be as well or better attained without such interference.

There is much useful work that temperance societies might do in addition to that of spreading abroad a knowledge of their subject. They might do a very great deal by providing amusement of a high class in connection with temperance hotels. They might try to provide comfortable tea- and coffee-rooms where people could meet and chat in the evenings—where, indeed, they could get everything that a public-house provides except strong drink. Above all, they might try their very best to get the liquor laws, the laws against drunkenness, put in force just as they stand—to have public-houses keenly watched by the police and under thorough control, and to have those houses that are badly carried on, and especially those that supply liquor to persons that are not perfectly sober, closed at once. It would cost much hard work to get all this done, but if it were done the troubles arising from strong drink would be greatly lessened.

Ought the State to provide such things as public parks, botanical gardens, museums, public libraries, and galleries of pictures and statues ? Is it right to expend money raised for State purposes on such things as these ? The answer is, " Yes, most certainly." The work of making grand collections of objects of art and of science, of laying out and keeping in order handsome parks and gardens, of providing for public use the best books that can be procured, is one of the noblest in which the wealth and power of the State can be employed. For such things as these bring within reach of all men, down to the very poorest, some of the purest, the most refined, and most ennobling pleasures that men and women can feel ; while it is quite certain that if the State did not provide the people at large with the means of enjoying these pleasures many would never be able to enjoy them at all. Such delights would belong almost entirely to a few rich people, while the great mass of human toilers and sufferers would never have a chance of lightening their labours by the enjoyment of what is most beautiful in art or in nature. We may be quite sure that a moderate amount of money spent by the State for purposes of this kind is spent in doing useful work for the community, work which would not be done so well—or, rather, would not be done at all—if the State did not itself take it in hand. Well might the great Greek orator and true lover of his country lament the declining greatness and nobleness of Athens when he found that the State was completely neglecting all work of this kind, that, while private luxury and private wealth were fast increasing, the public buildings, gardens, and pleasure-grounds were going to decay through State neglect. This orator says in one of his speeches, " In the olden days the State herself was wealthy and flourishing. Then your great men had houses no grander than those of other people, while the public buildings were so magnificent that nothing could surpass them. Now your great men are building splendid houses for themselves, while the State buildings which you put up and whitewash are so paltry and miserable that I am almost ashamed to speak of them." There can be no doubt that when a settled State fails to provide objects of natural beauty and collections of works of art for the delight and instruction of all its members it is neglecting a very important duty. One of the results of this and similar kinds of neglect will probably be that the poorer members of the State, feeling that the rich have all the advantages arising from State action, while the poor have none, will no longer take pride in the State's work or feel much interest in the State's welfare.

Having now dealt with the State in a general way—having traced its growth and described its work—we shall go on to treat of the different branches of our subject under the heads of Human Wants and how they are satisfied, Law, Government, the Lessons of History, and Individual Conduct.

# PART II.—HUMAN WANTS.

## CHAPTER VI.

**INTRODUCTORY.—HUMAN WANTS, AND THE EFFORTS MADE TO SATISFY THEM.—LABOUR, WEALTH.**

In order to obtain a satisfactory knowledge of, and to be able to reason about, the efforts that are made to satisfy human wants, you must begin by learning the exact meaning of several common-looking words that everybody uses and that but few thoroughly understand; that is, you must endeavour to get clear ideas about such things as labour, wealth, capital, wages, and rent, and their relations to one another. Until you know what these things really are, you can make very little useful progress. If you were told that in order to produce much wealth we must get the help of capital, you would probably be unable to understand the statement thoroughly. Perhaps you would not even know that there is any difference between capital and wealth; and, if you did, you might not know what the difference is. The first thing you have to do, then, is to get the exact meanings of certain easy-looking but really difficult words determined. Fortunately, while you are doing this you will also be learning a great deal about the whole of the subject, and will be mastering what is really the most difficult part of it; and, if you do this part of the work well, you will find the remainder of it easy and pleasant.

There are many different modes of showing the meaning of the words referred to—some are good and some bad : the most obvious plan would be to state at once the sense in which the words are to be used. This is a short way, but a bad one; for the chances are that as little would be known of the meaning of such a word as *capital* after this sort of statement of it had been read and studied as was known before. The plan adopted here will be to lead you gradually to find out for yourselves, by the help of suitable stories and word-pictures, the meanings of the words referred to : when you have done this, you will find little difficulty in grasping the definitions given afterwards. The first term to be dealt with in this way is *labour*.

## Labour.

It is a cold winter's morning ; the sunshine is pretty bright, but there is a keen wind blowing from the south-west; you dip your hand into the sea to pick up a piece of seaweed, and you find that the water is very cold. It is low tide, and you see far out on a sandbank a Maori woman gathering cockles. Her work must be very unpleasant, because, to say nothing of the cold, a wave comes in every now and then and drenches her thoroughly. Now, why does this Maori woman do this kind of work, and at such an unsuitable time? The reason is, that her store of potatoes is used up, the weather has been very rough for many days, and the consequence is that she is nearly starving. She has a WANT—the want of food for herself and her children ; and she is making an EFFORT to SATISFY this want.

You are in town, and you notice an absurd man slowly pacing up and down the street, carrying two boards, one in front of him and the other at his back. On these boards you may see printed bills stating that Smith and Co.'s stock of drapery must be cleared out in ten days. Why should this " sandwich " man, as he is called, carry these boards ? Does he enjoy the fun ? Not at all. You can see by the look on his face that he is very much ashamed of having to make a show of himself, and that the hardest part of the *effort* he is making arises from his having to endure this shame. Why, then, does he make such an effort ? Because he has *wants*—he wants food, and clothing, and shelter. He is probably a poor broken-down man, who could not gain a living by ordinary labour, and therefore he gets Smith and Co. to satisfy his want of money for the purchase of these things by first satisfying their want, which is,

that a great many people should know that Smith and Co. are
selling off their stock.

As you pass down the street you see a neatly-dressed
man with thoughtful look come out of a house; he steps into
a buggy that has been waiting for him; he drives on a couple
of hundred yards, and then gets down and enters another house.
Who is this man, and what is his business? This is a doctor,
and he is visiting his patients. He does this work all day
long, and all the year round. But this visiting sick people day
after day must be very troublesome and unpleasant: why does
he do it? He is making an *effort* to *satisfy* his *wants*, by
satisfying other people's want of a doctor's help. The patients,
of course, supply the means of satisfying the doctor's wants by
giving him money for his attendance. Some of the principal
wants of the doctor are a comfortable house, good furniture,
books, good clothes; but there are many other things that he
wants, and that his efforts enable him to get.

You should notice that the efforts of all these three people
are made—that their work is done—in order to satisfy their
own or somebody-else's wants, and that the work of each of
them is more or less unpleasant either for the body or the
mind. All work of this kind is called labour.

Labour, then, is bodily or mental *effort* that is more or less
unpleasant, made in order to *satisfy* somebody's *want* of something that he thinks useful or desirable. If we may make the
word "usefulness" mean the power to satisfy a want, to give
pleasure, or to prevent pain, we may say that the object of
*labour* is to create *usefulness*.

### Wealth.

If you were asked to say what is the meaning of the term "a
wealthy man," you would be likely to answer, "A man that has
plenty of money." In ordinary conversation this answer would
probably do well enough; but now, when you are trying to get
clear ideas about wealth, you must find a better. A man who
has plenty of money of his own is certainly wealthy; but a
very wealthy man may be entirely without money.

Mr. Jones is a farmer. He owes no man anything. He has
two thousand acres of land, all well fenced and in first-rate

order. He has a fine house and beautiful furniture, a large garden full of well-grown fruit-trees in full bearing. He keeps a carriage, and has several fine horses. He has five hundred healthy sheep and ten cows, and his barns are filled with grain and hay. But he has no money; he has just given his last half-crown to a man out of work. Yet you would hardly say that Mr. Jones is not a wealthy man! You see, then, that, though money is wealth, wealth may not be money.

What, then, is the proper answer to the question, What is wealth? Perhaps you will say to yourself, " Mr. Jones could, if he wished, sell his grain, his sheep, and his fruit, or a banker would let him have money if he asked for it; therefore a wealthy man must be one who can easily get plenty of money." If you said this you would again be partly wrong. A wealthy man can easily get money; but he who can get money easily is not necessarily a wealthy man.

Signor Bianchi, the great singer, sometimes receives £500 for singing in the opera for a single week. Before now he has been paid £100 for singing one song. During the last ten years he has earned more than £50,000. Few can get money more easily than he. But he has nothing except his voice that he can call his own. What he earns is spent at once, and his debts are very large. Do you consider him wealthy?

You must have noticed, now, that Mr. Jones, who is wealthy, has a great quantity of desirable things, and that he can exchange what he has for other things that he may wish to have, while Signor Bianchi, who is not wealthy, has only a very useful voice, with which he can earn a great deal of money, but which he cannot exchange for other useful things. Perhaps, then, you will say that a wealthy man is one who has a great quantity of things that are desirable, and that can be exchanged. This reply would be much better than your former ones; but still it is not quite correct.

Many years ago the town of Geelong, in Victoria, was without any water except what was brought from the River Barwon in water-carts. It was found to be very troublesome work to carry the water in buckets from the rivers to the carts. A man therefore put up a pump, and charged so much a barrel for the water. Hundreds of barrels of water were taken into town every day, and the water in the river cost the man nothing. Now, there is hardly anything more desirable than water, and it can easily be exchanged if necessary : how was it, then, that the possession of this pump, the right to draw up and sell as much water as ever he liked, and the actual sale of very large quantities, did not make him a wealthy man ? Why could he not charge a high price for each barrel instead of a low price ? The reason was that anybody that liked could get from the river as much water as he wanted without paying for it : though water was *scarce* in town there was as much in the river as the most thirsty man could desire. In fact, the man was paid, not for the water, but for the use of his pump and for his labour in raising the water. But, on the contrary, if a man who was not in debt owned a spring that was the only means of supplying water to a large town he would be really wealthy : the supply of water would then be limited, and, as people would be obliged to have water, and as he would be the only one that could let them have it, he might charge a high price for it, and would be a very wealthy man indeed until other means of getting water could be found. His water would not only be desirable and capable of being exchanged, but *the supply of it would be limited.* You may now see that a wealthy man is one who has a great quantity of desirable things that can be exchanged for other things, and that, at the same time, cannot be obtained by everybody without any trouble. The word WEALTH, then, means a quantity of *desirable* things that are both *transferable* and *limited in supply*.

### The Acquisition and Use of Wealth.

We may properly finish this chapter with a few words about what seems to be a mistaken idea with regard to the possession and use of wealth. All men, except, perhaps, a few philosophers, would like to have wealth, and all men show by their conduct that they think it a good thing. But many people think it is more honourable to live on wealth that has been stored up by one's parents or ancestors than it is to live on that which is obtained . by one's own daily labour — that in some way or other it is more respectable *to live on one's means* than to earn one's daily bread. It is hard to see why. Wealth is indeed a good thing. It is an honour to a man if he has, by patient and steady industry, and by just and honest dealings, stored up enough to keep him from want for the rest of his days. The man who has become wealthy in this way is generally a good man all round—one who will use his wealth in such a manner as to promote the good of others as well as his own. But when a man makes wealth his only object, when he becomes hard and cruel through the pursuit of it, his fellow-men begin to despise and, perhaps, to hate him, and wealth is, to him at all events, a very bad thing. Again, when wealth is used by a man solely to gratify his own tastes—when he spends his time in idleness and luxury and never thinks how he may benefit his fellows—though, as we shall see further on, his wealth will probably do much good to others, to him it does nothing but harm. It is, indeed, very hard to see why persons who live on their means in this fashion should be considered more respectable than those who earn their bread by hard work. A man who has in his time done much honest work of any kind may have the comfort of knowing that he has been of real use to the world, and that there is far more real dignity and nobleness in toiling on year after year in some disagreeable and laborious trade than in wasting time in senseless visiting and idle chatter, and at last leaving the world without ever having been of the slightest real use to any creature in it.

# CHAPTER VII.

## WEALTH.—PRODUCTION : PRODUCERS, LAND, LABOUR.

AFTER studying the last chapter you ought to have a pretty clear idea of what wealth really is. In order to impress this idea upon your minds, we shall take a few simple cases and apply to them the tests afforded by the definition of wealth. The term " wealth " is applied to those desirable things that are both transferable and limited in supply.

Well then, there is a horse going along the road with a man on his back : is that horse wealth ? Of course he is : the man finds him a desirable object, the horse could be sold, and you cannot get as many horses as you like for nothing. As you ride along from Lake Tarawera to Fort Galatea you may sometimes see large numbers of wild horses. Are they wealth ? No. They are limited in supply, for they cannot be caught without great trouble ; and they are desirable—that is, any one that can ride well would like to have some of them : but you could not transfer them ; you would have to go to great expense and trouble in catching them and making them your own before you could sell them to another person.

Is a character for honesty wealth ? No ; for, though a good character is very desirable, and a man that has such a character finds it very useful, seeing that it causes him to be trusted by his fellow-men, and though men with such characters cannot always be met with when they are wanted, yet this good character cannot be handed over to another person, and so it is not wealth. A fragment of rock that had formed part of a ship's ballast, and had been landed after having been carried round the world several times, would not be wealth, because, even if it happened to be the only thing of its kind in the world, and could easily be transferred, no one would be foolish enough to think it a desirable thing, or to give anything in exchange for it. Lastly, sand on a sea-shore may be of some use, and portions of it can be transferred; but it is not wealth, because any one can get as much of it as he likes for nothing; unless, indeed, some person (or body of persons) has a right to sell it.

We should remember, however, that a thing may be wealth at one time or place and not at another. Water is wealth in our large towns : it has been brought into them in pipes at a great expense, and people have to pay rates for it. Sea-shore sand, too, is wealth when carried inland to be used for garden-paths.

## Producing and Producers.

Now that we know what wealth is, we must find out how it is produced, after first learning what we mean by the words *produce* and *producer*. To *produce* means *to lead forth* or *to bring forth;* and this is just what the producer does. He creates nothing—by himself he really makes nothing : he only *brings things out* to the state in which we want them.

A Chinaman goes round the town selling cabbages that he has produced. What has he really done ? He bought seeds from a seedsman and sowed them, and then, when the young plants were large enough and strong enough, he planted them out in rows. After a time he hoed the ground up around the plants, and at last was able to cut his cabbages and bring them to your door. He has done comparatively little : he merely put the seeds and young plants into places where the powers of Nature—in the sunshine, the rain, and the soil—could act upon them; and these powers have done all the rest. Man seldom does more than a very small part of any work : the powers of Nature, such as heat, gravity, and electricity, do the most of it. What man does is to get these powers to work for him, to change things that he does not want into things that he does want. In favourable seasons fruit is so very plentiful and so cheap that it does not pay the grower to bring it into town and sell it; as fruit, it is nearly useless to him, but its form may be changed and then he will be able to get people to buy it. He purchases sugar, mixes this with the fruit, pound for pound, calls in the aid of that great natural power *heat*, and the fruit and the sugar become jam. All that the owner of the fruit does is to place the fruit and the sugar in a favourable position for the power of Nature to act upon them, and this power does the work required.

To PRODUCE, then, is not to create, but to alter the condition of certain matter, so that a useless thing may become useful, or that what is already useful may become more useful still. *The producer* is he who does this work, or arranges things so that Nature does it for him.

As we go on we shall find that one of the chief features of man's progress is that he is gradually getting the powers of Nature to do more and more of the work that he wants done, and that every man who secures more of Nature's help by inventing a useful machine, or by noticing what happens when certain things are mixed together, enables all men who come after him to satisfy more of their wants with less effort.

*Instruments of Production; Wealth sometimes produced entirely by Natural Agents.*

Having learnt what wealth is, and what producing is, we go on to inquire what things are needed for the production of wealth. A woman at Fryer's Creek, in Victoria, was one day strolling along the banks of a little stream that runs into the main creek. There had been a very heavy flood a day or two before, and all at once she saw lying before her something that looked like a very yellow piece of clay. She stooped down and picked it up, and found that it was a nugget of gold thinly covered with mud. It weighed more than 17oz., and she sold it for about £65. Of course this nugget was wealth; and the question is, How was this wealth produced? The nugget had been formed in the bowels of the earth by heat and other natural powers. The rain had gradually washed away the earth that covered it up; after long ages, perhaps, the last coating of soil had been removed, and there was the nugget all ready for the first passer-by. Now, who or what produced it? Many writers on this subject would say that it was produced by land and labour, meaning by *land* the powers of Nature working on the land, and by *labour* the woman's act of stooping down to pick it up and make it her own. But do you not think that her labour formed a small part—an extremely small part—of all the work done? Do you not think that it would be almost safe, in all cases in which mere chance enables a man to make his own with the smallest possible trouble what Nature has placed ready to his hand, to consider Nature or its powers the only producer? A very important case of this sort will have to be dealt with by-and-by; it is therefore desirable that you should remember this one.

*Natural Agents the most important Instruments of Production.*

The instances of the Chinaman and his cabbages, and the fruit-grower and his jam, will enable us to understand that there is no case in which the powers of Nature do not render very great assistance in the production of wealth. Where these powers seem to do but little in helping us with the work we are engaged in, we may be quite sure that they have done a very great deal in preparing things for us to work with. If you were asked to say what help the Chinaman gets from the powers of Nature when he is digging up his ground to grow cabbages you would probably say, "None at all." But such an answer would be quite wrong. Does the Chinaman turn up the ground with his hands? No; he uses a spade. Well, where did the handle of that spade come from? What caused the growth of the tree from which it is made? Then, again, where did the iron or steel blade come from? Countless ages before he was born, that iron, no doubt, was really produced for the Chinaman's use in Nature's great workshop, the bowels of the earth.

Further, it would be of little use for the Chinaman to be ready and willing to work unless he had matter to work upon. The ground is that matter. But how did it come to be there? Perhaps, untold centuries ago a range of hills was formed by the wondrous forces in the interior of the earth, and then the work of preparing the Chinaman's garden by the slow but ceaseless action of Nature's powers was begun. Ever since, the action of sun and wind, frost and rain, has been causing soil to be brought down to the low-lying land: the work is at last completed, and the Chinaman is not only able to dig, but he has a piece of ground to dig in.

If you think this over carefully, you can hardly help seeing how very much we owe to the powers of Nature. What was it that did all the work of providing for us matter that we could adapt to our wants? It was the powers of Nature. They gave us kauri, totara, and rimu for our houses, coal for our fires, iron for our railways, to say nothing of the bread we eat, the water we drink, and the raiment we wear. In the end, we are driven to conclude that the powers of Nature are the most important instrument of production.

### Land the principal Natural Agent.

It is not very convenient to be constantly speaking of the powers of Nature; it would be far better if we could find some. short word that would express our idea equally well. You may have noticed that nearly everything we have mentioned in this chapter has something to do with land. Cabbages and fruit come from the land. The nugget had been hidden away in the land. Timber, coal, and iron are all from the land. Most of the powers of Nature that help us so much act in or through the land in some way or other. For instance, warmth and rain, which do a great part of the work of providing us with food, are connected with the mighty powers of the sun, but they have to act on the land before they help us much. It has therefore been agreed to use the term "land" as meaning not only the land itself, but the powers of Nature, so far as they are in connection with the land, and act upon or through it so as to help us to produce things that are desirable, and also transferable and limited in supply—that is, so far as they assist us in the production of wealth. Also, the term "land" is made to include rocks, streams, and even lakes. We are now able to say that LAND is one of the things needed for the production of *wealth*: it gives us the matter of which wealth is formed. The term includes land, water, and other things, as well as the powers of Nature acting in or through them.

# CHAPTER VIII.

## WEALTH.—PRODUCTION: LABOUR, CAPITAL.

The things—the material objects—that land provides for us are, in their natural state, seldom exactly what we need. The kauri-tree is a noble object to look at, but it is of very little use where it stands. The usefulness of coal while it is in a mine is very trifling. It is much the same with some of the powers of Nature. Electricity, for instance, has been made to give most powerful aid to man; but that is since it has, so to speak, been caught and tamed. Our forefathers knew electricity only as the lightning that was able to set fire to a haystack, to destroy a ship or a fine building, or to kill a man or two now and then.

### Labour an Instrument of Production.

In nearly all cases the help of labour must be called in before the things provided by land can be turned into wealth —before they can be made desirable, exchangeable, and limited in supply.

The coal in the mine, now of little use to anybody, will have had its usefulness vastly increased when it has been hewn by the miners, lifted to the pit's mouth, and carried by rail and steamer to the place where people want it to make fires with. This increased usefulness is given to the coal partly by the natural power, heat, which drives the machinery at the pit's mouth and the engines of the railway-train and the steamer, but partly also by the labour of the miners who bring it to the surface, and of the persons engaged in carrying it by railway and steamer.

4

Again, kauri-trees in the forest have some little *usefulness*. A man owning a very large piece of ground thickly timbered with kauri would certainly be wealthy—he would be in possession of a large quantity of what is desirable, transferable, and limited in supply. But his wealth would be a mere nothing compared with what it would be if all these trees had been cut down, if the timber had been made into boards, doors, and window-sashes, which had been removed to some town where these things were wanted. Of course this increase of wealth would have been caused by the application of labour to the material provided by the land.

Here it is necessary to caution you against a mistake that is very commonly made with regard to labour — you must beware of thinking that the amount of labour bestowed on a thing is the sole cause of its price being high or low. That would be a serious error to fall into, as you will find further on. Just now it will be sufficient to remind you that the woman who found the nugget at Fryer's Creek got just as much for it as a man would have received if he had worked for it for three months. You may see clearly that it was not labour bestowed on that particular nugget that made its price high. You will easily understand, too, that if a man offered you the usual price — say, half-a-crown — to take a message to a person two or three miles away, and you went by a roundabout way, and made a twenty-mile journey of it, you could not expect the man to pay you an additional half-crown for the hard work you had done. The man would pay you the price of the *service* you had rendered him, without taking into account the amount of labour you had expended in performing it for him.

There are two principal ways in which labour takes part in production : the first is, by altering the form of things so as to render useful what would otherwise be useless. A kauri-tree when standing has some little *usefulness*, because it is raw material; when it has been cut down, trimmed, and cut into logs, it is more useful, and people would give far more for the timber than they would have given for the tree when it was standing ; and when it has been made into doors and window-sashes it is very much more useful still. Now, what is it that has increased its usefulness? The labour that has been bestowed upon it has done this. It has altered the *form* of the wood of the tree till, instead of being nearly useless, the wood has become highly useful.

The second way in which labour takes part in production is by removing things from places where they are not wanted to places where they are. You will remember the case of the man who put up a pump on the banks of the River Barwon, and the different degrees in which the water was useful according as it was where it was wanted or where it was not wanted. A man living close to a river-bank would give you nothing for a barrel of water. Why should he give you anything for it? Could he not use the whole river if he liked? When the Barwon water had been raised by labour at the pump so that it would run into the barrels on the water-cart, people were willing to pay sixpence a barrel for it. Labour had moved the water from a place where it was not wanted to one where it was wanted. When the water had been taken into Geelong, and was ready to pour into people's own tanks, the price of it was 7s. 6d. a barrel. Here, again, the water had been moved from a place where its usefulness was small and the supply unlimited to one where its usefulness was great and the supply very limited.

We may say, then, that *labour* is the second of the instruments needed for the production of *wealth,* and that its chief office is to increase the usefulness of things provided by *land*— (*a*) by changing their form; (*b*) by removing them from places where they are not wanted to places where they are wanted.

### *Wealth produced by Land and Labour alone.*

There are many things that can be produced by land and labour alone that must in strictness be called wealth. For instance, a Maori woman might get up early in the morning, pull a few flax leaves and make a small *kete,* then go down to a sandbank, fill the bag with cockles, and sell them to a European for a shilling. The fact of her being able to exchange them. would show that they were wealth, although they had been produced by land and labour alone. But only very little wealth can be got in this way—in fact, only the very lowest savages would be content with such things as they could get by using land and labour only.

## Capital.

For the production of any considerable quantity of wealth a third instrument is required, as the following illustrations will show : A family of six Maoris, all able to work, have in their potato-storehouses a good crop of potatoes and some maize. These people are very poor, and they live on potatoes and fermented corn, with an occasional meal of fern-root, cockles, fish, or pigeons. It would be wrong, but not very wrong, to say that they have no clothes. The next planting-time is a long way off, and they are talking about selling a good part of their potatoes and corn and buying some decent clothing for themselves. The father sees a prospect of getting two or three pounds of tobacco in the course of the transaction, and is strongly in favour of selling; but the mother, who has gone through very hard times in consequence of similar sales in previous years, is in favour of keeping everything they have. At last, after a long talk, it is agreed that the potatoes and corn shall be divided into five equal parts. Two of these are to be sold, and the money is to be spent on clothing and tobacco; two parts are to be kept for food; and the remaining portion of their crop is to be planted when the proper time comes round. It is decided also that they shall begin work at once, and clear and prepare enough ground for the whole of their seed-corn and seed-potatoes, in order that next year they may have plenty to eat and be able to buy as much clothing as they may require.

The potatoes and corn formed these Maoris' wealth. To what use was this wealth put? The whole of it, except what was spent on tobacco for the father and a few fine ribbons for the mother and her girls, was used for producing more corn and potatoes : the serviceable clothes that they bought were used to keep them warm and strong; the potatoes and corn were used to feed them while they were preparing the ground; when the proper time came the corn and potatoes that had been reserved were planted in order that more corn and potatoes might be produced. That is, they used all their wealth, except what

went for tobacco and ribbons, to assist them in further production. Wealth used in this way is called capital.*

## Unproductive Consumption.

You may notice here that these Maoris might have used
their wealth in a very different way—they might have said to
themselves, " We will sell all our potatoes and corn, buy flour,
sugar, and spirits, invite our friends, and have a thorough good
time; and then trust to fish, fern-root, and cockles for the rest
of the year." If they had acted in this way they would have
consumed their wealth *unproductively*—that is, they would have
utterly destroyed it, without producing more wealth to take its
place. This way of disposing of wealth is called *unproductive
consumption*. You can hardly be too careful in noticing what
is the real difference between the use of wealth as capital and
the unproductive use of wealth. In both cases the wealth is
consumed entirely, but when it has been used as capital new
wealth takes its place; when it has been used unproductively the
wealth entirely disappears.

## How Capital assists Production.

Let us suppose now that a Maori family have acted
foolishly, that they have consumed the whole of their wealth
unproductively, and that they find themselves unable to get
food in the way they expected. What can they do? They
must either starve or go and work for some one who can pay
them for their labour.

You may suppose them to be employed by a storekeeper—to
pack gum, perhaps. How could the storekeeper pay them for
their work? He would pay them with his capital—with the
wealth that he was using for further production. He would
buy their labour, which would cause the *usefulness* of his gum
to increase, and would make the gum worth more after it was
packed than it was before. But perhaps these Maoris would go

---

* If you find any difficulty in understanding why the potatoes and corn
should be called *capital*, you may get over it by thinking of the Maoris as being
both their own employers and their own servants. As employers they allow
their wealth to be consumed to assist production—that is, they use it as capital;
as labourers they receive wages which enable them to subsist.

and dig gum for themselves. Even then they would have to be helped by the storekeeper's capital; the gum itself would be of no use to them—they could not eat it. They would have to sell it to the storekeeper, who would pay for it with part of his capital.

You should now begin to see that one of the principal uses of capital is .to allow the products of land and labour to be bought and paid for before these products are thoroughly fit for the final use for which they are intended. We know that the storekeeper does not want to *consume* the gum himself : he bestows a certain amount of labour upon it, and then sells it to the merchant; the merchant, employing more labour upon it, sends it to England and sells it to the varnish-maker; the varnish-maker, after more labour has been bestowed on it,* sells it to the varnisher, who at last is paid for his labour and for the varnish itself by the owner of the house in which the varnish is used. From the time the kauri-gum is dug by the Maori until it is used to varnish a house in England it is worth more and more as each labourer makes it more useful; and the capital of one man after another pays for the gum and the labour, till at last the owner of a house settles up the whole thing by paying for his varnish and using or *consuming* it—that is, putting it to the final purpose for which it was made. Thus you may see how capital assists labour in production through being employed in purchasing things not yet ready for the consumer.

### Fixed Capital.

Do you see that very tall chimney over there ? Do you think it pretty ? Do you think that any one would care to buy such a chimney ? No one would buy it unless he wanted a very powerful fire for making bricks with, or for some similar work. Then the owner must have spent his money in the purchase of what is of very little use except for brickmaking? Just so. Will he ever get his money back? Probably. When ? When he has made and sold a great many bricks : every sale of bricks gives him back part of what he spent on the chimney. We may say, then, that the owner of the chimney paid for the pro-

---

* Of course the varnish-maker mixes the gum with other substances.

ducts of the land, labour, and capital used in making the bricks of which his chimney is built, and for the labour of building it, in order that he might have a chimney to help him to produce more bricks. The money so paid was his capital, and it was paid for a thing that was of little use except for further production. Capital put into the form of buildings or machines that will last a very long time is called *fixed capital*. It is quite easy to see why it is so called.

### How Capital assists Production.

A party of miners are sinking a shaft in a quartz claim on the West Coast. They are all poor, and could not manage to live if they were not paid for their work by the shareholders who own the mine. Another party of men are working not very far away; they are digging in shallow ground, and, though they too are poor enough, they need no help from any shareholders. How are we to account for the difference? · The first party are gradually producing a shaft, a thing that is of no use in that district except for the purpose of producing gold, and this shaft produces no gold as yet. Here comes in the use of capital : the shareholders pay for the shaft little by little, because they hope by-and-by to produce gold by means of it. That is, they turn their wealth into capital, and expend it on what is of no use except for aiding further production. The second party, on the contrary, produce gold at once, though in small quantities. In their case capital is hardly wanted. Nobody, you see, wishes to have a shaft for its own sake, but every one wants gold, and is glad to give useful things in exchange for it. In the one case an unfinished article of no use except as capital is being produced, and nothing but capital can pay for it. In the other an article that everybody is anxious to have is produced all ready to hand, and very little is required for the work of producing it. It ought now to be clear to you what capital is, and also what its principal use is.

CAPITAL is *wealth* used to assist in further production, which it does principally through being employed in the purchase of those products of land and labour, or of land, labour, and other capital, that have not yet been put into the form in which they are used by the consumer.

# CHAPTER IX.

## WEALTH.—CAPITAL AND WAGES.

You ought now to be able to understand that capital is stored-up wealth used to help production, and that it is very largely employed in buying things that have been partly produced or *brought forth*, or that are of no use except for helping to produce something that will be useful. To impress this more deeply on your minds, you may proceed to consider two or three simple instances of the use of capital along with labour.

### *Production : a Grocer's Capital and his Assistant's Labour.*

A grocer's capital consists to a large extent of sugar, tea, coffee, and similar things, bought and stored up in his shop in boxes, drawers, and bottles, in such a way that they may always be easily got at when they are wanted. They are almost ready for the use of consumers, but not quite. When customers come to the shop to buy goods it is necessary that they should have an opportunity of seeing them, that they should be told the price of each article, and that the things they require should be weighed and packed up in neat and convenient parcels. Now, a grocer generally employs a man to do this work, which is the very last that has to be done to the goods before they are handed to the consumers. The grocer pays his assistant, perhaps £2 a week, for doing this work, which is that of removing the goods from a place where they are less useful to a place where they will be more useful. While they remain in the boxes, the work of production—of getting them ready for the consumer—is not quite finished; but when they are placed in the consumer's hands it is thoroughly completed. The grocer, then, has used his capital in purchasing in large quantities sugar, tea, and other things when they have been *only partly produced;* his assistant does what little is needed to complete the production; after this work has been done, the grocer pays the assistant for his work of increasing the usefulness of the goods, and the customers buy the goods and pay for them. Thus the customers return to the grocer the capital that he laid out when he bought the goods from the merchant and the capital employed in paying the assistant for completing the work of production; they also pay him something more which is generally called profit. Of this profit we shall speak further on.

*Capitalists do not advance Means of Subsistence to Labourers.*

A wealthy man takes a contract for making a road, and employs a number of labourers on the contract, giving them each 7s. 6d. a day for the work they do. Now, does not the contractor do more for these men than merely pay them for their help in producing something that will be useful? Does he not *advance* money to them? Does he not really give them their living before they have completely earned it?. Whether the work pays the contractor or not, they will not suffer. They are sure to get the benefit of their labour; but the contractor may actually lose by having employed them. Is it then quite fair to say that all that the contractor does for them is to pay them for what has been partly produced by them? Does he not give them something in advance? Not at all : they give *him* something in advance, because workmen are generally not paid till the end of the week, and all the work of the former part of the week remains unpaid for till Saturday comes. It is only in very rare cases that the capitalist pays for labour in advance.

This is how the matter stands : When a man is about to take a contract he reckons up how much he will have to pay for horses and carts, for tools, for labour, and for the interest on any money he may have to borrow while the work is going on; how much he ought to charge for the risks of bad weather, of rise of wages, and accident ; and how much he ought to get for the use of his knowledge of this kind of work, for his trouble and

anxiety, and for interest on any money of his own that he may
have to lay out. He adds these all together, and then he sends in
his tender for the whole amount. Now, it is quite plain that he
will reckon up his probable payments for labour just as he will
reckon up his probable payments for horses. He will say to
himself, " I can buy a horse for £20 ; this horse will cost £10
for forage ; he will earn £25 by removing so many yards of
earth ; I shall be able to sell him for £15 when the work is
finished : I shall therefore gain £10." He will also say in just
the same way, " I shall get a man for three months for £30 ;
his work in removing earth will be worth £35 : I shall gain
£5." In each case he reckons on buying a certain thing and
selling it again at a higher price. The only difference is that
in the one case he will buy a horse that will do certain work for
him, perhaps remove the clay from a cutting, while in the other
he will buy at once the product of a man's labour, perhaps a
heap of metal ready for road-making purposes. And, just as
the contractor pays for the horse when it has been handed
over to him, so does he pay for the products of the man's
labour, not before the work is done, but after. Notice, too, that
when the labourer gets his wages at the end of each week the
contractor merely pays him for something that he has produced
—perhaps it is a heap of clay that the contractor's carters can
easily remove, or perhaps it is a ditch by the roadside ; at all
events, it is something that the contractor has reckoned before-
hand to be worth the money to him, because it will aid him in
completing his work. We may say, then, that capital is used in
this case, as in former ones, to purchase the unfinished products
of labour and land, and that it is exchanged for other wealth,
not before, but after production.

### Is Capital advanced in Mining Enterprises ?

Again, here is a tunnel running into a hill. Near the mouth
of the tunnel there is a large quantity of quartz. If you
examine this stone carefully you will find here and there small
specks of gold on it. The three men who got this stone out of
the ground have used all their provisions, and they have no
money. The gold in their quartz cannot be extracted without the help of a costly machine. They have therefore found

that it is useless to keep on working unless they can by some means get help of this sort. They have partly produced a large quantity of gold; but unless they can get capital they are very little better off than they would have been if they had done no work at all. This, then, is the course they adopt: They go to a wealthy man whom they know, and ask him for assistance. This man comes to see the tunnel. Small quantities of the quartz taken from different parts of the heap are broken up with hammers, and are found to contain a great deal of gold. The man then says, "Give me two shares in your tunnel, and I will pay you two thousand pounds." The bargain is struck and the money is paid. Now, it would seem at first sight that this man advances money to enable the miners to live, and that what the shares bring in to him will be a payment for money lent; but it is not really so. The tunnel and the quartz are an unfinished product of land and labour, the capitalist buys two shares of this unfinished product, thus paying for the labour that the men have spent in finding the quartz vein, and in making the tunnel, and also for what may be called the "unfinished" gold, all of which are useless if nothing more is done. What has been produced so far can be used for further or more complete production or *bringing forth*; otherwise it is quite useless. You should now see for yourselves that it is only in rare cases that the capitalist advances money to labourers. What he really does is to buy what is useful for further production, but requires more to be done to it before the principal use to which it may or can be put ceases to be that of assisting further production.

A great deal of capital is paid away in the form of wages; but it must be quite plain, after what has been said, that, so far as the capitalist is concerned, such payments are made for the unfinished articles produced by the labourer, and are of exactly the same character as those made for a horse or a machine that is to be used to assist in production.

## Wages.

You should understand that the term "wages" as it is used in this book has a meaning rather wider than the ordinary one, just as the word "labour" has an extended meaning. When you

hear the word " wages," you at once think of a servant or a workman, who is paid so much a day, a week, or a month ; ordinarily,
you would hardly speak of a Governor's wages, or of the
wages of the head of a Government office ; you would then use
the word " salary." But, when dealing with a subject like ours,
it is found very convenient always to use the same word for
the same thing, and also always to call the same thing by the
same name. In this book the word " wages " will mean what is
given in exchange for labour, or, more exactly, the reward of
labour. We are also accustomed to connect wages with money.
Wages are generally paid in money, but they might be paid
in something else. A brickmaker, for instance, might be
allowed so many bricks for every week's work. A fisherman,
working for another fisherman, the owner of the, boat they
use, might be paid with, say, a quarter of the number of fish
caught. A miner might receive for his work a share of the
gold obtained. In all these cases, what was received would be
payment for labour, and wages are the reward of labour.

Some of the old writers on this subject seem to have thought
that the wages of productive labour are taken *out of* capital, that
when wages are paid capital is made less, and that the loss
cannot be made good until the article on account of which
the wages have been paid is sold. This is plainly a mistake.
Capital used to pay wages merely changes its form. A
capitalist may at the beginning of a day have £100 in money,
and at night he may have paid this money away in wages, and
the labourers may have spent it all in bread, meat, beer, clothes,
and tobacco ; but then, of course, the capitalist has something
instead of his £100. Perhaps some cloth, which in the morning
was worth only £500, is now, on account of the labour spent
upon it, worth £610, and in a condition to be further improved
the next day and many succeeding days by the same workmen.
The fact is that capital is one of the most changeable of things,
unless, perhaps, when it is in the form called fixed capital. You
will easily understand the reason of this when you remember
that the principal use of capital is to purchase the incomplete
products of land and labour. Take what occurs in the wholesale
confectioner's trade as an illustration of the changeable nature
of capital. To-day, the confectioner's free capital is money ; to-

morrow, it may be money and sugar; the next day, money, refined sugar, and acid drops ; the next day, refined sugar, acid drops, and lolly-sticks ; the next day, money, lolly-sticks, comfits, and tin boxes; and the next day, money only. You will easily understand how this might happen, and will see that much of the capital was, all the time till the last day, in the form of articles that needed to be improved by labour before they were fit for the consumer.

## *Wealth not necessarily Capital.*

Though all capital is wealth, all wealth is not capital ; and what is capital to-day may not be capital to-morrow. An express-driver's horse is capital because he is used in the production of wealth; but if he is sold and used as a lady's carriage-horse he continues to be a part of wealth, but he is no longer capital. A violin may be capital to a music-seller while it remains in his shop; but it ceases to be capital when it has been sold to a customer. If, however, the purchaser is a teacher of the violin, and he uses it to help him to earn his living, it is still capital to him.

# CHAPTER X.

## POSSESSORS OF WEALTH. — CAPITAL, INSURANCE, WAGES OF MANAGEMENT, INTEREST, PROFIT.

The owner of wealth may deal with it in five principal ways—he may hoard it up, consume it unproductively, lend it, take risks upon it, or employ it as capital.

### *Why few People hoard their Wealth.*

Very few people hoard wealth nowadays. Sometimes a miser or other stupid person will take a fancy to store up gold, silver, jewels, or clothes without making use of them. In some Eastern countries, where the Governments are either weak or dishonest, men cannot always safely make use of their wealth, and therefore they hide it in caves or other secret places, or perhaps conceal it about their persons; but with us wealth may always be used so as to produce more wealth. Now, the fonder of wealth a man is, the more anxious he is to increase his stock of it; so at the present time even misers will almost always lend their wealth to a banker or some other person who will make excellent use of it.

### *The Unproductive Use of Wealth not necessarily a Bad Use.*

A great deal of wealth is consumed unproductively. Every time that a man drinks a glass of beer or smokes a pipe of tobacco, he consumes wealth unproductively; unless, indeed, these things enable him to do productive work better, which is doubtful. All the clothing that a man wears out beyond what is necessary to keep him healthy and able to do his daily work,

and, indeed, all that is spent on any kind of luxury or amusement, or that does not assist in the production of wealth, is
unproductively consumed. But we must not make the mistake
of supposing that the unproductive use of wealth is always a
bad use. It may be either good or bad. The object of all efforts
is to satisfy *wants*. Wealth satisfies one of these wants ; but
this want is not the only one—it does not even belong to the
highest and noblest class of wants. Any honest act that tends
to the satisfaction of a lawful want is not bad, but good. In
certain cases the unproductive use of wealth satisfies some
of our loftiest wants and wishes. For instance, the wealth
used by the State in making the lives of old, infirm, and weak-
minded people as happy as they can be made is unproductively consumed. None of the wealth so used will ever produce
more wealth ; no part of it will ever come back to the State
again. Very few people would say, though, that wealth so used
is not well and nobly used. We must remember, then, that all
that is meant by the term " unproductive use of wealth " is that
the wealth consumed does not produce more wealth.

## *Loans.*

The third way of dealing with wealth is to lend it to some
one who will pay for the use of it. A man that decides to
employ his wealth thus may lend it to some one that will consume it unproductively, or to some one that will use it in
purchasing unfinished products of land, labour, and capital, in
order to produce more wealth—in other words, to some one
who intends to use it as capital.

## *Distinction between the Capital of an Individual and the Capital of a State.*

Here you should notice the difference between the *capital*
that is used to increase the wealth of an individual, and the
capital that is used to increase the wealth of the State as a whole ;
as far as the lender himself is concerned, wealth lent in order
that more wealth may be returned for it may fairly be called
capital, but we cannot tell whether we should consider it part
of the capital of the State until we know how the money is

going to be used. If the borrower is going to buy racehorses, and wine, and fine clothes, and things of that sort with it, it surely is not capital to the State. These things will be used up soon, and there will be nothing left in the place of them. It is quite true that the man who has lent the money may be repaid ; but it will be with some of the land belonging to the borrower, or with some other wealth not produced by the consumption of what has been borrowed. But if the money is used in the purchase of some machine that will assist in the production of more wealth, then the money lent is certainly capital, not only to the individual that lends it, but also to the State as a whole.

The best plan will be to admit that it is quite right for those who lend money on interest to call it their capital, whatever use may be made of the money, but to hold that those who are discussing the State should call no wealth capital unless this wealth is used in the production of more wealth by being employed in buying the products of land, labour, and other capital, in order that these may be made more useful.

### Insurance.

Taking risks is the fourth way of using wealth. If a man had £10,000, he might undertake to pay one neighbour £500 if his house were burnt down; to pay another £1,000 if his ship were lost; and to pay £2,000 to the wife and family of a third immediately after his death — each of these persons agreeing to pay the wealthy man a certain sum every year. The service that this wealthy man would render these people would be that of making them feel that in case of death or misfortune they or their families would have something to fall back upon. This is a very great service, and it is quite right that it should be duly paid for. The service is called *insurance*, the wealthy man is said to take a *risk*, and the payment is called a *premium*. This kind of work is seldom done by individuals; it is generally undertaken by a company. In New Zealand the State has taken the matter of life insurance in hand.

This is a very safe way of using wealth, though at first sight it does not seem to be so. Experience has taught us that any one man may die during any year, and that it would be very unsafe to insure only one person; it is quite easy to see that, unless the premium were much higher than premiums usually are, the gain would be small if the insured person lived, and that if he died the loss would be great. But it has also been found that out of a certain very large number of persons about the same number die in one year as in another. Suppose, now, that it has been found that in a certain town twenty-five out of every thousand die in a year, and that some one agrees to pay £100 for each one that dies, on the condition that he, the taker of the risks, shall receive £3 at the beginning of the year from each one of the thousand. Then for every thousand people he will have to pay out £2,500, but will receive £3,000, and will therefore gain £500. The calculations that have to be made are very much more difficult than this, because a great many things have to be taken into account. When a man insures his life he agrees to pay so much every year, and till he dies interest on the money paid by him is constantly being obtained by the company; because it does not keep this money idle, but lends it out. Also, the ages of people, their state of health, and many other things have to be thought of. Still, this simple illustration will enable you to understand the way in which insurance works. Houses and ships are insured in much the same way as lives are.

### May Wealth employed in Insurance be called Capital?

Now, should wealth thus used be called capital? Here, again, you may say that it is capital as far as the company is concerned; but you must not consider it capital except in so far as it assists the production of wealth by causing people to venture to engage in works that they would not undertake if the risks were very great. It is plain that, if a house worth £1,000 is burnt down, a thousand pounds' worth of wealth is destroyed. It is well for the owner that he is insured, and that he has saved £1,000; but the taker of the risk loses £1,000, and the State as a whole is poorer by that amount than it was before. No individual or company can suffer by the destruction of wealth without the State's suffering too. Insurance, therefore, does not directly assist in the production of wealth, nor does it even prevent its destruction.

5

### Insurance of Property equalises Risk.

But it is not only those who insure lives, ships, and houses that have to do with insurance. Nearly every man that enters into business or lends money has to receive premium for insurance. You may take an extreme case as an illustration of the principle : A gunpowder-maker runs a great risk—at any moment his mill may be blown into the air; does he get nothing for running this risk? Of course he gets paid for it; you may be quite sure that when he sells his gunpowder he adds a good deal to the price of it, just on account of this risk. There are few trades so dangerous as the gunpowder-maker's, but there is some risk in all kinds of business. People trusted with goods may turn out to be dishonest; your neighbour may invent a new machine that will enable him to make and sell goods much cheaper than you can sell them; or the men you employ may ask for higher wages than you can afford to give them, and you may have to shut up your shop. Thus, then, there is always some risk in business, and unless people could get paid for this risk few would be found to take it. Unless people are paid for doing unpleasant things they will not do them. The payment for risk in the employment of capital is *insurance premium*.

### Wages of Management.

You will remember that it was said in the last chapter that the reward of labour is called wages. Wages paid for some kinds of labour are much higher than those paid for others. Further on you will see why this is. But even now you can understand that a man who manages a business, whether it is his own or somebody-else's, must be paid good wages for his work. The more difficult the business is to manage the higher the wages must be. Suppose that a man with £10,000 found himself working hard year after year and getting payment only for risk and interest—no more than he could gain by lending his money; do you think that that man would go on working in this way? No; he would lend his money, and do some other work that would pay him for his trouble; or perhaps he would remain idle.

### Abstinence : Interest.

In many respects the man that lends another money in order that he, the lender, may get more money by-and-by, is in the same position as the man that buys the unfinished products of labour in order that he may, by making them more useful, get more for them eventually; that is, he refrains from consuming his wealth unproductively, and expects some reward for so refraining. If then you can determine the nature of the act of lending another man money for a certain reward you will also determine, generally, the nature of the act of using capital, and will be able to say why the reward for this act may be claimed. Suppose, then, that a wealthy person lends a tradesman·the sum of £1,000, in order that this tradesman may at the end of the year pay him £75 in addition to the principal sum. The lender, besides refraining from consuming his wealth unproductively, gives the tradesman the right to consume it. In so doing, the lender makes an *effort* that no one would consider pleasant if it were not for the reward, the *satisfaction*, that is to follow the making of the effort. At the same time the lender performs a *service* to the borrower, and this service is paid for with the extra £75 given to the lender at the end of the year. The effort that the lender makes is called *abstinence*, and the reward paid to him for the service is called *interest*. And, generally, it may be said that ABSTINENCE is the effort required· in employing *wealth* as *capital*, and that INTEREST is the reward of *abstinence*.

You are now prepared to understand that *capital* is produced by land, labour, and abstinence, and that *interest* is the reward of *abstinence* just as wages are the reward of labour.

### *Interest on Capital may be justly demanded.*

Some people think it very unfair that wealthy people should demand interest for the use of money. But it is surely just as right that a man should wish to be paid for putting up with the disagreeable feeling of having his money in another person's possession and of having to abstain from using it, as that a working-man should wish to be paid for the labour of his body in chopping up a load of wood, and for refraining from using this labour in some way that would be more pleasant to him. You will see, too, that it is just as right that a man should pay for the service he receives from the man who lends him the money that enables him to build a good chimney as it is that he should have to pay for the service rendered him by the man who chops up the wood that is to be burnt in the fireplace.

There is another point, too, that those who object to interest do not consider. A man who has wealth might purchase cattle with it, or plant timber-trees with it. In time his wealth would increase with no effort on his part, except that of abstinence. If it is fair that the increase should be his property, it is also fair that he should be paid for his abstinence by the person to whom he gives up his chance of increasing his wealth in this way.

### Interest and Time : Compound Interest.

You will also see that time is a most important thing in all matters relating to interest. If a man ought to be paid £1 for doing without £20 for one year, he ought to be paid £2 for doing without it for two years, £10 for ten years; and so on. Also, if he is not paid the interest on his money at the end of the first year, he ought to get interest upon this interest, the two kinds of interest taken together forming what is called compound interest. This is one of the things that make large works such as railways, manufactories, and similar undertakings so expensive. During all the time that they are being got ready for use there is not a penny returned from them, and the total amount of the free capital of the country is lessened by the amount spent on them, unless, of course, they are being constructed with wealth borrowed from abroad. When they are ready the capital that is spent upon them is returned very slowly, and it may be many years before it comes back, if it comes at all. When the total cost of a railway is properly reckoned, allowance is made for the slow wearing-out of the works, in such a way that, as parts of them require to be made new, the capital that has been expended on those parts, and the profits on it, shall have been returned along with the profits obtained on the actual working of the railway.

### The full Reward for the Use of Capital may fitly be called Profit.

You will now readily see what is the reward for using wealth as capital. When a wealthy man uses his wealth as capital, and uses it with success, his reward is PROFIT, which is nearly always made up of *interest, insurance premium,* and *wages.* Briefly we may say that *profit* is the reward of success in the use of *capital.* Some writers on this subject think that it is well to say that the only reward for the use of capital is interest, and that payment for risk and for wages of management ought to be left out of account when mere capital is being dealt with. No doubt this view is, strictly speaking, correct : interest is the reward for the use of capital ; while payment for risk only helps to make the interest on capital in different employments equal, and wages of management are payments for labour and skill and not for the use of capital. Still, as 'these two things are always connected with capital in one way or another, it is very convenient, especially in a book for beginners, to take interest, risk, and wages of management together, and call them *profits.*

In the next chapter we must, by means of one or two simple examples, test the truth of what has been said about capital in this chapter.

# CHAPTER XI.

## CAPITAL; KNOWLEDGE AND SKILL; CAPITAL AND PRODUCTION.

You may now study two or three more illustrations of the growth and use of capital. A man had worked for a long time with rough tools as a sort of bush-carpenter. Through being frugal, however—through keeping from spending the whole of his wages on food, drink, clothing, and tobacco—he gradually got together some *wealth* in the form of money. When he had saved £30 he visited the neighbouring town, where he was strongly tempted to spend his money unproductively on drink and other pleasures, often falsely so called. He resisted the temptation, however, and wisely decided to buy something that would help him to produce wealth more rapidly : exercising *abstinence*, he bought a set of first-class tools, and thus used his stored-up wealth as *capital*. He was now able to do work of a better kind, and so to produce much more wealth than he could have produced before. The extra wealth thus earned was *profit* on his capital. This profit was made up of three things— (*a*) the *interest* he would have had to pay if he had borrowed £30 to purchase his tools with; (*b*) his *premium* for *insurance* against the consequences of the wear and tear of his tools, and also against the risk of breaking or losing them, and having to replace them with new ones; and (*c*) his extra *wages* for managing and using better tools. This, however, was not all the advantage he gained from having first-class tools, as we shall see further on.

The case of a blacksmith working in a very rough smithy and with very poor tools (as smiths used to work on the gold-diggings in the early days), and deciding after a time to build a new smithy and make new tools *for himself*, would be almost exactly like that of the carpenter. The only difference would be that, instead of giving his stored-up wealth to a seller of tools, he would pay it away to the butcher and the baker who would supply him with food during the time that he was building his smithy and making his tools. The smith would put his wealth into the form of flour, bacon, tea, and sugar, which he would use as food while working, and would thus turn his wealth into capital just as the carpenter did when he bought his tools ; each of them would use his wealth for purchasing things to aid him in further production.

There is yet another way of looking at the matter ; you may consider the smith as being both capitalist and labourer. As a capitalist he purchases the tools that he produces, and as a labourer receiving wages he purchases from the butcher and the baker the articles that he requires.

You may finish this part of your work by considering the case of a man whose wealth is equal to £10,000 in money, of which he lends £5,000, and uses the remaining £5,000 as real capital. The money lent is in the hands of a banker, who gives the man the common rate of interest for it—let us say 6 per cent. This brings him in £300 a year. With the other £5,000 he buys a boot and shoe factory in full working order. Of course he does not want this factory for any other purpose than that of producing more wealth by means of it ; indeed, it would be of little use for anything else. The £5,000 spent on the factory is therefore *capital*. On this he gains a *profit* of, say, £900 a year, which is made up in some such way as this : (*a*) The *interest* on £5,000 is £300 ; (*b*) *premium* for insurance against risk of loss through dishonesty of customers and from accident, £200 ; (*c*) *wages* for managing the business, £400. The £300, the interest on the money he had lent, being added, this man's total *income* would be £1,200. A large part of this he might *use unproductively*, in providing luxury and amusement for himself and his family ; but he would most likely add something to his wealth every year. What was so added would be *savings*. No doubt you will say that a man acts wisely in using only part of his wealth in his business and allowing the rest to be out at interest in perfect safety; for in this way he " provides for a rainy day."

*Land, Labour, and Capital not the only Instruments of Production.*

You have now seen that in order that wealth may be produced *land* is always necessary, and that, except in a few doubtful cases, *labour* also is needed. You have seen, too, that land and labour without the aid of *capital* cannot produce much wealth. You have now to learn that *knowledge* and *skill* are also important aids to production. Perhaps the best way to do this will be to consider a number of instances in which increase of knowledge and skill have led to the increase of wealth.

*Knowledge and Skill aid Production of Wealth.*

In the very old times it was sometimes most difficult for men to get a living. Wild animals soon began to learn how clever men were, and to keep a good distance away from them. At last some one found out that certain kinds of wood were very tough, and that if pieces of this wood were bent and then let go they would at once spring back to their former position. It was known, too, that the sinews of certain animals became very tough and strong when they were dried. Then the thought came into some one's mind that it would be possible to make with the tough springing wood and the strong sinews a weapon that would serve for killing animals from a distance; and, very soon, bows and arrows were made. Animals that before could be only looked at were now killed. Increase of knowledge caused increase of wealth. Knowledge led people to make the weapons, and with the weapons they procured more food.

In olden times it was extremely dangerous for ships to go far out of sight of land, because if bad weather came on and prevented the sailors from seeing sun, moon, and stars they would not know which way to steer their ship, and would run the risk of being wrecked. It was found out by-and-by that a needle might be made magnetic, and that it would then always point nearly to the north. Soon a compass was made, and ships were able to go on distant voyages, carrying things to places where they would be worth more than they were where they had been grown, and bringing back large quantities of very useful things in exchange. Thus the wealth both of the places that the sailors went to and of their own country was greatly increased. In a similar way we send kauri-gum, which is of small use in New Zealand, to England, where it is of great use, and receive in exchange iron rails perhaps, which would be very dear if they were made here, but which, when they are sent from England, can be sold here at a very cheap rate.

Fifty years ago it took a man a couple of days to make a common pair of boots; now a good workman can make many pairs in a single day. Increase of knowledge has enabled men to make machinery do quickly what human hands do very slowly, and so to produce more wealth with less trouble.

Fifty years ago it was a whole day's work for a man to reap an acre of wheat, and perhaps another man was needed to bind up the sheaves. A knowledge of the natural powers of steam, and skill in making machines, have enabled one man to reap and bind the wheat from a great many acres in a day. This saves much useless toil, and so sets free great numbers of men to produce wealth in other ways—perhaps by digging for gold, or by helping to make more machines.

The knowledge of the fact that when compressed air is set free great cold is produced, and skill in making machines for compressing air and setting it free at the proper time, have greatly increased the wealth of New Zealand, by enabling large steamers to take frozen mutton from New Zealand to England, where it is much wanted and dear, and to bring us in return things that are worth much more to us than mutton is, seeing that we have very many more sheep here than we want to use for ourselves alone.

About a hundred years ago an Italian doctor found out that by gently touching a frog's leg in a certain way with two kinds of metals at the same time he could make the leg move sharply. This set him and others thinking; their thinking caused them to try various experiments with copper and zinc, and other pairs of metals. Thus they gradually obtained a little knowledge of the action of the metals, then more knowledge, till now at last we have the electric telegraph as the result of this knowledge. You will easily understand that the telegraph is a very important part of the wealth of the State, and that it is of great use in increasing this wealth; perhaps nothing, except the railways, gives more help in the process of moving things from where they are not wanted to where they are wanted. The telegraph is therefore an important part of the State's capital as well as of its wealth.

Thus you see that knowledge and skill are and have been most important aids to production, and, though they cannot quite be ranked with land, labour, and capital, it would be a very great mistake to leave them out of the list of things that assist in production. How are we to account for the gradual increase of knowledge and skill? Progress in knowledge has been caused almost entirely by man's power of storing up and using the knowledge of those that have gone before him, and by his being thus put into the way of observing and finding out new things for himself. This was fully explained in Chapter II. But increase of skill seems to have been caused mainly by the *division of labour*, about which we must now say a few words.

### Combination of Labour.

Before division of labour was possible men must have learnt the advantages of combination of labour; they must have learnt that "many hands make light work." In the earliest times everybody had to do for himself whatever he wanted done. Even a few years ago the Australian blacks never helped one another : every man gathered grubs for himself ; any one that wanted an opossum had to climb up a gum-tree and get one ; if he felt that he would like a black snake, a "turkey," or an emu, he had to catch and kill one for himself. The Maoris, on the contrary, appear to have always understood the advantages of the combination of labour. This has enabled them to increase their wealth by building fine *whares*, making large canoes, planting crops regularly, and in other ways, all quite unthought of by the blacks. Simple combination of labour still takes place in many parts of New Zealand. Neighbours in turn assist one another in getting in crops, in mustering sheep, and in ploughing. A very simple form of combination is to be seen in the case in which a bushman cannot lift his log on to the skids, and two or three others come and help him till the work is done.

*Division of Labour : the Advantages and the Disadvantages connected with it.*

Division of labour takes place when two or more persons do *different* parts of a piece of work that one might do by himself. If, for instance, three miners are working in shallow ground, each of them might throw up wash-dirt from the hole, carry it down to the creek, and wash out the gold. But probably they will do the work thus : One will throw up the wash-dirt, the second will take it in buckets to the water, and the third will wash out the gold. The advantages will be—(a) that each will learn to do his work well and quickly ; (b) that time will not be lost in going from one kind of work to another ; (c) that each man will do the work best suited for him—the heaviest and strongest man will throw up the wash-dirt, the steadiest and most cautious will wash out the gold, and the third, having no special qualifications, will do the least important work—he will carry the buckets. It is quite certain that the work will be much better and more quickly done in this way than it would if each did the same kind of work ; but there are evils connected with this plan too. There will be an entire want of change, and so the labour will be more wearying and tiresome ; and, of course, if the miners break up their company and work separately they will each be able to do only one part of the work well. This last kind of disadvantage is sometimes found to cause great inconvenience.

*Effects of Extreme Division of Labour.*

A Maori that has been brought up in his settlement is able to do a great many things pretty well. He can cultivate ground, he can build a whare, he can manage a canoe, he understands horses and can ride fast over any kind of country. In fact, he can do almost anything that he is required to do. The consequence is that if it is necessary for him to do any new thing he very soon learns how to do it ; his hand, and eye, and mind have been *trained* by many kinds of work, and the task of learning to do quite new things is a mere trifle to him. In England, on the other hand, men who live in towns can very often do only one or two things. It is true that they do these things extremely well—constant practice has made their *skill* very great. If a man has been taught to make one certain part of a watch, and nothing else, after a few years' practice he will make that part very fast and very well. But, if a machine is invented to do the work even faster and better than he can do it, he will be thrown out of work, and be unable to get a living until he has learnt a new trade. Many of the people from large English towns who come out to New Zealand are nearly as helpless as babies would be, because they have been doing only one kind of work all their lives—working some machine, perhaps, or making a small part of some article—and know not how to do anything else. These people often suffer great misery while learning to do the hard work that is required in the colonies. A man who has been making pins' heads all his life finds it very hard to learn how to put up a good strong fence that will keep out cattle and pigs. All this shows that if division of labour is carried very far it is good for the work but bad for the workman. People everywhere are beginning to see how necessary it is that all children should be taught when they are young how to use their eyes and their hands, and that they should also learn to do hard bodily work; so that when they are older, and happen to have to undertake a new kind of work, they may be able to master it easily and quickly. Very soon it will be acknowledged that the eye that sees and the hand that works must be trained at school, as well as the mind that remembers and thinks.

### Division of Labour extremely beneficial.

Nevertheless, Division of Labour is an excellent thing. How long would it take a man to build a small brick house if he had to do everything himself? What would it cost, and what kind of a house would it be when it was built, if he had to make the bricks, get the lime for the mortar and burn it, make a trowel and the other tools needed, cut down the trees and work them into boards, make the glass for the windows, smelt the iron for the locks, make the paint and the paper, and do hundreds of other things? It would take a long lifetime; the cost of labour, to say nothing of interest, would be thousands of pounds; and the house when finished would probably be fit only to be pulled down again at once, because no one could live in it. For, while doing so many different things, the workman would have had no chance of obtaining skill in doing anything—the whole of the work would be done badly. But by division of labour, which allows each man to learn to do one or two things quickly, cheaply, and well, and by combination of labour, a good house, that will last for a very long time, can be built for four or five hundred pounds in a couple of months, or even less.

*Division of Labour between Countries; Capital renders Division of Labour possible.*

Division of labour also takes place between different countries. Sugar could be grown in New Zealand, and flour could be produced in Fiji. But Fiji is unsuitable for wheat-growing, and New Zealand for sugar-growing; so Fiji sends sugar to New Zealand in exchange for flour, and New Zealand sends flour to Fiji in exchange for sugar. Thus Fiji and New Zealand get the benefit of each other's soil and climate. We should remember that there must be a fair supply of capital to make really useful division of labour possible. A carpenter's plane or a bricklayer's trowel would never be made by people who did not want such things for their own use, unless it was thought that stored-up wealth would be used to purchase them. It is by people with capital that they must be bought, if by anybody, because such things are worth very little except for the help they afford in the production of more wealth. If, then, there were no capital, there could be but very little division of labour. In the same way, foreign trade could not be carried on without a large amount of capital. Tea could never be used in New Zealand unless some one had enough wealth stored up to enable him to purchase the tea from the tea-farmer or the tea-merchant, and also to make it useful to New Zealanders by bringing it within their reach.

# CHAPTER XII.

RENT: WHAT IT IS; ITS AMOUNT; WHOSE IT IS.

THE next two words that you have to master will require much careful attention. They are by no means uncommon words, but they are both used in many different senses; in this book an attempt will be made to use each of them in one sense only. The word you have to deal with in this chapter is "*rent;*" and you will first learn which of its meanings are to be rejected, and which one is to be adopted.

*Payments received for the Use of a Building may be Profit.*

Suppose that the Government, in order to encourage fishermen to settle in one of the West Coast Sounds and follow their business there, permitted any fishermen settling in that Sound to take possession of an acre of land wherever he chose. Suppose, too, that a man took advantage of the Government's permission, and built a couple of comfortable cottages, one for himself, and one for his brother, whom he had asked to come from England and be his partner in the business of fishing and curing. If, now, for some reason, the brother did not come, but another fisherman went to the Sound, it is very likely indeed that this second fisherman would say to himself, " Why should I build ? Here is a cottage that will just suit me. I can do better by fishing than by wasting my time in building a house." The end of the matter would probably be that he would agree to pay the other man so much a week—perhaps 5s.—for the hire of the second house, and that he would live in it and go on with his fishing at once.

Now, the question is, What is this 5s. a week that is paid for the use of the house ? You will probably answer at once that it is *rent*. That is the way in which the word is commonly used ; but that use of it will not suit us. The first fisherman built the house with his stored-up wealth in order that he and his brother might use it for the production of more wealth—that it might keep them warm and comfortable and healthy while they were engaged in fishing. Another man comes along and uses this wealth in the way it was intended to be used, and pays the first fisherman 5s. a week for the use of this *capital*. What, then, is this payment? Plainly it is *profit* ; it is not rent:

### Payments supposed to be Rent may be Wages.

Again, it may be that no part of a sum paid yearly for permission to use a building is rent. In a certain city there is a large public building called a Town Hall. This has been built with the ratepayers' money and is intended for the use and convenience of the people living in the city. Every Saturday morning the teachers from the different schools in the city meet in one of the rooms belonging to the Town Hall, to improve themselves in various ways, and to help one another to learn the best ways of teaching. As other meetings are held in the room during the following week, the room has to be cleaned on Friday evenings, and got ready for the teachers, and it has to be put into order again on Saturday evenings. This work is done by the person that takes care of the building. The teachers have to pay £5 a year to the managers of the business connected with the hall. Now, what is this payment? Many people would say at once that it is the rent that the teachers pay for the room. It is certainly not *real rent*. It is wages ; for the charge is made to enable the managers to pay the man that has the care of the buildings for his labour in cleaning and preparing the room that the teachers make use of.

These two examples will show you that many payments that seem to be rent are really wages or profits. Now that you have some idea as to what rent is not, you may go on to learn what it really is.

### Rent is what remains of Produce after Wages and Profits have been taken from this Produce.

Two brothers take up two pieces of poor land side by side. They have each the same amount of wealth. They are both

very frugal and cautious, and they expend their wealth entirely
on the cultivation of their land. They both work in the same way,
and they each get the same quantity of land under crop. At
the end of the second year, the results of the work having been
reckoned up, it is found that, while each brother has earned 6s.
a day as wages (this being the current rate of wages at that
time and place), and has made £75 profit on his capital (at the
current rate of interest, insurance, and wages of management),
the elder brother has 200 bushels of wheat left, while the
younger has not a single bushel. Thus, these two brothers
have used the same amount of capital and the same amount of
labour ; but the elder brother's land, being the better piece,
gives more than what is required to pay his wages and profit,
while the younger brother's land, being of a poorer kind, gives
wages and profit and no more. Well, then, reckoning the
corn as being worth 4s. a bushel, what are you to call the £40
that the elder brother has in hand after taking his wages and
profits out of the produce ? It is what you are to call rent.
You have, no doubt, been accustomed to look upon rent as a
payment, and you may find it difficult to understand why this
£40 should be called rent ; if you feel this difficulty you may
get over it by considering the elder brother as being both
owner and tenant of his land : as tenant he pays, and as owner
he receives, £40 as rent.

Again, a farmer works on a piece of ground that is not
his own. In the year, this ground yields £500 to be divided
between himself and the owner. Out of this he keeps for
himself £300 for his own wages and for profit on his capital,
and pays £200 to the owner of the ground. Now, what is this
£200 ? " Rent," you will say. Perhaps it is ; perhaps it is not.
It all depends upon the amount of capital that the owner (or perhaps a previous owner) has spent upon the land. If he has
spent so much on it that £200 is only a fair return on the capital, he does not get a single penny of rent, he gets only profit.*

---

* In Chapter XXIV. these *rent-like profits* are dealt with much more fully,
and it is shown that, as a rule, the elements that compose them become so mixed
up that it is impossible to separate them. For many practical purposes such
compounds are rent ; for others, profit. Perhaps time is an important element
in the case. If a piece of ground has been newly cleared and broken up it would
seem rather absurd to call the return for this work rent ; it would seem equally

But if he has spent, say, £1,000 on the land and buildings, and £100 is the ordinary profit on this, then he gets £100 as rent. You will now begin to see what rent really is. RENT is what is left of the produce of land when wages and profits have been taken out of it.

### *Possession of any natural Advantage may lead to the Receipt of Rent.*

But the word "*rent*" relates not only to income from land, but also to any income that may be obtained through the possession of a natural power or natural condition which a man may get benefit from, or turn to his own advantage. Two milkmen bring milk into a large town for sale. Both of them are careful and frugal men. They are both honest, too, and make only a· proper use of their pumps. Their expenses on the farms are almost the same, and each of them owns the farm that he works. Each sells 150 quarts a day, at 4d. a quart. But one lives only a mile from town, while the other lives seven miles away. The milkman that lives seven miles away merely makes a fair living; while the one living close to the town is fast becoming a wealthy man. What causes the difference? It is this : A great part of the time of the man that lives far off is taken up in driving to and from the town, so he has to keep an extra labourer; his horses wear out very soon through having to travel twenty-eight miles a day, and he has to keep two extra horses; his cart needs repairs very often ; and when he is away the work does not go on so well as it would if he were at home. The man that lives near the town, you see, has a great advantage over the other, and this is entirely owing to the *very short distance* that his farm is from the town. It is through this that he saves £75 more a year than the other man does. Now, what shall we call this £75 ? There is only one name for it, seeing that it is paid to one who possesses *a natural advantage*, and that it is through this advantage that he gains £75 a year : we must call the extra sum "rent." We shall see before we have done that this kind of rent nearly always comes

---

absurd to give the name profits to the return from improvements made a century ago. Perhaps the safest plan is to look upon the extra return derived from land on account of permanent improvements as *profits on fixed capital.*

6

to be attached to land. In this case the effect would be that, if the two men let their farms, the one near the town would be let for £75 more a year than the other one would.

## Rent compared with Wages and Profit.

You will now understand that the possessor of a natural advantage may receive rent on account of it just as a landowner receives rent from land; and that, as wages are what is gained through labour, and as profits are what is gained through abstinence, so rent is what a man gains through being the owner of land, or the possessor of some natural advantage. You will see, too, further on, that the man who is the owner of land takes as rent *the whole* of the produce of the land, and of the labour and capital employed upon it, when enough has been taken out of this produce to pay the wages for the work done and the profits on the capital spent upon the land. You are prepared also to notice a striking difference between wages and profits on the one hand, and rent on the other. A receiver of rent may grow rich without either toiling or spinning, without either labour or care; while a capitalist is nearly always worried and anxious, and a labourer is hardly ever free from fatigue of mind or of body. Wages and profits always have to be *earned* by some kind of hard work or by sacrifice of comfort; but, though the title to receive rent is often thoroughly sound, you will see as you go on that rent itself cannot be *earned*, for it is always the result of the operation of the laws of Nature, and is part of the free gift of Nature to mankind. That individual men do not always get their full share of the gift results entirely from man's own arrangements, and perhaps these arrangements are the result of man's lack of wisdom.

## Determination of Amount of Rent.

Consider now, once more, how the amount of rent that land will produce may be determined. A farmer has 40 acres of land that he has brought into cultivation himself, and that is all his own. This land may be divided into four lots. You may call these lots A, B, C, and D. Each of them contains 10 acres. Suppose, now, that the farmer can grow only wheat, but that he does this in the best possible way. At harvest, A yields 300 bushels, B yields 200, and C 100. D is very poor land, and yields only 50 bushels. The farmer finds that, taking one year with another, the expense of working any lot is equal to the price of 100 bushels, that 100 bushels will give him wages for his labour and profit on his capital expended upon the lot. What will he do? He will work lots A, B, and C, and he will not work lot D. He will work C because it gives him wages and profits and thus pays him for his trouble. A and B he will of course work, because A will give him 200, and B 100 bushels, over and above the cost of working them. These 300 bushels, which would, at 4s., be worth .£60, are his rent—that is, what he would gain through being the owner of the land. Thus, then, you can find out the *amount* of rent of any piece of land by first finding out how much more it will produce, with a certain quantity of labour and capital, than can be obtained from the poorest land in use at the time and in the neighbourhood. Lot C returned wages and profits, but yielded no rent at all; Lot B, with the same labour and capital, produced 100 bushels more than C did; therefore the rent of B would be the price of 100 bushels, or .£20. In the same way, the rent of A would be .£40; while, of course, D would give no rent at all. You may notice that if corn became any dearer C would give rent; and, if it became very much dearer, even D might yield rent. In both cases the owner of the land would get all the advantage unless wages and profits rose too—a very unusual thing; as rent rises wages and profits generally fall, as you will see when you have studied the effects of increase of population on rent and on wages and profits respectively.

*Reasons why Nominal Rent is often higher than the Real Rent.*

If this farmer went into some other business, and let his land, what rent would he ask for it? Besides the profit on the capital that he has put into the farm, he would, of course, expect £60 as rent, for he would know that this was what the land would bring in above the cost of cultivating it; he would know, also, that working-farmers can always be found to take land if they think they can get from it the usual wages of labour and profit on capital. Farmers are ready to do this because they know that that is all they could expect to get either from farming or any other business. But the owners of land often get more than their profits and real rent for their cultivated land, because what a man seeks when he takes a farm is not so much a means of getting profit on his small capital as a place where he can have constant work and where he can house his family in comfort. In nearly every society there are many people in this position; and the consequence is that a man who owns a small farm and wishes to let it can nearly always get more for it than the real rent. In some cases, indeed, he might get as great a share of the produce as the new farmer could give after keeping enough to provide for the bare wants of himself and his family.

### Nominal Rent not always as much as the Real Rent of Land together with the Profits on Capital expended on the Land.

On the other hand, there are cases in which landowners cannot get the whole of the real rent of their land, together with the profits on the capital expended on it; this occurs generally when there has been unwise expenditure on the land. In some countries it is considered a very honourable thing to own grand estates. This sometimes leads to the giving of very high prices for land or to the expenditure of a large amount of wealth upon it. Such estates cannot be expected to yield profit on the large capital expended on them. Perhaps, however, you may justly say that it is unfair to call all the wealth expended on such land capital; part of it is, without doubt, wealth unproductively consumed, from which no return can be expected.

### To Whom does Rent rightfully belong ?

The next question you have to answer about rent is: Is it fair that all the rent of land should go to the owner of the land; and, if not, to whom should it go? In the case of labour and capital you are able to answer such questions as these at once. If one were asked to say who ought to receive wages, he could reply at once, "The man who makes an effort and performs a service—the labourer—should get them." It is quite plain, too, that the capitalist who has stored up wealth, very likely through his own labour, and who does not use it merely for his own enjoyment, but for the production of more wealth; who takes the risk of losing his wealth while assisting labour; and who works very hard in managing his business—it is quite plain that he should have his profits. But about rent you cannot yet be so certain. You must learn a great deal more about it before you can give an answer, and it will be better for you to leave such a difficult subject until you have nearly finished this part of the book. But even now you may safely say that, if a man has lawfully become possessed of a piece of land, the rent of that land *fairly and justly* belongs to him until his title has been rightfully extinguished.

# CHAPTER ·XIII.

## EXCHANGE: VALUE AND ITS CAUSE; PRICE.

You have now to deal with another very difficult word, VALUE. Like *rent*, the word *value* is used in many different senses.. You must learn, if possible, to use it in one sense only. In common language you may say that a good name is of great *value;* that courage is a *valuable* natural gift; that a friend's advice is often of great *value.* In all these cases you will see that the words *value* and *valuable* might be replaced by *use* or *useful.* Now, though it is quite true that value very often, perhaps always, depends on some kind of usefulness, yet that is not the special thing that you have to think about when you make a strict use of the word *value.* When the word is used in books of this sort it refers not to merely useful things, but to things that can be *exchanged.* Many able writers, seeing how very hard it is to confine the word to this peculiar sense, have proposed to add one or more words to it to limit its meaning; others, again, think it would be well to have an altogether new term. But if it is at all possible to use the old word it will be advisable to do so, especially as its strict meaning exactly answers the purpose. If you can by any means make the word *value* do the work you want it to do, it is far better to use it than to employ such terms as "value in exchange," or "ratio of exchange."

The word value comes from an old Latin word that means *to be strong, to be well,* and, also, *to · have sufficient strength.* Now, if you were asked to say what is meant, even in common language, by such an expression as " £20 is the value of my horse," could you not reply that it means that in a bargain £20 would have the same *strength* in the exchange as the horse would have? Or, again, if it is said that the value of a sovereign is the same as that of twenty shillings, does not this mean that if an exchange were being made the power of the sovereign would be equal to that of twenty shillings; or that if you went to buy sugar with a sovereign its strength in exchange would be exactly the same as that of twenty shillings, seeing that the grocer would give you just as much sugar for the one as for the other? Well then, we shall always try to make the word VALUE mean *strength in exchange.* You will now understand why the meanings given at the beginning of the chapter were not suitable; if you take the first sentence in which the word was used—" A good name is of great *value* "—you will see at once that a good name cannot be exchanged, and that therefore it can have no value if the word *value* is used in the strict sense.

### How the Value of a Thing may be found; Price.

In order to find the value of anything you must learn what it will exchange for; though you would not be able even then to say that one thing is the value of another thing, as that an ounce of silver is the value of a teaspoon, or that 6d. is the value of six ounces of acid-drops. Value means strength in exchange, and you could not say that the strength in exchange of six ounces of acid-drops is 6d., though you might say that the value of 6d. is equal to the value of six ounces of acid-drops. But' it is not very safe to reckon value from one exchange only; if you want to find the true value of any article you will have to notice what its strength in exchange is as compared with that of many other articles under various circumstances. A boy might be very anxious to get two ounces of acid-drops from another boy who had some, and he might be willing to give 1s. for them; but that would not show their true value,* which a boy might learn if he went to a shop, where he would find that the strength of 1s. in exchange was equal to that of twelve · ounces of acid-drops. The true value of anything is its strength

---

* It would show neither the *market value* nor the *natural value* (which will be explained in Chapters XVII. and XVIII.), but what may be called a temporary value depending on altogether exceptional circumstances. Other examples of this kind of value are given further on in this chapter for the purpose of illustrating the causes of value.

in exchange for things in general. If you had a watch and wanted to know its value you might find what it was by going to the greengrocer's, and asking how many cabbages he would give you for it; you might learn from the butcher how much beef, and from the grocer how much sugar, you could get for it; at last you might go to the chimney-sweep and ask him how many times he would sweep your chimney for it. You could thus, no doubt, get a good general idea of your watch's strength in exchange. But this would be a very slow and troublesome way of finding its value. We have, however, a means of finding out what the value of anything is without putting ourselves to so much trouble. There is one article that everybody will give and everybody will take in exchanges, and that is money. Money enables us to measure value pretty exactly. If you took your watch to two or three buyers of watches, and found that you could get £7 for it, and if a grocer told you that he charged £1 a bag for his sugar; besides learning that the value of your watch was equal to the value of seven sovereigns you would know at once that you could get seven bags of sugar for your watch—that its value was seven times as great as that of a bag of sugar. It has been found convenient to have a special name for the value of anything in relation to money. The money that an article will exchange for is called its price. You may say, then, that the PRICE of anything is the quantity of money for which it will exchange.

## Service is the Cause of Value.

You have next to learn how value is caused. In Chapter VI. it was shown that human *wants* lead to *efforts*, and that it is through these efforts that *satisfaction* is obtained. But it is not the effort that actually satisfies the want. There is a link wanting between the effort and the satisfaction; an effort must be well directed or it will not result in satisfaction, even when one makes an effort to satisfy his own want. Suppose that your watch is very much out of order and you take it to the watchmaker. A week after you call for the watch and are told that it is not ready. The next week you call again, and the watchmaker hands you the watch and tells you that he has done his best, but has been quite unable to make it go. He has made a great effort, no doubt, but he has not satisfied your want, which is that your watch shall be made to keep correct time. Accordingly he does not expect you to pay him anything. You then take the watch to another tradesman, who puts it right for you in three days. He makes an effort, renders you a SERVICE, and satisfies your want, and you pay him 10s. for his *service*. Now, notice that what you consider to have strength in exchange (to have value) equal to that of your 10s. is not the effort—you paid the first watchmaker nothing for his effort·—it is the *service* that has value. If a man lost a horse and offered a reward for him, no one but the man who, by returning the horse, had rendered the service and satisfied the want would receive the reward. It is very possible that other men would have made great efforts to find the horse, but these efforts, having led to no service, would be without value. You see, then, that it is *service* that gives *value* to effort.

It may be well to consider here the case of a lawyer or a doctor. As the lawyer gets paid whether he wins your case or loses it, and as the doctor takes a fee whether his patient lives or dies, you might think that in their case, at all events, it is the effort that is paid for and not the service. The position of the doctor and the lawyer differs from that of the watchmaker in this.: If the watchmaker knows his trade he can tell whether your watch can be mended or not ; and if it can be mended he ought to be able to do the work.· But a human body is a kind of machine that no one fully understands. What seems at first a very simple disease may cause death ; and all that can be expected of the doctor is that he should do his best. It is for the *service* of attending a sick person, and for doing his best to help him, that the doctor is paid. In the same way the law is a very difficult thing to understand ; and a person going to law with another often makes mistakes in telling his lawyer about his case, or lets him know only part of it. In short, the lawyer's work is nearly as difficult as the doctor's, and all that can be expected from him is that he will *do his best* for those who come to him. It is for *this* service that he is paid, and the winning or losing of the case has little to do with the matter.* It will be seen, then, that service is always the foundation of value; it is, indeed, the cause of it. There are, however, some things to be considered before we can say that value—strength in exchange—depends entirely on service.

### The Relation of Scarcity to Value.

The Maoris find potatoes just about the most useful of all things; without them they would lead a very hard life indeed, especially those who live far away from towns. Now, let us suppose a Maori and his family living near the head of the Wanganui River to have had a very poor potato-crop, and to be starving. If you took a bag of potatoes to their *whare* these people would be ready to give you for it everything they possessed—their mats, their blankets, even their clothes; if you next took them a ton of potatoes they would probably be willing to give you a large piece of their ground for it; but, if you then sent another bag of potatoes, they would hardly care to have it. Here, you see, the first service would be very great, because the want would be sore; the scarcity of potatoes would be so great that the value of the service of supplying them would, to these Maoris, be greater than the value of all that they possessed. The second service would be still great, and the Maoris would consider its value equal to that of a large piece of their land; but when the third effort was made there would be no longer a want, there could be no service, and the potatoes would be without value. Now, we may learn two things from this example: The first is that *mere* usefulness, like *mere* effort, is not the cause of value; and the second is that, as scarcity decreases, and as wants become easy to satisfy, the value of the service that satisfies them becomes smaller. A woman annoyed by mice will perhaps give 5s. for a good cat, but she would hardly give 10s. for two good cats, and she certainly would not give £2 10s. for ten good cats.

---

* This may be stated in a somewhat different way: Doctors and lawyers, on account of the complex nature of the subjects that they deal with, cannot be expected to undertake the curing of a patient or the winning of a case; the service they offer is the mere giving of advice. If you are sick, or have had a wrong inflicted on you, you *want* advice from a skilled person; the doctor or the lawyer gives you this advice; this is his *effort*. The receiving of this advice is your *satisfaction*. The effort of the doctor or of the lawyer satisfies your want, and is therefore a *service*.

### Mere Scarcity is not the Cause of Value.

If you were going into the Urewera country and took with you, among other things, a good barometer, worth, say, £5, with the intention ·of exchanging it for greenstone ornaments and other curious things, you would find that, though there was no such thing as a barometer in the country, though barometers were even scarcer than were potatoes in the Maori whare referred to in the last example, yet no Maori would be willing to give you much for it. No one would feel a *want* for such a thing ; your *effort* would have rendered no service, and your barometer would have no strength in exchange. From this and the former illustrations we learn that *mere* usefulness, *mere* effort, and *mere* scarcity are not causes of value unless they give birth to a want that nothing but a service can satisfy.

### Value does not reside in Objects, but is the Result of an Operation of the Human Mind.

But the most important 'lesson to be learnt from these illustrations is that value is not a real thing or quality that is to be found in this article but not in that ; that value does not, so to speak, *reside* in things constantly, but is the result of the work of the human mind in comparing a want with the effort that would be required to satisfy it. If a man wants an American organ, the price of which is £30, he will ·weigh, in his mind, this want against the effort that he will have to make in parting with £30, or perhaps against the efforts that he has had to make in earning it. If the want wins the day, the *value* of the organ *to him* will be £30 ; if not, he will keep his money and do without the organ.

Still, though value is the result of the mind's work in weighing a want and a satisfaction the one against the other, it would be wrong to say that such things as usefulness, amount of labour required, and scarcity are not causes of value. They are causes, but not of the first class, like service, which has been shown to be the foundation of value ; they are second-class causes. In the case of labour, for instance, if things that are very useful can be got with very little labour—as potatoes can —a very large quantity of them is sure to be produced if it is wanted, and this large production satisfies the want, and so the value is sure to fall. If potatoes were very scarce in Auckland in any year, and the price rose to £20 a ton, next year so many would be grown that the price would be very low. On the other hand, anything that costs a great deal of labour to make would be sure to have a high value, or else would cease to be produced; because labourers will not work without pay, and no one will pay them for labour if there is no chance of getting the money spent in wages repaid through the sale of the things produced.

# CHAPTER XIV.

## EXCHANGE: BARTER; MONEY.

When a person has more of a thing than he wants he will either store it up, throw it away, or exchange it for something that he has not enough of, or that he thinks it will be well to have more of. If Jane keeps fowls and pigs but no cow, and Mary has cows but no pigs or fowls, Jane will very likely have more eggs than she wants, while Mary will have more milk and more butter than she herself can use. The chances are, then, that Jane and Mary will make an EXCHANGE. Jane will give some of the eggs she does not want to Mary, and Mary will give some of her spare milk to Jane. It is probable that Jane will require milk every day, and butter often, while Mary will want eggs only now and then; they will therefore talk the matter over, and perhaps it will be decided at last that, in order to make the exchange fair, Jane shall give Mary a leg of pork whenever Jane's husband kills a pig. This mode of exchanging common things is called BARTER.

In some places labour is paid for with goods. A man employs a number of men and pays them their wages in flour, meat, clothes, and such things. This is called the TRUCK SYSTEM; and a very bad system it is. It enables a dishonest man to really reduce the wages of his workmen, by giving them articles of poor quality, that cost him little, and charging the price of good things for them; if the workmen complain, their employer can discharge them, and get others, who will submit to be thus wronged and cheated.

If all exchanges were such simple matters as the dealings of Jane and Mary with regard to their spare eggs and milk, barter might answer the purpose well enough; but it would be quite impossible to conduct by barter the exchanges that require to be made in a large town, and in nearly all cases it is far better to make exchanges in another way. If you were a shoemaker in a town where all exchanges were made by barter, and you had nothing but shoes and enough meat for your own use, and you wanted bread, sugar, and a hat, your only way of getting these things would be to put three pairs of shoes under your arm and go all round the town to find a baker, a grocer, and a hatter that wanted new shoes just then. Perhaps you would be unable to find any customer. One of the bakers, however, might tell you that though he did not want shoes he would like to have some meat, and that none of the butchers in town wanted his bread. You would then go to look for a butcher that wanted shoes, so that you might get meat to give the baker for bread. If you succeeded, there would still be this difficulty: You would have to take a large quantity of meat in exchange for your shoes; and, after you had exchanged some of the meat for loaves, you might find that no grocer or hatter wanted meat. After all your trouble you would find that of the things you had wanted you had got only the bread, while you had had to take home a large quantity of meat that you did not want. It is quite plain that barter is a very poor means of making exchanges.

### Various Kinds of Money.

Nearly all peoples, therefore, that do much exchanging, or are ever so little above the savage state, have found out a better plan than this. They make exchanges by means either of money or of a sort of credit. The Maoris seem to have managed in this way: If a man saw that his friend was short of food of any kind, he would send him some of this food as a present, but it was always understood that a present of somewhat greater value was to be made in return when it was needed. This we may fairly call a system of giving a kind of credit. We always find, when the plan of using money as a means of making exchanges has come into use, that the *money* used is some article that everybody is glad to have. It is said that in some of the South Sea Islands cocoanuts have been used; in parts of Africa little shells used as ornaments serve for money; in others, glass beads. Anything that everybody wants, and that can be easily exchanged, might be used as money—potatoes, for instance. If a Maori wanted a pipe and some tobacco, he could take a *kete* of potatoes to a neighbour, and exchange them for what he wanted. If the man who had sold the pipe and tobacco did not want the potatoes just then, he could take them to another Maori and exchange them, or some of them, for a melon. You understand that the potatoes would serve as a means of making exchanges just as coppers would. But potatoes would be but a poor kind of money, for several reasons. If a man sold a horse for *potato-money*, he would not be able, as he is now, to put his money into his pocket and carry it about with him; he would require a horse and cart to take it away, and, perhaps, would have to dig a big hole for it, or to build a shed to protect it from the wind and rain. Then, again, his *potato-money* would soon spoil; if he could not soon get it passed on to somebody else, the potatoes would surely rot, and would have to be given to the pigs. Besides, the value of potatoes is always changing : this year there might be a large crop and their value would be small; next year the crop might be small and their value would be great. If a man were to say, " My old horse was worth five tons of potatoes," you would have to ask in what year the horse was worth that, or else you would not know whether the horse was a good one or a bad one. *Potato-money* would have one good point about it that gold-money has not : a load of potatoes could be easily divided, even into single potatoes, and you could always manage to pay nearly the exact price of anything with them ; and it would be a very worthless thing that you would have to pay less than a single potato for.

### What should Money be made of?

By noticing what defects would be found in *potato-money*, you are now able to see what qualities a really useful kind of money should have. (*a.*) It should be much prized by everybody. (*b.*) It should be easy to carry about. (*c.*) It should be of a kind that will not readily spoil or rust. (*d.*) It should be made of material that could be easily divided into pieces of very small value and of moderate size. (*e.*) Its value should change as slowly as possible. (*f.*) It should take up but little room in proportion to its value. You will easily understand that metals are almost the only things that have all or nearly all these qualities, and that there are only two of them that are really very suitable. More than two thousand years ago iron was used for money in the Kingdom of Sparta, in Greece; but iron could never be a good metal to make money with. If iron money were in use, and a man went to a store to buy a few things, he would need to have a wheelbarrow to carry his money in. Lead is a great deal too soft. Copper is better than iron and lead, but it is suitable only for small purchases.

Gold and silver are really the only two metals that have most of the qualities that a substance used for money should have. Gold has one serious defect; if it were divided so that each piece was of very small value, say of the value of a penny, these pieces would be so small that they would be very easily lost. This defect is made up for by the use of silver and copper money.

The last lesson will have enabled you to see why gold is so highly prized—to understand the cause of its value. The *first-class* cause is that those who give other persons gold perform a great service for them. The *second-class* causes are that gold is useful to everybody, either for money, for ornaments, or for other purposes, and that it is scarce, through very much labour being required to obtain even small quantities of it.

## The Uses of Money.

You are now quite prepared to see what the work of money is. Its chief work is to enable us to make exchanges conveniently, and you learnt in the last chapter that it is also of great use in enabling us to compare the value of one thing with that of another. You may say then, shortly, that MONEY is useful as a means of making exchanges, and as a measure of value.

To impress this on your minds it may be well to give an example. I have a great quantity of apples, and wish to buy a violin. The music-seller will not, I know, want a load of apples, but the fruiterer will. What the music-seller wants is money, or the power which that money will give him of buying what he wants. I therefore take my apples to the fruiterer, who gives me money for them, and then I take the money to the music-seller, who gives me a violin for it. Thus I exchange my apples for the violin by means of the money.

But money also measures value. I am told by the music-seller that the price of the violin is £5, and other people tell me that this is a fair price. I learn from the fruiterer that the price of apples is 3d. a pound; I then know that 400lb. of apples are *worth* £5, and I know, too, that the violin and 400lb. of apples have the same strength in exchange, that is, the same value. Thus, then, money is not only a means of making exchanges, but also a measure of value.

### *To what Extent Gold, Silver, and Copper are Legal Tender.*

In New Zealand, a person to whom a large sum is due must take gold when it is offered in payment of a debt, whether he wishes to or not. But if you owed a man £1,000 you could not pay him with half-crowns or shillings, unless he was willing to take silver. Any debt up to 40s., however, may be paid with silver, and any debt up to 1s. with copper money. The quantity of silver in twenty shillings is not worth a sovereign; it is not even worth quite 17s. The copper in a penny is worth far less than a gold penny would be. It is found that making silver and copper coins in this way prevents them from being melted down and used for other purposes; it would be a very foolish man that would melt down twenty pounds' worth of shillings when he could not get quite £17 for the silver.

### *The Values of Gold and Silver vary slowly.*

Although the values of gold and silver are very steady, it is not to be supposed that they do not vary at all. In the thirteenth century one ounce of gold would exchange for no more than ten ounces of silver; now one ounce of gold will exchange for fifteen and a half ounces of silver, and sometimes more. This fact shows why it is advisable that gold coin should be chosen as the only legal tender for payment of a large debt. Since the values of gold and silver vary, it would be impossible to make a sovereign that would always be worth just twenty shillings. If a man with much wealth could pay a large debt with either gold or silver, he would find out which of the two, say sovereigns or shillings, were just then under

7

their proper value,* and would pay his debt with the other. Besides this there would be another inconvenience. People from a foreign country, say France, would take every chance of getting the coins that were under their true value, in order to take them to their own country. If the gold in a sovereign were really worth twenty-one shillings in silver, and a French-man could always get a sovereign in England for twenty shillings, sovereigns would surely be taken in large quantities from England to France, and France would gain and England would lose a shilling on every sovereign that passed from the one country to the other.

### Is it a Bad Thing to send Money out of the Country?

But you must not think from this that it is always a bad thing to send money out of the country; it would certainly be foolish to let gold coins leave the country in the way just described, but quite often the very wisest thing to do with money is to send it right away to a foreign country and let it stay there. As long as a man keeps his money in his pocket it is of very little use to him; it is when he exchanges it for other wealth that the use comes in, and it is just the same with the State as it is with the indi-vidual. Before the middle of the last century most people thought that a country possessing much gold and silver must be richer than one that had but little, and that for a country to send away gold and silver, or to allow them to be sent away, was very great folly. Money is wealth in a very convenient form; people that have money can nearly always buy what they want with it; and it is a common fashion to speak of wealth as money, as when we say, "Mr. Jones is worth £30,000," though perhaps he has nothing but land and houses. It seems probable that this way of regarding money misled our forefathers, or prevented them

---

* If the quantity of gold in ten sovereigns would exchange for two hundred and five shillings, and if at the same time two hundred shillings would by law be sufficient to pay a debt of ten pounds, then it would be right to say that sovereigns were under their proper value; for the "legal value" of the coined metal would be less than the strength in exchange of the material of which coins were made. In such a case no one would pay his debts with gold coins; he would try to exchange the gold in them for silver coins and to pay his debts with the latter. But, seeing that it is unlawful to melt down or deface the coinage, the real effect would be that all the gold coins in the country would be exported to foreign parts, where they could be sold for their *proper* value.

from considering whether money is indeed always the best form of wealth or not. However that may be, the result was that nearly every one believed that it was a good thing to keep gold and silver in the country, and a bad thing to send it away to foreign parts.

The truth is that gold and silver are mere *goods*. Like other goods they have their uses. They can be made into money, or ornaments, and they can be used for a few other purposes. Now, how do we act if we have too large a quantity of other goods? If we have too much wheat, too much wool, or too much mutton, what do we do with it? We send it away to England and get it exchanged for such things as we really want, railway iron, or knives, or calico. Just in the same way we send our gold to England or Australia, and get useful things in exchange for it. England keeps as much of this gold as she needs for money or for ornaments, and sends away the rest of it to countries that have no gold-producing colonies, and thus pays for cotton, silk, or other useful things that she wants. If gold and silver have been coined — turned into money — is the case different? Of the coins now in New Zealand a certain number are wanted as a help in making exchanges. All that we have beyond that quantity are quite useless to us in their present shape, and will be so long as they are not wanted for making exchanges. The very best thing to do with all such money is to send it away as soon as possible, and get things that will be of some real use in exchange for it. So then, if you are asked if it is not a good thing for us to keep our money in the country, you may answer, " Yes, we must keep as much as we want to help us in making our exchanges, but the best thing to do with all that we don't want is to send it away and exchange it for something that we do want."   .

We may now consider what would take place if we constantly sent goods to foreign countries in exchange for money and kept all this money in the country — every penny of it. The effect would be that prices would rise throughout the country, and the value of gold—its *strength in exchange* — would fall. People having sovereigns and finding prices rising would be anxious to buy what they wanted before prices rose still higher; first one, then another, would be willing to give more sovereigns for a horse or a house than it had been usual for people to give, and at last nearly everybody would be anxious to exchange his sovereigns for really useful things, while few would care about exchanging their goods for money unless they got a large quantity of it for them. Thus prices would keep on rising till the money in the country was just enough to carry on all the work of exchange. Now, no one would be any the richer for this. The produce of the country would not be increased by keeping the money here. How could it be? As long as the money continued to be money you could use it for nothing but making exchanges with. On the other hand, every one would suffer through so much wealth having been allowed to lie idle when it might have been sent to a foreign country and exchanged for something that would have quickly produced additional wealth. People would probably very soon learn that it is sometimes a bad thing "to keep the money in the country."

### *Money is part of the State's Fixed Capital.*

It seems as if money might almost be called part of the State's Fixed Capital. It is, in truth, a sort of machine for making exchanges with. Like machines, money wears out very slowly. Money, while it continues to be money, is, like a machine, of little use except for its own proper work. Just as a machine will do a great deal of work of the same kind and suffer little through doing it, so will a small quantity of money serve for making a great number of exchanges without being much the worse for it. If you consider what a large number of exchanges a shilling may help to make in a single week, you will understand that the amount of money needed in a country is very much smaller than most people think. Further, just as every improvement in the way of working a machine at a smaller expense without spoiling the work sets capital free to do better work, so does every means that is found out of carrying on the work of exchanging by using a smaller quantity of coin enable the State to employ more of its wealth either as capital or as a means of increasing the comforts of the members of the State. We shall see in the next chapter that it has been found possible to lessen this fixed capital—the amount of wealth that is in the form of coined gold and silver—by the use of bank-notes, bills, and cheques instead of gold and silver, that is, by making pieces of paper do much of the work of real money.

### Credit assists the Work of Exchange.

The subject of *Credit* will be dealt with pretty fully in the next two chapters—on Banking and Business; but it may be well to say here that, besides coined money and *paper money*, credit affords great help in the work of exchanging. Credit is an excellent thing when properly used, because it enables those that have little wealth of their own, but are skilful in causing wealth to produce more wealth, to have a chance of making use of their skill. We shall have to show, however, that credit often may be, and sometimes is, the cause of very great evil.

# CHAPTER XV.

## EXCHANGE: BANKS AND BANKING.

In most cases there is no difficulty in telling what a merchant or a shopkeeper buys and sells. We know that the tailor buys cloth, and then, after having increased its value by his labour, which has made it suit the wants of his customers, sells it in the form of coats, trousers, and waistcoats. The grocer buys sugar, tea, soap, and candles from the merchant in large quantities, and sells them in small parcels to suit his customers. But what does the banker buy and sell, and what service does he render to those who deal with him? You should first try to find out what he sells; when you know this, it will be easy enough to say what he buys. It will be well, perhaps, to consider a simple transaction that took place between a banker and his customer. Mr. Smith, a builder, went to his banker and said, " I want £1,000 for three months." Mr. Smith was a regular customer; the banker knew that he was an honest man, and that he had two houses nearly ready for sale; so he said, " You can have the money." Three months afterwards Mr. Smith paid the banker £1,020, and the transaction was concluded.

### What does a Banker deal in ?

Now, what did the banker sell? Do you think it was the money? No; it was not the money, for Mr. Smith gave this back to the banker with £20 more. This £20, which was the banker's profit, was paid for the use of the money for three months. Then, what does the banker sell? Clearly it is the right to use money. But if I am a grocer and give you the right to use my tea and sugar for three months before you pay me back—not exactly the tea and sugar, but the money that I charge you for it—what should I be said to give you? Credit. Then, if a banker gives you a right to use part of his wealth during three months, on the condition that at the end of that time you return it to him along with his profit, which is the payment for the service rendered you, he gives you *credit*, and you pay him for giving you credit. Well then, you see that what the banker really sells is credit. The next question to be answered is, What does the banker buy, and how does he pay for what he buys? You may be quite sure that, just as the tailor bought cloth and sold it again in a more convenient form, and just as the grocer bought tea and sold it again in smaller parcels, so what the banker buys is of the same nature as what he sells. He sells credit, and credit is what he buys. Sometimes, indeed, persons who sell credit are so wealthy that they do not buy it at all; but such persons are not really bankers, they are money-lenders. There are always people that have money which they cannot conveniently use themselves, and who yet do not like to let it lie idle. Now, the banker is ready to buy the use of this money and to pay the owners of it interest. The banker pays these people for allowing him to be their debtor—that is, for *credit*, because he hopes to sell this credit again for a larger sum. Thus, we see that a banker is really a dealer in credit; he not only sells credit, but also buys it.

### Current Accounts.

Then, again, most people who are engaged in business are constantly paying and receiving money, and they would find it inconvenient to keep money in their chests, for it might be stolen; or in their pockets, for they might lose it. They therefore leave the money with their banker, and, when they wish to make payments of any kind, write orders (or *cheques* as they are called), which the banker continues to give money for as long as he owes these customers anything. Now, the money of such customers as these cannot be greatly depended upon. One day the banker may have a great deal of it, and the next day very much less, and therefore he pays these customers no interest for their money. What he does pay for the credit they give him is the service of keeping their money safe and of enabling them to carry on their business conveniently. But still, though any one customer may draw out all his money on any one day, it is found that all such customers will not; one will take out money, but another will pay it in. It will very often happen that one customer will draw out his money by paying another customer with a cheque, which will be immediately paid into the bank again. In this and similar ways it comes about that a banker has nearly always a large sum of money in his hands from customers of this kind, and that he is able to make profit by selling the use of this money to other customers who want it. Accounts of this kind between a banker and his customer are called "current accounts." It will be seen directly that these accounts are very useful to the banker in another way.

### How Banks are established; Banking Capital.

Now that you have learnt what it is that the banker buys and sells, you may go on to consider how the business of banking is started and conducted, and then to gain information about different kinds of work done by banks. It is not every man or even every company that could start a bank. If, for instance, you said to yourself, "This banking seems to be a fine business—I will be a banker," you would not find the plan answer; you would have no customers. People would not sell you the use of their money unless they knew that you could pay them for it, and, besides, they would probably have grave doubts as to whether they would ever again see a penny of the money itself; and those who might be foolish enough to try and borrow money from you would find that you had none to lend. Before you could begin banking you would have to make it plain that you were so well off that it would not pay you to cheat people, and also that any tradesman who had the means of repaying you could get money advanced to him for three or four months if he wanted it. If you could do this you would soon find persons, both sellers and buyers, who would be willing to deal with you in regard to the use of money. In these colonies, which do not yet possess large quantities of stored-up wealth, there is often serious difficulty in starting a bank, but this difficulty is generally got over in this way : Several wealthy men, having agreed to start a bank with a capital of, say, £250,000, promise to take a certain number of shares in the bank, and undertake to be answerable either for the amount of their shares or for all debts the bank may contract. The law prescribes how this is to be done. Perhaps many shares are taken up in England, or even in foreign countries. At last all is ready, bank officers are appointed, offices are opened, and the bank is soon in full working order. The shareholders probably give their own business to their own bank from the very first; but other people, knowing that the shareholders are wealthy and well able to pay all the bank's debts, will also soon begin to take their business to the bank.

You will see now that the very first thing that a bank has to do is to establish a good character, and to make people see that it can be thoroughly trusted; when once it has done this it can carry on its business mainly with other people's money. The amount of money actually paid in by the shareholders—the bank's real capital—is generally not very large; if nothing but this real capital could be used, the profit, if there were any, would be very small indeed. It is from the "banking capital"—the money borrowed by the bank in the course of its business—that most of the profit is made. You see, then, how true it is that a banker deals in credit—in the right to use other people's wealth.

### Bank-notes.

Besides the two ways that have already been described of making profit through the use of other people's money, there is another of equal or perhaps greater importance. Banks issue notes as tokens for gold. In the transaction described at the beginning of this chapter Mr. Smith did not get his £1,000 in gold, but in the bank's notes. A bank-note is a piece of paper having printed on it the banker's promise to pay £1, or £5, or £10, or £50, whenever the amount named is asked for. So long as the bank ·is solvent these bank-notes are just as useful to Mr. Smith as gold would be. People will take them in payment for their bricks, timber, and paint, or for wages, because they know that they can get gold for them whenever they wish to have it. Now, when once these notes have been sent out of the bank a considerable time may pass by before any of them are taken back to the bank to be exchanged for gold, and it is quite plain that till they are taken back the banker is being paid for the use of other people's money. The banker, you see, does not really give Mr. Smith any money; he gives him only promises to pay money, and for these promises he receives payment at the rate of £20 per quarter, or £80 per year. You understand, then, that as long as this goes on, and, indeed, as long as any of the notes given to Mr. Smith have not been brought to the bank to be exchanged for gold, the banker is using for his own benefit the money of those who hold these notes and do not demand gold for them.

*Only a Limited Number of Notes can be kept in Circulation.*

You must not think that a banker can issue as many notes as he likes. It is profitable work, this issuing of notes, if it is properly managed ; but there are many things which limit the number of notes that can be kept going round from hand to hand. It is true that the banker can send out a great many of his notes, but he cannot keep them out.

The chief advantage of the use of notes is that it lessens the quantity of gold and silver required for the work of buying and selling. Gold can be procured only by great labour; scraps of paper can be procured for next to nothing. If these scraps of paper can be made to do the work of buying and selling, a great advantage is gained. If one hundred thousand pounds' worth of gold would be needed to carry on the exchanges in our town, it is plainly a good thing if by using paper we can manage the work with five thousand pounds' worth of gold and a few pounds' worth of paper, because we can then send away a great part of £95,000 in gold to other places to be exchanged for things that will be really useful to us. We may thus do our work of buying and selling just as well as it was done before, and have in addition ninety-five thousand pounds' worth of something that we could not get before. We might, if we wished, use some part of the £95,000 in making a railway or a harbour. States have sometimes tried to carry the use of paper money beyond its proper limits. Some attempts have been made to cause notes to be considered real money without being exchangeable for gold on demand, but all such attempts have failed more or less. People will not long continue to take one-pound notes as money unless they feel sure that they can turn them into sovereigns at any time. When they know that they can do this they look upon the notes as being as good as gold.

If a banker issued more notes than were needed for carrying on the business of his town or district, by lending too freely and so giving out more notes than were needed for the work of making exchanges, his notes would soon pass into the hands of some one that did not want to use them, and would just come back to him at once. Hardly any one keeps more cash than he wants for present use ; and most people take all their spare notes to the bank and "deposit" them with the banker in order that they may get interest on them. So perhaps if a banker, over-anxious to do business at a time when trade was dull, lent his notes to tradesmen who could not then make such a profitable use of the notes as would enable them to pay the banker his interest for the use of the notes, and if the notes passed into the hands of wealthy persons, who then *deposited* them with the banker, it might easily happen that the banker would be punished for lending too freely by having to pay interest on his own notes, which, when not in use, are *to him* mere scraps of paper. Again, hardly any banker has command of the whole business' of a district. When there are several bankers in a place, though they take in one another's notes, they never pay them out again ; they arrange for frequent exchanges of notes. Now, the banker that has issued too many notes is almost sure not to have enough of the other bankers' notes to exchange for his own, and in that case he has to pay the difference in gold. You see, then, that what may be called unnecessary notes come back to the banker who issues them, either through "depositors" or through other bankers. Current accounts afford great help to the banker in putting his notes into circulation.

### Banks sometimes lend Money on Mortgage.

We must now describe briefly one or two of the most important parts of a bank's business. Banks sometimes make what are called dead loans—that is, they lend sums of money for a considerable time on mortgage on land or houses, or on other kinds of property, such as shares in a mine or a bank. By a mortgage a great many of the owner's rights to a piece of land are handed over to the bank until the amount of the loan, along with the interest agreed upon for the use of the money, is paid. This kind of business, however, is not thought to be proper for a bank. The best kind of bank business is the discounting of bills. We must learn what bills are, and what is meant by discounting them.

### Bills and their Uses.

A bill is a stamped paper in some such form as this :—

£50 . 0 . 0.                    Auckland, 10th January, 1887.
Three months after date pay to me or my order the sum of fifty pounds ; value received.                    John Jones.
Mr. William Smith.

If William Smith writes across the face of this paper, "Accepted, payable at" say "the Bank of Polynesia," and then signs his name below it, the bill is complete. This bill means that William Smith acknowledges that he owes John Jones fifty pounds for goods or wages, or for something of the same kind, and that he will pay the money into the bank for John Jones not later than the 13th April (three days' grace are allowed), so that it may be ready for him at that date. Besides fixing the exact date of payment, this bill enables John Jones to make use of the amount that William Smith owes him. For instance, if John Jones owes Charles Brown £50, he can pay his debt by handing over the bill to Charles Brown. Before doing this, however, John Jones signs his own name on the back of the bill. This means that, if William Smith does not pay the money, he will pay it himself. Perhaps Charles Brown wants the money at once ; if so, he may go to the bank and get the bill *discounted ;* that is, the bank will, when he also has signed his name at the back of the bill, pay him perhaps £49, keeping the other £1 for *discount.* A bill, then, is a means of turning debts into a kind of bank-note that can be used for many of the purposes for which money is used. The banker makes his profit by giving money for the bill. It is very convenient to get a debt acknowledged by means of a bill, because if there should be a lawsuit about the debt the Court would consider the bill a sufficient proof of the debt. A bill, however, is not the only kind of proof.

These bills are very useful in trade. If a small tradesman sold one hundred pounds' worth of goods that he had made, and had to wait three months for his money, he might not be able to buy the material for a new lot of goods until the end of that time. But if his customer gave him a bill for the money, he could get this discounted by a banker, purchase new material, and go to work again at once. This simple illustration will show what a very useful thing a bank is. The discounting of bills, however, is often done by persons who are not bankers. When a bank bill is not paid at the date specified, the bill is said to have been *dishonoured*.

### Remittances.

Banks also arrange for the sending of money from one town to another, or even from their own country to very distant foreign countries. Banks have branches in various places, and in places where they have no branches they have accounts with other banks. Thus they can arrange for the payment in one place of money that has been received in another, very often without sending any money at all. Suppose that thirty Frenchmen in New Zealand wish to send home £10 each to friends in France, or £300 in all, and that ten Frenchmen want to send out £20 each for phormium, and six wish to send £20 each for kauri-gum, £320 in all, it is plain that the banks could so arrange the matter that if £20 were sent to New Zealand from France it would suffice for settling the whole business. Of course the banks get paid for this kind of work.

You might be told a great deal more about the useful work that banks do, but you now probably know enough to enable you to form a good idea of the New Zealand banks and their business.

### Savings-banks.

There are, however, banks of another kind, and something must be said about them. These are banks that enable the State to put to a good use the savings of people who are not wealthy. Some of these banks are connected with the Post Office, some are not; and most of them are excellent banks. When money is lent to the Government through the Post Office, interest on deposits up to £500 is regularly paid. These banks offer many of the advantages afforded by ordinary banks. Many of them also lend money on mortgage. Those who deposit their money in savings-banks may feel quite sure of getting it back again. They may also be sure that if they use these banks regularly they will gradually teach themselves the habit of saving their loose money instead of wasting it, and of providing for the future—a very highly important habit, for the cultivation of which too high a price could hardly be paid.

# CHAPTER XVI.

## EXCHANGE : BUSINESS ; CREDIT TO CONSUMERS.

THIS is a very simple but very important chapter ; it would be well if more space than is available could be devoted to it ; as it is, only a few points can be dealt with, and these must be treated very briefly. " Business " really means the state or condition of being busy, or work that keeps one busy ; the word is sometimes used in this way, as when we say, " As soon as the *business* was finished the meeting broke up." This, however, is not the most common meaning of the word ; *business* now generally means, in ordinary language, work connected with buying and selling— the exchanging of goods for money. It is in this sense that we shall use the word.

### *The Draper's Shop.*

You may consider, first, a very simple case of a man who is *in business*, and try to find out what his real work is, and why and how he does it. There is a draper's shop. In the shop-windows we see many beautiful and useful articles arranged in a neat and attractive way ; many of the things have tickets fastened to them to show that they may be had at a low price. You can at once understand what these shop-windows and the tickets are for ; they are intended to make passers-by understand that if they want drapery goods they can purchase them there, and that the things sold in the shop are good and cheap. The shopkeeper knows, too, that many people will immediately *want* anything that strikes their fancy ; and it is to his advantage that people should be caused to want the articles that he has for sale. The goods in his windows suffer through being exposed to sunshine and dust and damp; but the draper knows that he gains more through attracting customers to his shop than he loses by exposing his goods. The advantage derived from advertising, of course, depends on the same principle. When you have entered the draper's shop you see some customers busily engaged in examining the articles that are shown to them by the shopmen; other customers are paying for things that they have purchased; one or two buy and take away things without paying for them; and here is a man who appears to have bought nothing and yet is paying the draper a pretty large sum of money. What is the meaning of it all? What is the work that the draper does, and how does he get paid for it?

### The Draper's Stock.

In the first place, how does the draper determine the quantity and the quality of the goods that he will require for his shop? He finds, by looking over his account-books for previous years and reckoning the amount of money that he has received during each of those years, that there are no very great changes in the amounts of his sales in successive years. Mr. Jones may buy less this year than he did last; but then Mr. Smith may buy more. Mrs. Brown, who has dealt with him for many years, may take offence at something and, in future, buy her goods at the shop over the way; but then Mrs. White, who has always dealt at the other shop, may leave it and come to him. Again, the other shop may have got in a lot of very good hats which it can sell very cheap, and so take away some of his chance customers; but then our draper may have been able to buy shirts at such a low rate that he can sell them much cheaper than the other shop can, and so take away some of its chance customers. On the whole, then, he finds that there is generally little difference from year to year in the quantity of goods required to meet his customers' wants. If, now, he finds that he requires fifteen thousand pounds' worth of goods in the year, how is he to spend the money? What ought he to order from England? This is a matter about which he has to be very cautious. As you know, there is a thing called Fashion. Fashion is a great tyrant, and must be obeyed. You would find few boys or girls in New Zealand who would be strong-minded enough to go to a party or to church dressed in an "old-fashioned way." You know that Fashion is very fickle. A dress that would have kept one quite warm and comfortable three years ago is now, though quite unworn, only fit to make dusters with. Well, then, the draper has to study fashion with the greatest care, and the moment that he sees it is about to change he must get rid of things that are going to be old-fashioned, and procure, as soon as possible, what the new fashion demands. For the draper lives by successful *efforts* to *satisfy* people's *wants*, and it is for doing this that he is in the end paid. Many New Zealand drapers, in order to be able to get the most suitable kinds of goods, employ buyers who live in England but have been trained to understand what kinds and quantities of goods their employers will require : these goods they buy and send out to New Zealand as they think they will be needed.

### *The Draper renders important Services.*

You will see, then, that the draper is a very important person, and that we could hardly do without him. Just consider the kind of service he renders. A Maori wants a good warm striped blanket, of a kind made only at Peebles, in Scotland. The draper enables him to satisfy his want without sending to Peebles for what he wants, without running any kind of risk, and by paying only a reasonable price. A man wants a box of paper collars of a particular pattern : the draper can let him have it. A lady wants a silk dress from the looms of Lyons : she can get it from the draper. The kind of service rendered by the draper, therefore, is this : He makes it possible for any one to go to his shop and obtain at once, and at a reasonable price, things which, if procured direct from the maker, could be got only with great delay, expense, and risk. But his customers are not the only people to whom the draper renders service. He himself is a customer of the makers of the things that he sells, and by using his capital in the purchase of things that require to be moved to where they will be *useful to the consumer* he renders a service to the makers that they would find it impossible to perform for themselves. Part of his reward for this service is that he pays only *wholesale* prices for his goods.

8

*How the Draper is paid for his Services.*

You must now consider how the draper is paid by his customers for the services that he renders them. You saw that some of the customers paid him *cash* or ready money for his goods, and thus returned to him what he had paid for the things, along with his *profit* on them. Other customers bought without paying, and one paid without having apparently bought anything; these were regular customers who had *accounts* at the draper's—that is to say, they were, or had been, purchasers on credit. The draper has their names in his books, and when they buy anything he writes under their names a statement of the things that they have bought. At the end of the month, quarter, or year he sends out accounts of all the purchases made and their total amounts, which these customers are then supposed to pay him. It generally happens, though, that some of these accounts are never paid. Thoughtless or dishonest persons often run up accounts that they can never hope to pay, and so the draper never gets his money *from them*. The amount of money lost in this way in the course of a year is sometimes very great, and, if the drapers who give credit lost this amount entirely, they would all be ruined. The money therefore must be paid by somebody. Who pays it? There can be only one answer: The paying customers. The draper does not say straight out to these customers, "I have lost £1,000 this year by trusting careless and dishonest customers, and you honest people must make good this loss." But still the effect of his losses is, that he cannot afford to sell his goods at such a low rate as he could sell them at if he were paid for everything sold, and that he has in the long-run to charge his paying customers the price of the goods that they purchase, together with the price of the goods that the dishonest customers have had; that is to say, the honest people have to pay a high price for their goods, so that the draper may not lose much by his careless trading. Now, how is it that this bad system has not been done away with long ago? It is not difficult to find the correct answer to this question. The answer is, that the State, to a certain extent, gives its support to the system.

*Credit: Evils caused by it.*

What has been said in the chapter on banks and in the pre-

vious part of this chapter will have enabled you to understand
that there are two entirely distinct kinds of credit. One kind is
that given to a merchant or a tradesman to enable him to carry on
his business with profit and without loss of time : this is a most
useful kind of credit, and, if it were done away with, the State,
as a whole, would suffer greatly. The other kind is that given
to people purchasing things intended for their own private use.
Credit of this sort may sometimes be of real service to a man who
lives by wages ; it would be hard if a person whose salary is paid
at the end of each month could not get necessary things during the
month : but generally it is very hurtful. Even the most careful
people are sometimes tempted to buy more than they can afford,
when they know that they will not have to pay for it at once ;
and it often happens that those who are at all careless or
thoughtless find themselves deeply in debt without well knowing
how they came to be so. Maoris often get into trouble in that
way. There is going to be a great feast, or a tangi, or a
wedding. The Maoris have some land, and can get credit ;
they get it, and it ruins them. After the feast is over they find
that they can never hope to pay the debt without selling their
land ; they become utterly careless and hopeless, and soon go to
utter ruin. The same sort of thing, in a milder form, happens
to Europeans also, through their buying things that they can
never hope to pay for.

### Should the Law protect Careless Traders ?

The State interferes in almost any case in which credit for
goods has been given, if it is called upon to do so. It makes no
distinction between the useful and the hurtful kind of credit.
If a man has bought goods from another man, the State will force
the debtor to pay his debt. It would seem that the State acts
unwisely in this matter. The tradesman who gets credit is a sort
of middle man between the maker of goods (or the merchant) and
the consumer. The goods of the maker are given to him in
trust, and this kind of trust has been shown to be of service to
the State as a whole. It is, therefore, plainly the State's duty
to try to prevent this trust from being broken, and to punish
those who break it, and also to decide disputes who may arise
between traders in the course of their business transactions.

But the case of consumers is very different. Credit given to them is, on the whole, very hurtful to the State, because it tends to make people thoughtless and careless, and to induce them to run into debt, and it thus tends to hinder the State from reaching a higher stage of progress.* Do you not think, then, that it would be well if the State were to refuse to interfere between tradesmen and people who purchase from them things for their own private use? As it is now, the tradesman knows that if a customer is unwilling to pay for goods sold to him he can be summoned to Court and made to pay. This knowledge makes the tradesman careless, and leads him to give credit when he should refuse to sell except for cash, and in the end, as we have seen, honest people have to suffer. It seems almost certain that if the State said to tradesmen, "You may give credit if you like, but you must not expect the State to assist you in getting payment for your goods unless you can show that the purchaser obtained them through fraud," the effect would be to make tradesmen much more careful and much less liable to misfortune than they are, to make customers much more frugal and cautious, and to prevent honest people from being compelled to pay the debts of those who are dishonest.†

Large businesses are conducted on the same principles as smaller ones are, but it would take a book much larger than this to give you even a general idea of the kinds of work carried on by them, and of the methods by which it is done.

We may finish this chapter with a table showing the principal dangers that business men are exposed to.

*Dangers and Difficulties that Business People have to meet.*

The principal difficulties and dangers that people in business have to encounter may be classified as follows :—

1. Dangers that arise from want of wisdom and care on the part of tradesmen themselves.

---

* See Chapter IV., page 29.

† Perhaps, if a law were passed providing that the Courts should take no proof of debts under £50 except a (new and special kind of) bill or promissory note, running for not more than two months, endorsable only by the first receiver of it, and payable only to a bank, all the good points in the credit system would be preserved, and nearly all the bad ones would be done away with. The effect would be that none but perfectly solvent or very trustworthy people would be able to get much credit.

2. Dangers that arise from the faults of others.

3. Dangers that are the result of misfortune, and cannot be avoided.

Class 1 may be subdivided as follows : Dangers arising from

(*a*.) Buying badly: (1.) Buying things that customers do not want: a storekeeper in a Maori district who bought a large quantity of knives and forks would never sell them. (2.) Buying things in too large quantity: if a tobacconist bought half a ton of snuff he would have it lying on his hands for a long time ; few people use snuff now. (3.) Buying things at too high a price : having dead stock means, at the least, the loss of the interest on its value.

(*b*.) Selling things of poor quality at a low price, and so spoiling future trade. Many people have a kind of weakness for buying things cheap, and are attracted to a shop where prices are low ; but, when once a purchase has been made, the quality, not the price, is considered by the customer. Bad quality in an article purchased at a shop gives the purchaser a bad impression of that shop, and very probably prevents him from again visiting the place where he bought the article.

(*c*.) Selling particular articles of good quality at too low a price, in order to attract trade. Small profits and quick returns make good trade, but there should be a return and a profit on every article. If the price of one thing sold at a shop is very low, customers will expect other things to be equally cheap, and will be displeased if they find that they are not.

(*d*.) Selling things at a low price to beat rival tradesmen. This is a dangerous sort of game ; two or even three can play at it. If a weak rival is beaten a stronger may come in his place. Let well alone.

(*e*.) Neglecting to let people know the nature of one's goods. Modesty is a good thing, but it does not answer in trade. Truthful advertising greatly benefits a business. Lies, on the other hand, seldom answer their purpose in the long-run, even in business ; nor does any kind of dishonesty.

(*f*.) Having much trade-capital in the form of book debts. One who has too many debtors is not likely to be able to pay his own creditors. If a tradesman spoils his credit he can no longer buy on easy terms.

(*g*.) Failing to arrange a plan that ought to secure a profit at the end of the year. A business man who works without system is nearly sure to come to grief in the end.

(*h*.) Neglecting to keep proper accounts. A tradesman should be able to see at any time with very little trouble whether he is gaining or losing, and so to make changes when they are needed.

(*i*.) Making promises that cannot be kept. If a customer is promised a coat on Tuesday and does not get it till next Saturday week, he will probably try a new tailor next time. A tradesman who allows his bills to be dishonoured may expect soon to have to pay cash for all his material : a bill is a *promise* to pay.

(*j*.) Living at too expensive a rate : making the extent of one's business rather than the profits actually gained the measure of one's personal expenses.

(*k*.) Not taking the greatest possible care to avoid being injured by the dangers included in Class 2. These dangers arise from the dishonesty and foolishness of certain classes of customers, but also, and perhaps chiefly, from the carelessness and unbusinesslike habits for which many people are remarkable.

The dangers mentioned in Class 3 will very seldom occur.

If a man insures goods sent to him by sea his business will not be much affected by the loss of them. Fire insurance will do much to protect him against fire. Still, there are calamities that cannot be avoided ; when these come they must be borne. But a business man who has gained for himself a character for industry, prudence, and honesty has but little reason to fear even when serious misfortune comes upon him.

# CHAPTER XVII.

## VALUE: DEMAND AND SUPPLY.

You ought by this time to understand that Wants are the cause of Effort, and that efforts that satisfy wants are services; and also that the value of a service depends not only on its mere usefulness, but also on the difficulty with which it can be obtained by the person that feels the want.

*On what Causes does the Value of a particular Service depend?*

You may say, shortly, that the value of a service depends (a) on its usefulness, and (b) on the difficulty of getting it performed. If, then, a man feels a want, these two things—the usefulness to him of the thing he wants, and the difficulty of getting it—will both take part in deciding whether he will or can satisfy his want or not. If a man wants a watch of a certain kind he will, very likely, think the matter over and come to the conclusion that the usefulness of the watch will be equal to that of £10. He then goes to a watchmaker, and if he finds that the price of the watch is *not more* than £10 he will buy it, but if the price is higher than £10 the difficulty of getting the watch will prevent him from satisfying his want.

There are, then, two causes that determine whether a sale will take place in any particular case or not: one is the usefulness of the thing to be sold, and the other is the difficulty in the way of obtaining it. Now, these two causes depend upon two different persons, the buyer and the seller. The buyer decides for himself what the usefulness of an article to him is. The seller decides for himself what amount of difficulty there shall be in inducing him to part with it. It is plain that the seller can make this difficulty as great as he pleases; but there are two things that will generally guide him in fixing a price. He will want to gain something by the sale, and will therefore wish, at any rate, to get more for a thing than it cost him; but, if he is a dealer, he will also be anxious to sell, and will therefore try to avoid fixing a higher price than he thinks he is likely to get. If the seller finds that he can make nothing by selling a certain article he will soon cease to *supply* it to his customers, and if the buyer finds that the money that he has to pay for an article is more useful than the article itself he will cease to ask for it—to *demand* it.

### Buyers and Sellers: Demand and Supply.

There are, of course, at least two persons concerned in every sale. Each of these has a want; each seeks to have this want satisfied. There is very little real difference between a buyer and a seller; but it is usual and very convenient to treat them as belonging to two different classes—to call those who wish to exchange their money for goods *buyers*, and those who wish to exchange their goods for money *sellers*. When persons have the power and the wish to buy goods at a certain price there is said to be a *demand* for these goods at that price. If people are willing to sell goods for a certain price there is said to be a *supply* of them at that price; the demand comes from those who wish to buy, the supply from those who wish to sell. The buyers ask for a certain service; the sellers are willing to render it if they can agree with the buyers about the price to be paid for the service—in other words, if the sellers and the buyers can hit upon some amount of money that they can all agree to consider as having a value equal to that of the service.

### Values are not constant.

Questions of value would be easy enough to deal with if values were always and everywhere constant; but they are not. If a ton of potatoes at all times of the year were worth £10, if it had the same value in a town as it has on a farm where potatoes are grown, and if the values of other things were equally constant, we could always say at once that so many potatoes could be exchanged for so much flour, and there would be an end of the matter. But, as it is, we find that the price, which for our present purpose we may take as being the true value of potatoes, is constantly changing. One year potatoes may be worth £10 a ton, and the next year only £5 ; in the very same town they may fetch £4 in March, and £8 in September. At Dunedin they may be worth £6 a ton, and at Sydney £10. It is such changes in prices that you have now to consider, and your object should be to find out, if you can, the causes of changes in value.

### Market Value.

The first thing to be clearly understood is that even when the word "value" is used in the strict sense, and is made to stand for strength in exchange, it may still have two somewhat different meanings. If you say that the value of a pound of apples is now sixpence, and it is found that a pound of apples and sixpence can be exchanged for each other, you use the word correctly enough. But it may be that at the very same time, in a town twenty miles off, two pounds of apples will be given by any fruit-seller for sixpence. In that town the value of a pound of apples is threepence. Again, in the month of April the price of apples in Auckland may be twopence a pound, but in December, before the new crop begins to come in, the price may be sixpence a pound. It is plain, then, that the value of apples changes with the time when and the place where the apples are sold. This kind of value is called the *market value*.

### Natural Value.

The values of most things change in this kind of way, but some more slowly and some more quickly. Bread is not always and everywhere in New Zealand at exactly the same price. The price of a 4lb. loaf is sometimes 6d., sometimes 7d., 8d., 9d., 10d., or even more ; but if you took the prices paid for all the loaves used in New Zealand for many years, and divided the amount by the number of loaves, you would find that the *average price* is about 7½d. Now, this price may be taken as being, as nearly as possible, the *natural value* of a 4lb. loaf during the period. You are to try to find out what determines, first *market value*, and then *natural value*.

*Law of Demand and Supply.*

*Market value* depends chiefly on *demand and supply.* Let us suppose that the price of pigs of a certain size and weight is now £3. It is summer-time, and people do not care to eat much pork. But, as the weeks roll by, first one person and then another will begin to ask the butcher for pork ; many people, too, will think it well to have some bacon for the winter. Many pigs are killed, but more are wanted. Then the owners of pigs begin to think that by-and-by pigs will be scarce and hard to get, and that people will be willing to give more than £3 for them, perhaps £4 or even £5. They determine then to keep their pigs, and to wait for the good time that is coming. Thus they increase the *difficulty of getting* pigs. But the butchers find that their customers must have pork, and that most of them are willing to pay a little more for it. They therefore offer the owners of pigs more for them, perhaps £3 10s. Some owners will sell ; some will not. Soon all the £3 10s. pigs will be gone, and then the butchers will offer £4. But now the pork will have risen in price, because butchers, having to pay more for pigs, will charge more for it. Many of the customers will say : "Pork is now too dear. We must use mutton instead." So the demand for pork will grow less, and very likely there will be just enough £4 pigs left to make the *supply* equal to the *demand.* *If so, the price of pigs will remain steady at £4.*

But now the pork season is passing by. The demand for it rapidly grows less. Great numbers of young pigs are nearly ready for the market. Many owners are anxious to get money for their pigs, and, finding that these extra pigs cannot be sold for £4, begin to offer them to the butchers for £3 10s. The butchers reduce the price of pork a little, and for a week or two more pork is eaten and the price of pigs remains steady at £3 10s. Then, for the same kind of reason, the price of pigs falls to £3. But now at last the end of the season is drawing very near, and the owners of pigs find that if they are to sell their pigs at all it must be at a still lower price, and they determine to take £2 10s. During nearly all the summer the supply of pigs may remain equal to the demand for them, and the price of pigs will then be steady. But when March comes round once more the owners begin to say to themselves : " Next month people will begin to eat more pork again, so we must keep our pigs unless we can get a better price for them." Pigs are no longer supplied at £2 10s., so the price rises again to £3 — that is, to what it was when we started.

Now, from this example we can get all the chief laws of demand and supply. These are here stated :—

(a.) Higher price causes a smaller demand, but a larger supply.

(b.) Lower price causes a larger demand, but a smaller supply.

(c.) Greater demand raises the price if supply remains the same.

(d.) Smaller demand reduces the price if supply remains the same.

(e.) Greater supply reduces the price if demand remains the same.

(f.) Smaller supply raises the price if demand remains the same.

(g.) When supply at a certain price is exactly equal to demand at that price, the price remains steady.

You would do well to find out for yourselves actual cases to which these rules could be applied.

### Limitations of the Law of Demand and Supply.

Market value does not always depend entirely on demand and supply; several other things have more or less effect upon it; old customs and town regulations, and the convenience of buyers and sellers, may be mentioned as things that interfere with the effects of demand and supply to some extent : A lawyer's fee is 6s. 8d.; a cabman may not charge more than his regular fare, even if cabs are few and passengers are numerous; and the price of a single paper box of matches is nearly always a penny. But, on the whole, it is not far wrong to say that market value depends on demand and supply.

### Cases in which Supply cannot be increased.

It may be well to just mention here that there are some things whose value depends almost entirely on the difficulty there would be in obtaining them. The things referred to are those that either cannot be increased at all in number or quantity, or that admit of only slight increase. Old Maori carvings and weapons, and land in the middle of Auckland or Dunedin, are things of this kind ; the Terraces at Roto-mahana also belonged to the same class. The value of the Terraces would, if the question of selling them had arisen, have depended almost entirely on their being the only things of their kind in existence. If any person had wanted to buy the Pink Terrace he would have had to give exactly what the owners asked for it, or else to do without the Terrace. There could be no such thing as increased supply. Actual sale would merely have shown that some one's idea of the useful-ness of the Terrace came up to the owners' idea as to how great they might make the difficulty of obtaining the Terrace. Such cases as this may well enough be left out of our account, as they are neither numerous nor important.

### A General Rise or Fall of Values is impossible.

Before leaving this subject of market value and supply and demand, it will be well for you to consider carefully an important difference between price and value. There may be a *general* rise or fall of prices; there cannot be a *general* rise or fall of values. Value is strength in *exchanging for things generally ;* therefore there cannot be a general rise of values. Suppose that 2lb. of apples are of the same value as 4lb. of potatoes, or 1lb. of biscuits, and that any of these could be exchanged for ½lb. of gunpowder. If now the value of potatoes and apples fall, so that 3lb. of apples or 6lb. of potatoes will exchange for 1lb. of biscuits and ½lb. of powder, then this very fall in the value of potatoes and apples raises the value of the biscuits and gunpowder and increases their strength in exchange with respect to potatoes and apples. Plainly, what holds good in the case of these four articles holds good also in the case of any number of articles : in order that the value of some articles may rise, the value of other articles must fall. Therefore a general rise or fall of values is impossible.

### There may be a General Rise or Fall of Prices.

Price, however, means strength in *exchange for money* money is made of silver or gold, and silver and gold are *good* that are produced by labour, land, and capital, just as sugar is produced by them. What was said in Chapter XIV. showed you that gold and silver, like other goods, change in value; indeed, the value of either or both of them might change very greatly. If a large number of new gold diggings like those at Ballarat were discovered, the value of gold would fall very much indeed. If the value of gold—its strength in exchange—fell, you would of course have to give more gold for all articles that you buy than you do now: that is, there would be a general rise in prices. We are to remember, then, that, while there cannot be such a thing as a rise or fall of all values, there may be a general rise or fall of prices.

There is one other matter worth noticing here. It does not present the slightest difficulty; but people may be met with who find real difficulty in it. It will be sufficient to state the fact; you will be able to see quite easily why it is a fact. While the sovereign continues to be the standard coin the ordinary price of uncoined gold can never change much, even though the value of gold should fall very considerably. If the value of a sovereign fell till it was equal to that of a shilling, gold would still be worth about £4 per ounce, as it is at present.

# CHAPTER XVIII.

## VALUE; COST OF PRODUCTION.

THE preceding chapter has taught you that *market value* depends mainly on demand and supply. In this you are to learn that *natural value*, which market value has a tendency to approach and is seldom equal to for long, depends mainly on the cost of production.

### *Wages of Labour and Profits of Capital form the Principal Part of the Cost of Production.*

You have already seen that land, labour, and capital are required for production : now you are to inquire how much of the total cost of production is due to each of these things. And first take some common article and try to determine roughly what part of its price has to be paid for the work done by land, labour, and capital respectively. Here is a tin dish. Where was it purchased ? It was bought at a store, and the storekeeper received 3s. 6d. for it. Did it cost the storekeeper 3s. 6d.? No ; but he had to make his profit on the capital that he had spent in purchasing it and bringing it within reach of his customer ; he gave only 2s. 9d. for it, or 3s. including the cost of carriage. No doubt the storekeeper bought the dish from a tinsmith. Where, then, did the tinsmith get it ? He made it. Whence did he get the material ? He bought sheet-tin from a merchant, who got it from England, where it had been made of iron from the Black Country and of tin from Cornwall. What payments, then, have had to be made for it ? The tinsmith has had to be paid, say, 9d. as wages for his labour in making it. He has also had to be paid interest on the capital used in buying the unfinished material, and he has received something on account of his risk in connection with the sale of the dish, of his work in managing his business, and of his skill as a workman ; perhaps 6d. in all. Then the merchant had to get his profit. The sailors of the ship that brought the dish to New Zealand had to receive their wages. The owners of the ship, the merchant in England who bought the material, the manufacturer of the material, his workmen and clerks, the miners, those who made the miners' tools—these people, and perhaps many others, have had at some time or other to receive wages or profits, part of which has had to be made good at last through the sale of this tin dish. Perhaps 9d. would cover these payments, and then 2s. 9d. of the price, which was 3s. 6d., would have been paid to labourers and capitalists. You must have noticed that in this long story the two words *wages* and *profit* continually occur, and that 2s. 9d. of the whole price of the tin dish has had to be given as payments of wages and profits. Further, you can see that if the whole work of producing the tin dish, except that of finding the material, had been done by one man for the person that supplied the material, the latter would have had to pay the former a very large part of this 2s. 9d. for wages and profits.* You may conclude, therefore, that wages and profits form a very large part of the cost of production.

### Rent and Production.

But rent and land have not been mentioned. Had land nothing to do with the production of the tin dish ? You may be pretty certain that both land and other natural agents took a full share of the work of producing it. It was shown in Chapter VI. that there are very few kinds of work that we could do at all if it were not for the amount and kind of help that natural agents afford. You may be sure, too, that the owners of the natural agents that had owners would have to be paid for the use of them. Therefore rent in one shape or another would be included in the *price* of the tin dish. You can already see, then, that the 9d. remaining from the price of the dish (3s. 6d.) after 2s. 9d. had been paid for wages

---

* The person that had to supply the material would have had to pay the whole of the 2s. 9d. for wages and profits if he had not had a right to some profit on the cost of the material. Probably 1d. would be enough to allow for this.

and profits very probably went for rent. But this very important question still remains for you to answer: If we grant that rent formed part of the *price*, does it follow that rent formed part of the *cost of production* of the tin dish?* In order to be able to answer this question you will have to study the *law of rent and production*. This is one of the most difficult matters that we have to deal with; but if you carefully attend to the explanation given, you will be able to understand it. It will be well, however, for you to be on your guard against the error of supposing that the principles stated in this explanation can always be applied at once to any case in which rent has to be dealt with.

### *Allowances usually have to be made when General Rules are applied to Particular Cases.*

If you were asked to work an easy sum in the rule-of-three, you could no doubt do it at once, but your answer would probably be only *generally* correct; and if you applied the sum to a particular case you would find that you would have to make allowances of some kind before your answer would be of much use. Let us consider such a sum. "If five men can trench a piece of ground in four days, how long will it take eight men to trench it?" The answer, of course, is, "Two days and a half." Now, this answer is *generally* true; but if you apply it to any actual case you will find that allowances will have to be made. Such allowances would depend on the intelligence of the men, the shape of the ground, and the nature of the soil. For eight men might be able to have better division of labour than the five can; they might be able to arrange the work so that three could dig the subsoil, and three the surface-soil, while the other two mixed or arranged in the proper way what the others had dug up. Or eight men might be too many for the work, and might only get into one another's way. Or, again, the eight men, having to work a shorter time than the five have to work, might be able to work much harder. Any, or perhaps all, of these things would make some difference, perhaps a considerable difference, in the time the work would take. Thus, you see, the correct general answer to

---

* The same question might be asked with regard to wages and profits had we not traced, step by step, the items paid for wages and profits in the course of the production of the dish.

your sum might be incorrect when applied to a particular case. Is the rule-of-three useless then? Not at all. It gives us the correct general principle, and when we have got this we must make allowances to the best of our ability. The defect is not in the rule, but in ourselves, if we expect it to give us certain, when it can yield only probable, results. Nearly all calculations except those that deal with mere figures—such, for instance, as 2562 × 3809—or with things that are always perfectly uniform, have the same defect; and yet no one thinks applied arithmetic a useless thing.

*Allowances have to be made when the Law of Rent is applied.*

When we are trying to find a general answer to questions about rent, we have to suppose that we are dealing with men that are all of one kind, with men who wish to get as much as they can, honestly, but with as little trouble as possible; that every man not only knows how to make, but is also able to make, the best use of his labour and capital, and that he will always be ready to leave his friends and the place where he was born in order to better his condition; that labourers or capitalists will not combine in order to get more wages or more profits; that there are no ties of friendship between the owners of land and those who hire land from them, and that the owner of land will always insist upon getting the very highest rent he can; that landowners, capitalists, and labourers are thoroughly and completely free to do what they like with their land, capital, and labour, and that the owner and the capitalist have no power over the labourer; that labourers cannot emigrate to another country; and that machines and division of labour do not, as time goes on, lower the cost of the production of food. But not one of these suppositions is quite true. Men do not always try to gain as much as they can. A labourer cannot always leave a place where wages are low and go to another place where they are a little higher. The owners of land do not always insist upon getting the last penny of rent; and so on. Still, not one of these suppositions is so far from the truth as to be able to make the conclusion that will be arrived at untrue, any more than, because it is possible that all men will not work alike, the supposition that they will do so makes a rule-of-three sum

9

useless if it deals with men's labour. Well then, you have to try to find out what the Law of Rent and Production is under the circumstances mentioned, and then to apply the corrections as well as you can. You will probably find that a careful consideration of this law leads to very saddening conclusions, even when all necessary allowances have been made. Many people have been led to believe that the State, the people of New Zealand, could not find a more important subject to think about and master than the Law of Rent and Production, and the best means of dealing with some of its consequences.

### Profits on Capital used in Farming will tend towards the Current Rate of Profit.

You may now go on to study this Law of Rent. The first thing that you have to do in this inquiry is to learn that profits on capital, however the capital is employed, tend towards one current rate. Let us suppose that 2s. is the regular profit that can be obtained by master-tailors for every pound employed by them as capital. Then in no kind of business will capitalists long continue to get *more*. If it were found that more profit could be made by selling hats than by selling coats, all tailors would wish to become hatters, so that their capital might yield them, say, 2s. 6d. instead of 2s. Many master-tailors would become hatters. More hats would be produced, and the increased supply would probably cause hatters' profits to fall below 2s. Tailors would no longer wish to be hatters; they would leave off making hats, and return to their old business, or go into some other. In time the supply of hats would be lessened, the price would rise, and profits also would again rise to about 2s. on the pound, the common rate of profit. We see, then, that, just as there is a natural value to which market values always tend, there is also a regular rate of profit to which profits in all businesses tend; and that, if 2s. is the regular profit on £1 in all other businesses, it must also be about the regular rate of profit on capital used in farming.

### Rent, as a Rule, forms no Part of the Cost of the Production of that from which it is taken.

Now, suppose that a farmer with a wife and two grown-up sons owns 100 acres of very poor land, which he clears and farms

in the best possible way, and which yields him just £100 profit
on £1,000 of capital (his only wealth), the whole of which he
uses in working his farm. · Then this is at the rate of 2s. for
£1, which is what we have supposed to be the regular profit on
capital. At the end of the year he takes stock and finds himself richer by exactly £100 than he was at the beginning of
it. Another farmer in the same district owns 100 acres of very
good land, which he works just as the other farmer does; but
this land yields £300 profit on the £1,000 of capital that is
used in working the land. Then this is at the rate of 6s. for
£1, which is 4s. more than the regular rate of profit upon
capital. The annual stock-taking shows this farmer that he is
richer by £300 than he was at the beginning of the year.

In each of these cases the capital used was the same. The
first farmer got the regular profit on his capital, £100. The
second got £100 profit, and £200 besides. This £200 must
have been rent; it could have been nothing else, as was shown in
Chapter XII. The owner of the poor land sold all his wheat at
4s. a bushel, and this, as we reckon, gave him his wages and the
profit on his capital. His wealth had gone through three changes :
at first it was in the form of money ; then it was in the form of
buildings, improvement of the land, tools, seed-corn, and food
and clothing for his use while he was working ; then it took the
form of wheat ready for sale, tools partly worn out, buildings,
and improvements ; and at last of buildings, improvement of the
land, seed-corn for next year, and tools partly worn out, and of
a certain sum of money which he had received for the corn.
Now, this money had to pay him for his risk in putting his capital
into buildings, tools, seed-corn, and food and clothing ; the
interest on the wealth that he had used to produce more
wealth ; and his extra wages for managing the business. That is,
the one part of this money gave him his profit. The other part
of the money was paid for food and clothing for himself and his
family to enable them to perform the necessary labour—that is,
for wages. Thus you see that the whole of the return from the
land was used for wages and profit ; so that wages and profit
formed the whole of the cost of the production of the corn, and
rent formed no part of it.

Now, if this farmer got 4s. a bushel for his wheat, 4s. was

probably the ordinary price, for if the price had been higher it is not likely that he would have sold it for 4s., and if it had been lower you may assume that no one would have given him 4s. for it. The other farmer, then, also got 4s. a bushel for his wheat. "Surely," you will say, "the cost of production was not 4s. a bushel in this case too, seeing that the farmer obtained so much more wheat with the same amount of capital and labour." No, it was not; because the rent—that part of the price of the produce obtained by the farmer through the superior quality of the soil—was as good as secured to him from the produce *before* the work of production began at all.* If this farmer were to let his land to another person, would he not expect at least £200 a year for it? Of course he would, because he knows that the land will give him the ordinary profit and £200 besides, and that it is always possible to get some one to take a farm that will return the regular rate of profit. If, then, the owner can get a rent of £200 from some one else for the use of his land, do you not think that this owner will be thoroughly sure that he can make £200 more than it will cost him to produce his crops, before he determines to use the land himself?

*Rent is included in Price, but does not fix it.*

Now perhaps you will say, "Yes, what you have said is very true; we see that the general cost of production must depend on the amount of wages and profits paid for production; but what about the price? Surely the farmer that has good land could, if he wished, sell his corn cheaper than the farmer that has poor land could sell his; you say too that the difference between what is got from the good land and what is got from the bad land is rent; and therefore rent must be part of the price." You are quite right; rent is included in the price the farmer receives for his corn. It must be out of the price that the owner of the land is paid his rent, the capitalist his profits, and the labourer his wages, for there is no other source from which these payments can come. The fact is that the *price* of *food* and its *cost* are very different things and depend on different causes. *Price* depends mainly on supply, which becomes more difficult, and

---

* Of course a failure of crop might cause total loss of rent, wages, and profit; the average harvest is referred to.

on demand, which increases, as population increases. *Cost of production* depends mainly on the wages and profits that have to be paid for producing, as we have learnt in the present chapter. It may be added that in the case of *food* the difference between the *price* and the cost of production may be very considerable. You may say, then, that rent is very often included in the price that has to be paid for an article, but that it has nothing to do .. with fixing that price—that it adds nothing to the cost of production, and adds nothing to the price; which, indeed, depends on demand and supply.*

---

\* It is plain that if the State, acting as a whole, grew on Crown lands all the corn that is used in the country, the average cost of a bushel of corn would be equal to the average amount paid per bushel for labour and capital employed in producing it. If taxes are left entirely out of account, there is no reason why the cost of production of corn grown by members of the State on private land should not likewise be equal to the wages and profits paid in the course of the production. If you bear this in mind, you will find the following table of use in enabling you to understand the reasoning in this chapter. In this table it is assumed that the cost of producing a bushel of corn on the poorest land is 2s.; and that all the land used for growing corn may be divided into three equal-sized blocks, having productive powers which enable the land to yield 20, 30, and 40 bushels per acre respectively, with equal expenditure of labour and capital. It is improbable that such conditions could be found anywhere, but not impossible ; they are assumed for the sake of simplicity.

*Table showing Relations between Cost of Production and Price.*

|  | On A. | On B. | On C. | On A, B, and C together. |
|---|---|---|---|---|
| Land used in producing corn gives .. Total cost of production to the State or the owner of the land | 20 bush. 40s. | 30 bush. 40s. | 40 bush. 40s. | 90 bush. 120s. |
| Average cost per bushel .. .. | 2s. | 1s. 4d. | 1s. | 1s. 4d. |
| Price per bushel—the cost of production on the poorest land in use, and what would be from the tenant-farmer's and the consumer's point of view the cost of production in each of the respective blocks | 2s. | 2s. | 2s. | ·2s. |
| Rent paid on each bushel, or the difference between the true cost of production and the price | 0d. | 8d. | 1s. | 8d. |
| Rent per acre in each block .. .. | 0s. | 20s. | 40s. | 20s. |

After studying this table you will easily understand that, if enough corn for all wants could be obtained from C, B would not be used; the price of corn would be equal to the cost of production, and there would be no rent. But as soon as B has to be used to increase the supply and make it equal to the demand, the cost of production on B fixes the price, and then C yields a rent equal to the difference between the cost of production on B and C. Thus supply and demand fix price, and price and cost of production between them determine the amount of rent that will be yielded by a given piece of land.

Thus, then, you have seen that rent *must* always be yielded by good land if poorer land is being cultivated ; and that the owner can *secure* the rent for himself before he allows his land to be used for farming, and can fix his rent high enough to leave his tenant no greater share of the produce than will pay the wages of the labour, and the profit on the capital required for working the land. In this way all land can be brought down by rent to the level of the worst land in use, before capital is used on it for farming. From this it is plain that the cost of producing corn differs from its price by the amount of the rent yielded, and that therefore rent forms no part of the cost of production.

What is true with regard to the produce of a farm is at all events *generally* true with regard to the produce of a mine. You may safely say, therefore, that the rent that may have been paid to the owners of the mines from which the material used in making the tin dish referred to in the beginning of this chapter was taken, formed hardly any part of the cost of the production of the dish, although rent was included in the price paid for the dish.

*The Natural Value of an Article depends on the Cost of producing it.*

You will see by-and-by that taxes add to the cost of production. But, leaving taxes and one or two other matters out of account for the present, you may say that WAGES and PROFITS are the two things that make up the COST of PRODUCTION, and that rent generally has but little to do with it. Rent, however, may add somewhat to the general cost of food-production in a district where land that would, if used for farming, give rent, is used for something else than the production of food. If for instance large pieces of rich farm-land at some little distance from a considerable town were to be taken for building factories on, or for chemical works or ironworks which would spoil a good deal of the surrounding land, the cost of food-production in the district generally might be somewhat increased ; because poorer land than any now in use would probably have to be cultivated, in order to produce the quantity of food that would have been grown on the rich land taken for factories. You may try to work this out for yourself ; it is not very difficult to do it. Taking account only of things of which a very considerable quantity can be produced, you may learn, from what has been said in this chapter, that, if one thing, such as a cake of tobacco of a certain size, will nearly always exchange for more money than another thing, such as a box of matches of a certain size, will exchange for, the cake of tobacco requires for its production more labour, or more expensive labour, or more abstinence on the part of the person that bought it in an unfinished state, than the box of matches does, unless the one is more heavily taxed than the other. Now, as this holds good with regard to all articles that can be produced in quantity, it is plain that their average or natural value depends in the main on the amount that has to be paid in wages and profits for their production. As it has been shown that in the main the cost of production is made up of the amounts paid in wages and profits for production, you may thence conclude that the natural value of any article depends mainly on the cost of producing it. You can now see why it is that the market value of anything tends to become equal to its natural value. (1.) People will not long continue to produce an article that will not return them the cost of production; therefore, if the market value of an article is below its natural value, people will gradually leave off producing it, the supply will become less, and the market value will rise. (2.) If an article returns more than the cost of production, a larger quantity of it will be produced, the supply will increase, and, as soon as it becomes greater than the demand, the market value will fall.

# CHAPTER XIX.

## LAW OF RENT; HOW WEALTH IS SHARED.

WHAT has been said in the two previous chapters has shown you that the market value of any article depends mainly upon demand and supply, and that the natural value depends on the cost of production. You have learnt that the cost of production of any ordinary article that can be increased in quantity if required, and that is not taxed, is equal to the amount required to pay the wages of the labourers and the profits of the capitalist who took part in producing it. You have also seen that rent forms no part of the cost of production, and that if one farmer produces wheat at 4s. a bushel and just manages to get his wages and profit out of it, while another, also selling his wheat at 4s., gets wages, profit, and rent, this rent forms no part of the cost of production, but is (on an average of harvests) secured to the owner before production begins. You have seen, too, that, as a rule, rent *adds* nothing to the price of an article, though it be included in the price.

### *Necessity for using Land other than the Best increases Cost of Production and gives rise to Rent.*

But, though it would generally be wrong to say that real rent forms part of the cost of production, it is quite true that cost of production is the cause of rent. In a new colony, at the very beginning, everybody can get as much good land as he wants for almost nothing, but when the number of people increases all the best and most convenient land gets taken up, and by-and-by people have to work on land from which a given amount of capital and labour will bring in a smaller return than it would from the land first taken up. For, even if the new land is quite as rich as the other, it will be further away from where the produce is required, and to get this produce to a place where it is wanted will cause expense that is not incurred in the case of land nearer the market. Thus, in one way or another, the land occupied by the first colonists will give a greater return than can be got out of the new farms. The old farms, you see, cannot produce enough to feed all the people that have come to the colony, and therefore the poorer lands *must* be worked, even though the cost of working them is much greater : people cannot do without food; nor, again, would they stay in a colony unless they could get suitable wages and profits there. Thus, then, as the colony grows larger, and land more distant from the towns is worked, the cost of production rises—more has to be paid in wages and profit * in order to produce a certain quantity of food—and the better lands, which can be worked at smaller cost, begin to give rent. Of course, if the country begins to export food, the increase of rent may soon become very rapid, because the more food there is grown the poorer the *worst* land that is used will be, and the greater will be the difference between the cost of production on it (the price that the corn grown on it will fetch) and the cost of production on the best land. In any case (even if wages fall considerably), as time goes on and poorer land gets worked, so does rent increase, and the man who has been lucky enough to obtain possession of much land in a convenient situation may sleep if he likes and yet grow rich. Others labour to make a living; they build up the wealth of the colony, and in so doing they help to increase the riches of the owner of much good land; but he may, if he likes, receive everything and give nothing.

You see, then, that it is the extra cost of production for a larger number of people, which arises from the necessity for working poorer or less convenient land, that is the cause of rent. In the case of a young country containing an abundance of good land, increased distance from a market is the most important cause of the increase of rent.

---

* This does not involve a rise in the *rate* of either wages or profits, but simply an increase in the total cost of production of a given quantity of food through more capital and more labour being required to produce it.

*If in any Country the Population in the Towns increases, the average Cost of Food produced entirely in that Country increases also, unless the Methods and Means of working the Land improve in proportion to the Increase of Population.*

You might think that it would be better to use more capital on good land near towns than to take up poor land or land that is a long way off. No doubt this might be done to a certain extent with advantage. Quite near to some of our large towns there is much land now lying nearly idle that might perhaps be put to a good use. But, unfortunately, after land has once been properly fenced and tilled, extra capital does not make it yield extra produce in proportion to the capital put into it. If you had a small plot of ground, say the sixteenth of an acre, dug up and planted, the ground would produce a certain number of, say, cabbages; if you then spent £2 in having it trenched you would find that the trenching did good, and that your next crop would be much larger. If you now spent another £2 for breaking up the soil and passing it through a coarse sieve there would be further improvement, but not so much as there was when you spent £2 in having the land trenched. You would find the same thing happen if you went on spending sums of £2 upon the land; every £2 would do some good, but less than the previous £2 had done. We may say, generally, that, after a certain moderate amount of capital has been spent on land, every additional equal sum spent brings a smaller return. You will see, then, that, sooner or later, increase in the number of people in a country must make 'it necessary to take up poor lands, and that the poorer and more distant the land is that it will pay to take up, the higher the rent of good and convenient land must be.*

---

* It may be said that all this would be right enough if it referred to a country whose population was already large, and whose methods of working the land did not improve with the increase of population, but that it does not apply to New Zealand. It might be said that New Zealand now exports large quantities of food to the utmost parts of the earth, though her population is increasing with great rapidity, and that the price of food is lower in New Zealand than it was thirty years ago, when none but the best land, situated near the best harbours, was in use. This is all quite true; but still the law of rent may be silently and steadily doing its work. It is far more likely that improvements in the method of working the land (for instance, with reapers-and-binders), the opening-up of roads, and the improvement of harbours, are retarding the operation of the law, than that they are abolishing the law itself. Unless still more effective machines than those now in use are invented, machines which will allow very poor lands

*So long as the Cost of Material remains constant, the Cost of Articles manufactured from that Material decreases as the Number of Articles Manufactured increases.*

We may just notice here that there is one great difference between things that are produced from land mainly and those that are produced with much less help from it. Take a sewing-machine, for instance. The cost of the iron and steel in a sewing-machine is small. But that of the instrument, when it is complete, is great. Now, to make *one* of the best sewing-machines would cost a great deal of money, probably thousands of pounds; but, when once all the tools and machines required for making one machine have been provided, hundreds of them can be produced at little extra cost, and the more that are produced the less will the last one cost. You will see, then, that, while the cost of corn becomes greater in proportion as more of it is required, sewing-machines cost less in proportion as more of them are required, and that, as increase in the number of people will cause more machines to be needed, increase of population will lower the price of sewing-machines. You will also easily see, without further explanation, that, while the price of corn is fixed by the cost of that portion of it that it has been most difficult to produce, the price of sewing-machines of a certain quality is fixed for the time by the cost of that which it has been least difficult to produce; and that, as people go on learning to make these machines more easily, the price of them will keep on falling.

*Populous Countries that manufacture largely may be fairly prosperous, though Rents are high.*

Perhaps this explains why it is that some very populous countries, like England, are so well off as they are, although

(such, for instance, as the gum-fields or the Kaingaroa Plains in the North, or the shingle-plains in the South) to be worked as profitably as fair land is now worked, the increase of population must soon bring us up to the point at which we shall not be able to produce corn at a sufficiently low cost to afford us a profit when we send the corn to foreign countries. Is it likely that we shall be able, do what we may, to prevent the cost of production from steadily rising as it does in other countries that are, so to speak, fully under the sway of the law of rent? The fact is that objections like those above stated merely amount to this: New Zealand is a country with wonderful natural resources, and immense improvements have taken place in the methods of working the land; these two things together are delaying the appearance of the most painful effects of the law of rent. These effects, however, will be seen in due time, unless the history of New Zealand is to be different from that of any country that has as yet had a history.

so much of all that their land produces goes to the owners of land as rent. England produces large quantities of useful articles made by machines, such as cutlery, tools, and other machines, which rent affects far less than it does the produce of land, or than it affects things that cannot be produced without a very great deal of labour, and therefore of food to support the labourers that help to produce them. If a country produces little more than corn, butter, bacon, eggs, and such things, then a large portion of the produce will go for rent, and the people must be miserably poor. This is what is the matter with Ireland; at all events, it is one of the things from which she is suffering. But when a country makes large quantities of things by machinery, which is worked mainly by such mighty natural powers as those of steam and falling water (which powers happily, no one has yet been able to make prisoners of, and so get rent from), not only is a great quantity of useful things produced at a very low cost, but also large quantities of these things can be sent away to countries where there is still plenty of rich land, and be there exchanged for corn and other produce, which would be very expensive if they were produced at home.

## How Produce is shared.

There can be very little doubt that rent is an evil; but it is an evil that must be borne. There are no means of escape. Rent cannot be done away with. If there are two pieces of land side by side, and the poorer of the two would yield the ordinary profit of capital, then the other would yield rent to somebody. The question that remains to be decided, then, is, "Who should have this rent?" You must try by-and-by to answer this question cautiously, wisely, and justly; in the meantime it will here suffice to state once more the law of rent, which is: RENT is that portion of the produce of land that is left after the cost of producing it from the poorest land in use has been taken from it. The owner of the land, whoever he may be, takes this, whatever it may be. Here it may at once occur to you to ask whether it would not be right that the labourer who has worked in order to aid production should have a share of this rent. The answer to this is that as a labourer he has no right to any portion of the rent. Suppose that two labouring-men, with similar strength and skill, are working near each other. Their wages are 7s. 6d. a day. One is working for a farmer and planting turnips; the other is mending a road. If you think that the farmer's labourer has a right to a share of the turnips, you ought also to think that the other man has a right to a share of the road. Of course the labourer has a share in the road, not because he works on it, but because he is a member of the State; and if the farmer's man had any right to the turnips it would be for exactly the same reason. In the same way it might be shown that the capitalist has no right to rent or to any part of it.

We have now to see what share of the cost of production (which is all that is left of the produce of land after the rent has been taken out of it) will go to the capitalist, and what share to the labourer. Suppose that a farmer had a piece of very poor land that would pay him his wages and his profit and no more, and that in one particular year he decided that he would not work this piece himself: what would be the highest wages that he would give a labourer for doing the work? Clearly, such as would leave for himself the ordinary rate of profit on his capital, say 2s. in the pound. Labouring-men's necessities would determine the lowest rate at which he could get the work done. That is, the farmer would not give more than what would leave for himself the usual profit, and the labourer could not take less than what would keep him from starving. We may say, then, that the LABOURER's share of the produce would be something between what would keep him from starving and what would allow the capitalist the ordinary rate of profit, and that all that was left would belong to the farmer CAPITALIST. In almost all cases the LABOURER and the CAPITALIST receive from the produce of land only what is left after everything except the total cost of production from an equal-sized piece of the poorest land in use has been given to the owner of the land as rent. From what has been said in this and the previous chapter you can understand that as time goes on, and the *price* of produce increases, the landowner's *share* of the produce must increase, while the share of the labourer must decrease. In the next chapter it will be shown that the rate of wages depends mainly on demand and supply; and in Chapter XXI. it will be shown that, as population increases, the supply of labour tends, from various causes, to be greater than the demand ; which means, of course, that wages tend to fall. You may therefore add to what has been said with regard to the shares of the landowner and the labourer that, while both the landowner's proportional share of the produce and his rent tend to become greater as population increases, the labourer's proportional share of the produce and also his wages tend to decrease.

### The Current Rate of Wages and Profit generally determines what Quality of Land shall be the poorest in use.

You must not, however, fall into the mistake that has been made by some writers of supposing that, because the amount to be divided between the labourer and the capitalist is equal to that required to produce the common rate of wages and profit from the poorest land in use, the quality of the poorest land in use *fixes* the amount to be divided as wages and profit. It is generally just the other way :˙ the amount to be divided as wages and profit usually decides what is the worst kind of land that can be used.

If very large and rich gold-diggings were to be discovered in New Zealand only the best land in the country would for some time be worked, because in that case wealth would be so easy to obtain in other ways that people would find it no longer pay them to grow corn at 3s. or 4s. a bushel ; they would import it from countries where it could be got at a low price. If a man could make £2 a day at gold-digging he would not work on a farm for 6s.; and it would not pay the farmer to give more for work on 'any but the very best land. In England, as we have shown above, the making of goods by means of machines causes the corn that is used to cost the people much less on the whole than it would if they grew it all themselves ; therefore no land will be culti-vated except such as will produce it at' the price for which it can be got from abroad. You saw in the previous chapter that the rate of profit in one business is the rate of profit in another. It is equally easy to show that the rate of wages for one kind of work that does not need any special skill in the labourer is the same for all work of a similar kind. You can, therefore, have no difficulty in understanding that it is the rate of wages and profits in other occupations than farming that decides what the rate is to be in farming also, and therefore decides too what is to be the worst kind of land used. But in a country like Ireland, where, on the whole, very few things are made by machines, where people are very much attached to the district in which they were born, and where a great part of everything that is produced goes for rent, the quality of the poorest land in use does probably fix the amount of agricultural produce that is to be divided into wages and profit, to the extent of making these much lower than they are in more wisely governed countries.

# CHAPTER XX.

## WAGES.—HIGH AND LOW WAGES; WAGES OF SKILLED LABOUR.

WAGES are the reward of labour. Labour, like goods, has a market value and a natural value. The market value mainly depends upon demand and supply. The natural value depends on the cost of bringing up labourers and of supporting them after they are brought up in the lowest degree of comfort that they will consent to put up with. This value may be measured in wages by the amount of wages that the poorest land in use will give after the ordinary profit of capital has been taken out of the produce from it.

### The Market Value of Labour.

The market value of labour depends mainly upon demand and supply. You remember that the market value of anything is what it will fetch at any given time and place if it is freely offered for sale. You are now to see if what is true of the market value of such things as eggs and butter also holds good in the main with regard to the market value of labour. You will have to bear in mind all the time, however, that men have minds and wills, and that it is in their power to refuse to allow their labour to be the object of bargain and sale, while eggs and butter have no such power.

Let us suppose, then, that it is winter-time; that there are a great many men in town, and that there is but little employment for them. The demand for labour is small, and the supply is large. A man takes a large contract for making a road, and wants a hundred men to work for him. That is, he wishes to purchase their labour, or the unfinished products of it. Wages are at, say, 6s. a day—that is, all the labouring men that are employed are receiving this amount; but only a few of them are working, because there is no more capital that can be used so as to give the ordinary profits while wages remain at 6s., and men will not work for less. All those capitalists that can afford to give 6s. are already giving it, and, as. no working-man will take less, the labour-market is closed. The gate of the market is, so to speak, shut and locked, not because capitalists *will* not give 6s. a day—they cannot give it—but because the labourers think 0s. a day better than 5s. or 4s, However, the contractor gets one hundred men to work for him at the current rate of wages. Then another large contract is taken by another contractor, and one hundred more men are wanted to build a bridge. Only sixty can be got. The demand for labour is greater than the supply. But the second contractor has to get his work done in a limited time or else be fined; his machines are on the ground, and are being seriously damaged by the weather; and he has borrowed money from the bank, and is paying interest on it. Therefore he must push on with the work, even though he lose some of his profit; so he offers 6s. 6d. a day. Men leave their employers and flock to him; but this makes the other employers anxious to secure men to do their work, and so they offer 6s. 6d. also, and, soon, a general rise in wages takes place; business in town becomes more lively; the summer will shortly be here; one capitalist sees how to make profit by employing labour, and so does another; but labour is scarce, and wages rise to 7s. a day. Men working on farms are tempted to remove to the town in order that they may get a share of the good things that are going. Shearing-time comes on; wages rise to 7s. 6d., and people from other parts of the colony are induced to come and get the increased wages that are being given. Just then, unfortunately, the news arrives that wheat has fallen 6d. per bushel, or frozen meat ½d. a pound. Capitalists will lose money, they know. They must reduce their expenses and not start any new work. The banks are certain that the loss will injure, perhaps ruin, many of their customers, and they have therefore to be very careful about giving credit. By-and-by, too, the shearing is over and the harvest is past. So the demand for labour decreases while the supply remains very large; wages fall till they reach 6s.; they would fall still further, but men have perhaps decided not to sell their labour at a lower rate, and capitalists think that they cannot make their profit if they

10

pay such wages; so the labour-market is again closed. Thus you see to how great an extent the market value of labour depends upon supply and demand. So far we have been dealing with the wages of unskilled labour only, of wages given for work that men can do without special training; further on something will be said about labour for which the labourer must be specially trained, or for which he must possess some special qualification.

*How some painful Effects caused by the Law of Demand and Supply might be got rid of.*

Those labourers that have been prudent during good times and have saved up their spare money can manage to get on during the dull season; but those that have squandered their extra earnings have now very hard times indeed. It is plain that even those labourers who make it a rule to save nothing might squander away all their wages with much greater enjoyment than they now get from the process, if they made it a rule that their weekly expenditure should never exceed their *average* weekly income. In this way they could get rid of a year's earnings within the year just as they do now, without having to pass through periods of great misery once or twice a year. And if labouring-men always took the market value of their labour whatever it might be—not necessarily what was offered them by any chance employer, but what was decided upon by themselves and the employers after consultation—they would make higher average wages than they do now. But, of course, it is for labouring-men to decide what wages they will work for and what they will refuse to work for; when they will work and when they will remain idle.

*High Wages and Low Wages.*

The words *high* and *low* as applied to wages are used in several different ways. Sometimes the words are made to refer to the share of the produce that the labourer receives. A man who gets a large share of what is produced would be said to receive high wages; he who gets a small share would be said to receive low wages. Thus, if a man produced in a day something worth 1s. and received 10d. for making it, his wages would be high, and if he produced something worth £10 and received £2 for his work his wages would be low. This seems to be an absurd way of using these words.

Wages may also be considered high or low according as the quantity of goods that may be bought with them is great or small. Thus, in a country where gold has a high value and everything else a low value, you might purchase with a sovereign what in another place would cost you ten. In New Zealand, for instance, you can buy more meat for 1s. than you can buy in London for 2s. 6d. If wages are 7s. a day they will become really *higher*, in this sense, when we can buy things cheaper, and really *lower* when things cost us more. Therefore, if you are told that this plan or that plan will make. wages higher, you should always consider whether it will also make things dearer in proportion. If it does, the high wages will be of no advantage to you. The proper thing for a labouring-man to consider is not how the highest money-wages may be obtained, but how his labour may be made most productive to him, how he may get most bread, meat, clothing, &c., in return for his labour — that is, how he may get high real wages. A heavy tax on bread and meat would at once make money-wages rise in New Zealand; but no one would gain much by the rise, and in the end everybody would lose heavily. Labouring-men would gain nothing by the rise in money-wages, for there would at once be a general rise of prices, seeing that the cost of production, reckoned in money, would be raised. Another effect would be that much of the trade between England and New Zealand would cease, and New Zealand would be a great loser thereby. As it is, New Zealand finds it rather hard to sell her wheat and her mutton in England at paying prices; but if wages, generally the most important part of the cost of production, rose much she would not be able to sell them at a profit at all. If, on the other hand, some plan could be devised for taking off most of the taxes that labouring-men now have to pay, money-wages would fall; but so would the cost of production, and therefore the prices of many things that working-men have to buy would fall too. Less capital would be needed for carrying on business, and therefore less money would have to be paid for interest; *and therefore* prices of goods would fall more than the price of labour, *and therefore*, also, real wages would be higher. There would be another advantage to New Zealand : the fall in money-wages (accompanying the rise in real wages) would enable New Zealand to send many things to England that she cannot now send because the cost of producing them here is greater than the price that England would give for them.

A pretty safe way of using the terms "high" and "low" wages" is to make them mean money-wages, and to be very careful not to think that higher wages would mean gain and lower wages loss ; or perhaps it would be still better to always use the terms "money-wages" and "real wages" in their proper sense.

### Rate of Wages and Price of Labour.

There is another thing that you ought to be careful about when speaking of wages, and that is, not to confound the expressions *rate of wages* and *price of labour*. The rate of wages in England some years ago was about three times as high as it was in Ireland. It is said, however, that the English labourer was expected to do three times the amount of work done by a labourer in Ireland ; thus, then, although the rate of wages was so different, the price of labour was exactly the same. Perhaps this is only a particular instance of the working of a general law.

Again, if in one country men work ten hours a day for 8s., and in another eight hours a day for the same money, the rate of wages is higher in the second than it is in the first ; but, if the men working eight hours do as much work as those who work ten—and they probably do—the price of labour is the same. It may be remarked, however, that there is one case in which it is impossible for this kind of difference to occur. If a machine produces a certain quantity of goods in a certain time, it is quite plain that the labour of the man who works it for ten hours must both cost less and be lower in rate than that of one who works for only eight hours for the same wages.

### Day-work and Piece-work.

Wages are the reward of labour, but it is, beyond doubt, fair and just that the reward should be in proportion to the service rendered. A man who removes ten thousand bricks should get twice as much as the man who removes only five thousand. If the first service is worth £2, then the second is worth only £1.

Wages are commonly paid by the day. Now, one man who is honest and active will move perhaps ten thousand bricks in three days, while another who is careless, and perhaps lazy, will take six days for the work. Each of these men will render the same amount of service, but the idle man will get twice as great a reward for his service as the industrious man will get for his, if their wages are paid by the day. Is this quite fair? Does not this seem to show that payment for work *by the piece*, or *by the job*, as it is called, is much fairer than payment by the day? Would it not be well if the system of payment by the piece were adopted in all cases for which it is suitable? The plan of paying fixed wages or salaries is always more or less unfair, though in some cases it is the only one that can be adopted. Here is another way of looking at the thing : If a man has ten labourers working for him, he says to himself, " These men will do five pounds' worth of work for me in a day. I must deduct £1 as profit on my capital, and this will leave 8s. for each of them." Now, some of these men will work much harder than others and will produce much more, and the effect will most likely be that one or two will receive about the value of their service, and the rest will get either more or less than this value. This is, of course, unfair. But, if each were paid for what he had produced, each would receive the exact value of his service. This seems fair.

### Trade-unions.

In many towns workmen combine and form what are called trade-unions, to protect themselves from unjust treatment by their employers. Wealth always gives power, and a single working-man is generally no match for a capitalist. If the labourer does not work he must starve ; but the capitalist is not obliged to use his capital : he may withdraw it and use it in maintaining himself. But, if a number of working-men combine, they can nearly always prevent injustice being done to them as a body, or to any one of their number. A trade-union therefore is a very good thing, and the forming of these unions is one of the best things that working-men have ever learnt to take in hand. But, as is the case with many other good things, a trade-union may be made very bad use of. When the men belonging to a union try to force capitalists to give them a larger share of what has been produced by labour and capital than belongs to labour they do a very foolish thing. The capitalist has exactly the same right to his profits as they have to their wages, and, besides, if he is not allowed to get these profits, he will of course make use of his wealth in some other way : perhaps he will no longer employ it as capital, but will live on it.

### Strikes and Lock-outs.

The question is, however, What is the capitalist's proper share? This question can be decided in two ways. The union and the capitalists may fight the matter out, each side trying how much it can compel the other to give. This is done by *strikes*, in which the workmen refuse to work for less than a certain amount of wages; and by *lock-outs*, in which the employers stop their business and refuse to pay their workmen a higher rate of wages than that which will allow capitalists to make what they consider a fair profit. There can be no doubt that a strike always causes a dead loss to everybody concerned in it, except perhaps one or two paid officers of a union, who find it to their interest to keep up strife when it might be put an end to. *A strike* is perhaps a rather foolish means of deciding such a question, and in all cases a strike causes great suffering to the workmen : still, it is always quite right for men to fight manfully against what they honestly believe to be injustice. But a far better way of deciding such a dispute would be for capitalists and persons chosen by the union to meet and talk the thing over, and to try to come to some agreement. If they fail to do this, they should call in some outside person, who thoroughly understands business and in whom both sides have confidence, lay their case before him, and ask his advice. By this means strikes and lock-outs, and all the misery that they cause, might generally be prevented.

### Abuses connected with Trade-unions.

Unions often act very wrongly in the following ways : (*a*.) Sometimes they will not allow men to do piece-work. You have already seen that if the aim of trade-unions is to secure justice to the working-man they ought to encourage piece-work in every possible way. Perhaps the real reason why piece-work is objected to is that it gets work done quickly, and workmen are afraid that if work is done fast there will be no more left for them to do. This is a great mistake. The more wealth there is produced, the more can be produced, and the more work there will be. Besides, no man can benefit himself by working hard without causing benefit to other people through the increase in the community's wealth. A steam-engine works hard, and very fast, and it increases not only its owner's wealth, but everybody-else's. It enables people to buy things much cheaper than they could be bought if they were made by hand, and so a steam-engine at work always does something towards raising the rate of *real wages*. You may be sure that the more people can " work like a steam-engine " the better it is for them and for everybody else. (*b*.) Unions of the men of a single trade sometimes try to limit the number of workmen by refusing to work with those who do not belong to the union, and will not allow people to belong to it if they have not been apprenticed. Such unions sometimes succeed in keeping up wages in their own trade, but it is done by making people pay more than the proper value for the goods produced. Thus the union taxes the nation without an Act of Parliament, and interferes with the freedom of men to do what pleases them provided that what pleases them does not interfere with the freedom of others. Perhaps the State should discourage this kind of thing as far as it can by protecting from any kind of insult or injury those men that wish to work at a trade without belonging to a trade-union.

### *Friendly Societies.*

There is one kind of work done by some trade-unions, and by what are called friendly societies, that is excellent. The members pay so much a week when they are well, and receive so much a week when they are ill. This mode of " providing for a rainy day" is admirable ; a man who belongs to such a union, who insures his life, and puts money into the savings-bank from time to time, has, when evil days come, little cause for fear.

*Cases in which there is some Difficulty in deciding whether Payments are Wages or Rent, or whether they are Wages or Profit.*

The money paid for labour, whether it is paid to men who keep the roads in good repair, to shoemakers, to watchmakers, to teachers, to doctors, or to clerks in Government offices, is not all *true* wages. Indeed, part of it is often more like rent, and part of it is more like profit. If two young men, each having had the same amount of money spent upon his education, are trained to be doctors, and both obtain the same rank as doctors, the one that has the greater natural power of observing the signs of disease and thence learning exactly what is the matter with his patients, will succeed in curing more sick people than the other will. In time this will come to be known, and many more people will go to the abler doctor for advice. Perhaps he will be able to earn £500 a year more than the other will. Now, what is this £500? It is not wages or profit. The other doctor, plainly, will get the same wages and profit. This extra payment, then, must be made to the abler doctor because he has a certain natural advantage that he lets other people have the benefit of, and therefore this part of his income must be something very like rent. The difference between it and true rent is, perhaps, that rent can be received only on account of articles of wealth—that is, of things that have value. This special power of the doctor's is not wealth, for it cannot be exchanged; he alone can use it. The services that he renders have value, but his power has not.

Again, if two boys are born with just the same natural powers, but one receives a good education, which perhaps costs his father £2,000, he may be able to earn £1,000 a year as a lawyer; while the other, not being able to get any education, remains an ordinary labouring-man, and never earns more than £100 a year by his labour. Now, what is the extra £900 that the lawyer gets? Is it not very like profit? The father has expended money on the son's education with a view to make him an able and clever man by-and-by, and the son receives the reward of the father's abstinence. The difference between this reward and true profit is very small. It is perhaps this: The son's education cannot be handed over to another, and therefore it is not capital or even wealth; the father has not turned his wealth into capital; and therefore what is earned by means of the education cannot be profit. It is more like the income from wealth that has been used in purchasing an annuity. Even in the case of ordinary labourers degrees of strength and education cause great differences in the wages earned, and all such differences must be caused by extra payments that are, more or less, like rent or profits.

*Causes of the Different Rates of "Wages" of Skilled Labour.*

Many of the differences we find in the rewards given for different kinds of labour may be explained by reference to such extra payments, but supply and demand have always much to do with the rate of wages in any particular trade. It is not easy to get an appointment as headmaster of a high school; the cost of first-class education is very great, and but few are clever enough to do the work; among a great number who may start to learn the business, only very few can succeed. Men fitted to be headmasters are very scarce, and therefore the extra payment for a headmaster's work is high. Any one with health and strength can use a pick-axe and shovel; navvies, therefore, are very plentiful, and their wages are low. A man who wishes to be a bank-manager must have shown himself to be very trustworthy and honest, besides being clever; no one unless he was thought to be very wise and prudent as well as clever would ever get such a position. Such men are not common, and therefore the supply is small, and a bank-manager is paid a high salary. Very few like to be chimney-sweeps or dustmen, for the work is very dirty; the supply of men who are willing to be chimney-sweeps and dustmen is therefore small in proportion to that of ordinary labourers, and so chimney-sweeps and dustmen get better wages for their disagreeable work than an ordinary road-man gets for his more pleasant work. People like to have regular work, and if they can get it they will take it at low wages; but a man who has sometimes to work very hard and then to be idle will get high wages. Lumpers, as they are called, and porters have to be paid much higher wages than day-labourers. Some kinds of work are badly paid, because persons that have failed in other businesses can take them up. Thus, a man who has failed as a doctor, as a lawyer, or as a teacher may make a good clerk. Therefore clerks receive lower wages than we should expect if we considered only the cost of their education.

# CHAPTER XXI.

## POPULATION AND WAGES.

It is plain that the number of people in a country cannot continue to be too large for the food-supply of that country to support; but this food-supply may either be grown in the country itself, or it may be purchased from some foreign country with articles of wealth that are not food. England does not grow enough corn to feed all her people, but she makes iron rails, cutlery, and such things, and sends them to America, New Zealand, and other places in exchange for corn: thus England has a food-supply that she could hardly grow for herself. The quantity of food that can be produced in any country of course depends chiefly upon the nature of the country itself. One of the small islands in the Pacific could not produce more than a small quantity of food. White Island, in the Bay of Plenty, with its barren soil, could produce hardly any.

### *The Growth of an Isolated Population will in time be checked.*

If a boat-load of men and women, escaping from a leaky vessel, were to land on one of the small but fertile islands to the north of New Zealand, and were to decide to live there, shut out from the rest of the world, this is what would happen on that island : The people would for a long time increase in number; but the rate of increase would slowly grow less. For the first century perhaps the increase would be rapid, during the second it would become slower and slower, and during the third there would perhaps be no increase at all.

### *The Positive Check.*

When a lot of rabbits are placed on a small island a similar thing happens. At first there is plenty of food, and the rabbits increase very fast; but after a time there are more rabbits born

than can be supported by the quantity of food that the island
can produce, and therefore large numbers of the rabbits that are
born die of starvation and disease. The number that will die
from these causes will be just enough to keep the number that
remain alive on a par with the power that the island has of producing food on which rabbits can live. Starvation and disease,
then, would be a positive check to the increase in the number of
rabbits.

### The Preventive Check.

But man, though he is like a rabbit in some respects, is very
unlike him in many others. The existence of the rabbit depends
entirely on outside circumstances : if there is enough food for
him he will live ; if there is not enough he must die. But man
can, to a large extent, make outside circumstances suit him, and
he can also suit himself to outside circumstances. Thus the
people on our island would certainly not depend entirely on the
cocoanuts and bananas that Nature provided for them ; they
would cultivate the ground and make it much more productive,
and so they would be able to put off the time when the positive
check from starvation and disease would prevent their number
from increasing ; and at last, when they began to see that, do
what they would, they could no longer make the island support
more inhabitants, they would, unless they were very foolish
people, make a check of their own that would keep the positive
check from coming into operation at all. They would say : More
children are being born here than we can provide for ; therefore some of us must go away and find another island, or we
must make it a rule that people shall not get married till they are,
say, thirty years old, so that they may have smaller families ; anything is better than for us all to live in misery and constant fear
of starvation. Men, then, differ from rabbits in this : that they
could, by means of a preventive check devised by their own
wisdom and foresight, do away altogether with the fearful positive check caused by starvation and disease. What has been
said shows what man could do if he chose : the following
sections will tell what man too often does.

### Man generally invents a Check of his own.

History shows us that there have not been many cases in
which the food-supply of a country has been really limited by

the nature of the country itself. We do not know what may take place in the future, but in the past food-supply and, consequently, population have generally been limited by man's carelessness, or by his folly, long before the restraints that the natural conditions of the country might cause have begun to work. The more we look into this matter the more clearly we see that man in his foolish way so arranges matters that, long before there is any real reason why the increase in the number of people should stop, Starvation and Disease have to come to the front and say, "You people are so ignorant and foolish and selfish that we cannot let any more of you live. There are enough of your sort here already."

### Ignorance and Idleness are Checks.

The soil and climate of Italy are far better than the soil and climate of England and Wales, yet in the two last-named countries there was in 1872 about one inhabitant for every acre and a half of land, while in Italy there was only one for every three acres. What can be the cause of this difference? The people of England and Wales are industrious and fairly educated, while Italy is noted for its swarms of beggars and for the ignorance of its lower classes. Perhaps, however, the cause lies still deeper than this. It may be that the idleness is caused by the fact that the people have very little inducement to be industrious, and that bad laws and bad government have a great deal to do with the matter. Let us consider the case of two other countries in order to find out if this is so.

### Bad Land-laws are a Check.

Belgium has a population of very nearly one person to every acre of land, but there is not nearly so much poverty in Belgium as there is in many countries where there is very little crowding-together of the people. In Ireland there is not one person to every four acres. A few hundred years ago Belgium was not a better country than Ireland; indeed, it was not nearly so good; it has been made what it is by its people. How is it that Belgium can now support such a dense population, while Ireland can hardly support one four times as sparse? We need not search very long in order to find an answer to this question. In Belgium the laws and customs allow the land to be nearly all parcelled out into small farms. These are cultivated by their owners, who get the full benefit of their labour, and so have good reason to be industrious, thrifty, and prudent. Speaking generally, we may say that land in Ireland has been the property of a small number of people who have got out of it, in the shape of rent, all that it has produced, except what has been little more than enough to keep the tillers of the soil alive. These labourers have grown hopeless and careless through knowing that whatever they might do would be for the good of the landlords, whose agents would merely raise the rent if they saw that the peasants could pay more. It is said that during the Irish famines, while large numbers of people were dying from the want of something to eat, food was still being sent out of the country in large quantities in order that the rent of the land might be paid to the owners of the land. The starving men and women who had grown this food had to be fed by the charity ·of the people of England, Scotland, and America. What country could be expected to maintain a large number of people under laws that allow such à state of things as this to exist?

Probably, this is how it has come about that, while in Belgium every little patch of land has been made rich and fertile by care and hard work, the Irish people have been afraid to do any good to the soil lest the results of their labour should be lost to them, and should enrich only those who appear to already have too large a share of the produce. This is why the population of Ireland is scattered, while that of Belgium is dense. No doubt, if Ireland manages to end her troubles by getting fair and sensible land-laws and customs, she will be before very long just as thickly peopled as Belgium is, and will be able to support in comfort nearly twenty millions of people instead of five or six millions.

### The Maori Check.

It would be quite easy to show that *old* New Zealand never had as great a Maori population as it was capable of supporting. The Maoris in the old times brought the positive check into operation long before Nature said it was wanted. Tribal jealousies, war, and the thriftless and idle habits produced by the feeling that what was wrought for would probably never be enjoyed by the workers, constantly kept the people too near the starvation-point, and prevented the increase of population.

*Man's Ingenuity displayed in the various Means he adopts to bring the Positive Check into Operation prematurely.*

If we carefully examined the history of other countries we should find that in many cases· population has been reduced or kept small through bad government, bad laws, or bad customs, and that it is only in very few countries that the *positive check* has really been brought into work by Nature and Nature's laws. This is because man with his greed and his folly acts as if he were taking great trouble to have the check in operation long before Nature says that it is needed—just as if he thought it a ·good thing, whose working ought not to be waited for, but should be hastened on as much as possible.

*Benefits derived from Increase of Population.*

This is very much to be regretted, for a large population is in many ways a capital thing for a country and for the people in it. If everybody were sensible and prudent it would be the best of things. The more people there are in a country the more the comfort and convenience of all can be promoted. Compare the New Zealand of forty years ago with the New Zealand of the present day. Then there were no railways, no telegraphs, no large steamers, no fine towns, no libraries, no museums, no places of amusement, no hospitals, no universities, no botanical gardens, no great public buildings ; and very few roads, bridges, schools, churches, or comfortable houses. How is it that we have been able to get all these things, and scores of others that add to our comfort, convenience, and happiness generally ? It is the increase in the number of people that has enabled us to have them. We may be quite sure, too, that if this increase went on, and if our wisdom and foresight were also somewhat increased, our comfort and happiness would be still further added to. There is another reason, a very important one, why it is desirable that population should continue to grow larger : a large population can produce wealth much more readily than a small one can. The number of people in England has increased enormously since the year 1800, but wealth has increased very much faster in proportion, and England is now able to lend, and does lend, her wealth to various countries all over the world. To New Zealand alone she has lent in one way or another more than £70,000,000.*

*How the Positive Check might come into Operation even in the case of a wealthy and prosperous Nation.*

It is, however, always necessary to bear in mind that there may be a great production of wealth with, at the same time, a small production of food ; and that a country that produces great wealth, of which very little is in the form of food, is always unsafe unless it has a large and well-secured foreign trade. People must eat or die, and if they do not themselves produce food they should so arrange matters that they may always be able to buy it readily; · otherwise, in the event of a great war, they may suddenly find themselves without a proper supply of food, and so be brought face to face with the positive check in its most frightful form.

*Has our State yet invented a Check ?*

As New Zealand is well suited for food-production it is nearly impossible for its people, for ages to come, to suffer from a limited food-supply through war ; but they may, and perhaps do, suffer in a mild sort of way from some of the checks that are caused by man's folly. If, through want of wise land-laws, private owners are allowed to keep good land idle for their own pleasure, or to save themselves trouble while they are waiting for the value of their land to rise, the effect is, as was shown in Chapter XIX., to cause poorer land to be cultivated at a greater cost, and to raise the price of most kinds of food through this extended cultivation.† Of course, if this kind of thing were

---

* Between the years 1875 and 1885 the average yearly *increase* in the wealth of England was at least £150,000,000, or 3½d. a day for each inhabitant.

† The reason why we as yet hardly feel the pressure of such evils, if they exist, is that we still produce abundance of food, and that in regard to many articles of food the world is our market, while the world, fixing its own prices, fixes them, fortunately for us, higher than our cost of production. When, however, our population rises above a certain limit (which is probably not very far off) the cost of production will have so increased that we shall no longer be in a position to sell these articles of food at the world's price and at a profit, but shall very likely have to buy some of them at that price increased by the cost of freight. By that time perhaps the Law of Rent will have become thoroughly effective, and then, it may be, we shall feel the full effect of evils caused in the way indicated in the text.

carried very far, even in a country so richly endowed by Nature as New Zealand is, it would greatly increase the cost of living, and would bring the positive check a step or two nearer to us than it ought to be.

*Population and Wages; why Real Wages do not always increase with the Growth of Population.*

We may now consider how wages are affected by increase of population. It seems to be quite plain that, as the wealth-producing power of a young country increases with the increase of population, and very much faster,* real wages should also increase as population increases. Real wages do not thus increase in all cases, but it would be very difficult to show why they should not. Let us try to discover the causes that may hinder this increase, even though we may be unable to suggest any remedy. The causes which in a new country prevent real wages from increasing so long as the general wealth of the State increases, are these: First, the increase of real rent. It has been already shown in Chapter XIX. that real rent must always begin to be paid *to somebody* as soon as it is found to be worth while to cultivate any but the best and most convenient land. In some countries this rent goes to persons to whom the State has given the ownership of the land; in others it goes to the Government officers, the king, and his nobles. Many people now believe that in a new country where the rent-producing power has been entirely created by the State—the whole community—rent should belong to that community, and should be used to pay the community's expenses. At present these expenses are paid by the people generally in addition to the rent which is received by owners of land. Thus, then, all the produce of land, labour, and capital must be reduced by rent and taxes as a first charge —one that, as a rule, is constantly increasing †—and what tends to keep real wages from rising is that the greater part of the

---

* Of course there is a limit; but, generally, in a young country, increasing division of labour, increasing facility of communication and transport, and increasing use of powerful machinery cause wealth to increase very much faster in proportion than population increases. Under such circumstances, supply of labour ought seldom to exceed demand.

† A very similar effect would be produced if the rent went to the State; the difference is that, if all true rent belonged to the State, taxation would probably be unnecessary. It will be shown in Chapter XXVII. why, in New Zealand at all events, all rent cannot be taken by the State.

advantage arising from the improved condition of the country and its increase in wealth goes to the owners of land. To put it in another way : What the labourer earns as a man working for an employer he receives; but what he earns as a member of the community by helping to increase the wealth of the State as a whole he does not receive : this would be part of the reward of his labour—may we not almost say, of his *real wages ?* —if it were not converted into rent and eventually given to the owners of land in the country generally. A part of what might be a labourer's real wages goes for taxes; but it will be shown in Chapter XXIV. that he gets a return for this.

The second reason why real wages do not increase as might be expected is that through land being in the hands of private owners it is not all put to the best use. If men could at once go and take up unused land anywhere, some of the good land now lying nearly idle would be made proper use of. This would tend to render the increase of true rent less rapid, and would make the supply of labour in towns somewhat less and the demand for it somewhat greater than it is, and thus the difficulty of getting a share of the increased wealth would be made less. By allowing good land. to remain unused in this way a State may make a large island into a very small one, and so bring the positive check much nearer than it ought to be.

The third reason why real wages do not always increase with increase of population is that immigrants are not always dealt with in the right way. The real use of immigration is to bring about the placing of people where they are wanted— that is, on unused lands—and not in towns, where there are often too many people already.

The fourth reason is that in nearly every community a large proportion of the people are careless and imprudent. People that ought to be spreading themselves over the country crowd into towns; they "come there to stay," and they do stay. Their children marry young and without a thought as to how they are to provide for a family. Soon, the town has more people than it can provide · for. The law of supply and demand produces its usual effect : wages fall, and people are glad to work for the merest living. There are two remedies for this. Young people must swarm off into the country ; and sound views about marriage must get spread abroad,

11

and must also sink down to the very foundations of society. It must come to be considered wrong and disgraceful for a young couple to get married without having a good prospect of being able in some way to provide for a family, to bring up their children comfortably, and to give them a proper idea of what a home should be. Young people who have been brought up in this way will not be likely to rush into hasty marriages; they will look before they leap. It may be that these remedies cannot be applied : if so it is to be regretted, for they seem to be the only ones that can prevent one section of the community from dragging a large part of the whole population down towards its own level.

# CHAPTER XXII.

## PROSPERITY AND DEPRESSION; RICH AND POOR.

A NATION seldom grows richer and richer, or poorer and poorer, quite steadily; its progress is something like the rising of the tide. When the tide is coming in on a stormy day great waves run far up the beach, and then the water goes back almost as far; it is only by watching the water for a considerable time that one can see that progress is being made, and that the tide is really rising. So it has been with New Zealand. There have been times when it has seemed that the country was going to grow wealthy all at once, trade has been good, work has been plentiful, and every one has been in good spirits. But a change has come; tradesmen have found themselves unable to sell their goods, workmen have been unable to get work, and every one has been inclined to think that the country was fast going to ruin. It is only when we take account of a long period that we can know for certain that real progress has been made. If we compared the New Zealand of 1886 with the New Zealand of 1884 we might say that our tide is falling, but if we could compare the New Zealand of the years 1850–56 with the New Zealand of 1880–86 we should at once see that a great advance has been made—that the tide has risen. Now, what is the cause of these waves of prosperity, and why are they followed by bad times— by what is called "depression"? They are caused in much the same way as the waves of the sea are caused. In a sheltered inlet where there is no wind, the tide rises quite steadily; there are no waves. So, there would be no waves of prosperity and depression for a community of perfectly careful and prudent men, men who could not be made rash and imprudent by the hope of suddenly becoming rich, who could not be induced to risk the loss of the good things they possess for the mere chance of getting something better : such a community would grow rich surely, but slowly and steadily; they would be content with fair and regular gains, and their tide of prosperity would rise as quietly and gently as does the tide in a well-protected harbour. The causes of the great ocean billows are the wind and storms that violently rush over the sea and gradually deepen the furrows on its surface. The motion that has been given to the water out on the ocean does not cease near the shore; the waves are therefore carried on over the sand, or up the face of the rocks; these with quiet but resistless might gradually stop the motion of the water, which, by its own weight, falls back with resounding roar, to and even below its proper level. Similarly, men's minds are always ready to be acted upon by what seems to be a chance of getting wealth easily and quickly. If, for instance, a new gold-field is discovered and much wealth is produced, people are not content with the enjoyment of this wealth, they assume that the golden stream will continue to flow, and they gradually come to believe that it is much larger than it really is, and that it is going to do all sorts of wonderful things for them. Tradesmen order from merchants very large quantities of goods, hoping to exchange them for gold that is to be obtained by-and-by; land is bought at high prices in order that it may be sold for higher prices in a year or two; a great deal of wealth is turned into fixed capital in the shape of fine buildings, broad roads, and handsome bridges. The wealth produced is not enough for all the grand schemes that have been started; but the banks advance money freely, and more money can be borrowed in England. In one way or another a great many people manage to get all their own and much of other people's wealth locked up in some kind of undertaking. But now the yield of gold falls off, or it becomes plain that the supply is far too small to do all the great things expected from it. The wave has reached its greatest height, and it rapidly falls back. Tradesmen cannot sell their goods. Land can hardly be sold at any price. The banks have to refuse help to their customers. The crash has come; the wave has broken and fallen back; a time of depression has arrived; and people find it hard to make a living. They are now sadder but wiser. They have learnt a lesson, and will remember it until the next wave of prosperity comes, and then—they will forget what they have learnt and will act just as they did before. So the thing goes on, and will go on until men have learnt to look before they leap.

### Is Unproductive Expenditure good for Trade?

Here is the place to say a few words about the effects of races, sports, festivals, and exhibitions, which often for a short time give increased employment to a portion of the people of a town. Sports and festivals that take people away from their homes and their work do no good whatever in the way of increasing the trade of the country. They merely take wealth from one set of people and give it to another set, of whom there are not a few who consume much and produce nothing. Now, the wealth so consumed would almost certainly be used as capital if it were not thus handed over to non-producers, and then it would assist further production : as it is, the wealth is really destroyed and nothing is produced to take its place; and, of course, what people would have produced if they had remained at home at work is not produced if they are amusing themselves. On the whole, then, races, sports, and festivals, which are supposed by many to be "good for trade," do great harm to trade by causing the loss of wealth that would almost certainly become capital; in any case, they cause a dead loss of wealth to the community as a whole, and benefit only persons in certain occupations in particular places. Of course we understand that people are not mere machines, to work right on till they are worn out; men and women must have change and amusement. But it is well for us all to bear in mind that if we have amusement we must pay for it, and not to believe that we can both enjoy fun and do good to the trade of the country at the same time—that we can eat the cake and have it too.

### The Nature of the State's Increasing Prosperity; why Poverty increases along with Wealth.

When a great wave of prosperity and the depression that follows it have come to an end, things are not left quite as they were before; when the quiet stage is reached, it is found that, though real progress has been made by the State as a whole, it is usually the rich who have become richer; the poor are just as they were—perhaps they are somewhat poorer; at all events, the condition of the poor has not improved at the same rate as the wealth of the rich has increased. Now, how is this? There are two reasons for it. First, the number of labourers in towns increases very fast, through too early marriages, through labourers being unable to take up and work land in convenient positions on their own account, and through their unwillingness to remove from the towns, where they are merely in the way, to the country, where they are much wanted, or where, at all events, they could soon make room for themselves. Thus it turns out that the local demand for labour becomes smaller than the supply; money-wages in the towns begin to fall, or work is not to be constantly obtained; after a time, real wages must certainly fall, because the price of food is sure to rise. This rise in the price of food is the second cause of the want of improvement in the condition of the poor. The rise in prices affords the means of paying the increase of rent caused by the increase of population and the need for working poorer land to feed the new members of the State. The land is owned by private persons, and it is they who get the benefit of the rise in rent. These, then, are the causes that tend, even in a young country, to make the rich grow richer and the poor poorer. It is very hard to see how, under our present system of distributing wealth, this state of matters can be greatly changed for the better. The very rich must go on growing richer, and the very poor poorer, till a new and better system can be found. In the meantime the State has to do the best it can for those who feel the pressure of the system most, and the best it can for itself in its relation to them. But all the time the State should keep a sharp look-out in order to discover, if possible, a new and better way.

### How Poverty is dealt with by the State.

All that we can do here is to describe briefly the plans that have been proposed for helping the very-poor, or that have been already tried; and to point out the course recommended by those who have studied this subject in order to find out how to help the poor to help themselves, and so in the end to do away with poverty. The very poor may be divided into three classes. To the first class belong those who are or have become poor through misfortune, and cannot help themselves. Such are orphan children, and persons suffering from disease of body or mind, or through accident. In this country orphan and destitute children are provided for by means of industrial schools and orphan homes, and by the boarding-out system. This last is a very good system. For a small weekly sum, which is paid by the State, foster-parents receive orphan and destitute children and treat them as if they were their own. The welfare of these little ones is carefully looked after by kind ladies appointed by the State to do the work. Thus these children have many of the comforts of home provided for them, and have a fair chance of growing up to be useful men and women. They are educated at the public schools, and when they are old enough they are put out to work, much in the same way as they would be if they were being brought up by their parents. It is found that in a great many cases the foster-parents and the children become almost as warmly attached to one another as parents and children generally are. If any of the destitute children have parents, these are keenly looked after by an officer of the Government, and are made, as far as they are able to do so, to pay for the support of their children. Other persons belonging to this class are dealt with in the manner described in the next chapter.

The other two classes of the very poor are, on the one hand those who are able to work and would rather do so than beg, and on the other those who are able to work, but would rather beg. A good plan of dealing with both of these classes is one that was tried in Holland at the beginning of this century. There, large numbers of poor people were placed on poor land, and made to work on it until it became good enough to keep them in comfort. Of course, during the time that such people were getting the land ready they would have to receive much support from the State; but when once it was ready the State would be freed from the burden for good and for all.

It is always quite right both for the State and for private persons to help those who are in misfortune, if it is seen that the help is really wanted, and that it will be properly used. But there is this difficulty : When the State gives alms to deserving people, those who are not deserving soon come to look upon this kind of help as their right, and the effect is that some of them manage to live without doing a full share of the State's work. These people never pay any taxes (though somebody has to pay taxes for them, seeing that they consume many articles that are taxed), and so the industrious hard-working members of the State have to keep the idle ones. It is a good plan for all who give assistance to the poor to insist on getting some work done in return for the help, if the persons receiving it are able to make such a return.

### *Remedies for Pauperism.*

Those who have studied this subject most deeply think that the evils of pauperism must be remedied by the following methods, if they are to be cured at all :—

(*a*.) By means of education of various kinds the tastes of the people must be improved, so that all shall take delight in higher things than drunkenness, gambling, expensive dress, and luxury that cannot be afforded ; and young people must be trained to refuse to do without these higher things, and to be unwilling to marry unless they can make sure of having a good share of comfort.

(*b*.) Opportunities must be afforded to the very poorest of getting small pieces of land which they may turn into farms, and arrangements must be made to enable them to work these farms till they are able to pay for the farms and for the assistance granted to them.

# CHAPTER XXIII.

## HOSPITALS, LUNATIC ASYLUMS, PRISONS.

If one of the wise men of old could rise up and see the world as it is now, the first feature of our social life that would strike him as being strange and wonderful would be the increase of comfort and convenience brought about by improvements in those arts that depend on our knowledge of the powers of Nature. But, after he had got over his first feelings of surprise at the work done by our steamers, railways, and electric telegraphs, and had studied the people for a time, he would probably find the growth of humane and benevolent feelings among people of all classes, rich and poor, educated and uneducated, the very hardest thing to understand and explain. He would remember that in the olden time poor people who were sick or insane, and all classes of criminals, were, as a rule, either utterly neglected or treated with the most horrid cruelty. He would call to mind how, in his days, soldiers who had been wounded in battle were often left to die on the field unless they were of high rank or had special friends who were willing to care for them. He would remember that the lunatic was left to wander about starving and uncared-for, or, if troublesome, was chained and perhaps beaten; that prisoners were kept in loathsome dungeons, tortured in every possible way, and at last slaughtered without mercy. If he were a Greek he would perhaps remember how surprised the polished Athenians were when one of their poets took the trouble to say that even a slave was also a man; if he had lived in imperial Rome he would be able to tell how prisoners, almost unarmed, were made to fight with armed soldiers, or how they were thrown to hungry wild beasts to afford amusement to the civilised but brutal people of Rome. But now, in one of our modern States, he would find all this altered. He would learn that sufferers from sickness or accident, however poor they may be, are treated with kindness and humanity. He would learn, too, that when a great State goes to war a complete hospital, with well-trained nurses, nearly always accompanies its armies to take proper care of the wounded and the sick. He would hear that lunatics are well cared for, and that great skill, knowledge, and kindness are used to cure them if possible, and that if they prove to be incurable very much is done to make them comfortable till death comes to set them free. But what would perhaps astonish him most of all would be to find that even prisoners—men and women who have broken the laws of the State—are treated with a large amount of kindness, as well as with necessary severity. It would take this wise man a long time to find out the cause of the change, and if he were left to himself he would, perhaps, never discover it. Is it possible for us to find out what the cause is?

### *The Cause of the Growth of Humane Feelings among all Classes of the Community.*

It is not usual in works of this kind to refer to the subject that has now to be dealt with, but one of our principal objects is to show you how we came to be as we are, in order that clearer ideas of the meaning of what is now going on around us may be within your reach. If for any reason this means of getting at the truth should be neglected, the results obtained will be imperfect and misleading. You should, then, endeavour to find out what is the true cause of the growth of humane and benevolent feelings among men, before you study the institutions that these humane feelings have brought into being, or that have had their character completely changed through the existence of such feelings. Nearly nineteen hundred years ago there lived a Teacher who, by some means which it is unnecessary for us to enquire about here, was gifted with a marvellous knowledge of men, of their weakness and their folly, of their tendency to evil and of their capacity for good, a knowledge that has neither before nor since been surpassed or even equalled. The accounts of him that have been handed down to us show that this Teacher had the greatest sympathy with and affection for all men, both in their joys and in their trials and sufferings, and an earnest desire to help them to get clean away from wickedness and ignorance. By his conduct, and by his treatment of those who came to him to be taught, he showed that he made no distinction between rich and poor, clever and foolish, between those who had lived low, vulgar, and wicked lives and those who had been respectable. All were allowed to come to him and learn what he had to teach them. One of the principal methods of instruction used by him was to tell short, interesting stories full of meaning. Among these well-known stories the following may be mentioned: "The Lost Sheep," "The Prodigal Son," "The Good Samaritan," "The Pharisee and the Publican," and "The Merciless Creditor." All these stories are of very simple construction, and when they have been heard once or twice they can hardly be forgotten.

These stories teach, among other things, the foolishness of all kinds of pride and vanity, the wickedness of harsh conduct to the helpless, and the nobleness of generosity, kindness, mercy, and forgiveness. These stories form part of a book that has for nearly nineteen centuries been read more or less in churches and in private, and that has for the last three hundred years particularly been very much in most people's hands at one time or another. Besides this, these stories have been carefully taught and explained to young children, and now there are many millions of people who know them nearly by heart through having been so taught them in early youth. Now, if you remember that the book in which these stories are to be found has been more reverenced than any other book in the world; that the stories are in themselves of the greatest beauty and interest; that the knowledge of them is so widely spread: when you think that the care of the sick, of the insane, and of the erring, even of those who have erred wilfully, is almost directly enjoined by them; when you find that the change that is taking place agrees almost exactly with the teachings contained in the stories; and when you can find no probable cause outside of a group of facts of which the influence exercised by these stories is one of the most remarkable, is it not reasonable to suppose that this wonderful growth of humane feelings among all classes of men must to a very large extent have been caused by the stories told so long ago by this great Teacher? Is it not reasonable to think that these stories have for long ages been slowly working their way into the hard and merciless hearts of men, and that now at last they have got in, and we are beginning to see some of the results that their teaching is fitted to produce ? If this is not the correct explanation of the growth of humane feelings in modern times it would, perhaps, be hard to find a better one.

### The State's Relation to Dangerous Persons.

The State cannot in any case consult the particular interests of single individuals,—certainly not of those who by their fault or their misfortune are dangerous to others. The State's first duty is to provide for the safety of all. Therefore, if a man has small-pox, or is insane and believes that it is his duty to kill somebody, or if his moral sense is so imperfect that he breaks the law by injuring others in person or in property, he must be placed in a position in which his fault or his misfortune will cause the least possible mischief. The difference between the old feeling with regard to dangerous persons and the new one is, that in olden times the only object aimed at was to get rid of such persons in one way or another as soon as possible, and, in the case of criminals, to make them suffer as much as possible while being got rid of ; while the modern view appears to be that the safety of the members of the community must be secured by every means and at any cost, but that, when once this has been done, attention should be turned to the recovery of the sick or insane, or to the reformation of the criminal, as the case may be. It is now also thoroughly understood that, while cruelty to an insane man or to a criminal very seldom does him any good, reasonable kindness and thoroughly fair treatment often bring about the desired end. It would be very near the truth to say that the State, in order to secure the safety of its members, has to deal with three kinds of disease—disease of the body, of the mind, and of what is called the moral sense. There is a proper kind of treatment for each of these diseases.

### Hospitals and Quarantine Laws.

The doctor knows how to deal with the first kind of disease, which is not often very dangerous to the community. All that the State does in connection with it is to try to prevent persons suffering from infectious disease from giving it to other persons, to see that arrangements are made under which poor people may receive proper treatment and attention, and, lastly, to bear a share of the expense in proportion to the amount of work done for the State as a whole. The first of these duties is performed in this way : If a ship comes from a foreign port with dangerous disease on board, the passengers and crew are landed on some small island and kept there, apart from all other people, till there is no longer any reason to fear that the disease will spread : at the same time the ship is cleaned and made thoroughly safe. In towns, too, similar arrangements are made for separating people suffering from infectious disease from those that are healthy. With regard to the second duty it is sufficient to say that, by an Act passed by the New Zealand Parliament a short time ago, the Government may appoint an Inspector whose business it is to visit hospitals; this he may do at any time without giving notice. The Inspector is to report to the Governor every year on the condition of all the hospitals he has visited. The State performs its third duty by granting money for the partial support of hospitals. It is very properly thought that the State should not do everything for the sick, but should leave room for the humane feelings of individuals to come into play. It is arranged, too, that the districts in which the hospitals are situated shall pay something towards the expense of supporting them.

The State gives towards the support of hospitals 10s. for every pound (up to £500) left by will to a hospital, £1 4s. for every pound given by private individuals, and £1 for every pound given by any local authorities.

### Lunatic Asylums and the Insane.

Those who are suffering from disease of the mind are dealt with in lunatic asylums. An asylum has to be somewhat like a hospital and somewhat like a prison. It has to be like a prison because most patients are more or less dangerous at times, either to themselves or to others. Formerly lunatics were horribly ill-used : the dark cell, the chain, and even the whip were freely employed in their treatment. But now, in our New Zealand asylums, no one ever thinks of using such things; even the canvas jacket with closed sleeves, and other similar means of restraining freedom, are seldom used. It has been found that appeals to the remains of reason that the patients possess, kindness, amusements, and ever-watchful care are far better means of keeping order, and in the end give far less trouble, than the cruel plans adopted in former days. At the same time, of course, due caution has to be used in order to prevent patients from running away. The asylum is like a hospital in this respect: The patients are sick, and require the care of a doctor who has made their disease a special study. There is one rather peculiar thing about insanity. In many cases the doctor can at first do a great deal for patients, perhaps cure them in a few months; as time goes on he can do less for them, though sometimes insane people get well after having been ill for many years. Generally, however, after three or four years the doctor is of little or no use to the insane; their minds have by that time been quite broken down by the disease, and there is nothing to be done for the patients but to make them as comfortable as such poor creatures can be made, and then let them wait for death. All this seems to show that there should be three kinds of asylums. One kind should be under the sole control of the ablest doctor that can be found. All insane persons should be sent to him the moment they are found to be insane, in order that proper measures may be immediately adopted in the case of all those that can be cured or improved. Those who have not been very greatly benefited, say, within a year, might be passed on to the second asylum, where they should be visited by the doctor pretty often and put through regular asylum treatment, which is really something like that of a school; the difference being, that the schoolmaster has to deal with *new* minds, while the doctor has to deal with *old* ones that have got out of order or have broken down and require to be built up again. The third kind of asylum should be merely a kind of refuge, and to it should be sent those who can never be cured. The asylum first spoken of would cost a very great deal, but there are two ways in which the plan proposed would tend to save expense. The hopeless patients would cost far less in a refuge than they would in an asylum, and a great many people would be soon cured if they could receive very close attention from a doctor as soon as they were taken ill. As you will learn, the early cure of a patient saves the Government more than £23 a year, and of course, if you take account of the fact that many of the people that are cured become producers at once, you must see that the saving to the State amounts to a much larger sum.

The number of insane persons in the lunatic asylums of the colony at the beginning of 1885 was 1,452. Reckoning all the people in the colony, we find that one person out of 391 was then in an asylum. The average cost of the patients is now a little less than £26 10s. a year, and, of this, about £3 5s. is paid back to the Government by patients or their relatives.

### Prisons and Criminals.

Now we have to say a few words about prisons and prisoners. In the year 1886 the number of persons who passed through the prisons of New Zealand was 5,590, but there were at the close of the year only 242 prisoners in penal servitude, and 208 "hard-labour" prisoners who had received sentences of one year or upwards. The number of people in New Zealand being taken into consideration, this is a very small number.

Crime, or the imperfect moral nature to which crime is owing, is a sort of disease, but not one that a doctor can deal with. A man may be a great criminal and yet be quite healthy in mind and in body. The gaoler is the proper doctor for the criminal's complaint; which is of this kind: While the criminal has evil thoughts and bad inclinations as most other men have—though the criminal's bad tendencies are, perhaps, much stronger—the feelings that restrain other men are in his case either weak or absent. These restraints are, first, a well-ordered respect for self, the fear of punishment and of the contempt of one's fellow-men, and dread of the loss of liberty. Some or all of these feelings are so weak in the criminal that they are not able to keep him from doing wrong. In the second place, the generous feelings, such as the desire to help one's fellows and to refrain from doing them any kind of harm, are in the case of the criminal so weak that his desire to have his own way quite conquers them. In the third place, the moral sense — which cannot be exactly described, though it exists in some form in most men and women—the faculty that gives rise to the feeling that it is a *duty* to do this and to refrain from doing that, has in the criminal hardly any strength at all. Now, you will easily see that this is a terrible disease, really far worse than disease of either mind or body. This is the disease that the gaoler has to try to cure. His principal remedies are work, discipline, well-ordered kindness, and hope. While in prison the prisoner is made to work hard and regularly, and to be thoroughly obedient. His own habits, it may be assumed, have been bad. The ordinary criminal has seldom been trained to work steadily on, or, if he has been so trained, he has got out of the habit and has learnt to do things by fits and starts as the humour takes him. His prison training will, after a while, make him used to doing the right thing at the right time and in the right way, and to working steadily on. If he is uneducated he will have to go to the prison school. If he has no regular trade he will be taught one, and this will fit him for getting an honest living when he regains his liberty. Then, in a good prison there is strict order. Any offence against it is followed by swift and certain punishment, and obedience to the law secures for a prisoner a fair amount of comfort. In prison, then, a man must learn to work and to obey law. If this training can be continued long enough it must produce a great change in a prisoner's character. But the training alone will not alter the inner mind of a man, it merely puts him into the way of working hard and behaving well if in some way the inmost feelings of his heart can be changed. This is the most difficult business that an earnest gaoler has to undertake. He has to help his prisoners to gain self-respect by showing them that he thinks them worth something—by making them feel that he is sorry for them, that he wishes them well, and that he is ready to help them as far as he can if only they can be persuaded to choose the right path. A gaoler who thus succeeds in making his prisoners consider him a real friend, though perhaps a rather rough one, is a good man, and his work is sure to be useful. Hope is a very important instrument in the training of prisoners. In our gaols hope is held out to the prisoners from the time they enter the prison until they leave it—the hope of shortening their imprisonment by good conduct, and the hope of earning a little while they are in gaol to help them to make a start when they are released. In many cases, too, there are officers belonging to the gaol whose duty it is to constantly hold out to prisoners the very best kind of hope. It will be seen that prison training must be a slow process if it is to succeed, for the gaoler has to perform the difficult task of effectively helping a man to get his real nature changed, and it is nearly always necessary that the gaoler should have plenty of time to do his work in. When, therefore, a man comes up for sentence a second time, and thus shows that nothing but long training can cure the perversity of his nature, the judge nearly always thinks it right, and for the offender's own good, that the sentence should be long enough to allow the prisoner to get the full benefit of prison training.

# CHAPTER XXIV.

## TAXES.

TAXES are payments demanded by the Government for the purpose of meeting the expenses of the State, acting as a whole. The State renders services to the individuals composing it, and carries on certain kinds of work that it is thought can be better done by the community as a whole than by private persons. As the State has no fund apart from that which is made up of the property, public and private, of all the people that compose the State, it is from this property or wealth that all payments for work done for the State must be made. Though we really know this quite well, we often talk as if we did not know it. We say, "The Government can afford to do this," or "The Government will pay for that," just as if the Government were an exceedingly wealthy and benevolent though rather foolish neighbour of ours, having a private purse out of which any amount of money could be extracted without the State's being any the poorer for it. We should do well to always bear in mind that the Government can but give back to us in another form what we have first given the Government in the form of taxes.

### *Expenses to be provided for.*

The expenses of the State acting as a whole may be divided into two principal classes. The first class consists mainly of payments for services. A very good example of this class of payments may be found in the wages or salaries paid to policemen, gaolers, magistrates, and judges. In order that the whole community may be protected from the violence and dishonesty of the few, men are selected to perform certain duties, and, as the time of these officers is quite taken up with public work, it is plain that they cannot grow food or make clothing for themselves, and that the State must, at the least, provide them with the means of getting these things. The second class of State expenses consists mainly of payments for railways, roads, bridges, and other public works, and of interest on money borrowed for such purposes. If the services rendered are well performed, and if the public works constructed really increase the wealth and comfort of the nation in proportion to the money spent upon them, it is manifest that the money paid to the Government by the tax-payers is well laid out—that people get as much in return for it as they do for any other money which they pay away, and that they ought not to consider it a hardship to have to make such payments.

*Total Amount of Public Expenditure and of Taxes ; Average Amount paid by each Member of the State.*

In this country the ordinary public expenditure amounts in all to about £4,000,000—£2,100,000 for services and £1,900,000 for interest on money borrowed and for special payments—that is to say, that on the average about £6 10s. has to be paid towards the public expenses of the State by, or on account of, every man, woman, and child in the colony, seeing that the total population of New Zealand is about 620,000. This sum of £6 10s. per head pays for protection, for the general management of the business of the country, for education, for *all* railway freights and fares (except on private companies' lines), for tele-graphing, for the carrying of letters, and for scores of other services. It also provides the interest on all the money, not yet repaid, that has been spent on railways and other public works undertaken by the State as a whole, and that have added so greatly to the comfort and convenience of the people. The New Zealand taxes, properly so called, amount to a much smaller sum—say, £1,900,000, or about £3 per head for the whole popu-lation. On the whole, it does not seem to be a very large sum that each one has to pay, always supposing, as was said before, that the services are well performed, and that the public works are really useful. It is very probable, at any rate, that less would have been obtained for the money that has been spent by the Government in New Zealand if the work had all been done by private individuals, and most likely much of the best work could not have been done at all if the Government had not taken it in hand.

*Difficulties in the way of a Proper Adjustment of Taxation.*

In a free State and under a good Government taxes are among the best and most useful kinds of payment that people can make ; but this is because such a Government arranges its taxation with great care and judgment, and in such a way that the taxes do the greatest possible amount of good to the State and cause the least possible annoyance to those who have to pay them. The principal thing that you have to learn in this chapter is to be able to recognise the distinguishing features of good and of bad systems of taxation. It is not always easy, however, to determine off-hand what the nature of a tax really is, or to find on whom the burden of it really falls. The Government might think it just to tax a certain class of people whose peculiar circumstances made it easy for them to escape the payment of other taxes, or, at all events, of the amount they might fairly be expected to pay. The Government might therefore try to impose a certain tax upon these persons, and yet this tax might actually in the end be paid by an altogether different set of people. A very simple and common case will give a general idea of the nature of the difficulty. It might seem at first sight as if a tax on imported boots must fall on the seller of the boots. If a storekeeper would have to pay 8s. for a pair of boots if there were no tax, and he now has to pay 10s. for them on account of the tax or duty, a thoughtless person would perhaps say that the extra 2s. must come out of the seller's profits; but a moment's consideration will show that the bootseller will get back the 2s. by charging his customer the extra amount when the boots are sold. It is probable that he will get more, for he will look for a return of the interest on the 2s., and for payment for the extra amount risked and for his trouble in getting the boots through the Customhouse, where the tax or duty on the goods has to be paid. In a simple case like this it is quite easy to see on whom the burden of the tax really falls ; but it is often a matter of extreme difficulty to determine who actually pays a tax that seems to be paid by certain persons or classes. Consideration of the case of the seller of imported boots and the extra charges he has to make through having to pay duty on the boots, will enable you to understand that the Government does not always receive all that the consumer pays on account of a tax. In some cases, indeed, when the merchant is put to great trouble through a tax (for which trouble he must of course be paid), the extra cost to the consumer is equal to or even greater than twice the actual amount of the tax. Taxes that are not paid at once by those who have to bear the weight of them are called *indirect taxes;* those paid directly to the Government by the person taxed are called *direct taxes.*

### Adam Smith's Rules of Taxation.

Adam Smith, a learned writer on this subject, who lived in the last century, framed a set of rules with regard to taxation which are so wise and sensible that they have ever since been taken as a kind of starting-point by all writers on taxes. These rules when put into very few words are — (1.) Members of a State should pay taxes in proportion to their ability—that is, in proportion to their wealth. (2.) Taxes should be fixed and certain. (3.) The manner and the time of payment of taxes should be made to suit the convenience of the taxpayer as far as possible. (4.) The work of collecting taxes ought to be made to cost both the Government and the taxpayer as little as possible.

The remainder of this chapter will be devoted to an examination of various kinds of taxes, in order that you may see how far these taxes conform to Adam Smith's rules, and that you may thus learn which are good and which are bad taxes.

### Income-tax : why it is unfair.

At first view it would seem that nothing could be fairer than an income-tax. Under a direct income-tax of, say, 6d. in the pound, one might be inclined to think, every man is certainly taxed according to his ability. A man with £100 a year pays £2 10s. in taxes ; one with £1,000 a year, £25 ; one with £10,000 a year, £250 ; and so on. Probably you would think it impossible to have a fairer tax than this ; but consideration of the working of the tax will soon show you that an income-tax may be very unfair indeed.

In the first place, a tax is a much more serious matter to a man with a wife and family and a very small income than it is to a man with the same income but no family; £2 10s. would deprive a poor family of many necessaries, while the same amount taken from the single man might mean only the loss of a few luxuries that could be easily done without, and that would hardly be missed. The difference between the effects produced by such a tax on a poor family and on a rich one would be still more striking : £2 10s. taken from a poor family might involve the loss of a certain number of meals or of necessary articles of clothing, while the family of a rich man who had to pay £100 a year in income-tax might hardly notice any difference in their father's expenditure. This difficulty has been met to some extent by remitting the tax on the first £50 or £100 of incomes. This makes the injustice press less hardly on those who have very small incomes, but it does not do away with it, as the following illustration will show : If two men have each an income of £350 a year, and one man has a wife and five children while the other has neither, the tax acts very unfairly. In the one case £350 is really the income of seven persons, and the tax ought to be entirely remitted, while in the other it is the income of only one individual. Yet the same amount is paid in both cases, and it seems almost as if the tax were intended to press as heavily as possible on the married man and his family, and to let off the single man as lightly as possible. An income-tax, then, breaks Rule 1. It also breaks Rule 2, for the payment of it is not certain, but depends to a large extent on the honesty of the person taxed; and dishonest persons may, and very often do, misstate the real amount of their incomes. In any case, the more honest a man is, and the more truthful, the more likely he is to pay more than his proper share of the general taxes. Thus, an income-tax may to a certain extent be a tax on honesty.

### Property-tax.

A property-tax is in several respects much fairer and better than an income-tax. In New Zealand it is a tax of so much in the pound on all that a man would have over £500 if all his debts were paid. From the way in which the tax is managed in this country, it is not easy to evade payment of it. The Government claims the right to buy a property if its owner objects to the amount of tax demanded. As the value put on property is generally somewhat below the true one, owners seldom object to pay the tax. Still, the same kind of objection may be made to a property-tax as was made to the income-tax : it presses much more hardly on some than on others. If a widow with three children has £95 a year coming in from a sum of £1,500, she has to pay property-tax on £1,000. Four have to live on a property which really has four owners, but only one gets the benefit of what is called the £500 exemption. A single man with the same amount of property pays the same amount of tax as is demanded from the widow and her three daughters. Another objection might be made to the property-tax : the tax is sometimes taken partly out of capital, and always out of wealth that is either capital or that might be used as capital, and therefore it may tend to prevent the purchase of unfinished articles intended to assist in further production. It must be admitted that a tax on that portion of wealth which is actually used as capital should be avoided as far as possible ; but a Government cannot avoid taxing wealth that might be used as capital, for such wealth is really the only thing that can be taxed : no taxes can be obtained from the wealth used for subsistence without reducing the number of people who have to live on that wealth. The objection to taxing wealth that might be used as capital is therefore an objection to all taxation. The principal reason why a property-tax must be considered very much fairer than an income-tax is this : The former is paid by persons who, if the tax is 1d. in the pound, possess at least 240 times the amount of the tax ; the latter may be, and often is, paid by men who possess no more than is actually required to pay the tax with, or who are even insolvent. Thus, under a property-tax people are called upon to pay according to their ability ; under an income-tax they may be taxed far beyond their ability. A property-tax conforms to Smith's first rule ; an income-tax does not. On the whole, then, and remembering that there is no kind of tax to which some thoroughly sound and reasonable objection cannot be made—some objection which can be met only by satisfactory proof that the advantages arising from the tax outweigh the disadvantages—we may admit that a property-tax is a fair and good tax.

## Land-tax.

A land-tax would be the most just of all taxes, provided that it could be put on land alone, and not on the wealth that has been expended in purchasing and improving it, and provided also that the putting-on of the tax were not a breach of an agreement that has been made between the State and the owner of the land.

A land-tax would be fair and just, because in levying it the State (that is, all the people) would merely be using what the State itself has created through the combined work of all its members in improving the country, and in increasing the population, and so causing the land to yield rent.

There is, however, a very great difficulty connected with the putting-on of a land-tax. It has been shown above that it is not always easy for the Government to tax the people whom it intends to tax. In the case of a land-tax the difficulty would be, as has been said, to tax land without taxing the wealth expended in purchasing and improving it; for in most cases the two are bound up together, and so much capital has been put into the land at different times and in various ways that it is almost impossible to separate the two. Suppose, for instance, that a man owns a farm that he has been working for ten years, that the farm is now worth £2,000, but that when the farmer bought the uncleared land he paid only £50 for it. Who could say how much of the £2,000 that the farm is now worth stands for the land, and how much for the capital? Who could separate the two? On the one hand, the increase of population in the district has greatly increased the value of the land, and, on the other, much of the capital put into the land has been returned to the farmer. Who could say how much the land-tax ought to be?* It appears, then, that, while a land-tax would be very just if its proper amount could be exactly determined, it is almost impossible to levy such a tax fairly. There is one excep-

---

* It may be added that there is a special difficulty in the way when the question of imposing a *new* tax on land is under consideration. Land is not always—perhaps it is seldom—in the hands of the original purchaser, and it would be very unfair to tax a man on account of the rise in value of a piece of land, when perhaps the original owner had reaped all the benefit of this rise in value by selling the land to the present owner at a price which might never again be realised.

tion however : land that is held by the original owner, and has never been used — unimproved land — might quite easily be taxed. The difficulties in the way of taxing land are got over to a certain extent, but in a rather clumsy way, through the property-tax. Those who wish to see landowners bearing their fair share of the State burdens may console themselves with the thought that, as land is, under our present laws, simply property, and as the value of land increases more and more as population increases, land will be more and more heavily taxed as time goes on through the medium of the tax on property, without any increase of the tax on capital.

It was shown in Chapter XX. that there are some kinds of wages that resemble rent, and other kinds that are very much like profits. This might lead you to expect that some kinds of real rent would be found to resemble profits. If a man bought a fifty years' lease of a piece of land for £1,000, and a large town happened to spring up around the land, his return for what he had spent on the land would be very largely increased ; instead of making only 5 per cent., he might get 50 per cent., or even 500 per cent., on the money he had paid for the lease ; then, though this increase might naturally seem *to him* to be profit on his capital, it would certainly be rent, because he would gain it through having become the possessor of a natural advantage. It is one of the good points of a property-tax that it causes the fortunate receivers of these profit-like rents to bear a due share of the public burdens. More will be said on this subject in the chapter on land tenure.

### Stamp Duties.

Stamp duties, which are taxes on receipts, cheques, and similar documents, are, when of reasonable amount, very satisfactory taxes. In this country they comply with all Adam Smith's rules, but in England and other places persons requiring certain kinds of stamps are sometimes put to a great deal of trouble in getting them ; in such cases, of course, Smith's third rule is broken. Stamp duties, however, have a bad effect when, through being excessive, they prevent land transactions. It is always desirable that land should be exchangeable as readily as possible. If a tax prevents sales it must have an evil effect.

## Legacy Duties.

Duties on legacies, too, are very fair and just. They are, of course, in accordance with every one of Adam Smith's rules as far as the person leaving money is concerned; and except a receiver of a legacy who has had some share in earning the money left—for instance, the widow of the person that has died—no one has any right to object to pay even a large legacy duty on property gained in this way. Some writers think that no one should be allowed to succeed to more than a fair living, and that when a very rich man dies most of his property should go to the State, which has done him the service of helping him to make a fortune, or at least of protecting him in the enjoyment of it.

## Taxes on Necessaries.

Taxes on common necessaries of life are, perhaps, the worst of all taxes, and the more necessary an article is, the worse is the effect of a tax on it. A tax on bread, for instance, would produce one of two results, both of them very bad ones. It might lower the condition of nearly all the working-men in the country, by causing them to have to pay for food what they now spend on extra comforts. Or, if money-wages rose, capitalists would have to give more than they had given before for unfinished products of labour; and so the cost of production would be increased, and it might be no longer possible to export goods and sell them at a profit. The final result would be just the same in the one case as in the other: working-men would be the chief sufferers.

## Customs Duties on Luxuries.

Customs duties on luxuries are the best indirect taxes. The tax on such an article as tobacco is a good example of taxes on luxuries. Referring to Smith's rules, you may say—(1.) If a man goes to buy tobacco he may be supposed to have money to spare, and he can hardly object to pay a part of the State's expenses. (2.) If he buys a cake of tobacco he pays a certain amount of tax, about the same as that paid in all similar cases. The storekeeper has already paid 3s. per pound to the State, and you may be sure that he makes the buyer repay him. (3.) No more convenient way of paying the money could be

found. So convenient is it that the buyer hardly ever remembers that he is paying the tax. (4.) The only objection that
could be made to the tax is that perhaps its collection costs
rather too much, because so many Customhouse officers have
to be employed to prevent smuggling and other kinds of dishonesty; but it would be hard to find a better mode of collecting the tax. Taxes of this kind should, if possible, be imposed in
such a way that the less necessary or the more hurtful the
taxed articles are, the higher the tax on them should be.
Things used merely to please the vanity of the users, such as
rings, grand dresses—" fine feathers " generally—and things
which on the whole seem to do people harm, such things as
strong drink, should be taxed more heavily than articles that are
not wholly useless for promoting health and general comfort.
A few remarks will be made, in the chapter on foreign trade,
with regard to duties imposed for purposes other than that of
paying the expenses of government.

# CHAPTER XXV.

## FOREIGN TRADE.

FOREIGN trade enables each nation that takes part in it to obtain on the whole, for a certain amount of labour, a greater quantity of the things that it requires than it could get if it had no such trade. England, France, and New Zealand could each produce iron, silk, and wool; but England has greater facilities for producing iron than either France or New Zealand has. In the same way France and New Zealand are better fitted for producing silk and wool respectively than England is. Now, by means of foreign trade England could get silk from France and wool from New Zealand cheaper than she can produce them. In the same way France could get iron and wool, and New Zealand could get silk and iron, at a lower rate than that at which they can produce them. Thus, if each country exchanges what it can produce most easily for what it could produce only with difficulty, it has the benefit of the advantages possessed by the countries that it trades with, and gives them the benefit of its own advantages in exchange. In this particular case England, France, and New Zealand would, with the same amount of labour, get more iron, silk, and wool by working together than they could produce if they worked separately—that is, their labour is made more productive by their foreign trade. As was shown in Chapter XI., foreign trade is a case of *division of labour*.

### Foreign Trade does not "give More Work."

You must observe that the advantage gained through foreign trade is not that it gives more work. If New Zealand produced its own iron and silk, people would have at least as much work to do as they have now ; the difference would be that the work would be less productive; people would be wasting a great deal of time in producing high-priced things that could be bought from England and France at a lower price, and the reward of their labour would be much smaller. If a man takes three days to produce what can be bought from another country for the produce of one day's labour, he should not expect more than one day's wages for his three days' labour. If he does get more, the extra amount must come out of the pockets of people who receive no kind of return for their money. The principal though not the sole advantage of foreign trade is that it benefits the consumers of the articles imported, by enabling them to purchase more for their money, or, more correctly, to get a greater reward for their own labour. Thus, in the case of labourers it of course increases real wages, if the labourers use any of the goods imported. It is very much like what would happen if the labouring-men in a country were earning 4s. a day, and a tax on certain goods that they were constantly using were to be suddenly removed. If the removal of this tax allowed them to buy these foreign goods at such a rate that it would cost them 1s. a day less to live than it did before, their real wages would, of course, be at once increased by 1s. a day. The contrary effect is produced when the labourers' power of purchasing foreign goods is decreased by means of a tax ; the tax raises the price of the things labourers use, and their real wages at once fall. There is no honest way of preventing the fall, except by the removal of the tax. If labourers do not use the goods imported they will still have a share in the advantage gained by the State as a whole through its foreign trade.

### The Cause of Trade between Countries.

It is important that you should learn and remember that it is not the mere fact that things in general are cheaper in one country than in another that causes trade between the two countries. What does cause trade is the fact that one or more articles can be produced in a country with smaller difficulty in comparison than other articles can be produced. If in New Zealand everything cost more labour to produce than it does in England, yet, as long as people remained in the country, if one article, say wool, could be produced with comparatively less labour than others, New Zealand would continue to produce wool and send it to England even if it cost a very great deal of labour to do it, because people in New Zealand would wish to get in exchange for what they produced with less difficulty things that required more difficulties to be overcome for their production. Thus it is plain that a country will always try to sell to foreigners the thing that it can make with the smallest comparative amount of labour, and that, generally, if a country sends away to foreign countries a large quantity of one particular article, that article is the one that it is best fitted for producing.

*The Object of Foreign Trade is sometimes thought to be to bring More Money into the Country.*

We sometimes hear it said that the use of foreign trade is to afford a market for what we can produce over and above what we need for our own use, and so to bring more money into the country—as if it was a good thing to produce wealth in order to exchange it for mere money, when probably there is quite enough money in the country already to do all the work that there is for mere money to do. People who talk in this way run the risk of losing sight of the principal reason for producing goods for export, which is that those who want and consume other articles of wealth may get them more easily than they could if there were no foreign trade, and these things had to be produced in the country. If we can constantly bear in mind that foreign trade is the means that enables us to have a share of the good things possessed by the whole world, and to satisfy our wants with the least amount of labour, it will save us from making many a mistake.

*Illustration of the Benefits derived from Foreign Trade.*

The benefits derived by two countries from foreign trade may be well shown by means of a simple example. A ship sails from New Zealand with a cargo of wool. This wool is worth a certain amount to the people of New Zealand. When it reaches England it is worth a great deal more. It is sold there for what it is worth, and with what it fetches a cargo of iron is bought. This iron is worth what the wool was worth in England, and when it reaches New Zealand it is worth a great deal more than it was in England. Now, what has been done? To say nothing of the sailors and others who have been profitably employed during the time the double voyage has lasted, the people of New Zealand have made two profits through the mere change of place of the wool and the iron—the first profit by sending the wool to England and selling it, and the second by bringing the iron to New Zealand. For the wool is worth more in England than it is in New Zealand, and the iron is worth more in New Zealand than it is in England. But England will have been benefited by the transaction too, for it will have got rid of its iron, which it produces with little difficulty, in exchange for wool, which it produces with great difficulty. To put it in another way: suppose that New Zealand sends Home ten thousand pounds' worth of wool, and that the clear profit made on it is 10 per cent. : if now the whole amount is laid out on iron, and this again gives 5 per cent. profit when sold in New Zealand, the total amount of gain is £1,550. This takes no account of the profit made in New Zealand by the New Zealand producer of wool, or of the profit made in England by the English producer of iron : these profits will probably amount to as much as that made through the *change of place* of the iron and wool. Thus we see that foreign trade must nearly always cause benefit to both the countries engaged in it. In this case England has a customer for its iron, and New Zealand a customer for its wool; both make profits, and both countries get wealth with less labour than would be needed to produce it at home.

### Foreign Trade always implies Home Production.

An important point is often overlooked. Many people, when speaking or writing about foreign trade, appear to forget that purchasing things from foreign countries means also producing things with which to pay for them. They say that it is far better for a country to make things for itself—to give employment to its own people—than to obtain them from the foreigner; as if any country ever found another country so foolish as to give goods without receiving something in exchange for them. Buying goods from a foreign nation always means producing goods to pay for them, and this of course means also that there are labourers paid for helping to produce them. The real question to be decided, then, is not whether we shall give employment to our own people or to foreigners, but whether we shall employ our own people in producing things that will pay well or things that will not pay at all.

Suppose, for example, that we were foolish enough to say, " In future we will buy no more iron from England ; we will produce our own iron, in order to give more work to our own people." What would be the effect of this ? A great many of the people who are now producing wool, a thing that does pay, would set to work to produce iron, a thing that would not pay ; and many others of those who are now doing various kinds of useful work would become ironworkers. We should get what iron we required ; but we should have to pay a very high price for it. Who would have to bear the extra cost ? Of course, the people who used the iron. Nearly everybody would have to give something towards it, and nearly everybody would have the satisfaction of knowing that he was paying a high price for what he might just as easily have been allowed to buy cheap. From this we may learn how the State would suffer if we took to producing our own iron. It would be exactly the same in the case of any other thing that we can buy more cheaply than we can produce.

### " More Work " is not always advantageous.

But it may be said that at all events more people would have work. Perhaps so ; but this increase of work would bring no advantage to anybody. It would be far better to give the extra men employed a regular salary without demanding service for it, and still buy iron where we could get it cheap, because then these men might perhaps go and do some useful work and produce something; under the other circumstances, they would really be producing nothing—their work would be quite thrown away.*

---

* By similar reasoning we are led to conclude that the plan of finding work for unemployed labourers in times of depression by means of special public works is better than that of securing constant work for workmen by means of

## Effects of discouraging Foreign Trade.

Suppose, now, that we determined to make everything for ourselves and to import nothing, what would happen? Just this: We should also export nothing; we should be a sort of world to ourselves. No other country would get the benefit of our advantages, and we should derive no benefit from other countries' advantages. If we did the same amount of work as we do now, we should gain far less by it. We should be something like a man who determined to make everything for himself, and refused to help or to receive help from his neighbours; and the effect would be that, in order to get what we want done, we should have to work perhaps twice as hard as we do now, and should find in the end that our work had not been nearly so well done.

But would not some advantages result from such a course? Yes; we should learn to do most things for ourselves, after a fashion, and should be quite independent of other countries. We should have all kinds of manufactures; we should probably be able to do a little of everything, but to do few things well, seeing that a great deal of our material would be of very poor quality. But is it not desirable for us to have as many manufactures as we can? Certainly it is; the more the better, provided that we do not have to pay too dear for them. It would be paying too dear if everything we used cost us nearly twice as much labour to produce as it does now, and this probably would be the case if we determined not to make use of any of the advantages that other countries possess. The plan has often been tried of starting manufactures by putting duties on foreign goods, so as to enable home workers to sell their goods at a price that would pay for making them. It seems to be a rather clumsy way of finding out whether a manufacture is suitable for a country or not, to make everybody pay a high price for many years for goods that ought to be cheap, when the thing could be easily decided in a few months. It is like taking a shovel

---

taxes on articles that can be bought from foreign countries at a cheaper rate than they can be produced in our own. For such public works certainly have some utility—may perhaps give a good return for the wealth expended on them, while the system of *making work* by means of taxes causes direct loss to the country in proportion to the amount of employment it affords. That is to say, the more effective the latter plan is in providing employment for a portion of one class of the people the more harm it does to the country at large.

to pick up a needle with. A far better and simpler plan for a State to adopt would be to establish new businesses on its own account, to keep them going for a few months, and then, if it was found that they would pay, to sell the businesses to private persons, or to give them up if it was found that they would not pay. A still better plan is to offer what are called bonuses to persons who succeed in establishing certain businesses. There is a special reason why a young country, at all events, should be content to buy from foreign nations what it cannot profitably produce, and why it need not be in such a hurry to establish manufactures as to do so by means of taxes. Of late years experience has shown, in America, Victoria, and other countries, that the effect of establishing manufactures in a country before it really wants them is to crowd people together in the towns, where, in order to exist, they have to keep up a constant struggle for wages with a few rich manufacturers, when they ought rather to be spreading themselves over the country, where they might be independent and make happy homes for themselves.

# CHAPTER XXVI.

## NATIONAL DEBT.

A NATIONAL debt is a debt owed by a State as a whole either to members of the State or to people in foreign countries. In England nearly all the public debt is for money lent by people belonging to the State; but our New Zealand debt is, for the most part, owed to people living in other countries, and especially to persons and companies in England.

*Ways in which National Debts are incurred.*

National debts are incurred in two principal ways: either some sudden danger threatens a country, and the ordinary revenue of the country is insufficient to provide for the increased expenditure thus rendered necessary for purposes of defence; or the State wishes to do some kind of public work for the benefit of the people, and is unable or unwilling to do it with the ordinary revenue, or by imposing an extraordinary tax for the special purpose. In such cases money is borrowed, and a national debt is begun. The greater part of the National Debt of England has been incurred to meet the expenses of the long wars in which she has been engaged, and especially the cost of the wars with France under Napoleon Bonaparte. The National Debt of New Zealand has been incurred partly on account of expensive wars between the Europeans and the Maoris, and partly on account of public works, such as railways, that are undertaken by the State.

*How Money is generally borrowed by New Zealand.*

The actual way in which money is borrowed by New Zealand is this: The Agent-General for New Zealand gives notice to people in England that this colony wishes to borrow so much money, perhaps £1,000,000, and invites them to send in tenders stating how much money they will actually pay for every £100 (at a certain rate of interest) that the Government of New Zealand becomes indebted to them for. The Government accepts in order the best offers received, if they are considered good enough, till the sum required is made up. The money is then paid to the Government, and thenceforth New Zealand has to pay interest on the money borrowed until this money has been paid back to the lenders. Of course the payment of interest does not in any way diminish the amount of the debt.

### *Ought a State to borrow?*

Is it well for a State to borrow money? Would it not be better to raise money as it is wanted by means of a heavy tax, and to have done with it; or, if this cannot be managed, would it not be better to do without the money than to run into debt? Every kind of reply, from "Yes" down to "No," might be given to the first of these questions, and the particular kind of reply to be given would depend on the answers to such questions as these: What seems to make it necessary to borrow, and for what purpose is the borrowed money to be used? At what rate of interest and from whom is the money to be borrowed? Who is to manage the spending of it? Who will benefit by the borrowing, and who will have to pay the interest on the money? Has the country borrowed enough already? If all these questions can be answered quite satisfactorily, the answer to the main question should be "Yes;" but, if they cannot, the plan of borrowing should be adopted by a State with very great caution. If you wish to understand this matter your best course will be to try to find out what answers might be given to each of the questions, and then to consider whether such answers are satisfactory or not. We may take the questions in the order in which they stand.

### *Reasons for borrowing.*

Let us suppose, then, that a State proposes to borrow money, and that the first question has been asked: *What seems to render it necessary to borrow money, and for what purpose is the money to be used?* If the answer is that a great war will probably soon take place, and if it does the country will almost certainly be attacked while the people are quite without the means of defence; that a large sum of money will be needed to secure the safety of the country, and that the only way in which the people can bear the expense is to borrow money for defence works, and pay interest on it,—under such circumstances you would have to say, " Let them borrow by all means if they believe they will be able to pay the interest on what they borrow, for the public safety must be provided for at all costs except that of loss of honour."

If the only reasons given for borrowing are, that trade throughout the country is very dull, that the people are hardly able to bear the burden of the taxes, and that it is thought that the bringing-in of wealth from outside may make business more lively and give the country a fresh start,—then it is most unwise to borrow. For it is almost certain that if any better reasons for borrowing existed they would be given; and, as no one can see clearly how the money is going to make the country more productive, it is very unlikely that it will really be more productive after the money has been spent than it was before. The only effects produced will be that, while the spending is going on, trade will be more lively and workmen will get somewhat higher wages—money-wages at all events—and a few lucky people will make fortunes. After the money is all gone the country will be much as it was before, except that the people will have to pay the interest on the additional money that has been borrowed. If the reason for borrowing is that it is quite clear that, if certain roads, railways, and harbours are made, the general wealth of the country will be increased by them to such an extent as to repay the cost of making them; or if, though it is doubtful whether a particular railway will greatly benefit the country as a whole, it is certain that it will in a short time repay the cost of working it and the interest on the capital that has been *fixed* in constructing it,—then the reason for borrowing is a good one, always supposing that the money can be borrowed at a reasonable rate.

If a State had decided to repurchase land, from owners willing to sell it, for occupation under a system of perpetual leases, it might quite safely borrow the money required to pay for such land. The natural increase of population would be certain to soon cause a return to the State, in rent, large enough not only to pay the interest on the money, but also to repay the principal within a reasonable time. It is probable that this is one of the best objects for which a State could borrow money.

### From whom should a State borrow?

If it has been proposed that the State should borrow, the next question is, "Who should be asked to lend?" If the country that intends to borrow is a poor one, and has less capital than is required for the purchase of such unfinished articles as can be made by its labourers for further production, and if the answer to this second question is, "From the people living in the country," we may be sure that the borrowing ought not to take place. For the effect would almost certainly be to *fix* the capital borrowed, and to increase the demand for *free* capital without greatly helping to increase the supply; in which case the rate of interest would surely rise, and so, therefore, would the cost of production. But if the State has great wealth and can command plenty of capital, no harm could arise through its borrowing from its own members to meet the cost of such a thing as a war: but, as a rule, a young country that wishes to spend money on public works should borrow it from an old and wealthy country; for a young country can generally make a better use of its wealth than an old one can, and it is seldom right for a young country to *fix* its capital at 4 per cent. interest when it can get an old country to do this and leave the young country at liberty to make 5 or 6 per cent. on its own capital.

### Who should control the Expenditure of Borrowed Money?

For all countries that borrow largely a very important question is, "Who is to say how the money shall be spent?" If this question referred to a free country ruled by a parliament it would really mean, "What is the best way of preventing money borrowed for public works from being scrambled for, and of preventing part of it from being wasted through being spent on works that are not yet necessary?" Perhaps a good way to answer this would be to say that if money for public works were not borrowed until *after* the purpose for which it was to be borrowed had been settled in the clearest and most definite way by the parliament (most likely through a house of representatives sitting as a committee), and if the parliament allowed no change to be made after the matter had been so settled, it would be quite safe to borrow if all the reasons for doing so were satisfactory. Perhaps a still better plan would be for the parliament to appoint commissioners, and to place them in a position somewhat similar to that of our judges, giving these commissioners full power to control the expenditure in every direction except that of incurring expense without the authority of the parliament.

*Who are to gain through the Incurring of a National Debt, and who are to pay the Interest on it ?*

Who will benefit by the borrowing, and who will have to pay the interest on the money ? There can be no doubt as to who will benefit most by borrowing for public works. It will be owners of land. There is no instance recorded in history of a permanent rise in wages through the execution of great public works; very often real wages fall as a country advances. Nor is there any record of any great rise in profits. On the contrary, profits, like wages, very commonly fall as a country progresses. Of course many workmen, by thrift and their own natural ability, become capitalists, and many capitalists grow rich, and some of the latter make enormous fortunes; but generally it may be said that the chief advantages that the ordinary labourer or the ordinary employer gains from a country's progress is that his comforts and conveniences are considerably increased. He is able to see more, to know more, and to travel about more; his share of the common wealth stands for more than it did before; but his own individual wealth is not increased. The owner of a considerable quantity of land, on the contrary, whether in town or country, grows rapidly rich as a country advances, because rent increases with the increase of population. Thus he has at the same time both his increased rent and also the full enjoyment of his share of the comforts and conveniences that are the common property of all. All history shows that this is a true statement of the case. If you are told, then, in answer to the question that you have asked, that things will be so arranged that a considerable part of the interest on money borrowed for public works will in some way be made to come from rent, you may answer that this is very just and satisfactory. In most countries it has been the practice, by one means or another, to cause the burden of taxes to fall heavily upon labourers—so heavily in some countries that labourers have to work many extra days in the year to pay for things that do not benefit and never have benefited them in the least. This can hardly be considered fair. You may be sure that only a small part of the taxes used for paying interest on money borrowed for public works ought to come out of wages and profits, seeing that those who earn wages and profits get but a small part of the advantage derived from public works. But it may be that there is no prospect of its being possible, after the public works have been completed, to obtain, through the increased value of the land, the means of paying the interest on the money that the public works will cost. If so, you may be sure that the money ought not to be borrowed at all, for rise of rent and of the value of land always goes along with a real increase of a new country's wealth. The object of borrowing money is to increase the country's wealth and its power of producing it; if borrowed money, then, will not do this there can be no reason for borrowing.

The rule that rise of rent and of value of land always goes along with a real increase of a new country's wealth holds good, too, in the case of older countries, except those that manage for a time to surpass other countries in regard to manufactures, and so become mainly manufacturing countries. In such cases food-production *within the country* ceases to be of first-class importance. As was shown in the previous chapter, a country will produce what it can produce with the *greatest* case, and this, in the present case, is manufactured articles. With part of the price received for these articles the country will procure most of its food from abroad. Then the rent of nearly all farms will be reduced, because most farms contain portions of very poor land, and of course it will no longer pay to work these portions when the price of corn is kept down through the bringing of foreign corn into the country. In such a case as this, then, there may be great increase in a country's wealth through its manufactures, and at the same time a fall in rent, especially in the rent of the poorer farms. The time is sure to come, however, when other nations will master the methods that have given a temporary advantage to the people of the manufacturing country, and then the law of rent will become thoroughly effective. The most striking example of this exception to the general rule is England, while proofs of the truth of the rule itself are afforded by Victoria, California, and New Zealand.

## When to leave off borrowing.

Has the country already borrowed enough money to meet all its real needs ? This question could be answered only after careful consideration of the answers to former questions. If such consideration should cause the answer to be, " Yes, enough has been borrowed," we should have to say, " Then for goodness' sake do not borrow any more ; " for, if you cannot use borrowed money properly, you are sure to waste it, and that will mean, of course, an increase in the taxes of the country without any adequate return.

## Does Immigration decrease the Burden of Taxation ?

There is one point that requires careful consideration in connection with the question of national debt, and that is, What is the effect of immigration ? Does it increase or lessen the weight of taxation ? The answer is that this depends on what becomes of immigrants after they arrive. If they crowd into the towns where no more labourers are required, they both lower wages, and, by lessening the constancy of employment, they lessen the power of purchasing luxuries—that is, the tax-paying power of the people already in the towns ; but if immigrants settle in the country they at once take a real share in *tax-producing*. It might perhaps pay the Government of a colony like this to place on cleared land poor people who have been too much crowded in towns, and to give them the means of keeping themselves going for a few months, in the way suggested at the end of Chapter XXIV., in order that they might become taxpayers instead of mere hindrances to tax-paying. There are, however, a great many practical difficulties in the way of giving effect to a scheme of this kind.

*How to leave off borrowing.*

It is worth while to inquire what would be the best plan for a young and rising country to adopt, if it had become convinced that enough had been borrowed, and had determined to leave off borrowing as soon as possible, and also to reduce its debt. Probably the best thing to do would be to borrow a little more money with which to complete as soon as possible all works that had been begun, and that would remain a burden on the State if they were not completed, and then to put a moderate special tax on the kinds of property that had been increased in value by the money spent on public works. But, as was shown in Chapter XXIV., it would be very difficult to ascertain the *true* taxable value of *land ;* it might, therefore, be on the whole more advisable to slightly increase the property-tax for this purpose, manufactories and machinery being exempted from payment of the increase. This would form a "sinking fund" for paying off the whole of the debt incurred for public works. (A sinking fund is of no use while a country is still borrowing—to have a sinking fund under such circumstances is merely taking borrowed money out of one pocket and putting it into another, and then pretending to be very saving.) The rest of the debt might fairly be allowed to remain as a charge for the present generation and for those that would come after them to bear. This would be a just course to pursue, because along with the debt the next generation would receive the great estate for which this debt had been incurred ; and, though it is not fair for one generation to ask too much from those that are to follow, they surely have a right to ask something.

*The Weight of a National Debt does not remain constant.*

One bad feature of a national debt that has to be handed down to future generations is that the real value of the amount that will have to be paid is very uncertain. At the present time the debt of New Zealand, including what has been borrowed by private persons and by local bodies, as well as what has been borrowed by the Government, is about £70,000,000. If prices generally should by-and-by fall very much through increasing scarcity of gold, then perhaps two or three times as much labour and capital may be required to produce the wealth necessary for paying off this debt as would now be needed for that purpose. For, supposing that a man can now produce in three days what would sell for £1, it might by-and-by, if a great fall of prices took place, cost him nine days' work to produce what would fetch the same price. The evil here referred to might under certain circumstances become manifest in a single lifetime, or even in a very few years.

# CHAPTER XXVII.

## LAND AND THE STATE.

In Chapter XII. you learnt that wages rightfully belong to the labourer, and profits to the capitalist, but you were not yet able to say what ought to be done with that part of wealth that is brought into being by the action of the powers of Nature. You were able to say that this actually does go to the owner of the natural agent that has been made use of, if it has an owner, but you were unable to say whether such natural agents as land ought to have owners, or who those owners should be.

You should now try to answer this question, which is, "To whom should rent belong?" but before doing so you should, perhaps, learn that in New Zealand the rent of land does really and rightfully belong to the private owners of the land, and that the State has no right to even think of taking it away from them against their will, without giving them full value for it. If you can once learn to take this view of the matter you will be able to discuss the general question of rent and ownership of land without running the risk of becoming anxious to get rid of the evils of private ownership of land by means of a still greater evil—the robbery by the State of the property of individuals.

*The Private Ownership of Land in New Zealand is the Result of a Bargain made by the State as a Whole with certain Members of the State.*

Fresh air, sunshine, the rivers, the sea, and the land are all alike Nature's gifts to mankind, and it is most desirable that every man should be able to get his full share of the use of them, provided that he does not prevent other people from getting their full share too. But men who become members of a State must consent to hand over to the State a portion of their private rights even in these matters, if cases arise in which the State thinks that private rights require to be limited for the general good. Many people think it is much to be regretted that our State, following the example of older States, has adopted the plan of *selling* large portions of its land to private individuals, and thus giving them the right of keeping for themselves what Nature has provided for all. It would perhaps be a great deal better for us if we had not sold our birthright : but we have sold it, and must put up with the consequences of the sale. In many old countries the State could take away the land from private owners with some show of justice, seeing that in these cases it could be said that the State had originally been violently robbed of the land, or cheated out of it, by the ancestors of the present owners, and that there could be no wrong in the State's taking back its own again. But here in New Zealand the case is very different : here the State with its eyes wide open has given its land over to private owners in exchange for other kinds of wealth. The State has said to settlers and others, " We want money to enable us to make roads and bridges, and to do other things : you want land. You take our land, and give us your money." Now, it would be extremely unfair for the State to say to these people, " We find that we have made a very bad bargain, and we wish to break it ; so you must give us back the land, and we will return you the money you paid for it." Of course it would be still worse to take away the land and keep the money too. It seems quite certain, then, that the State must abide by its bad bargains and just make the best of them. Perhaps the best way of doing this would be to profit by experience, and make no more such bad bargains.

*The Bargain does not involve an Obligation on the Rest of the Community to take special pains to increase the Wealth of Landowners.*

But, though the rights of landowners must be respected and preserved with the greatest care, it does not follow that the State is to go on blindly spending the wealth earned by labourers and capitalists when the effect is, in the main, merely to make landowners richer and richer : that is no part of the bargain. If landowners are not bearing it already, there can surely be no reason why they should not be made to bear the full weight of their share of that part of the public burdens which has been mainly caused by expenditure on public works, the effect of which is to increase the wealth of landowners while labourers and capitalists are, in comparison, but little benefited by them. We must remember that, though the total amounts of wages and profits earned by the members of a State are greatly increased by public works, the labourers and capitalists also increase as fast, or perhaps faster, but that as rent increases the number of rent-receivers may grow less, as has been the case in Scotland, and that thus it may come about that as a nation grows richer it may be only those who own land that are made wealthier, while all others become poorer. In that case it is only the individuals that own land who receive much lasting benefit from such public works.

### The Bargain does not involve a Right on the part of Landowners to bar the State's Progress.

It seems certain, too, that the rights of any particular landowner are not of such a nature as to make it wrong for the State to still keep, in some respects, a strict control over them. When it is found necessary to construct a railway from one place to another for the benefit of the State generally, the owner is compelled to sell his land at a fair price, for it would never do to allow one man to have it in his power to say that because he did not wish to give up his land a railway should not be made. In the same way, if it can be clearly shown that the nation would be greatly benefited by regaining possession of a piece of land, large or small, there can be no reason why the owner should not be compelled to sell it to the State for its full and fair price.

### Discussion of the Question of Ownership of Land and the State's Control over it.

We are now prepared to consider the general question : " Ought land to belong to private owners, and what ought to be done with rent ? " Were it not for the rights given to private owners, the State would hold just the same position with regard to land as it does with regard to streets, harbours, and roads. These things are required for the use of the whole community, and any one who blocks them up or prevents the fullest use being made of them has to be caused to move out of the way. If the State had not given private persons a *just* right to land, persons claiming the sole use of land might be moved aside with quite as little ceremony. Land seems to be no more a fit thing to be handed over to individuals as property than the air is, except for the one reason that it can be so handed over. All other objections that could justly be made to giving men property in the air we breathe, if the supply of air were limited, could also be urged against making land private property.

Land is the only property that lasts for ever. Is not "for ever" rather too long a time to part with it for? Who knows what may happen in that time? Land is the only source of material that the State can depend on having, and most of its members have, and will have, to live on and from the land in one way or another. Is it well to dispose of this land for ever in a way that may suit this generation, but that will certainly not suit all generations? As a matter of fact, alterations have to be made in one way or another. Would it not be well if our State had kept full control over the land as its own property, so that such alterations might be made at the most convenient time and in the most suitable manner? No matter what class of persons may be working the soil, it is surely always the State's duty to see that the land is properly used; and, indeed, if a State neglects this duty the time is sure to come when the growth of population and the poverty and misery arising from this neglect will compel the State to attend to it, and perhaps to inflict very great hardship and injustice in order to remedy the evils that have come into being. If the State owned the land it could do very much to prevent such evils from arising, and, if they did arise, to cure them without doing injustice to anybody.

If all the land is made the property of *some* persons, then all other persons are banished from it; except in the streets, roads, river-banks, and beaches, there is not a foot of ground on which they have a right to stand. It is always well for a State to consider its land-laws before such a state of matters as this comes into existence; it is so much easier to prevent evil than to cure it. There are, fortunately, many ways of lessening the evils that arise in this way, but all of them depend upon two principles : the State must always consider the land as being under its control to a very large extent even if it has ceased to own it, and it must see that whoever is allowed to have possession of land does not, either wilfully or by neglect, use it so that the State's progress is prevented by this use; and the State must also take care that the owners or occupiers of land pay their full share of taxes according to the ability which the proper use of the land should give them to assist in bearing the State burdens.

### *Schemes that have been proposed with regard to Ownership of Land.*

Many plans have been proposed for altering the arrangements now existing with regard to land, and putting all land entirely into the hands of the State. It has been proposed that, when more than a limited quantity of land is in the hands of one owner, the portion beyond the limit should be heavily taxed, but that the Government should be always ready to buy back such land at its proper value. It has also been proposed that the Government should take back at its proper value the whole of the land that is now in private hands, and pay interest on the purchase-money until this can be all paid off. It is said that these plans must answer well because rents in this country are sure to rise with the increase of population, and the Government would, by leasing the land, surely gain enough in a generation or two to pay off the whole of the debt, and that then all rent could be used instead of taxes. But these and all similar plans have a serious fault : they involve the taking from private owners, whether they wish it or not, property which is not yet urgently needed by the State. Those who favour these plans propose, for the sake of a mere opinion, to do that which nothing but very certain and very great advantage to the State could warrant—namely, to compel people to sell their lawful property when they wish to keep it. On this ground alone all those who still wish to consider themselves honest may safely condemn such proposals.

### *What should be done with Rent ?    Summary.*

We may perhaps now sum up what has been said in different parts of this book on the subject of rent.

In previous chapters we have learnt that rent is what is gained by the owners of natural agents ; that rent is not necessarily the result of any kind of effort, though it is sometimes secured through prudence and sound judgment; that, while wages and profits can be gained only by toil of hand or brain, rent may come to a man who sleeps, through the action of natural powers that know not what pain or toil is ; that rent is increased by the toil of labourers and capitalists, while wages and profits tend, through the operation of the laws that allow private ·· ownership of land, to decrease as population and wealth increase. We learnt, in the chapter on taxation, that it is just that taxes should fall on those who are best able to bear them ; and in the chapter on national debt we found that the only persons that have their wealth very greatly and permanently increased by public works are the owners of land.  On the other hand, it has been shown in the present chapter that where landowners, as is the case in New Zealand, have had given them by the State a perfect right to their land, the State can have no reason for treating them and owners of other property differently. They must be allowed free and full possession of what rightfully belongs to them—namely, their land and the rent that it yields. But, as their position is so much better than that of the other classes of the State, it would be hard to find a reason why the owners of land should not be made to bear·their full share of current State expenses, and of the payment of interest on money borrowed for public works, if they do not bear it already.

### How the State should exercise Control over Land.

A few words may be added with regard to the State's duty of seeing that all land is made productive.  It is quite certain that land is farmed best when it is divided into portions not too large for one man to manage.  Even in countries like England, where there are very large estates, the separate farms of which these estates are composed seldom contain more than four hundred acres; while in Belgium, and other countries that produce a large quantity of food for their size, nearly all farms are small.  It is quite certain, too, that the man who manages a farm will work best if he gets all the wages of management for working it.  Again, a man cannot do well

14

with a farm if he is in debt, for if he owes money he will not be able to keep his land in good order; he will have to get as much as he can out of the land to meet his present needs. He knows that it will be very bad for him if he ruins the land, but he thinks it will be worse to be turned out of his farm through not paying his debts; so he chooses what he thinks will be the smaller of the two evils, and ruins his farm by getting as much out of the land as he can.

Thus it seems plain, first, that it is hurtful to a State for single persons to hold large quantities of land; and, secondly, that it is an evil when persons holding land are prevented from working it properly through their being in debt. These evils would be greatly lessened in countries where they exist if, long notice of the change in the law having been previously given, it were made unlawful to sell or leave by will more than a certain limited quantity of land to any one person, and if owners of land were no longer allowed to mortgage it. The effect of this kind of State control would be that large estates would be broken up into properties of moderate size, and that a man who was too deeply in debt to work his farm with profit would have to sell it, most likely to some one that could work it properly. Many writers on this subject think that these two measures would do more to increase the general productiveness of land than any others that could be devised.

# CHAPTER XXVIII.

## HOW THE SATISFACTION OF HUMAN WANTS MAY BEST BE PROMOTED BY THE STATE.

We have now considered many of the most important facts connected with the satisfaction of human wants, and we ought to be able to form a pretty good idea of the principles by which a State must be guided if it aims at securing the welfare and the general comfort of all its people. We can now understand that if the members of a State are willing to live in fair accordance with the natural laws that have been explained in the earlier parts of this book, and yet the greater number of them fail to get the satisfaction of their reasonable wants to the fullest extent that the action of these laws will permit, there must be something wrong in the way in which things are managed, something that needs alteration. We are able to see, too, in what direction this alteration must take place, if it is to take place at all, and that it can be made in only one direction.

The laws that regulate the production of wealth are part of the uniform course of Nature; they cannot be altered. Nothing will ever prevent people from wishing to be as comfortable as they can with as little effort as possible. Increase of population will always in the long-run be followed by increase of rent. It will always be impossible to make a nation rich by means of bank-notes that do not represent wealth; and it will always be foolish for a nation to issue such notes and to consider itself any the richer for doing so. A people may be made richer by the cheapness and abundance of the things that they want, but never by dearness and scarcity. The laws which such things obey will always be the same until water begins to run up-hill and two and two make five.

But it is quite different with the laws in accordance with which wealth is shared by those who help to produce it. For instance, it has been shown in former chapters that, while one set of men may go to sleep, and remain asleep, and yet grow rich, another set of men may work as hard and as constantly as they will and yet most of them will find it hard to hold their own and not become poorer and poorer as time goes on. This is plainly to a large extent the result of man's laws, which give to one man a considerable portion of what another man earns. We have seen, too, that people are almost compelled to crowd themselves together in towns, where, on the whole, they do more harm than good, and really add little to the wealth of the State ; while, if the prevailing laws and customs encouraged them to spread themselves over the country, they would be able to do great things for themselves and at the same time to benefit the whole community. Man's laws can produce evil results ; man's wisdom, if he can manage to get any, can change these laws for better ones.

## Sudden Changes are hurtful to a State.

The first and perhaps the most important principle that a State has to observe when endeavouring to promote its own welfare and that of its individual members is that no sudden or violent changes should be made. If a man has been frostbitten people do not put him into a warm bath at once ; the change would be too sudden, and if his ears, his nose, or his toes had been injured by the cold they would be destroyed by such treatment. The proper plan is to rub injured parts with snow, so that the change from cold to heat may be very gradual : by this means the destruction of the parts would probably be prevented. In Victoria in 1851 a great many people went to the diggings, and in a short time made large sums of money, which they spent almost as quickly as they had gained them. When Maoris have received large payments on account of a land transaction, the money is very often all spent at once. In cases of this kind the change from poverty to wealth is far too sudden ; those who get wealth in this way have not been gradually trained to use wealth, and it does them more harm than good. If a man is suffering from too great pressure of blood in his brain, and he is very

freely bled, the pressure will be relieved, but the man will probably die because the relief has been too sudden. The blood-
vessels of the brain will, as it were, fall in when the blood has been
removed, and there will not be blood enough left in the man to
stimulate them and bring them to their proper condition again. If
a man had a clock that kept time pretty fairly, but always went
rather slow, and if he found out that the pendulum-rod was too
long, and therefore concluded that the pendulum was a nuisance,
and determined to remove it, he would surely find that this plan
would not answer. But if he very carefully shortened the pendulum-rod by means of the screw he would soon make his clock keep
good time. You will easily understand from these illustrations
that if any rule or custom of the State is altered more or less
change in the working of the whole machine will be caused. For
the State is a great machine, far less simple than a clock, and
perhaps as complex as the human body. It may be added that,
just as a small clot of blood in a certain part of the brain may
kill the strongest man, so may the sudden or violent alteration
of a standing law of a State produce very serious disaster.
James II. of England caused a revolution by merely directing
that a certain unlawful order of his should be read in the
churches. The French Revolution, which in the end led to the
pouring-forth of torrents of human blood, was actually begun by
the decision of the Third Estate, the representatives of the common people, that the nobles and clergy should sit and vote with
them. We may safely conclude, then, that no changes in a State
should be made rapidly or without very careful consideration.
People should have time to think about them, and even when it is
clear that changes ought to be made it is far better to give the
new laws a *tendency* in the desired direction than to actually
make the changes at once.

### State Laws that tend to produce too much Inequality should be altered.

The second principle is that, when it is possible, changes
should have a tendency towards the removal of special advantages
enjoyed by particular classes. For the purpose of explaining
what is meant we may take the inequalities that are constantly
being caused by the operation of the law of rent. In the

previous parts of this book it has been shown that the reasons why some men get all sorts of comforts without work, while others get all sorts of work without comfort, are to be found in the natural laws of rent and population, when the action of these laws is affected by human laws relating to private property in land and to taxation. It has been shown that as long as it is the case that, through the increase in the numbers of the people, increasing rents have to be taken out of the produce of labour on land, while taxes have to a large extent to be taken from the same fund,* so long will there be a tendency for the owners of land, as a rule, to grow richer, while, as a rule also, those who own no land will grow poorer. It seems plain, then, that States should carefully consider these laws of rent and population, and endeavour, slowly and carefully in accordance with our first principle, but surely in accordance with our second, to so arrange their own laws and customs that they may, in connection with these great natural laws, produce as little poverty and misery as possible.

### *The State should recognise the respective Advantages of Co-operation and of Competition.*

The third principle is that the State should allow full scope for the activities of individuals when this can be done without loss or injury to the State. In most countries the total amount of all kinds of work is done by means of two separate systems. The first of these systems is that under which the members of the State combine for a certain object, each member paying taxes in order that the work required may be done. There are many kinds of State work that are done, not for individual persons, but for the State as a whole, such as the work of the Governor and the Parliament. But the State also does work of a different description—work which, though it is decidedly beneficial to the State as a whole, yet in the first instance is of the nature of services to individuals. In such cases it can generally be said, in a rough way, that they pay most to the State in the shape of taxes who gain the most advantage from the service rendered by the State. Thus, for instance, a man with a large

---

* See Chapters XIX. and XXII.

family probably pays much more in the shape of indirect taxes than he would if he had a small family. But, on the other hand, the large family will probably cost the State more for education than the small one will. Thus, in a general way, amount of tax paid and of service rendered by the State maintain a certain relation. Of course it is absurd to suppose that people get their children educated for nothing : it is from the taxes paid to the Government that the Government provides for the education of children—from taxes of which parents have to pay an increasing amount according as the number of their children increases. The peculiar feature of the two kinds of work done for the State as a whole is that it is done, so to speak, in accordance with a fixed pattern, and that it is thoroughly done ; because persons employed by the State know that if they fail to observe the State rules they will cease to be employed at all.

The second system is that in which there is no Government interference, every man being left quite free to make what efforts he chooses in order to satisfy the wants of others, and so to procure the satisfaction of his own wants. Under this system each individual seeks his own advantage mainly ; his attention is directed, through the very nature of this system, not so much to the doing of good work as to the getting of the highest payment that the market will give him for it. But while each person is thus seeking his own ends he is really working for the State. All such matters as the supply of food and clothing are left in this way to private individuals, who *compete* with one another for the benefits that are to be derived from the performance of such services.

Each of these two systems has its advantages. Work done by the State as a whole, or Government work as it is called, is done without waste of effort. Two men or ten men working for Government never try to do exactly the same thing ; each one has his work allotted to him and he does it. Under the system of competition any number of men may be wasting effort in trying to do exactly the same work. If a house is to be built, perhaps twenty men will calculate the cost carefully and make out tenders, while only one can have to build the house. Thus much labour is wasted. If a Government wants a thing done it will have it done, and not employ more labour than is sufficient. If a service has to be rendered by private persons there are very often more men employed to do it than are at all necessary. In a large town a great many more people than are needed are engaged in driving cabs and attending to horses. One Government post-office and a few receiving-boxes will do the work of a whole town, but there are perhaps twenty booksellers' shops, while one or two large shops would do the work quite as well. Thus there is a great waste of labour and of capital in connection with this and all other trades.

But the system of competition has many very great advantages. As each tradesman's success depends on his being able to suit his customers, he takes great pains to do this. The officers in a Government shop would probably try to make the customers suit them. As customers in the long-run go to the cheapest shop, each tradesman does his best to be able to sell things cheap; and in the same way manufacturers find it to their advantage to make things as cheap as possible. Many useful labour-saving machines have been invented through the operation of this cause. At first, of course, the inventor of a machine gets the benefit of it; he gets more profit than other people. But soon the invention becomes the possession of everybody, and everybody has a share of the advantage. If shops were kept by the Government there would probably be little improvement of this kind; Government servants would do their work properly, but there would be little inducement for them to try to make things cheaper. It is clear that some of the State's work can be done better in one of these ways and some in the other. In each particular case the best plan should be found out and followed, and the State should constantly be extremely careful not to favour the system of Government work unless it is perfectly clear that that system will be the more advantageous. As a general rule it may be said that where there is only one plain definite thing to be done or to be managed for the good of the whole State, such as the establishing and working of a telegraph system, it is well for the State to do it. But where there are many different interests to be served, varying in the case of different people and different places, the thing is best left to private competition. Even for the sake of preserving individual liberty to the greatest possible extent, the State should be extremely careful not to render impossible the successful exercise in any lawful direction of the activities of any member or any class of society, without the very best of reasons for doing so : that is, the State should be very slow to decide that any particular work shall be no longer left for individual members of the State to do at their will, but shall be done by the State as a whole. This may be put in another way : it may be said that, generally, co-operation should not be employed until competition has been tried and has failed.

*The State should do its best to encourage the Growth of General Intelligence.*

The fourth and last principle is that the tendency of all State efforts should be to encourage, as far as a State can, everything that most men believe will be likely to increase the intelligence and the right feeling of the members of the State, and to discourage the opposites of these things ; but while doing this the State must carefully refrain from everything that will prevent men from doing what pleases them, provided that their liberty is not used to injure the State or its members.

# PART III.—GOVERNMENT.

## CHAPTER XXIX.

### THE PEOPLE; THEIR SHARE IN THE GOVERNMENT, AND HOW THEY GOT IT.

In the present part of this book you are to learn how we are governed, how those who do the actual work of government for the State are selected, and who the real rulers of the State are. But, before the Government of our own State is treated of, a few remarks must be made about government in general. In Chapter IV. it was explained that both law and government are necessary in every State, and that some person or persons must be intrusted with the power of saying what the law is and of making people obey it. In some States this power has been allowed to remain in the hands of a single individual; in others one class of the people has held it; in others, again, it has come into and remained in the hands of all the free members of the State. Even at the present time we find countries under the rule of individuals whose word is law to all their subjects, and who wield their power without being under any control except that which is exercised over them by their own fear of being dethroned or murdered if they rule too harshly. Russia, China, and Turkey have Governments of this kind. The government in some States is in the hands of a class, with an emperor, king, or, it may be, a president at the head of the class. In such countries a line could be drawn which would divide those who take a greater or smaller share in the government of the country from those who have no share in it at all. Such countries are Holland, Germany, and perhaps England; though · it is somewhat doubtful whether England should not now be placed in the next class, seeing that there is a far larger amount of power in the hands of the Government of the day than the Crown ever possesses, while the Government are the agents of the House of Commons and the members of the House of Commons are elected by nearly the whole people.

In a few States this power either remains with the people constantly, or returns at stated times into the hands of all the male members of the State that have reached full age. States having this kind of government might be divided into three classes : (*a*.) Those in which the people are directly governed by the people—that is, States in which the people make the laws, and themselves put them into force. This kind of government is very inconvenient, and it has never in modern times remained very long in use. (*b*.) Those States in which the power that is in the hands of the people is handed over by them for a certain time and for a certain purpose to men whom they themselves choose to hold this power. The United States of America, France, and Switzerland belong to this class. (*c*.) The third class differs from the second only in this : that the head officer of the State is not chosen by the people, but is, with their consent, selected by some person or persons outside the State in whom is vested the power of making the choice. When the State is a colony this power is generally in the hands of the principal ruler of the Mother-country : this is, as we shall see, a very satisfactory arrangement. Canada, New South Wales, and New Zealand have this kind of government.

It will be made plain as we go on that in New Zealand the people really have the government in their own hands, and that, if any one speaks to them about the State or the Government as something independent of and outside of themselves, they can say with all truth, " The State ! we are the State; and, as for the Government, we decide how we are to be governed and who shall govern us, and this means that we really govern ourselves and are indeed a free people." · No account of the Government of New Zealand would be worth much if it did not show how this power and this freedom have come to be in the hands of the people. The story of the birth and growth of English freedom is a very long one, and we must go to the history of other times and other countries to find out where this freedom of ours was born, what troubles it had to go through, and how it has at last become so secure and complete that it will be quite our own fault if we are not able to hand it down perfect as a priceless treasure to those who are to come after us. It would be well if we could tell the whole story, for it is well worth hearing, and, besides, to trace the growth of our freedom would be the very best way of showing what its real nature is and what special benefits we derive from it. In learning how we became free we should learn *how* free we are, and what power our freedom gives us. We cannot tell the whole story now—it is far too long; but we can do what is probably the next best thing: we can, so to speak, take peeps at our freedom in various stages of its growth, and so perhaps get an idea of some of the steps by which it attained to its present perfection. Though a doctor does not remain constantly with his patients, and merely visits them now and again, yet after a time he knows a great deal about their health and their constitutions. So we, though we have not, like the doctor, the advantage of previous experience, may yet hope to gain at least some general idea of the life-history of our freedom through getting glimpses of the condition of that freedom during important periods of its history.

The freedom enjoyed in New Zealand by Englishmen, Irishmen, and Scotchmen, aye, and by Maoris too, was born at least fifteen hundred years ago, most probably in Denmark or the North of Germany. At any rate, that is the place where it was when we first catch sight of it. It was not very strong at that time, and not a thing to be very proud of, but still it had many of its principal features even then. Just as when a man of middle age—meeting a stout young fellow with great bushy beard, broad chest, and strong arms, whom he has seen in bygone times as a little baby lying in his mother's arms; next as a weak and puny child, suffering from measles or whooping-cough; and then as a lout of a boy, sheepish and shy—can still trace in the man the features of the boy, the little child, and the baby, so may we find away there in the little State of the old land of the Angles, of the real old *England*, many of the very same features that the past history of the English nation reveals to us, and that we may now discern in our own State.

These English people lived in little townships surrounded by a rough fence and a ditch. Their chief was called an eorl (earl). He was the head man of the place. Around him lived his fellow-villagers, men related to him most likely, but not of such pure race as his own. Besides the eorl's relatives, there would be people from outside who had been invited to come and live in the township, and who had been made freemen of it. Perhaps marriage would sometimes cause such invitations to be given. The eorl would be the richest man in the place, and his wealth and his rank would cause him to be looked up to by all the others; besides this, if war came, he or one of his own rank would be chosen as leader. But he was the chief of the village not because of his rank, but because his fellow-villagers *acknowledged* him as the head. Within the village all freemen were equal. As the Maoris would say, all the freemen were *rangatira*, but the eorl was *tino rangatira*. Every freeman was a holder of land; but there was no ownership of land such as we now have. The bush and the pasture-land were undivided, and every villager had the right to turn his pigs or his cattle out on the *common*. The grass-land too was open, except during the grass season, and then each man fenced off some of it for himself. Only the land on which corn was grown was allotted to individual persons, and this land was equally divided. If the number of freemen became greater or less, the land was divided anew. Every matter relating to justice and government was settled at meetings of all the freemen. At these meetings it was decided which new-comers to the township should be made freemen; here, too, all arrangements about land were made; here all disputes between farmers were settled, in accordance with the *custom* of the township; here men talked over all public business, each profiting by the wisdom of all, and learning where his own opinions had been wrong. Maoris will see at once that these meetings were almost the same as their own runanga, and everybody will see that they had some of the features of our own parliaments. In all the customs and arrangements of this ancient people we can trace the operation of two great principles, which, though they have been considerably altered and improved, may still be seen working in our own State. The first of these principles is that all freemen are equal—that is to say, that it was recognised by custom in those days, as it is by the law in our own, that no distinction of rank or caste among the free members of the community should give one man or class of men a right to limit the freedom of others, unless with the consent of the whole people. The second principle is that all freemen may claim a right to a voice in the management of public affairs. These principles have been altered and improved considerably. Now all men are freemen, in those old times many men were slaves; now the law regards the lives of all men as equally sacred, then values were placed on the lives of different persons according to the rank these persons held in the community.

When next we take a look at the English people we find them in England. About five hundred years have passed by ; England has been slowly but thoroughly conquered by the English people, who have in turn been frequently attacked by fierce warriors from Denmark and Norway, and have found it no easy matter to overcome them. But the Danes and Northmen have been overcome, for the present at all events. Still, many of the invaders have gained a firm footing in Northern England, and have now become peaceful settlers there. Changes have taken place, of course. The English people have become more civilised ; union, first among groups, and then among small nations that have grown up in England, has taken place, and this union has led to the formation of a great State ; a powerful, and truly great King, Alfred, with the assistance of his Councils of wise men, now rules the State ; but, with these and one or two other important exceptions, no very great alteration in the customs and institutions of the English people has taken place. The most important changes have been caused by war. The wars of the last hundred years have had the effect of making the freemen unable to protect themselves, and it has placed a great deal of power in the hands of the King and his servants. A custom has sprung up in accordance with which freemen hand their land over to the King's servants (or thanes as they are called), in order to get the thane's protection. The thanes give the land back again to the people on condition that they shall perform certain services in time of war. This, of course, soon leads people to feel that the thane is a kind of master and the freeman a kind of servant, and divides the free people into two classes, the lords and the lords' servants. Before very long a *lordless* man is looked upon as one whom anybody may rob or injure with impunity. The changes that have taken place then are,—that the *freemen* are no longer quite free ; that the land is no longer completely in the hands of the freemen ; and that the power of making laws and seeing them carried out is no longer in the hands of the whole of the freemen, but now belongs to a class having a powerful King at their head. Still, much real freedom yet remains to the people of England.

We now go forward two hundred years more, and find that the condition of the people has been altered, and for the worse. England and England's King, Harold, have been thoroughly beaten in a dreadful battle by William and his Normans, and a conqueror sits on the throne of England. William, having acquired the throne, tried to govern the people gently though firmly ; he found this impossible, so he ruled England with an iron hand. Englishmen could not be made to obey a foreign ruler in any other way ; a people well accustomed to freedom does not take kindly to foreign rule. Great changes now rapidly took place. The old English Courts of justice were almost done away with ; all real power was given to the King's Courts ; the Norman law and language were introduced into the Courts in place of the English law, part of the Norman law being that cases that had not been settled in some other way, could be decided by a deadly fight between those who had a dispute ; very large tracts of country were turned into forests so that the King might have plenty of hunting-ground, and it came to be considered a greater crime for a common man to kill a deer than for him to kill another man. But perhaps the most important change was that all land in England had to be handed over to the King, and received back directly from him. This was a very wise change so far as the securing of peace and order was concerned ; but it made the King extremely powerful, seeing that as the land was given back each man had to swear that he would be the King's man, and that he would render him certain services.

Thus every landholder in the kingdom became directly subject to the King, and was no longer the tenant of his superior lord only. This alteration greatly increased the King's power, while it lessened that of the nobles immediately under him.

At this time English freedom was, so to speak, weakly ; the nation was nearly enslaved, and it seemed very likely that freedom would die. But foreign rule did one good thing : it made the English one people, and when the bad times had passed away English freedom regained .some of its strength, and it was by-and-by found to have become too great a thing to be ever again in danger of being quite crushed out of existence. Even under the foreign Kings something was done for freedom, for in the reign of ·Henry II., about eighty years after the death of the Conqueror, the power of the clergy, which had been becoming altogether too great, was much reduced. In this reign, too, one of the most important safeguards of liberty, real trial by jury, was introduced in much the same form as that in which we now have it. The principal difference between the juries of those times and a jury of the present day is that the jurymen were then both judges and witnesses. It was about a hundred years after this that a jury became just what it is at the present time. More will be said about juries in Part IV.

We now go on to one of the most important periods in the history of English freedom. In the year 1215 the Great Charter was signed by King John, a rather able but thoroughly wicked man. The King did not sign this Charter of his own free will, but because the lords of England—barons they were called—were determined to be free, and had become strong enough to say so. This Charter is one of the most important agreements ever signed in England. Though it was obtained by the ruling class for their own advantage, yet it has been of the greatest use to all English men and women that have since lived, for it states in clear language what English freedom is, and it has therefore always been something that could be referred to whenever there has been any doubt about the meaning of the term. You will understand that this Charter did not give freedom ; our forefathers had had freedom long ages before ; but the consequences of the long wars with the Northmen before ·the Conquest, and the rule of foreign Kings, had made it somewhat doubtful what English liberty really was. This Charter made the matter so plain that even a child could almost understand it. The most important clauses of the Great Charter are those in which the King says, "No freeman shall be arrested or put into prison, or put out of possession of what he as a freeman holds, or be outlawed, or banished, or in any way destroyed, nor will we punish him, except by the lawful judgment of his equals or by the law of the land. We will sell to no man, we will not deny or delay to any man, either justice or right." You will see at once that these two clauses secure to every man two invaluable rights, his personal right and his right of property. These will be described pretty fully in the chapters on law.

John signed the Great Charter nearly seven hundred years ago, and it may well be called the bulwark of English liberty. The Charter has been confirmed by different monarchs a great many times since then. Since this Charter was signed a great many attempts have been made by Kings and their ministers to act in opposition to it. Such attempts have sometimes succeeded for a time, but in the long-run they have always been failures. One King lost his head and another his crown through making such attempts. You will see presently that the Great Charter does not allow a man to be taxed except by Parliament; nor can he be punished except by the judgment of his equals or the law of the land; therefore no man who refuses to pay a tax that has not been put upon him by the Parliament can be punished for so refusing. But still monarchs constantly tried by one means or another to raise money by their own authority and without the consent of Parliament, and Parliaments were constantly struggling to prevent this. By the time that Charles the First came to the throne, some two hundred and sixty years ago, it had been quite settled that a clause in the Great Charter that says, "No scutage or aid shall be imposed in our kingdom unless by the General Council of our kingdom," meant that taxes could not be raised without the consent of the Parliament of England. Still, Charles the First, like the Kings that had preceded him, did impose various taxes without the consent of any General Council. Now the Parliament determined to put a complete stop to these attempts of Kings to raise money without the authority of Parliament, and they drew up a paper

15

called the Petition of Right. After a great deal of trouble they got the King to assent to this and so to make it part of the law. This law directed that no man should be compelled to make any gift to the King or pay any tax without consent of Parliament, and that no freeman should be imprisoned for refusing to pay any such tax ; that no one should be compelled to feed and lodge the King's soldiers and sailors without payment; and that no one should be punished or put to death against the law of the land. The King, however, would not keep to the agreement he had made, and continued to interfere in many ways with people's personal rights and their rights of property ; he went on taxing by his own authority, and punishing and oppressing people in spite of the law. Civil war arose, and in the end the King was taken prisoner and put to death. But our freedom was not quite secured yet. James II., one of Charles's sons, tried to set aside the law and act in accordance with his own will; the result was that he had to escape to France, and his son-in-law, William, Prince of Orange, was appointed by the English nation to reign in his stead.

Then were passed the two Acts which made English freedom firm and secure, and placed it on the footing on which it now stands. No successful attempt, hardly any attempt at all, has been made to interfere with English freedom since these Acts were passed.

The first of these, called the Bill of Rights, besides confirming the liberties granted by the Great Charter and the Petition of Right, declares that the King has no power of suspending laws without the consent of Parliament; that he cannot make new Courts; that subjects may petition the King without being punished for doing so; that the King may not keep an army in the kingdom in time of peace without consent of Parliament; that the election of members of Parliament ought to be free; that members may say what they like in Parliament, or, rather, that no one out of Parliament may prevent them from so doing; that jurors must be properly chosen ; that it is unlawful to promise to give people fines that are to be paid by persons that have not yet been tried ; and that Parliaments should be held often. The second of these Acts is called the Act of Settlement; it provides, amongst other things, that no person paid

by the King shall be capable of being a member of the House of
Commons; and that judges are to receive fixed salaries and to
hold office as long as they behave properly, and that they may not
be dismissed except through action by both Houses of Parliament.
This last rule, you will see, makes the judges quite independent,
and enables them to do their duty without any kind of fear or
favour. You now have a pretty good idea of what English freedom
is, and how it has been obtained ; but you must remember that
it is only lately that English freedom has been becoming perfect.
The laws securing freedom have been perfect enough, but it is
only within the last few years that their scope and meaning have
been quite fully understood, and acted upon. You have learnt
that at the time when Alfred reigned freemen had had to give up
their freedom to a certain extent, and that it was almost completely
taken away from them during the reign of the foreign Kings.
Now, when the English people began to get their freedom back
in the reign of John, it was only the highest class that were
much benefited at first, and the condition of tradesmen and
labouring-men was for a long time but little improved. This
is how it has been : The freedom of the highest class has been
gradually creeping downwards ever since, and now it has very
nearly reached the bottom. Each class, as it has seen the one
above it becoming free, has struggled and toiled and fought to
get its freedom back too, and the whole work will now perhaps
soon be complete. It is greatly to the credit of the English
people as a whole, and shows what good stuff they are made of,
that, in this long-continued battle for freedom, the class that has
been at a particular time specially engaged in the contest has
always received important aid from many members of the classes
whose freedom was already secure.

One of the greatest struggles that have taken place began
more than five hundred years ago. The Black Death came to
England and carried off nearly half the nation. The demand for
labour was great, and the supply of it was small. Wages of course
rose. The upper classes wanted to keep them down, and to have
in their own hands the power of saying how much a man should sell
his labour for. Laws were passed fixing the rate of wages. There
was a long-continued struggle ; but in the end the labourers won
the day. There have been many somewhat similar struggles since,

but they have all ended in the same way, and Englishmen are again nearly or perhaps quite free, and their freedom, too, is a much higher and better thing than ever it was before; for we who are now free recognise that real freedom is freedom for all, and not merely for ourselves and those better off than ourselves. It is almost unnecessary to add that the freedom which is to be found here in New Zealand is our share of English freedom, and that it is because we form part of the great British Empire that we can be sure that this freedom is secured to us : we are not yet quite strong enough to defend ourselves against every foreign enemy that might choose to attack us. Thus, then, we have seen what the nature of our freedom is, and how this freedom has been obtained ; let us do all that we can to preserve it, and to hand it down to those who are to come after us.

# CHAPTER XXX.

## THE MINISTRY.

The Ministry has to do the greatest share of the real, actual work of governing the New Zealand State. It must therefore be very important for those who are endeavouring to understand the State and its work to get a clear idea of what the Ministry is, and of what it actually does—that is, if they wish to have a really useful knowledge of the institutions of the country. But before attempting to do this it will be well for you to understand that there is a special reason why the Government of New Zealand is a very useful and interesting subject for you to study. Many people seem to think that our Parliaments and Ministries are quite a small matter, and that it is not necessary for students to trouble themselves much about them, when they can just as well study the Ministries and Parliaments of the great English nation. But this is a very great mistake. The work done by our Parliament is most likely quite as important as that done by the English Parliament, and for this reason : Although New Zealand is as yet but a small State, it is going to be a very large one by-and-by. And it is with a State as with an individual : what one learns and does when he is a boy has a great deal more effect on his future character than is produced by what he learns and does when he is a man. Now, England is an old country, and its future has been, to a large extent, determined by its past. No single law and no single Ministry has very much effect in the way of fixing the destiny of England. Here, on the contrary, we are just beginning to make a mighty nation, and every new law that is passed and the action of every Ministry will seriously affect those who are to come after us. It is hard to imagine, then, that there can be any much more profitable subject of study for young New Zealanders than the Government of the State of which they are members. Knowledge is of no use unless it leads to action, and that knowledge is most useful which leads to the most useful kind of action. What was said in the last chapter shows that the Government of New Zealand is really in the hands of the members of our State. It is plain, therefore, that the future of the New Zealand State must largely depend on the soundness of the knowledge possessed by the members of the State with regard to the State's Government, and on the amount of wisdom with which this knowledge is used. It is certain that if this knowledge and wisdom are of a satisfactory character the future of the State will be satisfactory too. Useful knowledge is sure to lead to useful action. Let none of us, then, insolently pretend to look down upon our Parliaments and Ministries ; let us rather try to understand as much as we can about them.

We are to use the word *Ministry*, throughout this and the following chapters, as meaning those men who actively direct and control the whole business of governing the State —those men who, for the time being, are at the head of affairs. You will easily understand that if a large company of shareholders choose a board of directors to decide what business the company shall do, and at the same time choose a separate manager to give effect to the decisions of the directors ; and if the board of directors have no kind of power or control over the manager, who has been made responsible to the shareholders alone, work will not be done so satisfactorily as it will be in the case of a company that places the entire management of its affairs in the hands of a board of directors, and gives them the power not only of saying what work is to be done, but also of choosing and controlling the men that have to do it. You will understand that the people of New Zealand are to some extent in a position similar to that of the shareholders of a large company, and that they do not adopt the plan of choosing representatives to decide what work shall be done by the Government and of choosing a different set of independent officers to carry on this work : the other plan is followed — having chosen representatives, they allow the House of Representatives to do its own work in its own way. Now, the House of Representatives is, and most probably ought to be, a large body of men; but there are far too many members of the House for it to be convenient for them all to take part in the actual work of governing, and if all the members were Ministers it would certainly be a case of too many cooks spoiling the broth. They therefore content themselves with considering and deciding what is to be done, and selecting, in an indirect way, to be fully described presently, one member, to be called the Premier, who, with the other members of the Ministry, has to see that the work which the House may decide to have done is done properly, to propose matters for Parliament to consider — to announce a policy—and to manage the affairs of the country generally. The Premier selects other members to help him with his work, and they, with the Premier himself, constitute the Ministry. In the Premier and his Ministry, then, we find that the power of giving form to the wishes of the members of the House of Representatives and the power of giving effect to these wishes meet and mix. The Ministry, in short, is a committee chosen by the House of Representatives, who, with the help of the Legislative Council and the Governor, determine what work is to be done; and the Ministers are also the heads of the different offices that actually do the work. Now, how is a Ministry chosen, and what kind of persons are qualified to be Ministers? The people elect the members of the House of Representatives, and, if the electors themselves are, on the whole, wise and honest, and lovers of their country, the chances are that the members elected will also be, on the whole, among the wisest and most honest men that can be found in the country. At any rate, the opinions of the members will, when the elections have just taken place, be the opinions of the people of the country. But amongst the members chosen to represent the people there will be men who, as time goes on, will come to the front and show that they are specially wise and capable; and that, on the whole, they are the best able to explain and enforce the opinions of the people: opinions which they take a large share in forming. In time some of these men will come to be looked up to as leaders, and from among them, as a rule, all Ministers will be chosen.

In New Zealand every few years there comes a time when the Ministers holding office no longer satisfy the people. This may be through the faults of the Ministers themselves; perhaps it becomes plain that some of the Ministers, though they are clever enough, are not good business men, and that they do their work imperfectly. But it often comes about in some such way as this : All sorts of requests are constantly being made to Ministers; some of these are reasonable and are granted, some of them are unreasonable and cannot be granted. Now, those whose requests have been refused gradually increase in number as time goes on, and, as only few people have a very clear idea that it is a Minister's duty to refuse what he cannot properly grant, many people who were at first friendly to the Minister will come to look upon him as a personal enemy; thus in time quite a large number of those who supported the Ministry at first will think and say that the country must surely go to ruin unless this Ministry is changed. Also, after a Ministry has been long in office the people of the country seem to get tired of hearing the same names, and begin to think that it is about time that there should be a new set of Ministers. Members of Parliament, too, are affected in nearly the same way; and, besides, some of them may hold the opinion that they would make just as good Ministers as those who they think have already been in office long enough, and that it would on the whole be well that they themselves should now get a chance of showing what they could do in the way of managing the State's affairs. So now at last the Ministers find that there are more members in favour of putting them out of office than there are members who wish to keep them in; and most likely they will have to go out. Perhaps a member moves an address to the Governor to the effect that the House no longer trusts the Government, and that it wishes to have a new Ministry in whom it can place confidence. The member who moves such an address is nearly always a very able man, in whom a great many of the other members have great confidence. Unless a member was thus trusted, and had promises of support from a large number of other members, he would hardly be so foolish as to move such an address. Thus, then, you see, if the address is carried, this able man really represents the majority of the House, and if he becomes Premier he has in effect been chosen by the House to be the head of the new Ministry.

If in the manner described, or in some other way, the House

refuses to follow the Ministry, the Premier, after talking the matter over with the rest of the Ministry, will perhaps decide to yield to the wish of the House and resign. Then the Governor will probably send for the leading member of the Opposition and ask him to form a new Ministry. If this member undertakes to do so he will confer with some or all of those who voted with him, and, when it has been decided who shall belong to the Ministry and what offices they shall hold, the Premier will inform the Governor ; the Ministry will meet the House, and begin at once to carry on the business of the country. The member that moved the address to the Governor will probably be Premier, but some other member may take the Premiership. All the members of the Ministry will, most likely, hold some office. There will be a Colonial Treasurer, a Colonial Secretary, Ministers of Justice, of Lands, of Defence, of Native Affairs, of Education, of Mines, of Public Works, and so forth. But any Minister may hold any two or more of these offices. Most likely one or two of the Ministers will be chosen by the Premier from among the members of the Legislative Council.

The Ministers undertake to manage the affairs of their own departments, and to be answerable to Parliament for the proper conduct of them. All really important business, however, is done by the members of the Ministry sitting in secret council. These meetings are called " meetings of the Cabinet." Thus, then, you see that the people really rule New Zealand. The members of Parliament have to render to those who elected them a satisfactory account of their own conduct in Parliament, or else they will not be elected again ; and the Ministry who manage the business of the country have to satisfy Parliament or else be turned out of office.

It often happens, however, that there is great room to doubt whether the opinions of the House and of the people with regard to a Ministry are quite the same. When this is the case the Ministry will perhaps refuse to resign when told by the House to do so, and will ask the Governor to break up the House and have a new one elected ; the Governor seldom refuses to do this when the request seems to be reasonable. Thus you see that a Premier has very great power (which, however, the Governor can control if the Premier tries to make an improper use of it) ; the members really elect the Premier, but when once he has been chosen he can very often manage to turn the members out if he considers that they have not treated him fairly. He can appeal from an old Parliament to a new one—that is, to the people, who elect the new one. Of course the knowledge that the Premier can do this tends to make members cautious. They may be disposed to turn a Ministry out, but they know that, if the electors think that the House has treated the Ministry unfairly, the chances are that many of their number will not be sent back to Parliament again. This makes them very careful. Now that we have seen how a Ministry is chosen and how it is put out of office, we may go on to consider what the work of Ministers is, and to show that an occasional change of Ministry is not without its use.

The work of a Minister may be described under four heads. These are: (1.) His outside work. (2.) His work in the Cabinet. (3.) His work in Parliament. (4.) His office work.

(1.) The outside work of a Minister consists in travelling all over the country to see for himself what its condition is; noticing particularly how the work of his own department is carried on; listening to complaints and petitions; trying to find out how whatever is wrong may be best set right; and explaining to the people the Ministry's reasons for its actions.

(2.) In Cabinet the Minister has to make his fellow-Ministers acquainted with all important matters about which he has gained information on his travels, or by letters and reports; to propose measures necessary for the improvement of his department; to consider the proposals of his fellow-Ministers for the improvement of their departments; and to help to decide what new laws are required and to determine what business shall be brought before Parliament.

(3.) The Minister's work in Parliament is, besides that of an ordinary member, to take an active part in the work of getting the Ministry's measures passed through the House; to answer all questions that may be asked by any member about the work of his department; to try to learn, by listening to what members say, how the work of his department may be improved; to defend any officer whose work may be found fault with unjustly; and to give as much help as he can to his fellow-Ministers in the great work of keeping the Ministry in and the Opposition out.

(4.) In his office the Minister has to give directions as to what work is to be done, and to see that it is done; he has to answer to Parliament for the work of the office, and he must decide what he will answer for. Of course it is not the Minister's place to do any of the "office-work;" but the mere reading, considering, and signing of papers brought before him takes up a very considerable amount of time.

You will thus see that a Minister's work is none of the easiest: indeed, if it is done faithfully, it is about as hard work as a man can undertake; and if a Minister does not do his work well he will soon hear about his shortcomings from the Parliament.

We may conclude this chapter with a few words about changes of Ministry. Many people think that these changes must have a bad effect on the business of the country. Suppose that, say, a Minister of Marine has been in office for five or six years, and that by the end of that time he has come to know a great deal about his department, perhaps to remember the names of all the lighthouse-keepers; to know how much oil is burnt in each of the lighthouses, how much things should cost, and so on; and that he could write a letter about any portion of the department's business quite as well as any officer of the department. Under such circumstances does it not seem a pity that this Minister of Marine should have to give up his position because the Premier and the Parliament cannot agree about some tax, and that a new man, who, perhaps, hardly ever thought of a lighthouse in his life before, should be appointed in his place? It does seem so till one comes to think that what is wanted at the head of a Government department is not a man who knows the details of the special business of the department. The officers of the department ought to be able to attend to those details far better than any Minister, with his head full of other matters, can be expected to attend to them. What is wanted is a man with strong common-sense and a good general knowledge of business. These things will enable him to see at once whether things are done in a useful, handy way or in a slow and cumbrous way, and to know whether the forms of the office or the needs of the public are attended to most. Seeing, then, that strong common-sense and a general knowledge of business are the only things required in the head of a department, it must be a good thing to have a new man possessing this sense and knowledge, and having the power to examine everything, coming into an office and expecting to find many things going amiss. If the office-work is being well carried on, no harm is done by his coming. If it is not going on well, such a Minister can and will have what is wrong set right. It is through the fact that these changes of Ministry do take place now and again that the people are able to feel quite sure that it is nearly impossible for Government business to be carried on badly for very long. Whatever, then, may be the effect of a change of Ministry in other respects, it does little harm to Government office-work, and it may do much good.

Another reason why occasional changes of Ministry are beneficial is that, after a time, all men get into a groove, into a certain way of doing things. Ministers are just like other men in this respect, and if they remained in office too long very little progress would be made by the State. It is therefore a good thing, after one Ministry has been in office for a few years, for a new set of Ministers, with new ideas and with fresh strength, to take the place of those who have done all that they are for the present capable of doing to benefit the State. It is not pleasant for the old Ministers, but it is good for the State. Frequent changes of Ministry, however, are very bad things, because they prevent Ministers from giving the State the benefit of their ideas and their energy, and from making alterations that may tend to advance the State's interests.

# CHAPTER XXXI.

## PARLIAMENT: THE HOUSE OF REPRESENTATIVES.

THOUGH the parliaments of the present day differ in many important respects from the meetings held in the North of Germany fifteen hundred years ago, it is quite certain that these meetings of the people in the old land of our forefathers were the beginning of the system of parliaments. It seems certain, too, that by-and-by larger and more important meetings were held to settle matters that concerned many villages, and that questions concerning peace and war, the rights and duties of the people of one village in relation to the people of another village, and the welfare of the whole tribe or nation were dealt with at these meetings. It is true that we get the word "parliament" (which means a meeting for the purpose of talking) from the Normans; but long before the Normans came to England Great Councils, or Meetings of the Wise Men, as they were oftener called, were held in England to settle the affairs of the kingdom. Although England was pretty nearly enslaved under the foreign Kings, it is certain that such meetings were sometimes held even in their time. But it was in the reign of Henry III., or perhaps of Edward I., that these meetings were first called Parliaments, and had most of the external features that they have now. There was, however, no Ministry or anything like it, and the Parliament had little to do with the actual government. We may say, however, that real English Parliaments have been in existence for at least six hundred years; though real Ministries are of much more recent date.

Our House of Representatives stands for the English House of Commons. It is elected by the people, and during the period between two elections it holds a very large share of the power both of making laws and of carrying on the government of the country. But it hands over a great deal of its power, including that of putting an end to its own existence, to the Ministry, as was shown in the previous chapter. There are now (1887) ninety-one members of the House, besides four Maori members, one member for one district. Speaking roughly, therefore, there is one member for every six thousand persons. Of course this distribution may be altered as time goes on. The advantage of having one member for one district is that each district is thus likely to have its wants fully considered. If a large town had four or five members, the wants of the town as a whole would be well attended to, but the interests of some of its people might be neglected. Also, by this plan a greater number of people are likely to have as their member the very man that they desire. The disadvantage is that really clever and useful men, who would certainly be chosen by a town as a whole, may not have enough supporters in any one part of it to elect them instead of weaker men who have a great many personal friends in their own district.

The right to vote at elections may depend on two things—ownership of land and residence. (1.) Every European of the age of twenty-one years or upwards who has had in his possession a freehold worth £25 for at least six months is entitled to have his name put on the list of electors and to vote. (2.) Every European of the age of twenty-one years or upwards who has lived in the colony for a year may have his name put on the list of electors for the district in which he has lived for the previous six months, if his name is not on the same list through his owning land. (3.) Every Maori ratepayer who has a freehold of £25 may have his name put on the list of electors. All Maoris of the age of twenty-one years and upwards have a right to vote in their own districts at the elections of the Maori members.

Under the Constitution Act Parliaments should last for five years, but in 1879 the length of a Parliament was limited to three years; it has, however, been already explained that a Parliament may be dissolved before the limit of time has been reached. There is much to be said in favour of long Parliaments, lasting four or five years instead of three. The work done in Parliament is not a thing that can be understood

at once and without any trouble ; it takes some time to learn
the mere forms which it is the duty of the Speaker (or chair-
man) of the House to cause to be observed : in fact, it is
said that it takes new members at least one year to learn their
business thoroughly. Perhaps some members when they first
go to Parliament think that their work will be to get this old law
altered and that new law made, and that this is the chief work
that they will have to do ; but they soon find out that this is
hardly their work at all—that, indeed, they can do very little
in the way of law-making : by the end of the first session, however, they begin to see what their work really is, and how it must
be done. During the second year a Parliament generally does
its best work ; members know what they have to do, and they
do it. But during the third year members have to think so much
about the election that is coming on soon, and are so much
occupied with the task of preparing to meet the electors, that
they cannot give their full attention to the ordinary business of
Parliament. It would thus appear that our Parliaments have
only one year in which they can do much really useful work.
But, on the other hand, it may be said that the representatives
of a free people should not be intrusted with the people's power
for too long a time, without having to give an account of their
proceedings. If Parliaments lasted for five years, and if an unsuitable man happened to get elected, he might say to himself,
" The electors have put me in, and they cannot put me out ; I am
safe for five years at all events. I will look out well for myself
during that time, whatever comes, and if the electors do not like
it they must dislike it." But now, when such a man is elected,
he feels that he has not sufficient time to do himself much
good in any other way than that of serving the electors to the
best of his ability. In any case, the electors soon have a chance
of getting rid of a member who does not suit them. On the
whole, therefore, short Parliaments are best for a free people.

You may now go on to consider the kinds of work done
by the House. The first great work of the House of Representatives is to show what the mind of the State is, to make it
plain what the country thinks, what it complains of, and what it
wishes to have done. Between the end of one session and the
beginning of the next many events take place ; opportunities of

testing the working of new laws occur; the doings of last session are thoroughly talked over by people in all parts of the colony; the newspapers turn matters inside out, and say all that can be said for and against everything done or proposed during the previous session. By the beginning of the new session it has become plain that some things require further consideration in Parliament; but the country has made up its mind about other things, including certain evils that seem to need a cure of some kind. The Parliament declares what that mind is, and members generally, but more particularly, perhaps, the party that are opposed to the Ministry of the day, set about getting the evils cured: this they generally do by attacking what they consider the greatest of all evils — the Ministry itself. Secondly, a most important part of the work of the House is that connected with the choosing of Ministers—the trying to keep Ministers in or to put them out. You may think this strange, but it is true. It is by means of the great fights that take place between Ministers and their opponents that it is found whether Ministers are really doing good work, bad work, or no work at all—whether they really ought to stay in or to be put out. In these fights every good thing that a Ministry has done is brought forward by its supporters as a reason for keeping it in, and every piece of bad or imperfect work that it has done is brought forward by its opponents as a reason for putting it out. The whole of a Ministry's work is thus more thoroughly examined and sifted than it could be in any other way. The State as a whole gets the benefit. The people look on; they watch the fight and see the fun, but they are all the time learning the real truth. We see, then, that these party fights, which many people consider great evils, are the principal means by which we learn how we are governed. They really teach the people what ought to be done and what ought to be avoided.

We must not think, however, that this is the best *possible* way of governing a country. It most certainly is not. But it is, most likely, the best possible government for us. If all men were thoroughly just, honest, wise, and unselfish, this " party government " would be a rather stupid kind of thing; in fact, the system would not last a week. But while so many of us are more or less selfish and by no means too honest, wise, or just—so long as most of us continue to be more anxious that our own opinions, whatever they may happen to be, should prevail than that what is really best for the State should be done—it will probably be quite impossible to find a safer and better kind of government than party government. A ship goes best and is least strained when the wind is fair, because all the force of the wind is used to drive her in the direction in which the captain wishes her to go. But she does not travel so very badly when the wind is abeam. It is true that the wind then does its best to capsize her, but the sails and rudder if skilfully managed will make even the increased force of the wind useful, and the ship, though she may suffer some strain, will go ahead at a great rate, and at last reach her port.

Another branch of the House's work is law-making ; many people think it is the most important branch. So it is sometimes, as when some great difficulty occurs, or when the State is going to strike out and try to make progress in an altogether new direction. But this kind of thing occurs comparatively seldom. In most sessions of Parliament law-making is by no means the most important part of the business. Sometimes a whole session may go by without the passing of a single really useful law. Much of the Parliament's law-making, too, is rather badly done : not through want of a fair amount of care on the part of members generally, but because most of the work has to be done hastily, and because the number of members who are interested in any particular subject, and who have therefore taken the pains to master it thoroughly, is generally very small. But we need not now say any more about this, for it will be shown further on that what is called judge-made law is generally made in a much more workmanlike manner than are the laws passed by Parliament. Judges seldom make laws that will not work, or that spoil other laws, but Parliaments often do—for one reason, because members are not all lawyers ; for another, because there are so many members. The law-making of the Parliament, however, in spite of all its faults (most of which are quite excusable on account of the difficulty that attends the dealing with new questions), is really much more important than the law-making of the judges, for the Parliament may legislate in

16

any direction on almost any subject, and may abolish laws that have existed for hundreds of years, while all that the judges can do is to gradually and slightly modify laws that are already in existence. This is fully explained in Chapter XXXIV.

The last kind of work that we need deal with is the House's management of that part of the State's wealth that is devoted to the purposes of government. The House controls the expenses of the State as a whole, but it does it in a rather strange though very effective way. For any great object that seems likely to do good to the nation or to prevent evil from happening to it, the Parliament seldom objects to even run into debt if it seems necessary ; but there is no sin so great in the eyes of Parliament as for a Ministry, through mere extravagance and carelessness, to allow the expenses of the State to become greater than its income. For, though many members are very willing and even anxious that large sums of money should be spent in their own districts, where they of course think the expenditure is greatly needed, and though, whenever a Ministry tries to lessen any expense whatever, there is always a great outcry about its mean and stingy ways from the people of the district where the reduction is to be made ; yet if, when the accounts for the year are made up, it is found that the money spent is more than the taxes and other sources of income have brought in, the Ministry alone gets blamed for what has happened. In one sense this is just, because it is, in reality, only the Ministry that can propose to Parliament what sums of money shall be spent. The effect of all this on a wise Ministry is to make it very careful about the way in which the State's money is expended.

Altogether, then, the House of Representatives is about the most useful part of the State machine; and it is no less curious than useful, because it secures the welfare of the country by means of the disputes and disagreements of the country's picked men. Perhaps, as time goes on, some better contrivance for giving effect to the people's wishes may be discovered—one that will give more *service* with less *effort ;* but at present it is very hard to see how any great improvement could be made in one direction without causing loss in another. One great advantage connected with our system is that, while it gives us good government on the whole, the mode of working it tends to preserve our freedom, and even to increase it, if that is possible.

# CHAPTER XXXII.

## THE LEGISLATIVE COUNCIL; THE GOVERNOR.

It is best that laws should be made slowly and after a proper amount of discussion and consideration. Many evils in the State tend to cure themselves, but those that do not are nearly always of such a nature as to need the most skilful and cautious handling, because means that are used as a remedy for one of these evils may lead to other and greater evils. In most countries this principle has either been clearly understood from the first, or else sad experience has made the people learn that it must be attended to. The consequence is that in nearly all free or partially free States we find some contrivance for preventing the too rapid making of laws. This contrivance is generally a second Chamber, like the House of Lords in England, or the Senate in the United States.

The plan of having only one Chamber has been tried many times and in various countries. Among other nations, Spain, Portugal, Naples, England, and France have tried it. Every trial has proved it to be a bad plan. In France especially it was a very great failure. In that country it worked with advantage at first. France was groaning under the weight of a great mass of evils, the growth of many centuries : these evils had to be swept clean away, while there was not much that was worth preserving. Nothing but a great revolution could deliver the people from their thoroughly bad system of government and the other evils that oppressed them. A government by one Chamber works swiftly and surely, but unfortunately it goes on working when it ought to stop. The National Assembly did do away with the old bad system, but neither it nor the one-chamber Governments that came after it could leave well alone, and the *progress* of France never stopped until it had long been clear that it was a progress towards destruction; progress in this direction was at last put an end to by the ambition of a great soldier. The people, almost without knowing how it came about, found themselves, under the stern rule of Napoleon, completely robbed of their freedom and obliged at his command to pour out their blood in torrents in order to satisfy his desire for glory. Of course you must not think that every one-chamber Government would turn out quite so badly as this did, but still it is certain that such a Government always has a tendency to go too fast—to do things in haste and repent of them at leisure. Under such circumstances only one side of a question gets considered, and very often only a small portion of that one side. At any moment a pure one-chamber Government may become like a carriage going down-hill without a brake. At first the motion is particularly smooth and pleasant as well as fast, but the further the carriage goes the more those who are in it are jolted, and perhaps at last a great smash takes place. In some of the American States a plan has been tried that allows the management of affairs to be in the hands of one Chamber, but yet has some of the advantages that are to be obtained from having two Chambers. In some of these States any law or change that is considered to be of very great importance is proposed in one " parliament " in some such words as these : " This House is in favour of such-and-such a law, and passes it on to the next parliament to be dealt with." At the next election the proposed law of course comes before the electors, and if they decide in favour of it the new parliament passes it. The fault of this system seems to be that the power of deciding whether a new law shall be passed slowly or not rests with the House itself, and it is easy to understand that under these conditions the brake might be used when it was not much needed, and not used when it was really wanted.

In New Zealand the Legislative Council is the second Chamber. The members are chosen for life by the Governor, acting under the advice of the Ministry. Opinions are divided as to whether this is a good plan of choosing the members or not, but it seems to be pretty certain that it is far better that they should be chosen in this way than that the people should elect them. If two persons are riding on one horse, only one of the two can ride in front. Now, it is always well in such cases that there should be no doubt as to who is to take the back seat. A squabble after the riders had mounted would be inconvenient; and, besides, the horse might not like it. If the Council were elected by the people they would have *too much power of the same kind* as that possessed by the House of Representatives, and what are called *deadlocks* might occur, as they sometimes have occurred in Victoria and other colonies — that is, the business of the colony might be stopped because the two Houses had quarrelled about something and neither of them would give way. Ought the Legislative Council, then, to have either no power, or at any rate as little power as possible? Not at all; the more power that the Council has, of a certain kind, the better it is for the country. You will see presently what kind of power this is.

But is not the Council's power really quite as great as that of the House of Representatives, seeing that the Council's consent to the passing of a bill must be obtained before the bill becomes law? It is not so great. The Ministry is always able to have new members added to the Council, so that, if the Council refused to pass any law that the people had determined to have made, the Ministry could at once have a number of new members appointed who would vote for that law. Thus, in the end, the Council would always have to give way to the House and to the will of the people. The House of Representatives on the contrary, if it has the people with it, can always at last have its own way, because it has it in its power to refuse to grant any money, and so can bring the whole business of Government to a standstill.

But, though the Council cannot long continue to oppose the wishes of the rest of the State, it can and often does delay the passing of a law that it considers bad, or that it thinks should receive more consideration—because, for instance, it affects the rights of a large number of citizens. The Council, by "throwing the bill out"—that is, refusing to pass it—prevents it from becoming law, for the time at all events. Thus it is that the Council acts as a *brake* on the State carriage.

In the Council new laws may be proposed, read a first and a second time, considered in Committee, read a third time, and passed on to the other House, just as in the case of bills proposed in the House of Representatives, provided that such new laws do not relate to money. But the most important bills are generally introduced in the Lower House; and when they have been dealt with by that House they are passed on to the Council, which then considers them and makes such alterations in them as it may think necessary. After the Council has finished its work the bill is sent back to the Lower House. If the Lower House agrees to the alterations made by the Council, the bill is sent to the Governor for his approval. When this has been given the bill becomes an Act, and part of the law of the land. Perhaps, however, the Lower House may not agree to the changes proposed by the Council, and then there may be a *conference* of members from the two Houses; by this means a satisfactory understanding is often arrived at. The *revising* of bills passed by the House is probably one of the most useful parts of the Council's work. In the House everybody is in a hurry; perhaps members have to transact business specially affecting their own districts, or a trial of strength between the two parties in the House is coming on, or there is some other public business of great temporary importance to be attended to. But in the Council law-making is *the* business, and members have time to look after it, and it would perhaps be well if the Council had even more to do with this work than it actually has. If it came to be recognised that the work of the House of Representatives was merely to give the general idea of a new law, and that it was the duty of the Council to put it into proper form, the Council would perform this duty particularly well. This would not mean that the House was giving up law-making, but only that it was taking the right sort of steps to insure the passing of laws that would work. For, if the task of putting laws into proper form were once considered to specially belong to the Council, the members would, for the credit of their House, let no law pass through their hands without first seeing how it would affect other laws, and the general rights and duties of all the members of the State.

You can now perhaps discern what kind of power the Council has or ought to have; it is the power that wisdom and usefulness, together with an exalted position, always give to an individual or to a class. With this kind of power in its hands the Council will be able to do all its work in the best possible way; without this power its work must surely be imperfect. If it were fully recognised that the Council had a claim to the kind of power that superior wisdom gives, and it asked the nation to pause before assenting to a policy, the nation would certainly do so; if the Council proposed a law, the people would be nearly sure to think it worth while to have it passed, or, at all events, to give it very serious attention; even the House of Representatives itself would think long and carefully before refusing to take the Council's advice when it was given. The power that the Council has at any given time could, perhaps, be exactly measured by the amount of wisdom and of desire to do good work that are to be found among its members. It will be seen, then, that the appointment of members of the Legislative Council is a very important matter. The Ministry should be at liberty to choose the very best and wisest men in the country as members of the Council. It seems plain that every important class in the community ought to be represented in the Council—not only statesmen and men of wealth, but also doctors, clergymen, teachers, tradesmen, working-men, Maoris, and especially lawyers; and of course in every case the best men that could be got should be chosen.

### The Governor.

We have left the highest office till the last, although it is a very important one, because it was necessary for you to understand that in reality the government of New Zealand is in the hands of the people of New Zealand. Nevertheless, we are, both in name and by law, subjects of Her Majesty Queen Victoria, who holds her position as monarch of England by an Act of Parliament passed in the sixth year of the reign of Queen Anne. We are still, and nearly all of us hope that we shall long continue to be, connected with our Mother-country and its institutions, and we hold nearly the same relation to Her Majesty as we should if we were living in London. We are, however, much more closely connected with the Queen than we are with the Parliament of England. It is true that the Queen acts by the advice of her Ministers, but, for all that, our relations are with her and not with them. The Constitution Act passed by the English Parliament in 1852 makes over to us most of the powers that the English Government then possessed, except such as the Queen exercises in England. Now, the Governor is the Queen's representative, and does for us nearly all that the Queen does for England. The Governor, therefore, may be considered the head of our State; let us, then, endeavour to get a clear idea of the nature of his office and of the duties connected with it. It is the Governor, acting on the advice of his Ministers, who summons, opens, sends messages to, prorogues, and dissolves Parliament; who *executes* the most important State business and signs the most important State documents; and who, perhaps with the advice of his Council, pardons criminals when it is thought expedient to do so. Probably, his most important duty is to hold the balance between the Ministry and the House of Representatives (as it is the Queen's to hold the balance between the English Ministry and the House of Commons), to dismiss a Ministry that the House and the country disapprove of, but also to protect the Ministry from unfair treatment by the House.* He has other duties of a somewhat similar character, but this is the principal one that he is likely to have to discharge here. The Governor, too, is the mouthpiece of the State; he it is who can put the finishing-touch to a new law by giving his assent to it. If a law seems to him to be very important and to go beyond his own powers, he can reserve it for the Queen's assent, and, generally, it is his duty to protect the Queen's rights and interests in the colony. The Governor also performs duties something like those that would be performed by the ambassador of England if New Zealand were independent, and keeps England informed as to all matters that are likely to affect English interests. Besides this, the Governor is the head of society. When the Governor is a thoroughly good man as well as a good Governor his example has perhaps greater influence than that of any other man in the State; he helps to make right conduct fashionable, and in scores of ways produces a good effect on the people over whom he presides.

In some countries the head of the State is born to the posi-

---

* Of course it must be understood that when the Governor does this he is still acting on the advice of his Ministry.

tion. This arrangement does not seem to be quite the best, unless indeed when it has been sanctioned by very long usage : even then, though it may perhaps give a State a Queen Victoria for its head, it may perhaps give it a King George IV. It is not a thoroughly good arrangement even for those who are born to be kings or queens. The temptations to which a young man or a young woman of the. highest rank is exposed are such as the strongest head and the stoutest heart would find it difficult to fight against : how, then, can it be expected that a giddy youth or a thoughtless maiden should be able to resist them successfully and pass through them quite uninjured ? In some countries the head of the State is chosen by the people. This is not a good plan either. A Governor chosen by the people naturally has far too much power; the very fact of his having been elected by the people gives him great power ; and, besides, an elected Governor must have belonged to some party or he would not have been elected, but the party of the head of a State should be composed of all its members. The fact is that the head of a State should have but little real power except such as can be used only just when it is necessary that it should be used; but he ought to be a thoroughly wise and just man, with a complete knowledge of ˌState business, so that he may be able to use this power well when the proper time arrives. Now, we are very fortunate in being able to get just the kind of head that we require. Colonial Governors are always men that have been trained to transact public business ; and we may be sure, generally, that if they were not wise and just they would not have risen so high. They have, in most cases, travelled about the world a great deal and have gained much experience, and most of them are able to give useful advice to Ministers if advice is required. They can hardly belong to any party in the colony, seeing that all their interests are connected with England. It would be well, perhaps, for many other countries if they could get their heads *chosen* for them by some outside authority, much in the same way as our Governors are chosen.

# CHAPTER XXXIII.

## THE CIVIL SERVICE.

THE officers that actually do the work which the Parliament decides to have done are almost entirely under the control of the Ministry, who are, as has been shown, a committee of the House of Representatives. When these officers are spoken of as a body they are generally called the Civil Service, each member of the service being a Civil servant—that is, a servant of the State.* For the sake of convenience the work of the Government is divided into departments, each of which is, as a rule, managed by an "Under-Secretary," or other superior officer having powers similar to those of an Under-Secretary. But the Minister that has the control of each department really decides what its work is to be, and is responsible to the House of Representatives for the way in which this work is done. Of course in all important matters the Minister's decision is the decision of the Cabinet. Any Minister may have charge of one, two, or even more departments. But every Civil servant is, after all, under the control of the State as a whole. Taking the case of a policeman as an example, we find that if a policeman misbehaves himself in any way he has to answer for his misbehaviour to his Inspector. This officer is controlled by the Commissioner, the Commissioner is ruled by the Minister, the Ministry may be put out of office by the House of Representatives, and the members of the House may be dismissed by the electors. Again, if any Civil servant thought that he had been wronged by his superiors,

---

* Technically, perhaps, the expression "Civil servants" includes only those who have been appointed to offices by the Governor, acting under the advice of his Ministers; but the meaning of the term has not yet been thoroughly fixed. In the text, officers appointed by Parliament are spoken of as Civil servants; other officers, not appointed by the Governor, but who may be fairly considered servants of the State, are also included.

he could appeal for redress to the authorities one after another, until at last he came to the people, who alone have the power to settle any matter whatever quite finally. It is true that in most cases a Civil servant would find it very difficult indeed to raise his voice sufficiently to make himself heard by his real masters, the people; but, if he could manage to do this, he would most likely obtain redress, if he deserved it, after all other means had failed.

The best means of showing the amount and kind of work done by the Civil Service will be to take the departments one by one and give a brief account of its peculiar work. The words " department " and " office " will have to be used in a rather loose kind of way, but each of them will mean, generally, a more or less distinct branch of the public service.

*The Legislative Departments*, which are under the control of the Speakers of the two Houses, do all work connected with the meetings, business, and records of the Parliament itself. The General Assembly library is managed by a joint committee of the two Houses : this is the most important and valuable library in the colony.

*The Registrar-General's Office* registers births, deaths, and marriages, and takes all necessary steps to prevent the possibility of disputes with regard to the lawfulness of marriages contracted in the colony; it works that part of the Public Health Act which provides for the vaccination of children. It also registers doctors and dentists. The Registrar-General has the management of the census, which is taken every five years for the purpose of ascertaining the general condition of the colony, and of showing whether wealth and population are increasing or decreasing. The Registrar-General publishes every year a volume containing such information about the State as can be expressed in figures—information with regard to population, public health, immigration, trade, taxation, wealth, crime, education, and other important matters.

The business of the *Audit Office* is to see that no money is paid by the Government to anybody unless the payment is in strict accordance with the law. The head of the department, the Controller-General, is appointed by the Governor in the name of and on behalf of the Queen. Like the judges, he holds his office during good conduct, and can be removed by the Governor only upon an address from both Houses of Parliament; and no Minister has any control over him. No claim against the Government can be paid by the Treasury until the Controller-General has *passed* it. This officer has by law the power of compelling people, under heavy penalties, to appear before him and to answer on oath any questions and to produce any papers relating to public moneys, in order that he may be able to effectively perform the duties of his office. Speaking generally, we may say that the Audit Office performs the duty of controlling public expenditure by securing full compliance with all laws or parts of laws that relate to public money.

*The Agent-General's Department* is in London. This department transacts most of the business that the Government wishes to have done in Europe. It assists in most of the work connected with loans, purchases goods required for the use of the Government in the colony, and gives information to persons who wish to learn the best means of reaching New Zealand. Speaking generally, too, we may say that this branch of the Civil Service is of great use in preventing the spreading of untruths with regard to New Zealand and its people amongst the people of England. This department costs the State less than £4,400 a year, and the money it costs seems to be remarkably well spent.

*The Printing and Stationery Department* prints and publishes all parliamentary papers, statutes, debates, and official publications, such as the *New Zealand Gazette, Police Gazette*, &c., and also books on different subjects published under the authority of the Government. It likewise prints all departmental forms used by the public offices, executes all binding required, prints all the railway tickets used in the colony, and imports and prepares for use most of the stationery required for the use of the Government and distributes it over the colony as it is needed. "The State" was printed by this department, and it will easily be seen that it is a very good specimen of the printer's and the binder's work.

Most of the work hitherto referred to is in some way connected with the Colonial Secretary's Office. This office at the present time (1887) also deals with the following matters :—

Under the Electoral Acts it registers electors throughout the colony, prepares the rolls, and manages elections of members. of Parliament in so far as these elections are managed by the Government.

Under the Diseased Cattle Act it endeavours to prevent diseases of cattle from gaining a footing in the colony, under the Rabbit Nuisance Act it endeavours to keep down the number of rabbits, and under the Sheep Act to rid the colony of scabby sheep.

Besides these matters, the Colonial Secretary's Office deals with many others that could not well be attended to by any other department. Perhaps the most important of these is the working of the Public Health Act, which it at present administers with the assistance of the Customs Department and the Registrar-General's Office. It also administers the Aliens Act, the Lunatics Act, the Adulteration of Food Act, the Weights. and Measures Act, and the Animals Protection Act. This office deals with some matters connected with Road Boards, County Councils, and local bodies generally; it edits the Government *Gazette,* and conducts most of the Government correspondence with persons outside of the colony and with other States.

*The Treasury Department* receives all the revenue collected by the General Government of the colony. The revenue consists principally of Customs duty paid at the various seaports, and duties on beer and tobacco produced in the colony; property-tax levied at varying rates according to Acts of the General Assembly; railway receipts derived from lines open for traffic; stamp duty collected for defraying the cost of despatching letters and telegrams, of registering legal documents, such as titles to land, of conducting business in the Courts of the colony, and for many other purposes too numerous to mention here. Other sources · of revenue are rents and depasturing licenses paid by the lessees of large blocks of land commonly known as "grazing runs." The Treasury also receives the moneys paid for Crown lands that are sold either for cash or on deferred payments, and also such revenues as are obtained from the goldfields settlements, and from the duty of 2s. 6d. per ounce paid on all gold exported from the colony.

On the other hand, the Treasury makes all necessary pay--

ments to the public on receipt of proper vouchers which have first been approved by the various departments, and have then been passed by the Audit Office established for such purpose. The large majority of these payments are made by the issue of cheques which are sent to the claimants, and are payable at the branch of the Bank of New Zealand nearest the place where they reside. The Treasury conducts all the financial operations of the Government, such as the raising of loans, and the *conversion* of the public debt from one class of security to another; and it corresponds with the Crown Agents, the Loan Agents, and the Agent-General in England with regard to these and other financial subjects. The accounts of the General Government of the colony are made up in the Treasury, and are published quarterly and yearly for general information.

*The Property-tax Department* collects a tax upon all property in the colony excepting that which is exempt by law. Property of Maoris, whether land, money, or anything else, is exempt from the property-tax. A valuation of land, houses, and similar property is made every third year, and upon this valuation nearly all local bodies, excepting boroughs, levy their rates. This department also certifies to payments that are to be made by Government to counties, road districts, town districts, and boroughs, and manages one or two other matters that do not need to be mentioned here.

*The Friendly Societies Registry Office* registers these societies, and publishes useful statistics showing their financial position.

*The Government Insurance Department* insures lives, grants endowments, and does other work of a similar character in much the same way as the office of a private company would do it. This insurance office does no business outside of New Zealand. As the death-rate of New Zealand is lower than that of any of the other colonies of Australasia, it is plain that the Government office can afford to take lower premiums than those required by companies that insure lives in colonies where people die faster. Persons who insure their lives in the Government office, too, may feel sure that the sums assured will be paid when the proper time arrives, seeing that the colony is the *security* for the payment. The money received by the department for premiums is invested by a Board consisting of the Colonial Treasurer and five " Under-Secretaries." This money is invested in Government securities; in loans on mortgages, on policies, on freehold properties, and on borough and county securities; and in railway debentures. The funds in hand now (1887) amount to more than .£1,200,000, and the yearly revenue is nearly .£260,000. At the end of last year there were in force 24,644 policies, assuring £6,669,061. This department has been referred to in a former part of the book.

*The Justice Department,* which is under the control of the Minister of Justice, deals with all matters relating to the administration of justice. The Supreme Court, so far as it is not under the control of the judges, and all the other Courts of the colony except the Land Courts, are connected with this department, which also takes charge of the prisons of the colony. The working of the bankruptcy laws, and criminal prosecutions, are also managed by it. Coroners, whose duty it is to hold enquiries in cases of sudden death and of , fires, are under it. It administers the Licensing Act (publichouses) and the Probation of Offenders Act. It controls the sheriffs and other executive officers, and takes oversight of the work done by justices of the peace. It may be added that at present the Patents Office is connected with this department.

*The Crown Law Office* gives legal advice to all the executive departments of the Government, and drafts bills that are to be brought into Parliament. Its principal officers are the Attorney-General and the Solicitor-General.

*The Post Office and Telegraph Department* has two branches, which were separate till 1880, but now form one great department under one management. The Post Office branch controls all matters relating to the carriage of letters, post-cards, book-packets, parcels, and newspapers, and maintains all mail services, inland and by sea. It conducts the business of the Money-order and Post-Office Savings-Bank systems, and will shortly bring into operation a parcels-post scheme. The Post Office also performs a variety of Government business for other departments, including the insuring of correct payment of Treasury cheques issued to the public; duties of registrars of births, deaths, and marriages, and, at a large number of towns, of vaccination inspectors; the collection of property-tax; the making of payments on behalf of the Education Department on account of industrial-school work; Government insurance business; the collection of Customs duties at one or two places; the collection of fees for inspection of machinery; the issue of game licenses and collection of the fees; the collection of taxes under the Live Stock Acts, and rates under the District Railways Acts. At a few places this department undertakes partially the duties of land officers. The Telegraph branch controls the transmission of telegrams, constructs and maintains all telegraph wires, public and private, throughout the colony, and also manages the several telephone exchanges and offices.

*The Customs Department* collects the duties imposed through the *tariff* on goods imported into the colony, and the duties on beer and tobacco produced in it. It also collects the export duty on gold. To this department lighthouse dues, pilotage rates, various license-fees, and other moneys are paid. Customs officers are charged with the detection and prevention of smuggling and illicit distillation, and all prosecutions for these offences are directed by the department. Collectors of Customs at seven of the ports are Registrars of Shipping, and all the Collectors may hold inquiries as to wrecks and accidents to shipping. Returns of imports, exports, shipping, and revenue are compiled at the head office of the department, and are published yearly. This department has also charge of the quarantine stations.

*The Marine Department* manages the harbours that are not under Harbour Boards, and keeps the lighthouses, buoys, and beacons on the coast in good order. It manages the Government steamers, and examines all ships and steamers to find whether they are seaworthy and have proper accommodation for passengers; for places where there is no Harbour Board it provides pilots to take ships out of and to bring them into harbour; it corresponds with all Harbour Boards and controls all matters connected with foreshores; it examines seamen who are candidates for masters' and mates' certificates, and examines engineers for certificates; it inspects boilers and machinery, and enquires as to the causes of wrecks and other accidents to shipping. This department also conducts marine surveys, and attends to the correction of maps and charts of the coast.

*The Stamp Department* prints all stamps, including those required under the Stamp Act (the use of stamps is referred to in Chapter XXIV.), and it makes all arrangements connected with their use and distribution. This department also registers building societies and joint-stock companies; it collects the duties on the estates of deceased persons, protecting the interests of the Government, while the Public Trustee, whose duties are described further on, attends rather to the interests of the persons who succeed to property. A very important branch of this department is the *Land and Deeds Registry Office*, which keeps a correct account of all business connected with sales of land, and some other matters that by law require to be registered. The object aimed at is that, as far as possible, all titles to land and real property may be put on a footing of certainty, and that any one wishing to buy certain kinds of property may be able to learn with as little difficulty as possible who the real owners of the property are, and may not make the mistake of purchasing such things from those that have no right to sell them; also that the real owners of property may not run the risk of losing their property through wrongful claims. This office does for titles to land what the Registrar-General does for marriages.

*The Public Trust Office* takes charge of certain kinds of property intrusted to its care by the Government or by private persons; it undertakes business connected with the making of and giving effect to wills, and with various kinds of trusts, such for example as marriage settlements; and, speaking generally, it is willing to undertake most kinds of guardianship and trusteeship. It also deals in certain cases with the property of lunatics and of prisoners. The Public Trust Office is superior to ordinary trustees in two respects : there is no chance of its dying, or becoming unable to act, or leaving the colony; and, as no investment is made till it has been carefully considered by a Board of officers, and as all claims against estates have to be examined by the office and the Audit Department before they are paid, there is no reason to fear that an improper use will be made of property confided to the care of the Public Trustee. This office is again alluded to in Chapter XXXV.

*The Education Department* manages the public schools, but
17

not directly. The department's business is to see as far as possible that the Education Act is complied with by the Education Boards that have the actual charge of the schools, to examine and classify teachers and others, and to report to the Parliament year by year on the general progress of the work of education throughout the colony. This department, however, has the direct control over Native schools, industrial schools, and the Deaf-mute Institution, and it does a great deal of other work in connection with high schools and colleges, the University, public libraries, and with many other things that it is not necessary to mention here.

*The Native Department* deals with most of the important matters (except education) that concern the Maori race. It is the means of communication between the Government and the Natives ; it interprets Maori letters, and translates Government letters into Maori. Generally, the Native Department takes in hand all business that arises between the Government and the Maoris through the fact that the latter are Maoris and not Europeans. The Native Land Purchase Office conducts all negotiations for the transfer of land from the Natives to the Crown.

*The Native Land Courts'* business is to determine the ownership of Native lands, and to change the ordinary Native title into a title that can be dealt with under the land-laws of New Zealand. It is true that some of the rules with regard to land owned by Natives for which Crown grants have been issued are not exactly the same as those relating to lands owned by Europeans ; but still these lands are held in accordance with New Zealand law, and not under the ancient Native custom.

*The Mines Department.*—This department is under the Minister of Mines. It has the general management of the goldfields of the colony ; it attends to the inspection of gold-mines and coal-mines, and does its best to provide for the safety of those engaged in the work of mining ; and it also superintends the construction and maintenance of water-races.

*The Geological Department*, which is at present in some degree connected with the Mines Department, endeavours to spread as widely as possible information with regard to the mineral wealth of the colony and the places where it will most probably be found; it also publishes from time to time general information about the other natural resources of the colony; it has charge of the Colonial Museum and the Observatory, and it assists to a certain extent the New Zealand Institute and the Botanical Gardens. This department also collects information about the weather, and sends warnings to all parts of the colony when storms are expected.

*The Public Works Department* constructs the railways and public buildings undertaken by the Government, and makes roads in Native or sparsely-populated districts. The construction of railways of course includes getting them authorised by the Legislature by a special Act; making surveys; preparing plans of works; buying the land where the owners are willing to sell, and, where they are not willing, taking it from them by legal process under the Public Works Acts and paying compensation for it; the actual construction of the railway, with its bridges, stations, workshops, wharves, &c.; the importing of the rails and engines; and the importing or making of the carriages, wagons, and trucks. All railways and tramways constructed by local bodies, companies, or individuals have first to be approved of and authorised by this department, and then to be inspected and reported as safe, and fit for working, before they can be opened for public use. All disputes between local bodies as to which body shall maintain certain roads or bridges have to be referred to this department for settlement.

*The Working Railways Department* has the control and management of more than 1,700 miles of opened lines, divided into eleven sections, the number of which, however, will be lessened when the various links in the railway system are connected by extensions now in progress. This department has no control whatever over the lines until they have been handed over fully equipped with appliances, station-buildings, &c. All the new stock for the lines is now built in the workshops connected with the principal sections, at Auckland, Wellington, Christchurch, and Dunedin; and the maintenance of way and renewal of bridges and structures are attended to by the Working Railways Department. Some engines are also being built in the colony by private contract for this department. None but native coal is now used on the New Zealand railways.

The total revenue from the New Zealand railways for the year ending 31st March, 1886, was £1,047,418, and the expenditure £690,340, returning a dividend towards payment of interest on the cost of construction of £2 18s. 6d. per cent. The total number of passengers carried during the year was 3,362,266, and the number of men employed at the date mentioned was about 4,600.

The whole of this department, with its three branches, Traffic, Locomotive, and Maintenance, is under the control of a General Manager and an Assistant Manager, who are responsible to the Minister for Public Works.

*The Defence Department.*—The Minister of Defence deals with the internal and external defence of the colony, and administers the departments connected with harbour defences, the permanent forces (including the artillery and the torpedo corps), and the volunteers.

*The Police Department* is under a Commissioner, who controls the ordinary police and also the detective force of the whole colony.

*The Crown Lands and Immigration Department* makes arrangements for the sale or lease of land, and for the care of forests and other lands belonging to the Crown, and receives all rents yielded by them under the various systems at present in force. It publishes a work called "The Crown Lands Guide," which gives much useful information about this and kindred matters. This department, too, has under its especial care the hot springs of the country. It also has in hand the work of spreading information as to the best means of making use of the soil, and it is just now establishing a school whose special work it will be to teach its pupils what is known about such subjects. This department also controls immigration and receives nominations of persons who wish to be assisted by the Government to reach this colony.

*The Survey Department* does the important work of ascertaining exactly the position of a great many conspicuous landmarks in various parts of the colony, and, by measurements from these landmarks, determining the place of other natural features, or of convenient points selected by the surveyors. This of course renders it possible to correctly describe the whole of the country, for when this kind of work has been done it is easy to make a perfectly accurate map of a whole district, and to so define sections of it that disputes about the ownership of land can no longer arise between people through uncertainty as to the position and boundaries of their property. The information obtained by the department in the course of its work with regard to the geography of the country is spread abroad as much as possible by means of drawings, maps, and printed matter; and, with the aid of this and of the reports of the department's surveyors, people who wish to take up land can choose that which is likely to suit them best. This department also does much useful work in the way of making roads to and opening up land in new country. In fact the Survey may be considered as the Pioneer Department.

It will appear from this sketch of the work done by the Civil Service of New Zealand under the direction of Ministers that, even if the price of the services rendered is great, the services rendered are great also. It has been shown, however, in Chapter XXIV. that the price paid is not nearly so great as most people are in the habit of thinking it is, although a very simple calculation might convince them of their error. Having now described the means by which a very important part of the State work is done, we may go on to deal with an equally important matter— namely, the means that the State employs for regulating the conduct of members of the State towards one another and towards the State as a whole. This will be dealt with in the five following chapters on Law.

# PART IV.—LAW.

## CHAPTER XXXIV.

### INTRODUCTORY.—RIGHTS AND DUTIES.

In Chapter IV. it was explained that in every State there must be both Law and Government. From the five chapters preceding this one you have learnt something about the Government of New Zealand; in the next five the subject of Law will be treated of. Every one should have some knowledge of the laws of his country; he should have a general idea of what Law is, how it first came into being, how the general body of law has grown up, how new laws are made, what rights the law secures to him as an individual and what wrongs it protects him from, how the laws are put into force, what means are used for securing a right and preventing or punishing a wrong; and, generally, he should know what his rights and duties in respect to the law actually are. It is such a general idea as this that you are now to obtain.

#### What Law is.

At the very outset we cannot do better than to say what Law really is. Law is a collection of commands issued to the members of the State by its highest authority, for the purpose of regulating their conduct in certain respects. These commands are enforced by means of *sanctions,* or penalties which have to be suffered by those who neglect to do what the law orders them to do, or who do what the law forbids. Law differs from what is called Morals in this: *Law* tells each individual what he *must* or *must not* do; *Morals* tells each individual what he *ought* or *ought not* to do.

*How Law comes into being ; how the Necessity for Law begins to be perceived.*

There arc two principal ways in which law comes into being. It cither grows up, or it is made. People living together get into certain habits, certain more or less convenient ways of doing things, till at last they consider it wrong to do them in any other way;* these habits may lead to the establishment of rules, and at last those who break the rules that have thus grown up may be punished for doing so by the highest power in the community, whether the community is small enough to be called a tribe or large enough to be called a nation. Or, on the other hand, the law may be made by those who have the chief power, whatever may be the nature of that power, any breach of the law being punished by those who hold that power.

In Chapter III. it was shown that it might be possible for very savage tribes gradually to become civilised ; it was also shown that very little is really *known* about such matters. In this part of the book we shall leave these very savage tribes out of account, and deal with man only as we know him through history. It has been proved that after a certain period in the history of any society has been reached it is the family and not the individual that is the unit of the society ; and it is most likely that very many of our customs had their origin during the time when a father's authority was the only governing-power, and his word the only law. It must be always borne in mind, however, that the family was not necessarily what it now is among Europeans. It may have been what it was among the Maoris a few years ago, when the chief had a sacred character, and was the father of a family which might include many rather distant relatives and some members adopted from other families.

As families gradually unite a larger society comes into being. It is soon found that, though the life of this society goes on in a fairly orderly and satisfactory way, there are certain parts of the conduct of some of the members of the society, now partly released from the restraints of family rule, that give pain and trouble to the rest. Some of the actions of these trouble-

---

* This is custom ; it will be shown further on how customs become *true positive laws* by being adopted and *sanctioned* and perhaps recorded by the highest authority in the State.

some members give pain merely because they do not come up to the general idea of what is right and honourable; but other actions cause trouble to the society by making most of the members of it feel that if such actions are allowed there will be no safety for any one, either in person or in property. If a man is disagreeable, cross, and unkind, if he is hard and grasping, if he refuses to help those who are in distress, if he is idle and careless, his people will not consider him a good man; but this will be no reason for meddling with him or his affairs. If they do interfere it will be in the way of trying to persuade him that his conduct is wrong and that he *ought* to act otherwise, but no one will try to compel him to do so. But if one man insults and beats others, or steals other people's property, then all will feel that they are unsafe unless some means can be found of putting an end to such conduct. Moreover, disputes between neighbours will arise, now and again, with regard to their property, and the question who is in the right and who is in the wrong will have to be decided. As soon as the inconveniences arising from danger to person and from uncertainty with regard to property begin to be severely felt, the advent of law is not very far distant.

*Law arising from customary Modes of restraining unruly Individuals, and of settling Disputes; how New Laws spring up through the Decisions given by Judges.*

These two causes—the conduct of unruly members of the community and disputes between neighbours—will surely lead in time to the establishment of some sort of council, like the *runanga* of the Maoris, to decide what shall be done with such offenders and to settle such disputes.

In every case that comes before it this council will be sure to listen to the evidence of the persons who can give information with regard to the wrong committed, or who can tell anything that bears upon the dispute. The council will carefully consider the evidence, in connection with the customs of the people, and will at last decide how the offender is to be punished, or to whom the property in dispute belongs. Then, for the future all who have been present at the trial and all who have been told about it will look upon the decision as a rule, and the oftener any particular kind of ease is tried and decided in a particular way the greater will be the strength of the rule. After a very short time, when such a case comes to be tried, all that will have to be done will be to make sure that it is like those that have been decided before. As time goes on the number of rules made in this way will greatly increase, and at last it will be necessary to appoint some one who knows all the rules well, to act as judge. From time to time quite new cases will come up; then the judge will not be able to fit these on to the old rules, but will have to consider how he can best make his decisions agree with the rules that deal with cases most like them. When once a State has been formed, and has given birth to a Government, and these rules have been adopted by the Government as *its* rules, and when once the Government has affixed penalties to breaches of these rules, they become positive laws.* Then very probably some kind of code or collection of rules will be made, if the people have acquired the art of writing.

It is in this simple way that the great mass of the laws of every country has been made, except, of course, in countries like New Zealand, whose law had in the first place to be imported from the mother-country.

### Laws made by the Legislature.

The other way in which law is made is this : The highest authority in the State simply says, " In future the law about this or that matter shall be so-and-so, and those who do not obey the laws will be punished in such-and-such a way," and this authority's command becomes the law at once. In New Zealand, of course, the highest authority is the Parliament. The way in which laws are made by Parliament has been explained in Part III.

---

* But even before this there may have been positive laws ; for the judge's authority, which is the basis of " case law," is plainly derived from the sovereign authority, nearly always vested in early times, after the " father " has ceased to be the sole master and lawgiver, in the hands of all the members of a village community.

### Cause of the constant Growth of Law.

You will easily understand why it is that the law is constantly growing through the decisions of judges. In early times only the simplest kinds of cases have to be dealt with : but, as a nation progresses, new customs grow up ; new businesses are started ; new kinds of partnerships are invented ; cheques, bank-notes, and bills come into use ; merchants send ships to foreign countries, and establish trading-stations in them ; colonies are founded : all of these things may cause disputes at times, and these disputes have to be settled by the judges. Their decisions, as was before explained, in time become law, and so the law grows very fast, and becomes a most difficult thing to learn. But the law not only grows; it changes too, and would change even though the Parliament never passed a single Act. As a nation grows older it very likely becomes wiser; at all events, our nation has become wiser. The people become more humane and sensible, and their ideas of what is right and what is wrong change to a certain extent. The judges change too, and, though they are, of course, bound to keep close to the laws, yet in deciding cases they will always have a tendency to make their decisions agree as far as possible with the common-sense of the time. These decisions will be the grounds for new decisions still more in agreement with the thoughts of the people. Then, again, able lawyers write books about the law, and their opinions have some weight with the judges, because these writers often bring to light things that the judges may have overlooked. Judges decide, too, to a large extent, how cases shall be conducted in the Courts. As time goes on a great many of the rules in use are found to be unsuitable or troublesome ; accordingly the judges alter these rules, or make others instead of them. In this way nearly all that part of the law that relates to the carrying-on of trials and suits has been at one time or another either made, or more or less altered, by the judges. You will see now that the very common notion that all law is made by Parliament is quite wrong. It is true that the Parliament, including the Governor, represents the highest authority of the State, that the law is based on this authority, and that the Parliament can change any law; but it has not *made* the whole of the law, or even the greater part of it.

*Comparison of Laws made by the Legislature with " Judge-made " Law.*

Each kind of law has its advantages. If Parliament thinks that anything is wrong, and that a new law would set it right, it can pass a law, and it often does so with excellent effect; but very often a new law passed by Parliament spoils half a dozen old ones that there has been no intention of altering. On the other hand, a judge, when deciding a new kind of case, has to make his decision fit in with the old law as well as he can, and at the same time to be in agreement as far as possible with the common-sense of the men and women around him. Thus, what is called " judge-made law " or " case-law," and sometimes, though seldom correctly, " unwritten law," will nearly always work much better than laws made by the Parliament. But, on the other hand, again, judge-made law can never enable a nation to make progress in an entirely new direction ; a good law made by Parliament may and often does this.

*Legal Rights and Duties.*

The true and proper object of law is to establish and maintain rights, and to prevent or do away with wrongs. The first question we have to answer, then, is, What is a right and what is a wrong? In Chapter IV. the work of the State was described : a part of this work is to protect each and all from being injured by the action or the negligence of any individual or class in the society; to defend the whole community from injury by any individual or class ; and to make it possible for every one to do whatever pleases him, so long as what pleases him does not interfere with the freedom of others to do what pleases them, and does not hinder the efforts of the community to reach a higher stage of progress. This means, among other things, that the members of the State have to obey certain rules in order that all may be able to enjoy certain liberties and advantages. The general name for these liberties and advantages is "rights." You will presently learn much more exactly what a *legal right* is. In the meantime it may be said that the principal kinds of *legal rights* are personal rights and rights of property. A man's chief PERSONAL RIGHTS are—(a) the right to personal safety—

that is, to the free enjoyment of his life, his body, his health, and his character; (*b*) the right to personal liberty—that is, the power of going where he pleases, and freedom from any kind of restraint except such as the law itself may direct. Now, if the law gives men a right to the free enjoyment of, say, their health, it follows that no one may do anything to endanger his neighbour's health. A man may not make a drain, for instance, that will run under a neighbour's house, for by doing so he would expose his neighbour to a great risk of catching a bad fever. This neighbour would have a *right* to prevent the making of such a drain, and the law would protect him in the lawful exercise of that right, and, so far, he would be able to control the other man's conduct. A LEGAL RIGHT, then, is a certain amount of power given to one man by the highest authority of the State, which enables him to control the acts of another in some certain way. The person whose act is controlled, and who is liable to punishment through the law if he does not submit to the control, is said to have A DUTY. A legal duty may cause a man either to have to do a certain act or to refrain from doing one. Thus it is the legal duty of a banker to give gold for his notes, and it is every one's legal duty not to forge a banknote.

Plainly, the existence of rights makes wrongs possible; if a man has a legal right the man who interferes with him in the exercise of this right commits a WRONG. Wrongs will be dealt with pretty fully in Chapter XXXVI.

THE RIGHTS OF PROPERTY give a man free use of, and power to dispose of, all that he has acquired in accordance with law, and make him the sole master of it.

### How Rights of Property came into Existence.

It may be worth while to ask how these rights of property came into existence. We learn from history that amongst certain peoples all things were at first undivided and common to all, and formed a sort of single estate belonging to everybody, or perhaps we should say to every member of a tribe or group. But even then there must have been a right of property. If the *things* did not belong to anybody, the use of them did. That is, a thing belonged to a man while he used it; just as, although the seats at a tea-meeting belong to all those who go to the tea-meeting, yet every one has a seat that is his own while he is using it. But this sort of ownership would soon be found to be very inconvenient. No one would be at the trouble of providing anything that he could possibly do without if his property in it ceased the moment he left off using it. No one would care about building a comfortable house or making a good garment if he knew that the moment he left his house a stranger might walk in and use it, or that the moment he took off his garment some one else would probably put it on.

Thus it would very soon be found necessary for the comfort of everybody that whatever a man made, or obtained in exchange for something that he had made, should be his own whether he was using it or not.

Property in land must have sprung up in the same way. The soil produces little unless it is cultivated. No family would cultivate a piece of ground unless they could feel pretty sure of getting the crop as a return for their labour. This would gradually lead to a man's having a right to the piece of ground that he was cultivating, for he would naturally choose the best and most fertile land he could find, and would cultivate the same piece over and over again, perhaps for many years. Thus in time it would come to be recognised that a family *owned* the land that they occupied and cultivated. The right of property, then, would seem to have sprung from two things—(a) finding the material for a thing and making it; and (b) the constant use of a thing that had before been common property. This would lead to a third principle—namely, that he who takes a thing that no one else makes use of becomes the owner of it, and that it remains his till he shows by some act that he means to abandon it. Perhaps, too, we may add to this that the feeling gradually arose, after persons had begun to make things their own, that everything should have an owner. Every State, however, puts some limit to ownership. There are things so useful to all that each has to be prevented from making it his own. Streets belong to the State; so do harbours, large rivers, and roads; and many sound reasons might be given why land should be treated in the same way if all existing claims connected with ownership of land could be fully satisfied.

# CHAPTER XXXV.

## RIGHTS OF PROPERTY; TITLE.

LAWYERS divide things that may be held as property into Things Real and Things Personal.* These terms came into use in the old times, when property that could be easily moved about was thought little of; the old English law-books say very little indeed about such property. The writers of these books took great pains to explain correctly the rules that governed the possession of lands, houses, and the profits connected with them, probably because it was on the possession of such things that a man's importance most depended. They called these things *real* property; all other things, things that might go with a man or be carried wherever he went, were paid far less attention to, and were called *personal* property. The distinction between real and personal property still subsists, but it is of far less practical importance than it was formerly.

In New Zealand land may be owned in three different ways: it may be held by Native title, or through grant from the Crown, or through its having been lawfully acquired after being granted by the Crown. The possession of land by the Natives is entirely regulated by Native custom until it has been "passed through the Land Court"—that is, until the ownership has been decided in accordance with Native custom by a Land Court; the ordinary law cannot deal with it at all except in the way of protecting its owners in the possession of their property. When once land has been passed through the Court, and ownership has been settled, a grant from the Crown may be issued and the land can

---

* These terms referred to the nature of the legal remedy adopted for recovery: the remedy for deprivation in respect to real property was against the property itself, the *res*; the remedy for injury in respect to goods and chattels was against the *person*.

be dealt with in accordance with the special laws that are in force at the time. A great part of the land sold by the Natives has been purchased by the Crown; much of this Crown land has been sold, and some of it has been leased, to private persons. Sales of land by the Crown are made in different ways. Sometimes the purchase-money is paid at once; sometimes payment is made gradually; in some cases no payment at all is required, but certain improvements made on the land give all the rights that in other cases are obtained by payment of money. In any case as soon as all conditions required by the law have been fulfilled a Crown grant may be issued, and the land may become the property of the person who has fulfilled these conditions.

### Title to Property.

The special ways in which real property is held, or handed over from one person to another, would be an unsuitable subject even to attempt to deal with in a book like this; but the law-courts are tending more and more to regard *real* and *personal* property in nearly the same light. As, therefore, the general rules that govern rights to the one kind of property and those that govern rights to the other kind are becoming on the whole much alike, we shall make no further distinction, but go on to speak of Title to Property in general.

You must bear in mind that by the word "things" we do not always mean substances, but frequently only the rights connected with them. You are to understand, too, that by *title* is meant *right of property in a thing*, or, perhaps rather, the causes that give a man such a right. You may say that a title to a thing can be obtained in six different ways: (1) By taking possession of or holding it; (2) by invention; (3) by gift; (4) by will; (5) by contract; (6) by bankruptcy.

(1.) *Title by taking or holding Possession of.*—Any man may take possession of any wild beast of the field, bird of the air, or fish of the sea, except in cases in which there is a law forbidding him to do so; and if a man has once lawfully seized an animal that is wild by nature, and tamed it, or if he keeps it confined on his own property, the animal is his, but if it escapes it may be again treated as a wild animal. If a man lawfully kills a wild animal it becomes his own. If a man's property increases by the operation of nature the increase belongs to the owner of the original property. The young of animals and the fruit of trees are the property of the owner of the animals or of the trees. In the case of animals it is the owner of the mother that becomes the owner of the young ones. Under this head what is called "confusion of goods" is generally reckoned. If John and James are threshing corn with the same machine, and James, without John's approval or knowledge, mixes his corn with John's corn, then the English law gives the whole of the corn so *confused* to John. It does this to prevent fraud— to prevent one man, for instance, from mixing his inferior corn with another's good corn and then claiming a share of the mixture. It may be added to what has already been said under this head that, generally, if I possess anything my title holds good against everybody that cannot show a better title to it. Before you can take away my boat you must not only show that my right to it is not perfect, you must show that you have a better right to it. You must not rely on the weakness of my title, but on the strength of yours.

(2.) *Title by Invention.*—The Crown has no power to grant to any one the sole right to sell a certain article. That was settled by a law passed in the reign of James I. But an exception has always been made in favour of those who invent new manufactures, because to grant to such inventors the sole right to sell what they have invented does not interfere with a right possessed by any one else, and because such a grant encourages others to try to invent things that will be useful to the community. The right given by such a grant is called a *patent-right*, and the holder of it is called the *patentee*. The right is generally granted for fourteen years in the first place, though this time may be made longer. The inventor is allowed to *register* his invention, and this gives him all the rights of a patentee until it has been decided whether he ought to have the patent or not. Patent-rights are said to be given by Royal favour; but they are never refused in proper cases—that is, in cases in which the person applying for a patent shows that he is the true and first inventor; and that the invention is neither contrary to the law, hurtful to the State or to trade, nor generally inconvenient.

Copyright is a privilege of a similar kind. This gives an author the sole right to print and publish his own original book. In New Zealand the law of copyright affecting books is that the author, or the persons to whom he assigns his rights, shall have the sole liberty of printing for twenty-eight years from the day of first publication; and, if the author be alive at the end of that period, for the remainder of his life. Persons may hold copyrights for books, maps, pieces of music, drawings, plays, photographs, and many other things. Both patent-rights and copyrights may be given away, sold, or left by will.

(3.) *Title by Gift.*—Generally, a person may give away his property in anything with perfect freedom, provided that he is not under age, or insane, or deprived of his freedom. The law, however, is inclined to look upon gifts with some suspicion; and if a man, by giving his property to others, defrauds a creditor, the law will not recognise the gift. A man may also *assign* his personal property to another by what is called a *bill of sale.* This transaction ·is not usually a gift, for there is generally a *valuable consideration.* In any case, however, he who assigns his goods generally keeps possession of them, and merely transfers some of his rights with regard to them to the person to whom he gives the bill of sale. But if he does this in order to cheat his creditors, and they can prove it, the *bill of sale* will not deprive the creditors of their rights with regard to the property assigned.*

(4.) *Title by Will.*—Just as a man may give away his goods during his lifetime, so may he direct how the whole of his property is to be disposed of after his death, except such part of it as is required to pay the *legacy* duties.† This will (a) must be *written;* (b) it must be *signed·* by the person who makes the will, or by some one who does it for him in his presence and by his direction; and (c) it must be *witnessed* by two disinterested persons at the same time and in the presence of the testator and of each other. Any person may make a will if he is at least twenty-one years of age, of sound mind, and free from com-

---

* The bankruptcy law has many stringent provisions to prevent the operation of fraudulent conveyances or assignments.

† Legacy duties, under that name, are not charged in New Zealand, but duties in the nature of both legacy and succession duties are imposed. The State prevents the successors of a deceased person from dealing with his property until these duties are paid or provided for.

18

pulsion. In certain cases infants—that is, persons under the legal age of twenty-one years—may make wills. A male of the age of nineteen and married, or a female if married and not under eighteen, may make a will. Before the passing of the Married Women's Property Act a married woman's will would generally have been useless unless her husband had assented to her making it; but a material change has been made, and a married woman can dispose by will of her real or personal property as if she were a single woman. If a man dies *intestate*—that is, without making a will—his property, after the expenses of his funeral and all his just debts have been paid, is to be divided between his widow and his children, one-third to go to the wife and two-thirds in equal shares to the children. If there is no widow the children take the whole in equal shares. If there are no children the widow takes two-thirds and the intestate's father the remaining third. If his father is dead the mother takes this remaining third. If both father and mother are dead the third is equally divided among his surviving brothers and sisters. The whole of an intestate's property goes to his wife if he leaves no children, father, mother, brother, or sister surviving him. If there are neither children nor widow the whole goes to the nearest relatives. Some person is always appointed, either by the man that makes the will, or by the Court in accordance with fixed rules on the subject, to dispose of property after the death of its owner. In New Zealand there is an officer called the Public Trustee, whose business it is to look after the property of intestates. This officer will also, for a very small charge, manage all business connected with wills. A person appointed to give effect to a will is called an executor; but in cases where there is no will, or where no executor is named, the person appointed by the Court is called an administrator.

(5.) *Title by Contract.*—This is a very important part of our subject, because contract is one of the chief means by which *"rights connected with property"* come into being. Contracts in general might be classed in three different ways :—

The first and most important method of classifying contracts divides them into *special contracts* and *simple contracts*. Special contracts are made by *deed;* simple contracts by word of mouth, and, in some cases, in writing. Most contracts are of the latter kind; and for some of the most important written evidence of the contract is necessary.· For instance, any contract or sale ·by which land or any interest therein is dealt with is of no force unless there is some written note of the agreement, made and signed by the *party* to be charged, or by his lawful agent.

Secondly, contracts may be either express or implied. You may promise to give a tailor £5 for a suit of clothes, or you may simply tell him to make you a suit and send it home.. In the first case you promise to pay; in the·second you imply that you will pay the proper price for the clothes. Again, if you give a carrier a bag of sugar to take up the country for you, he implies, by receiving it, that he will deliver it safe, and not lose it or let it get spoiled by the rain.

Thirdly, contracts may be made either by principals or by agents. If John agrees to buy fifty dozen of eggs from James the contract is between the principals; but if John sends his servant to make the same bargain with James's shopman the contract is made by agents. John and James are bound by the bargain, for the law says, "He who does a thing through another does it through himself."

## Contracts.

A few words may now be said about some of the principal classes of contracts :—

*A Contract of Sale* takes place when the seller says that the price of his goods is so much, and the buyer agrees to give that price. If the sale is for ready money, and any part of the goods is handed over, or any part of the price, however small, is paid, the goods immediately belong to the buyer; but, unless the seller agrees, the buyer cannot take the goods away until he· has offered the whole of the price to the seller. ·What has been purchased in open market belongs to the buyer even if it has been stolen, unless the thief has been convicted : then the ·buyer can be made to give up the goods to the proper owner. This rule does not apply to horses or to certain other kinds of property. Generally speaking, a contract of sale is not broken through the goods supplied being of bad quality, if the buyer has had a fair chance of seeing· them for himself : the law says, "Let the buyer take care of himself." It is his own duty to see that he gets value for his money. But if a man sells another an ordinary article that is not fit for the purpose for which it is generally used, the contract has been broken.

*Contract of Bailment.*—An example of this kind of contract takes place when a visitor to a town delivers his horse to the keeper of an hotel; the implied contract is that the hotel-keeper will deliver the horse again when the visitor leaves.

*Contract of Insurance by Bills* has been alluded to in Chapter XV., where it is shown that *bills* are *negotiable*, and may to a large extent be used as money.

*Contract of Partnership* takes place when two or more persons go into business together. When a partnership has been entered into, the contract of one member of the firm, as it is called, generally binds each and all of the members with respect to any matter relating to the business in which they have engaged. This subject is too difficult to be further treated here.

*Contract of Guarantee* takes place in such a case as this: John tells James, in writing, that he will see him paid for all goods supplied by him to Thomas to the value of £20. Such contracts are of no use unless they are made in writing. If, at the time when the guarantee is given, James hears Thomas tell John that he owes James nothing, while at the same time Thomas really owes James £30 already, John cannot be made to fulfil his contract.

It may be said that generally no contract made by word of mouth, or even where there is a mere writing, is binding in law unless it is proved that there is a *consideration*—that is, unless something is given for something. If I promise to pay you £10 I ought to do so, but the law does not say that I must. The reason, probably, is something like this: John owes James nothing. John promises James £10. James had no right to this £10. Where there is no legal right there can be no wrong, so the law gives no remedy. Where there is a *deed*, however, the existence of a consideration is implied.

### Title to Property concluded.

(6.) *Title by Bankruptcy.*—When a contractor does an act which in the sight of the law shows quite clearly that he will have to break some of his contracts, the law at once compels him to satisfy all his creditors as far as he is able to do so, and also prevents him from making other contracts which might bring further loss, or might cause one creditor to be paid at the expense of the others. A very common *act* of bankruptcy is filing a schedule of debts in Court, and declaring inability to pay them. A man who cannot pay his debts or fulfil his contracts is said to be insolvent, and when the law would compel him to give up all his property to his creditors he is said to be bankrupt. Insolvent persons often make arrangements with their creditors to pay them as much as they can. Creditors are often glad to take, say, 5s. in the pound rather than go to the expense of making a debtor bankrupt. There are many cases recorded in which an arrangement of this kind has been made with an insolvent person who has afterwards been fortunate in business and has then shown himself to be an honourable man by paying all his debts in full. You have now learnt the various means by which men may obtain a title to property.

# CHAPTER XXXVI.

## RIGHTS OF PERSONS IN PRIVATE LIFE; PRIVATE WRONGS.

In private life there are three principal relations which the law takes account of—namely, those of master and servant, of husband and wife, and of parent and child. We shall deal with these relations in the order stated. But, first, we must say a few words about *slavery*.

### Slavery.

There is one kind of relation between human beings that does not now exist in New Zealand, that of owner and slave. Men may still be reduced to the condition of slavery for a period of years or for life (the State being, as it were, the owner during that period), but that is only when they have committed some crime which the law says shall be punished in that way, and we may say that no man is forced into this condition of slavery against his will. Men know what the law is, and if they break it of their own accord they must take the consequences. In the old times in New Zealand slavery was quite common; men and women were taken prisoners by warriors, and if they were not killed they were generally made slaves; then they had no rights at all, and might be treated just as it pleased their owners to treat them. One of the many benefits that the Maori has received from the pakeha is that it is no longer possible for him to be made a slave, for the English law hates slavery or anything like it.

### Master and Servant.

There are three principal kinds of servants—domestic servants, labourers or workmen, and apprentices. No one can be forced into any of these positions against his will unless he is the child of parents who are unable to maintain him, and thus or in some other way comes under the operation of the statutes dealing with destitute children; and even in that case he can leave his place on reaching the age of twenty-one years. A master is bound to properly lodge and feed his domestic servant, and cannot discharge him in case of sickness or accident without giving such notice or wages as the servant could otherwise claim. If a master neglects to properly provide for an apprentice, or unlawfully does him bodily harm, this master may be very severely punished. If a servant is guilty of gross misconduct, or wilful disobedience, or constant negligence, he may be discharged without notice, and if he steals any of his master's goods his theft will be considered by the law as much worse than a common case of stealing. If a master sees his servant being beaten by a man, he may assault the man in his servant's defence, and so may a servant defend his master. A master has to answer for a thing done by a servant in his absence, if the thing is done by the master's order, either expressed or implied. Thus, if I take my watch to a watchmaker to be repaired and his workman spoils it, the master must pay me for the damage done. Again, if you give your servant £10 to pay an account with and he loses the money, the creditor cannot claim the money from the servant; he must get it from you. For any *crime*, however, that a servant commits he must himself answer; it would be no excuse for him to say that it had been committed by his master's orders; nor is a master bound by what a servant does entirely without his authority.

## Husband and Wife.

The relation of husband and wife is looked upon by the law as a contract, and it gives certain rights, as other contracts do. Every person is at liberty to enter into this kind of contract unless certain reasons against his doing so exist. The principal reasons are these : A man having a wife, or a woman having a husband still alive, cannot marry again. A lunatic, while out of his mind, cannot marry. No person may marry a very near relative; for instance, a man may not marry his grandmother. The rules with regard to the marriage of relatives differ in different countries. For instance, in New

Zealand, if a man's wife dies he may marry her sister, but in England he may not do this. Most contracts are not binding if the persons making them are very young. Marriage is the most important of all contracts; yet the law allows persons to marry long before they can be expected to fully understand what they are doing. There is a limit, but it seems to be much too low. No promise to marry is binding in law unless the person making it is twenty-one years old at the time of making it.

Any person, then, may marry unless prevented by one or more of the four causes that we have mentioned. But it is not lawful for a minister or other officer, authorised by law to conduct marriages, to marry any couple without a certificate from a registrar. The certificate may not be granted for any one under twenty-one years of age unless the consent of the proper person has been obtained: this person is the father; if the father is dead, the guardian; if there is no guardian the mother is the proper person, if she is unmarried. The offences of making false statements with regard to age or of conducting marriages in an unlawful way may be severely punished. A marriage must now be registered immediately after it has taken place.

A man and his wife are for many purposes looked upon as one *legal person*. Before the passing of "The Married Women's Property Act, 1884," though there were some exceptions, it could be said generally that a man could not make a legal contract with his wife, and that a man and his wife could not bring an action the one against the other; and now, generally, in a criminal case they cannot give evidence the one against the other.* The old Roman law allowed a man to beat his wife smartly with a whip or a stick if she behaved very badly; for slight offences, however, only moderate punishment was to be used. Now, happily, this idea of the relation between man and wife has died out, and the tendency of the law is more and more to consider the two as equals. Under the Married Women's Property Act, a married

---

* There is a necessary exception to this rule as to evidence when the husband or the wife is the person directly affected by the crime. For instance, in a case of violent assault of a wife by her husband, the wife could testify to the acts done.

woman is capable of acquiring, holding, or disposing of any real
or personal property, just as she would be if she were a single
woman. She can also enter into any contract in respect of and
to the extent of her separate property, and she can sue or be
sued as if she were single. If she is carrying on trade or business separately from her husband she can, in respect of her
separate property, become a bankrupt. All the property that a
woman has at the time of her marriage and all that she may
afterwards separately acquire remains her separate property.
If a married woman has any sums in a savings-bank in her own
name, these sums are deemed to be her separate property until
the contrary is shown. A wife may insure her own or her husband's life for her own benefit. On the other hand, a husband
is no longer liable for debts incurred by his wife before her
marriage, except, generally, in so far as he has benefited
through the incurring of these debts. It is proper to mention
that, while the law takes away certain rights from a woman
who marries, it also gives her certain kinds of protection. A
husband is bound to maintain his wife; and if he refuses·to do
so, and she buys such things as are needful for persons in her
station of life, the husband will generally have to pay for them,
unless the wife. has left the husband of her own free will, or
has a separate allowance regularly paid. A wife, however, is
now bound to maintain a destitute husband, and also her children. A wife generally cannot be sued in Court unless along
with her husband, except in respect of her separate property.
There' are even some smaller 'crimes which she cannot be
punished for, if it be shown that they have been committed by
her in her husband's presence, as it is assumed that she has
acted under his active compulsion; but this must *appear*, for
she would not be excused, if her husband were 'absent, merely
because the crime was committed with his knowledge. If a
husband deserts his wife, she may obtain what is called a " protection order," which will prevent the husband's interfering
with her or her property if he should take it into his head to
return. In certain cases of misconduct on the part of the husband or the wife a divorce may be obtained by the injured party,
when the marriage will be dissolved.

## Parent and Child.

The relation of parent and child brings with it certain duties of parents to children, and of children to parents, and also gives parents certain powers over their children. These things are generally well understood, if they are not always acted upon. We need not do more than refer to one or two special points. Every man must maintain as part of his family his wife's children born before marriage, as in the case where a man marries a widow. In any case in which a child is sent to a reformatory, or is boarded out by the State, the parent must, if able, pay for the child's support. A father is, generally speaking, guardian of his children's property if they have any in their own right, and he has also the control of his children's persons; any one taking away a child from his parent or guardian by force or fraud is liable to severe punishment. The mother has no legal power over her children in the father's lifetime as against the father. The children of any parent who is unable to work are bound to maintain that parent, or to pay part of the cost of maintenance, according to their ability.

## Wrongs.

In Chapter XXXIV. it was explained that the existence of rights makes wrongs possible. You have gained a general idea of some of the principal kinds of rights, and you may now go on to consider the nature of the different kinds of wrongs. Wrongs may be divided into two main classes—first, those that merely need to be set right, and, second, those that require punishment. Roughly speaking, we may say that wrongs of the first class are injuries to individuals, which concern them principally; while the second class may or may not injure individuals, but are so hurtful to the community that the State forbids them, and makes it its special business to prevent them, and to punish those who commit them. There are, however, many wrongs that in some respects may fairly be said to belong to both of these classes.

## Private Wrongs.

Civil injuries, or private wrongs as they are called, are those that we are now briefly to consider. The work of setting such wrongs right may be done in two principal ways—namely, by agreement of the persons concerned in a dispute, or by an action in a Court of justice. Often, also, a person who is wronged may set himself right. This is the case sometimes when the action of the law is too slow to serve the purpose. If you see a man beating your child severely, the law does not expect you to wait till you can summon the man to the Police Court, but allows you, if you can, to set the wrong right by beating the man to the extent that is necessary for the protection of your child. If your horse has been borrowed and not returned to you, and you see him standing in the road some weeks after, the law allows you to take the horse and keep him. It does not allow you, however, to break into a stable and take your horse away by force, unless indeed the horse has been stolen. If my neighbour makes a great fire on his own land, but too near my house, I may go upon his land and put it out. The law does not expect me to wait till my house is burnt down before I do anything to set the wrong right. If your neighbour's cow breaks through into your strongly-fenced garden and is eating your cabbages, you may drive her off to the pound, to be kept there till you have been paid for the damage done. In all these cases *the law* allows you to set right the wrong that has been done to you.

Sometimes all the persons that have had a dispute agree to settle it in a friendly way : he who has done the wrong agrees to pay a certain sum of money, and the other says that that sum will satisfy him. In such a case the dispute has been settled by *agreement*. Another excellent way of settling difficulties connected with personal property is by *arbitration*. The person who has been wronged and he who has done the wrong agree to leave the whole matter to one or two *arbitrators*, who are really a kind of private judges. Where there are two arbitrators and they do not agree they call in an *umpire*. The decision of the arbitrators or of the umpire is called an *award*. This settles the whole thing as lawfully as if it had been decided in a Court of justice, and power is usually taken to enforce the award as if it were the judgment of a Court.

## Actions.

The other method of getting a wrong righted is *by an action*. An *action* is simply the lawful demand of one's right. As we shall in the next chapter pretty fully describe the way in which the work of Courts is conducted, it will be sufficient if we here mention very briefly the principal kinds of actions. An action may be a demand for redress of a wrong that comes either (*a*) from a breach of a contract made, or (*b*) from one of the three following things: (1) Neglecting to do something that a man is bound by law to do; (2) doing some lawful thing improperly; (3) doing some unlawful thing.

These are the grounds on which demands for justice may be made by a person who thinks he has been injured by the action or neglect of another person. There were formerly many different kinds of actions—actions for debt, on covenant, on promise, on detention, on trespass, and so forth—but these have now gone out of use, and any person may bring his action, stating his wrong in plain terms. All claims which a person may lawfully enforce are now made by action generally, without regard to the circumstances under which the claim has arisen. It may be added that generally no action can be successful if the person injured has allowed his claim for redress to stand over for more than six years.

# CHAPTER XXXVII.

## CRIMES; TRIAL; PUNISHMENTS.

THE word " crime " is often used to mean a dreadful or abominable act that not only hurts somebody and causes danger to everybody, but also shows a specially wicked and depraved mind in the person that commits it. If we said, in ordinary conversation, that John had committed a crime, we should very probably mean that he had done some very wicked deed that he ought not to have done and that he might have refrained from doing. Now, the meaning of the word *wicked* almost entirely depends on the feelings and opinions of the person that uses it. One person would consider it wicked to utter the smallest untruth; another would boast of his cleverness in escaping from a difficulty by telling a plausible lie, and would laugh at you if you said that you thought his conduct had been wicked. One thinks it wicked to give needless pain to any living creature ; another will call it sport to wing harmless sea-birds quite uselessly, and to cause them to suffer horrible agony perhaps for months. From this we may understand that· if the law undertook to prevent or punish *wickedness* it would have in hand a very difficult business indeed. The law wisely refuses to have anything to do with such a task.

### Crimes.

What the State does is this : It comes to the conclusion that a certain line of conduct that it believes to be the safest and the best for the community should be followed, and it then forbids in the clearest and plainest terms certain acts that would interfere with its plans, tries to prevent them by every means in its power, and punishes those who commit them. *Such acts are* CRIMES. It is very true that this is just the place where law and morals meet,—where what a man ought to do and what he must do are generally found together,—seeing that very many of the acts that the State calls crimes are also acts that are considered wicked by nearly everybody in a well-ordered State; but it is most important to remember that the very essence of a crime is not that it is a wicked act, not that it is hurtful to individual persons, but that it is *an act that has been forbidden by the State, and that subjects the actor to punishment.*

### Wickedness and Crime.

All wicked acts are not crimes, neither are all crimes wicked acts. For a man to intentionally wear out his wife's life by his ill-temper and unkindness is perhaps as wicked conduct as there could be, but it is no crime. When Maoris in past times forcibly and unlawfully took away a surveyor's instruments if they wished to prevent him from doing work that they wrongly believed would injure their title to land which had already been lawfully acquired by the Crown, they committed a crime, but certainly their action was not wicked. .Again, though most crimes do great injury to one or more individuals, some crimes injure only the State as a whole. If a man forged a Government security, and so defrauded the Government of a sum of money, the injury done would fall almost entirely on the State as a whole. We see, then, that a crime is merely a wrongful act which is forbidden by the State, and which the State, because it has forbidden it for reasons of its own, undertakes at all costs to prevent or punish.*

### Crimes and Private Wrongs.

We may now see why a distinction is made between crimes and private wrongs. If a man borrows money from me and refuses to return it, his conduct is injurious to me, but it does

---

* Among the more usual crimes are the following: Murder, rape, manslaughter, arson, bigamy, burglary, robbery under arms, horse-stealing, sheep-stealing, forgery, embezzlement, obtaining goods under false pretences, stealing from the person, larceny, receiving stolen goods, and indecent and violent assaults. For some of these offences the punishment is imprisonment with hard labour, for others penal servitude, for others again flogging and imprisonment, and for murder the punishment is death by hanging.

little harm to the State as a whole. The State therefore contents itself with providing means by which I may get the wrong righted, but it does not feel called upon to take steps to make the man pay his debt; it leaves that to me, thinking that, if I am so careless as not to make use of the remedy provided by the State, the injury to me must be very small, and that I have no right to complain. But, if a man sets fire to my house, the State at once takes the matter in hand. Believing that the act of setting fire to a house is so dangerous to everybody that, unless it is prevented by every possible means, there will be no peace or comfort for anybody, and that the safety of the whole State will be endangered by the violence of individuals, the State has forbidden the act, has made it a crime, and fixed a punishment for it.

## Police.

The State, then, makes it its business to prevent and punish crimes. In order to do this it uses various means : A police force is established, whose duty it is in the first place, by watchful care, to make the cases in which crimes can be committed as few as possible, and then, by their skill and courage, to make it almost impossible for actual offenders to escape punishment. In cases of sudden and violent death, when there is reason to suppose that the death may not have been the result of natural causes, an enquiry is held by a Coroner and a jury, whose business it is to determine, if possible, how and by what means the death occurred. Inquests, as they are called, may also be held to find out how fires have been caused. Courts are established to decide whether supposed offenders are guilty or innocent, and to determine what amount of punishment the law awards to those that are found guilty. Arrangements have also to be made for giving effect to the punishments awarded by the Courts, and for reforming the offenders and preventing them, if possible, from again committing crimes. In a great many instances persons committing minor offences are dealt with summarily by a Magistrate. Among such offences are drunkenness, vagrancy, indecency, and being a rogue and a vagabond. In the case of juvenile offenders many crimes that could formerly have been dealt with only by a jury, may now be disposed of in a summary way before Magistrates.

### How Liberty of Individuals is secured.

On the whole, people are well protected in the following ways from possible injury through the action of the police and other officers engaged in giving effect to the law: All crimes are described by the law with the utmost exactness; in all cases the answer to the question, "Is such-and-such an action a crime?" must be "Yes" or "No." There may be some difficulty in finding the answer, but when it is found it must be in that form. The police have no kind of control over any one's actions if these actions are not a breach of the law. The police, and indeed private persons, may, without any warrant, arrest any person whom they *see* committing any felony, and the police may do so on suspicion. They are also, in certain cases of misdemeanour and offences punishable summarily, allowed to arrest without a warrant, but in other cases it is necessary to have a warrant from a Magistrate *before* apprehension. After his arrest a prisoner must be brought before a Magistrate for examination without unnecessary delay. At this examination the accuser must make out a case against the prisoner. If the police show gross carelessness or malice in falsely accusing a prisoner they can be punished. An action can be successfully brought against any one who maliciously, and without reasonable or probable cause, charges another person with a crime of which that person is innocent.

### Bail, and Precautions against Unnecessary Delay.

When a Magistrate has decided that a prisoner should be tried by a higher Court, he must take reasonable bail if the offence is not of too serious a kind: that is, if any one will answer for the prisoner's coming to the Court to be tried at the proper time, and will bind himself to pay a certain sum of money if the prisoner does not appear, the accused must be set at liberty till the trial comes on. If the prisoner cannot get bail the trial must not be put off too long, and the Government may not *at its own will* change the time of the trial. Besides these rules there is the Habeas Corpus Act, which threatens with heavy penalties any judge or gaoler who refuses to take the steps required by law to prevent a prisoner from being unlawfully kept in custody. The kind of protection thus afforded by English law has already been referred to in Chapter XXIX.

## Jury.

Then, again, the law endeavours to protect a prisoner from being wrongfully punished, by directing that he shall be tried by his peers (that is, by his equals). Accordingly, after a man has been examined by a Magistrate, who has decided that the charge against the prisoner has been so far proved that he ought to be tried by a higher Court; and a grand jury has decided, from consideration of the evidence given at the previous enquiry,* that the indictment against the prisoner is a true bill to which he should be called upon to plead, he is brought before a judge and a jury, who go fully into the case. The jury may be taken as representing the State as a whole; they are chosen almost at random, and are generally a fair sample of the people amongst whom the accused has lived. The jury are sworn to give, in accordance with the evidence, a true answer to the question, "Is the accused guilty or not guilty?" and they must all agree in giving their answer. Many people think that it is not a good plan to insist on complete agreement. It is to be supposed that, out of twelve men chosen at random, one at least may very possibly be inclined to give an untrue answer, or may be ignorant or altogether foolish.

*Questions to be decided at a Trial, and who decides them.*

There are two different questions to be decided in nearly every trial. The first of these is—(a) What is the law with regard to such an offence as is said to have been committed? The second is—(b) Has the accused person actually broken this law? This second question may present itself in three forms : (1.) Did the act by which the law is said to have been broken really occur? (2.) Is the prisoner the person that did the act? (3.) If the prisoner did the act, did he do it in such a way as to break the law?

Let us suppose that (a) has been decided, and that the answer to it is that the law that is supposed to have been

---

* A *presentment* may be in certain cases made to the grand jury without any previous enquiry.

19

broken is that a man must not *attempt* to shoot another man.
Then, if John is accused of attempting to shoot James, the
three questions are—(1.) Was a gun fired at James? (2.) Is
John the man.that fired it? (3.) If John fired the gun, did he
do it wilfully? Generally, all such questions as (*a*) are decided
by the judge, while such questions as (*b*), (1), (2), and (3), are left
to the jury: that is to say, the judge determines questions of
law, while the jury decide questions of fact. The judge states
what the law is, and the jury decide whether John has broken
it or not. Or sometimes the jury decide whether such-and-
such an act has been done, and the judge states the law with
regard to it.

But there is another question that often has to be answered
first of all—namely, What part of the question that has to be
decided is matter of law, and what matter of fact? Now,
the judge always has to decide this question, and we may expect
that as time goes on more and more matters will have to be
considered questions of law, and fewer and fewer will be considered questions of fact — that is, the work of the judge
will increase, and that of the jury grow less. The only way to
prevent this is to make laws as clear and plain as possible; if
the laws are not plain the judges may be actually driven to
make juries mere dummies. Trial by jury is said to have
many faults, but it is too old and too highly prized to be lightly
given up until it can be very clearly shown that there is something better to take its place. It is not at all certain that some
better plan of securing people's liberty cannot be found; but till
it is found most people will think that the old system should
be interfered with as little as possible.

### Punishments.

The question of punishments to be awarded to those who
have been found guilty of crimes has been already touched upon
in Chapter XXIII. It is sufficient to say here that this matter
is to a great extent left in the hands of the judge, for the law
very often mentions the greatest punishment that can be given
for a certain crime, but leaves it to the judge to say how much
smaller it may be. Very severe punishments generally have a
bad effect, because they turn the attention of the jury from the

question of the guilt or innocence of the person to the consideration of what he will have to suffer if they find him guilty. This may make them anxious to find every possible excuse for letting him off altogether. When the punishments given are not severe they are much more certain, and most writers on this subject now think that in almost all cases of first conviction light punishments are in all respects better than severe ones.

The crime of wilful murder is punished with death. This is hardly the place to consider whether such a punishment should be inflicted in any case. A great many people think of it, however, in this way: Murder is a wrong that cannot be redressed. Hanging the criminal does no good to the murdered man, and, besides, it takes away the murderer's chance of repenting. The State should not be revengeful : it should prevent the murderer from having a chance of ever repeating the crime, and there the State should stop. Much may be said in answer to this. It is the State's duty to prevent murder, and the fear of death will do very much to prevent a man from committing murder. It is quite true that when a man has made up his mind to kill another he thinks very little of the consequences, but there can be no doubt that in most cases fear of the consequences does prevent a man from making up his mind to commit the offence. It is true a murderer might be kept locked up till the end of his days, but as a matter of fact he very seldom is. It is very doubtful indeed whether it would not be more merciful to hang a man than to keep him living on as a thoroughly hopeless prisoner, and this is the only way in which the State can really secure itself against a repetition of the crime, except by killing the man that has committed it.

### Pardon.

The Crown has the right of pardoning an offender after he has been tried, found guilty, and sentenced by the Judge. This right is often wisely exercised in cases where, all circumstances being considered, the operation of the law has been too severe ; and this is the only way in which, when a mistake has been made and a person has been wrongly convicted, the sentence passed upon him can be reversed.

This, then, is a brief outline of what our law does with

persons accused of crimes. In our next chapter some account will be given of the rules of evidence and of the part that lawyers take in trials. We shall conclude the present chapter with a very short account of the way in which civil cases are managed—cases that are not concerned with crime.

### Civil Trials.

The whole of a civil trial may be divided into two parts. The first thing to be decided is, what is the real matter in dispute between the two *parties*. The person that says he has suffered a wrong, the *plaintiff*, makes a statement of his case, generally with the aid of a lawyer; the *defendant* answers this statement in the same way, till the real point in dispute is arrived at. Then comes in the Court's work of deciding whether the facts stated on either side are real facts, and whether there are any rules in existence that can be applied to the case. Here, as in criminal trials, the Judge says what the law is, and the jury decides whether the facts are as they are stated, and, in most cases, what damages, if any, the plaintiff is entitled to. In many instances the *party* that loses his case is allowed to appeal to a higher Court ; or he may apply for a new trial. He may not do this on the ground that the Judge has acted unfairly, but only on the ground that a mistake has been made either in law or in regard to facts.*

---

\* It should be stated that juries in civil cases may be composed of four or of twelve jurymen. Sometimes, when a case turns on a legal point, it is settled without the aid of a jury, on a case agreed upon and stated to the Court, argument being heard from both sides, and the Judge deciding. In civil cases juries are not required to give a unanimous verdict or any verdict at all. After they have considered the evidence for a certain time, and there is no chance of their being unanimous, a verdict of three-fourths of the jury will be received. If the jury cannot agree to a verdict in twelve hours, they may be discharged.

# CHAPTER XXXVIII.

## EVIDENCE; COSTS; COURTS; CODES. LAW CONCLUDED.

As soon as it has been found, in any case brought before a Court, what the real point in dispute is, some method is needed for finding, in the quickest, cheapest, and most certain way, the value of the statements made by the witnesses who have been called to give evidence in favour of the different views taken with regard to the disputed point. Such a method is to be found in a system called the rules of evidence.

### Rules of Evidence.

The objects of these rules are—(1) To make the work short and simple by shutting out all evidence that from its nature is worthless; and (2) to fix the way in which evidence must be taken so that it may be as useful as possible.

The first thing to be decided is, which side has to prove its statements *positively*. This is often decided by the state of the case when it comes into Court. If John states that James has received goods from him and has not paid him for them, and James admits this, but states that he has an equal claim against John for horse-hire, which John denies,—then James has to prove that his claim is a good one, and that it is equal to John's claim. But generally what are called legal presumptions decide on whom the burden of proof lies. Such presumptions are—If a will is in proper form and appears to have been properly witnessed and executed, it is a proper will; if the opposite side deny that it is a proper will they will have to prove that it is bad.—A prisoner is innocent in the eyes of the law until he is proved to be guilty: if John is charged with stealing sheep, he is not called upon to prove that sheep were not stolen, or that if they were stolen he was not the thief; his accusers must prove

that the sheep were stolen and that he stole them : but if he
had the sheep in his possession he would have to prove that he
got them lawfully.—A person having housebreaking-tools in his
possession intends to use them for an unlawful purpose.—If a
person is proved to have destroyed a written paper that he ought
to have produced, the reason is that it would have told against
him.—A person who holds "a bill" has given something in
exchange for it,—there has been a *consideration*.

When the question as to where the burden of proof lies has
been decided in accordance with these and similar rules, other
rules are applied to make the work as short and certain as possible. One old rule was that the evidence of persons that had an
interest in the result of the case could not be taken. At present
*interest* in the result of a case is not a ground of objection to a
witness, but it is a fair matter for comment by the other side.

Of course, all evidence that does not bear on the point in
dispute is refused. If the point to be decided were, whether a
certain horse now in John's possession belonged to James, it would
not be evidence if George said that John was not a proper person
to have a horse, seeing that he had been fined some years ago
for treating a horse cruelly. "Hearsay" evidence is generally
refused. If John swore that he saw James taking a horse out
of William's paddock the evidence would be received; but, if he
swore that he believed that James had taken the horse, because
Henry had told him so, the statement would not be accepted
by the Court. This kind of evidence, is refused for two good
reasons : first, because it rests to a large extent on the witness's
opinion as to whether he has been told the truth or not ; and,
secondly, because the person who really gives the evidence is not
in Court to be cross-questioned by the other side. Some kinds
of hearsay evidence, however, are received, such, for instance, as
reports of what has taken place in another Court. Another rule
is that the *best* evidence must be produced. For example, if
an agreement to sell a horse has been made in writing, word-of-
mouth or what is called *parol* evidence that such an agreement
had been made would not be taken. Again, evidence with regard
to the nature of a receipt for money paid would not be received
unless there was very good reason why the receipt itself could
not be produced.

## How Evidence is taken.

We must now say a few words about the manner in which the evidence of witnesses is taken. The best plan is that of subjecting the witnesses to examination in open Court, the examination being followed by cross-examination. Cross-examination is used to discover the reasons for the witnesses' answers, and to show whether the answers are worthy of belief. In cross-examination leading questions may be put, but in examination-in-chief they may not. A leading question takes such a form as this : "Did you not look through the window and see the prisoner setting fire to a heap of paper placed near the wall?" This is called a leading question, because it is plainly intended to lead the witness to say "Yes." Evidence is generally taken on oath, but persons who object to make oath may now be required to *affirm*. Many people entirely object to the use of oaths in Courts; they think that oaths cannot bind people who do not mind taking a false oath if it seems safe to do so, and that those who would not take a false oath would almost certainly not tell a direct lie. They believe, too, that it is irreverent to invoke the Sacred Name when the object is perhaps to settle some petty quarrel between neighbours. Perhaps oaths really are useless in the case of truthful people, and fail to make liars tell the truth. In any case, it is clear that the punishments now inflicted for perjury or false swearing could be just as easily attached to telling lies in a Court of justice. There is a kind of difficulty that often occurs in Courts. Doctors and others are called to give evidence about matters that judges and juries cannot be expected to understand. In these cases the rule is that a *skilled witness's* evidence may be believed in matters relating to his own art. Where there is opposing evidence in such cases it is often difficult for the Court to find which is the more worthy of belief.

## Lawyers and Advocacy.

Law is a very large and difficult subject, and it would take any man several years to get even such a moderate knowledge of it as would enable him, if any one did him a wrong, or accused him of doing a wrong, to set about getting himself put right in the proper way. There is an old and very true saying, that a man who is his own lawyer has a fool for his client. Suppose that a man has a claim brought against him which he considers altogether unjust: if he determined to resist this claim, he would have to find out how the Court business was conducted and what had to be done in his own particular case; to get together all the evidence in his own favour and to learn the weak points in his opponent's case; he would have to state his facts in a plain and simple way so as to show that he was right and his opponent wrong; and he would have to know what rules of law were in his own favour, and to show that those that his opponent relied on were insufficient. Not one untrained man in a thousand could manage such a business: if such a man came into Court he would afford the clearest proof of the truth of the old saying; he would look, and indeed be, a very fool as far as his case was concerned. Nothing could help him unless the judge took pity on him and spent a great deal of time in trying to get to the bottom of the matter. Now, this is just what a judge cannot do unless under very extraordinary circumstances. If this kind of work were a judge's duty, perhaps a hundred judges would not be able to get through all the cases now dealt with in the New Zealand Courts. It will be seen therefore that lawyers and advocates who do the work of arranging and conducting cases in Court are most useful people, and that we could not well do without them. Some people think that the work done by lawyers is immoral—that to make the worse appear the better cause is, and always must be, wrong. No one admits the truth of this latter statement more fully than lawyers themselves, and if they see one of their number making it a business to take up bad cases and make them appear to be good ones they look upon him as mean, and unworthy to belong to their profession. It should be borne in mind that it is only in very few cases that all the right or all the wrong is on one side, and that were it not for the aid of lawyers it would be often quite impossible to decide how the least wrong might be done.

## Costs.

The Great Charter says that justice is not to be sold; and it may be asked why a man should have to pay the costs of a suit if he loses his case. It is, in many cases, through the fault of the law itself, which it is the State's work to make perfect, that things are so mixed up as to render it a long or a troublesome business to find what the law is. It may be true that the law is faulty only because the task of making a set of plain and easily understood laws that would meet every case is so difficult that no State can perform it properly; but, plainly, the State has no right to make the unfortunate person that has been proved to be least able to understand the law, bear the whole cost of a failure caused by the State's being unable to make plain and simple laws. It may be said in reply to this that in the great majority of cases it is not the law that is in question, but the facts; that these must be stated and proved by witnesses or other testimony; that it is this statement and proof that form the principal part of the expense; and that in very many cases disputes are not caused by real uncertainty either with regard to law or facts, but by the perversity of individuals, and that it is not a matter for regret when the penalty for such perversity takes the shape of the costs of a lawsuit. It may also be urged that the costliness of law makes people very careful not to commit wrongs, for they know that if they do commit them they may have to pay heavily for it. The expense tends also to prevent people from constantly going to law about trifles.

There is, however, one very sound objection to the system of costs : a rich man may get redress when a poor man cannot ; a poor man may have to put up with a wrong that a rich man could easily get righted. This objection is being gradually met in various ways—by making the law simpler and plainer, by reducing costs, by allowing important cases to be tried in the cheaper Courts, and by various other means that need not be mentioned here ; but perhaps it would, on the whole, be an improvement if at any rate costs of Court were quite done away with.

### Courts.

Courts are of different ranks, so to speak. In New Zealand, for instance, we have Wardens' Courts, and Resident Magistrates' Courts, District Courts, the Supreme Court, and the Court of Appeal. The great majority of cases brought into Court are of a very simple character, the facts being easy to discover, and the rules of law referring to them very plain. Other cases are more difficult and important; and some could not be properly settled in any but the highest Court, seeing that they are of such a character as to render it necessary to decide points that have not come up before, or to apply old laws to new kinds of cases. Now, the decisions given in such cases will afterwards become part of the law, and it is therefore most important that they should be dealt with by the wisest Judges and the cleverest lawyers that can be found. Perhaps it would be well to make all cases begin in a lower Court, so that they might be settled there if possible, and reach the highest Court only after the lower Courts had proved themselves unable to deal with them. In criminal cases the right of appeal might be allowed to the Crown as well as to the prisoner.

### Codes of Law.

We have seen that there are really three principal ways in which law comes into existence. Our Parliament makes laws, or statutes, as they are called; customs gradually arise in the State, judges have to take these into account, and gradually they become law too; lastly, we have seen that a great deal of our law has come into existence through the mode of working the law itself. These three kinds of law are to be found not only in our own but in every State, and in some countries it has been at certain periods thought desirable to gather together all the laws or a great part of them, and to form them into collections called Codes. In Rome, in very early times, such a code was made, and it was called the Laws of the Twelve Tables, because the laws were written on great slabs, which were set up in the Market-place, where everybody could see them. Many centuries after another famous code was made by one of the Roman Emperors. This is much admired and studied even at the present day. Napoleon did at least one good thing for France : he, with the aid of the ablest lawyers, had a code drawn up, which has made both law and justice much easier to get in France than it is in most countries. The work of forming a Code of Criminal Law has also been going on in New Zealand for many years, and it is perhaps not impossible that the work of putting the whole of the law into a code will be undertaken sooner or later. It might, then, be worth while to ask what are the chief advantages to be gained from such a code, and, also, how the disadvantages connected with it may be overcome. The principal advantage to be derived from a code is that the law would no longer be hidden away in musty books or in lawyers' heads, and that every man who wanted to get a clear idea of what the law on any particular point was would be able to do so by simply turning to the chapter that referred to the subject about which he wished to obtain information, instead of having to look for that information in vain, as is the case while the laws are so mixed up and confused that no one but a trained lawyer can understand them. A code would not make every man his own lawyer, but it would enable a man to get some idea of the work that his lawyer had to do for him. It is true that a code made in one age becomes in some respects unfit for the next age; but then, it enables everybody to see what changes are needed, and prevents the law from going on for centuries becoming more and more unsuited for 'the people whose lives it is supposed to regulate. Any custom that is decidedly bad will, if it is authorised in a code, be soon got rid of, because everybody will object to it. Thus the law will constantly be getting changed for the better. The law will be easier to understand, it will be better known and much more certain, and people will have less occasion to go to law, seeing that the cases in which they can make mistakes about their rights will be far fewer than they are now. Some writers on this subject seem to think that the laws will be changed so frequently that much evil will result. They believe, rightly, that no real experiments can be made in law-making, for if a bad law is once passed it becomes part of the whole system, and people soon get into the way of obeying it; therefore, they say, make as few changes as possible. But this seems to be a case in which a line must be drawn between constant change and no change at all. The proper drawing of the line must, like so many other things, depend on the wisdom and prudence of the members of the State, or, rather, of those who are appointed by them to make and administer the laws. At any rate, it cannot be wise to prevent the alteration of bad laws. It is true that the changes may not do very much good; but then, again, they may. Laws known to be bad can produce only bad effects.

### Conclusion.

We may well conclude this portion of our work by stating what the functions and character of law are, almost in the words of the writer from whom many of the best ideas expressed in this part of the book have been obtained : What steadies man and keeps him to his purpose, protecting all from the defects of each, and defending each against the pressure of all; kind and yet stern; standing for the past, the present, and the future; commanding all, yet whispering to each—is LAW.

# PART V.—THE LESSONS OF HISTORY.

## CHAPTER XXXIX.

### THE FUTURE.—WHAT TO AVOID.—CAUSES OF THE DECAY OF NATIONS.

In the previous chapters we have tried to show how State life begins, to describe the growth of a State, and to give a clear idea of what our own State actually is and does. We have given a pretty full account of the various means by which the work of the State is done and its life is maintained, and have endeavoured to explain why it is that the conditions under which we live are just what they are and not altogether different, and to show what results spring from one kind of social conditions and what from another. We have set forth the principal State customs and laws, both those that have come into being through the growth of the State, and those that the State has purposely instituted in order to secure its own safety, along with the welfare and progress of the individual men, women, and children that are members of it.

In order to do our work properly, we have often had to refer to the past, even to ages long gone by : by this means we have sometimes found it possible to explain things that we should have been unable to account for if we had kept our minds fixed on the present time and on the things that we see going on around us. We have now done with the present; what we wished to say about it has been said, and all that remains for us to do is to try to learn from the past a few more lessons that may serve as guides in the future. It is seldom either wise or safe to speak with certainty about what is going to happen : no one can know exactly what will come to pass next. "All the world's a stage," and Time is the great scene-shifter. No one can take Time's place. In social matters things do not occur twice in exactly the same way; similar events take place under altered circumstances, and the circumstances change so quickly that we cannot take proper account of them. If we could, it would probably be possible to foretell State changes just as it is possible to indicate the very minute when the next total eclipse of the sun will take place. But the sailor, though he cannot forecast the weather with any great certainty, expects and prepares for a dreadful storm when he hears the wind sullenly moaning afar off, and feels the rise and fall of his vessel as she is moved by a mighty swell; when he sees the black clouds gathering in the sky, and observes that the mercury in his barometer is all the while sinking rapidly—just because he has formerly seen storms follow these threatening signs. So we, by reviewing the past, and carefully noting what has happened when States have fallen into certain conditions, may learn what we ought to do and what we ought to avoid. We, too, like the sailor, are making a voyage, and our ship is the State. Our voyage, it is true, is a very long one and the crew will often change as time goes on, and we are all the while travelling from the past that we know something of to the future that we know nothing of: it is not a journey from one well-known port to another that we are making; it is really a voyage of discovery. But these features of our expedition render it all the more necessary that we should endeavour to obtain those things that can give us the most useful help. These are—wisdom, skill, and prudence based on knowledge gained through studying the histories of similar voyages. Let us, then, call in the aid of history, which contains our ship's log-book, along with those of similar ships, and see where and how some of the greatest dangers have been met with by other ships going on such voyages: especially let us try to find out why so many of these State ships have had to lie at anchor for long periods, till, in fact, they have become rotten and useless; and how it is that so many others have gone down with all hands on board.

### The Lesson that Egypt teaches.

Of all the nations of the world, Egypt has the longest history. During the last hundred years learned men have been

gradually finding out how to read and understand the writings
of the ancient Egyptian people. These writings have taught us
a great deal that is well worth knowing. We can here only
just glance at one or two points. Some five thousand years ago
Egypt was already a great nation. Under a king named Seno-
feru, who reigned about that time, the great mass of the
people, though poor, were happy. The rulers of Egypt had not
yet learned to consider the lower classes as being of no importance. No sign of regular training for war or of the existence
of a class of fighting men is to be found in the records of that
period. The greatest men of the age spent their time in
attending to the culture of the soil, and in directing the different handicrafts of the people. But even then a permanent
governing class was growing up, and this class was by-and-by to
help to bring the country to ruin. About fifteen hundred years
after this, or three thousand five hundred years ago, Egypt
reached the greatest height to which she has ever attained; but
now causes of decay had come into existence, and had already
increased to so great an extent as to cause her soon to fall
very rapidly from her lofty position. In the reign of Aahmes
Egypt had become a great military State. The war-horse had
become the most important animal. Egypt was no longer a
nation of farmers; she had become a nation of soldiers. The
governing classes and the priests had greatly increased in numbers. All offices were given by the King's favour. Justice
could no longer be obtained. No gentleman worked with his
hands. The mass of the people had very hard times; their
work was to pay taxes, to serve as common soldiers, or to erect
public buildings. As might have been expected, the heart was
soon eaten out of the nation. The power of Egypt appeared
to increase for a time, but all at once the nation began to
topple over—the head was too weighty for the weak body to
carry; its rise had been slow, but its fall was rapid, and it fell
to rise no more. That is to say, Egypt has never again been a
good country for the mass of the people; a time when it could be
said that the people, even though poor, were happy, has never
come again. Occasionally, indeed, the nation has regained something of its former splendour—generally under foreign rulers—
but it has never since been a happy nation. At present, through

has been now lying at anchor for more than two thousand years, and, as far as we can judge, has become thoroughly unseaworthy. It may be that China's condition is ,to some extent owing to the system of competition that exists in the country. Success in China means success at examinations. Men can do only so much work; if all the cleverest men in a country spend their lives in preparing for examinations in history and literature, they can have neither time nor strength for studying what is going on around them, and for trying to make the future better than the past.

### India.

India is and ever has been a grand country, and it is inhabited by an intelligent and keen-witted people; but the people of India have always been divided into sects and castes, unable or unwilling to combine for the common good. India therefore has been an easy prey to foreign conquerors. Her people, never having been able to make good their claim to the produce of their labour, have always had enough to do to pay the taxes needed to satisfy the greed of these conquerors and to pay rent to the classes that have established a right to the greater part of the produce of the land. While engaged in this work the people of India have had no opportunity of attending to such matters as the prevention of the famines which occur every few years and sweep off millions of the inhabitants. Perhaps England may in the end be able to do what she now earnestly desires to do—to teach the people of India how they may become fit to be freemen, and to be free as England's own people are free. England is now perhaps more anxious to do this than she was formerly, through having been herself taught, by a wide-spread and dangerous mutiny among the Sepoys, that governing an intelligent but down-trodden nation is not quite the safest kind of work. For a great number of years, while India was governed by a body called the East India Company, England taught India nothing except that a weak and divided multitude can expect but little consideration at the hands of a wealthy ruling class anxious to become still more wealthy; even if the nation as a whole, of which this class forms part, loves freedom and hates tyranny. Perhaps the English people generally got too much into the way of looking upon India as a country from which much wealth could be obtained, and as a place to which young men could be sent to make their fortunes. Perhaps also Englishmen forgot or did not know that this wealth and these fortunes could be obtained only out of the produce of the labour of a half-starved people. It must not be thought that England has been more unjust than other nations. It is quite the other way. Peoples that have come under the control of England have probably been better treated by her than they would have been by any other nation. But it generally takes nations a very long time to learn to be merciful and thoroughly just to races that are weaker than themselves—to treat a weaker people, for instance, as the English have treated the Maoris.

### France.

In the last century the people of France—although their country, taking it altogether, is one of the most productive in the world—had been reduced to great poverty and misery, partly by the long wars with England and other countries, undertaken chiefly to please the vanity of the King, Louis XIV.; partly by the extravagance and waste that prevailed in France under the government of Louis XV. and his favourites ; and partly by the luxury and idleness of the nobles. The lower and middle classes had had to pay the whole of the cost of this folly and wickedness of the kings and the nobles, without ever being allowed to take part in the management of affairs, and had had besides to put up with numerous hardships and vexations which it is not necessary to mention here. The condition of the mass of the lower class of French people had become most pitiable. Everybody saw that a change must take place; and at first nearly everybody tried to make the change gradual and safe. This was impossible. The injustice of centuries had to be swept away, and at once. The oppressed became for a time the oppressors, and, unfortunately, the innocent were too often punished with the guilty. At last, however, after passing through a terrible revolution, and a perhaps still more terrible despotism, France was saved, but in such a way as to teach us that a State is in very great danger when one class has run up a long bill that another class has to pay by making great sacrifices.

heavy taxation, forced labour, and useless war, the mass of the people of Egypt are in a pitiable condition.

## Greece.

Athens was once the leading State of the world, not indeed in power and wealth,—though she was able, almost alone, for a considerable time to keep the gigantic power of Persia at bay, and afterwards, with the assistance of Sparta, another Greek State, to humble it to the dust,—but in the nobler fields of manners, thought, and the fine arts. In these she was mistress and teacher of the nations. She and her sister States fell through petty local jealousies and distrust. Each province, and especially Athens, wished to be the first ; and each envied the success of the others. Had all the States of Greece, belonging as they did to one noble and highly-gifted race, combined and formed one powerful State, they might have ruled the world, and have civilised it long ago. As it was, they spent their strength in petty squabbles, and they sank at last, to rise no more.

## Rome.

Rome ruled the world for ages, and did very much to civilise it. She fell through two principal causes. First, her freemen allowed their love of party to become greater than their love for the State : the result was that the power which the people had gained after many a valiant struggle with a governing class fell first into the hands of individuals such as Sulla, Marius, Pompey, and Cæsar, and the Emperors who followed them, and by-and-by into the hands of the soldiers, most of them foreigners. The other, and perhaps the true and original, cause was the action of bad land-laws, and the failure of all attempts to really change them for the better. The Roman State was formed by the union of great families or clans. At first the State held a considerable part of the land, and received rent for it from those who made use of it. But much of the land belonged to the clans : part of this was treated as common, and some of it was portioned out as private property. The quantity of land thus disposed of was small. About an acre and a quarter became the private property of each household. By-and-by, however, a class of great landowners grew up. Lands were continually being acquired by conquest from neighbouring peoples : these were supposed to be retained as State lands, unless parts of them were distributed by the State itself; but, usually, large portions fell at last into the hands of wealthy individuals. Then, again, the Roman laws regarding debt were very severe, and, if a small landowner owed his neighbour money and could not pay it, the land would have to be handed over to satisfy the debt. Thus, in one way and another, through want of watchfulness on the part of the State, individuals gained possession of, or in some cases a claim to the use of, considerable portions of the State lands as well as of the lands of the clans. The lands were, to a large extent, worked with slave labour, the slaves often being prisoners taken in war. Many attempts were made to break down this system. Laws were passed limiting the quantity of State land that a single citizen might hold, and the number of cattle and sheep that he might run on the State commons. But these excellent laws were allowed to fall into disuse, and the bad customs, being at last recognised by the Courts and winked at by the State, gradually came to have the full force of laws. Thus it came about that immense estates swallowed up the small farms around them, and before very long Rome was ready to fall. Through these bad laws, enormous wealth and great poverty grew up side by side. The wealthy landowners became the slaves of luxury, idleness, selfishness, and vice ; and the old farmer-soldiers and their descendants had to crowd into Rome, where they gradually became a degraded city-population that had to be supported and amused with means supplied to a large extent by the tribute paid to Rome by foreign countries. Thus at last Rome fell because there were no real Romans of the old stamp left.

### China.

China was a great nation when England was still peopled by savages. She is a great nation still, but no improvement takes place in her condition. The Chinese long ago came to believe that they knew everything worth knowing, and that no good was to be got from contact with other nations. By discouraging foreign trade and keeping themselves to themselves the Chinese stopped the progress of their State ship, which

20

has been now lying at anchor for more than two thousand years, and, as far as we can judge, has become thoroughly unseaworthy. It may be that China's condition is .to some extent owing to the system of competition that exists in the country. Success in China means success at examinations. Men can do only so much work; if all the cleverest men in a country spend their lives in preparing for examinations in history and literature, they can have neither time nor strength for studying what is going on around them, and for trying to make the future better than the past.

### India.

India is and ever has been a grand country, and it is inhabited by an intelligent and keen-witted people; but the people of India have always been divided into sects and castes, unable or unwilling to combine for the common good. India therefore has been an easy prey to foreign conquerors. Her people, never having been able to make good their claim to the produce of their labour, have always had enough to do to pay the taxes needed to satisfy the greed of these conquerors and to pay rent to the classes that have established a right to the greater part of the produce of the land. While engaged in this work the people of India have had no opportunity of attending to such matters as the prevention of the famines which occur every few years and sweep off millions of the inhabitants. Perhaps England may in the end be able to do what she now earnestly desires to do—to teach the people of India how they may become fit to be freemen, and to be free as England's own people are free. England is now perhaps more anxious to do this than she was formerly, through having been herself taught, by a wide-spread and dangerous mutiny among the Sepoys, that governing an intelligent but down-trodden nation is not quite the safest kind of work. For a great number of years, while India was governed by a body called the East India Company, England taught India nothing except that a weak and divided multitude can expect but little consideration at the hands of a wealthy ruling class anxious to become still more wealthy; even if the nation as a whole, of which this class forms part, loves freedom and hates tyranny. Perhaps the English people generally got too much into the way of looking upon India as a country from which much wealth could be obtained, and as a place to which young men could be sent to make their fortunes. Perhaps also Englishmen forgot or did not know that this wealth and these fortunes could be obtained only out of the produce of the labour of a half-starved people. It must not be thought that England has been more unjust than other nations. It is quite the other way. Peoples that have come under the control of England have probably been better treated by her than they would have been by any other nation. But it generally takes nations a very long time to learn to be merciful and thoroughly just to races that are weaker than themselves—to treat a weaker people, for instance, as the English have treated the Maoris.

*France.*

In the last century the people of France—although their country, taking it altogether, is one of the most productive in the world—had been reduced to great poverty and misery, partly by the long wars with England and other countries, undertaken chiefly to please the vanity of the King, Louis XIV.; partly by the extravagance and waste that prevailed in France under the government of Louis XV. and his favourites ; and partly by the luxury and idleness of the nobles. The lower and middle classes had had to pay the whole of the cost of this folly and wickedness of the kings and the nobles, without ever being allowed to take part in the management of affairs, and had had besides to put up with numerous hardships and vexations which it is not necessary to mention here. The condition of the mass of the lower class of French people had become most pitiable. Everybody saw that a change must take place ; and at first nearly everybody tried to make the change gradual and safe. This was impossible. The injustice of centuries had to be swept away, and at once. The oppressed became for a time the oppressors, and, unfortunately, the innocent were too often punished with the guilty. At last, however, after passing through a terrible revolution, and a perhaps still more terrible despotism, France was saved, but in such a way as to teach us that a State is in very great danger when one class has run up a long bill that another class has to pay by making great sacrifices.

(*k.*) From the Government's making things dear when they might be cheap.

(*l.*) From the State's treating any class unjustly, either by imposing special burdens on them or by granting them special privileges.

Many readers may be surprised at finding no mention made here of the *positive check* referred to in Chapter XXI., and they may be inclined to think that the greatest and most frequent cause of danger to a State—*over-population*—has been wrongly omitted. The fact of the matter is that history does not teach us that over-population has ever really been a cause of danger to any considerable State. Reason teaches us that over-population might be a cause of terrible danger, but we learn from history that long before Nature's check to the increase of the number of people can even begin to work at all, much less to cause danger to any community that deserves to be called a State, man himself invents some means of checking this growth. This has been the case with both India and Ireland, for example ; for, though both of these countries are quite as well fitted for supporting a dense population as England is, neither of them is half so densely peopled.* We may say, then, that, while over-population is a very possible cause of danger, history has as yet given us no reason to say that it has been the actual cause of danger to any considerable State.

---

* England has about one person for every acre and a half, India one person for every three and a half acres, and Ireland not one person for every four acres. Even China has not one inhabitant for every two acres.

# PART VI.—INDIVIDUAL CONDUCT.

## CHAPTER XL.

### RIGHT CONDUCT OF THE INDIVIDUAL IS NECESSARY FOR THE WELFARE OF THE STATE.

Though a machine may be skilfully planned and have all its parts well constructed, yet unless the material of which it is made is good the machine is sure to break down before it has been very long in use. So, no form of government can work well unless the members of the State who have to live under it are intelligent and well-behaved. Well-devised laws and sensible customs will do much to secure right conduct; but something more than these is needed : the members of the State must have right motives if the laws and customs are to produce good results. If the members of the State have wrong motives, they will do what is right only when they think that right conduct will, on the whole, pay them better than wrong conduct.

*What is the Best Motive, and how are we to find it ?*

In this book we have already dealt pretty fully with laws and customs. In this, the final chapter, we are to say a few words about the motives that govern individual conduct, and to attempt to indicate the kind of motive that is most likely to make individual conduct tend towards the highest welfare of the State.

The question that we have to try to answer is a very important and difficult one. It is this : What is the *best* motive, and how are we to find it? How shall a man decide what he ought to do, and also why he ought to do it? By *motive* we mean that prevailing impulse to action which, whether it be the result of habits or the cause of their being formed, is the guide that regulates a man's conduct.

## Will the Consideration of Man's own Nature lead to the Discovery of the Best Motive ?

Experience has taught us that when we are searching for anything that we want it is generally well to see if that thing is close at hand, before we go to distant places to look for it. If a man wants his knife the first thing that he does is to put his hand into his pocket and feel if it is there. Let us also, in our search for the *best motive*, examine ourselves and see whether there is anything in our own nature that will enable us to decide what this best motive is. If we fail there, we must look for it in the outside world, in the circumstances that surround us ; if we cannot find it even there, we shall have to conclude that it must be found, if at all, in that mysterious region which lies outside of the area that our ordinary senses can take account of.

## Is our Desire to find Pleasure and avoid Pain the Best Motive ?

In the first place, then, let us consider what it is that generally makes a man act in one way rather than in another—what really seems to be the most powerful motive. It seems certain that man is, to a very great extent, ruled by two sovereigns, whose names are Pleasure and Pain.* Pleasure tells him what to do ; Pain tells him what to avoid. There can be no doubt that when a man is called upon to decide between two courses of conduct these two things, pleasure and pain, do very often decide the question for him. You should bear in mind, however, that when we use the words *pleasure* and *pain* we do not intend them to stand for real things. If we say that certain actions give pleasure to one man and pain to another, we mean that these actions are likely to cause pleasant *feelings* to the one and painful *feelings* to the other. Thus, in speaking of pleasure and pain, we refer to the sensations or emotions of the person affected by them, rather than to the object or action that causes them. Suppose, for example, that a man has fallen into the habit of drinking spirits. He knows that drink-

---

* Some writers think that Pleasure and Pain are absolute sovereigns, that they tell us what we must do, and that, in fact, we always obey them to the best of our ability. If this is so, it is useless to enquire what we *ought* to do. If I *must* do a certain thing it is a mere waste of time and trouble to enquire whether I *ought* to do it or not.

ing a certain quantity of rum will satisfy for a time the craving that he has for strong drink, and that the taste of the liquor and the excitement will give him a certain amount of pleasure ; and he knows well enough that pain will follow—bodily pain in the shape of severe headache, and mental pain in the shape of shame and sorrow for his folly. *You* understand that the pain will be altogether greater than the pleasure. But *he*, with his appetite and faculties disordered by his drunken habits, feels that the pleasure will, on the whole, be greater than the pain. The man's judgment is set wrong by his disordered appe-tites, but he acts in accordance with it. He places a couple of impostors on the thrones of Pleasure and Pain ; but when once they are there he becomes their loyal subject. It seems quite clear that the conduct of men is very largely determined in this kind of way ; but, happily, only few choose their sovereigns so very unwisely as the drunkard does, and, of course, the wiser the choice is the better the conduct will be. Let us remember, then, that, if it is true that pleasure and pain rule us—that the desire to get pleasure and to avoid pain is in very many cases our principal motive—their rule can bring good to us and to the State only in proportion to our *knowledge* and our wisdom.

Here, then, we have a very powerful motive. Is it the very best that we can find, or is it even always the most powerful ? Do we always say, " Let us try to get as much pleasure and avoid as much pain as we can, and seek for no other or higher motive," or *ought* we to say this ? The only answer is, If we can find no better motive we must be content with this, and be like the beasts of the field ; but, at all events, it seems to be worth our while to attempt to discover a better and nobler one.

*Does a Consideration of our Moral Sense lead us to the*
*Discovery of the Best Motive ?*

In order to do this, let us consider some instance of what all will allow to be good conduct, and try to find out the motive that leads to it. A not very uncommon case will answer the purpose best. It often happens that a wife who has been brought up in luxury, and has been used to have all her wants supplied with very little effort on her part, will, if she finds that her husband's health is suffering through the hard work that he has to perform, deny herself all the comforts and enjoyments to which she has been accustomed, in order that she may lighten her husband's work and at the same time allow her children to get a good education. In such a case, it may be said, it is merely " pleasure and pain " that give the motive, and the wife acts as she does because she feels that it gives her more pleasure to do what she considers right in helping her husband and her children than it would to continue to live as she did before, but with the feeling that she was doing wrong in allowing her husband and children to suffer in order that she might feel no discomfort.

This is true enough as far as it goes, but it suggests this further question : How has this feeling of pleasure in right-doing and of pain in wrong-doing come into existence? Whence did it come to us? The answer will probably be that man has a moral sense that urges him to do what he considers right, and to refrain from doing what he considers wrong ; that to act in opposition to his moral sense gives pain, just as acting in opposition to the sense of feeling by putting one's hand into the fire gives pain. If we now ask where this sense came from, we shall most likely be told that it has *grown up* in this way : In the earliest ages men found that some actions caused pleasure to the actor and to other people, while others produced pain ; and thus actions of the former kind came to be considered good, and those of the latter kind bad. As time went on, this mode of distinguishing conduct became part of man's nature through the habit having been transmitted from parents to children, and at last man came to feel that he *ought* to do certain things, and to refrain from doing certain other things—to have a sense of right and wrong, just as he has a sense that enables him to distinguish between a hurtful and a wholesome smell—and to feel *pleasure* in doing *right* and *pain* in doing *wrong*. It is easy to understand that those people whose actions were on the whole pleasant and beneficial to the largest number of people would have the greatest tendency to live and thrive, while those whose actions were of an opposite kind would have a tendency to be crushed out. Thus, then, men would gradually get, along with their moral sense of right and wrong, a desire to make their conduct pleasing and beneficial to the greatest number possible. Now, quite evidently, this desire would be a motive hardly differing from that caused by "pleasure and pain;" and, as in the case of a motive directly depending on pleasure and pain, it is plain that the usefulness, to us and to the State, of the moral sense and the resulting desire depends entirely on our *knowledge* of what is good and what is bad for ourselves and for others. We have now to learn, therefore, how far the amount of knowledge that we actually possess is able to assist our moral sense by showing us what kind of conduct is most likely to be beneficial to the State and to individuals.

*Is not the Desire to do the Greatest Amount of Good to the Greatest Number really the Best Motive?*

But some people have thought that a man *ought* to desire to do what he believes will produce the greatest good to the greatest number—that is, what he has learnt to endeavour to do while acquiring his moral sense—and that this is not only a sufficient, but also the best motive. Now, many writers have believed that a man may best help the greatest number to obtain the greatest happiness, and so do the greatest good to the State, by fully exercising all his own faculties as far as he can do so while thoroughly suiting himself to the circumstances that surround him—that the less he is like a fish out of water the better it will be for him and for other people, and the more he will be doing what he *ought* to do. Can we then find here that best motive that we are searching for? Certainly not. There is perhaps hardly a motive at all. We have here merely a statement of what men have been compelled to do, and what a man must continue to do if he wishes to live as long and as *comfortably* as possible. The doctrine that a man's motive should be a desire to gain and to give as much happiness as he can, and that he can produce the greatest measure of happiness by trying to suit himself to his surroundings, amounts to this: If a man is to be as useful and comfortable as his faculties and circumstances will allow him to be, he must try to be as like other people as possible, to offend nobody, to sneak through life as quietly as he can, and to believe that everything is going on in the best possible way; and he must carefully abstain from thinking about such a thing as progress. This is the only kind of motive that is to be got out of the doctrine.

What we want to learn is, what kind of motive a man ought to set before himself as the best; how a man may best kill the evil will that is in him, if it is evil, and get the good will; how he ought to shape his constant painful strivings to be different from what he is, so that he may attain to that which is *best*. The doctrine of "the greatest good to the greatest number" in all its forms only tells us, in a rather loose kind of way, without hinting what happiness is, that our aim must be to give the greatest happiness to the greatest number; and in one of its forms it tells us, without any warrant whatever, that if we act according to our lights, and leave others at liberty to do the same, each will secure for himself the greatest happiness that is possible for him. Now, it is probably very true that in the end the best motive, if we could find it, would lead up to the greatest happiness of the greatest number; but the principle is quite useless as a motive or as a rule of conduct for men so ignorant as the best informed of us are, though it might serve well enough for beings of a higher order, gifted with far greater powers than we possess of learning what in the end will produce happiness and what will not, and of determining whether leaving every man to do what pleases himself will really bring the greatest possible happiness to the greatest number. We do not object to the "greatest happiness" principle, and cannot; a great part of this book is based upon it—that is, we have been endeavouring throughout to discover how the greatest happiness to the greatest number is or may be produced. All that we say is that there is no reason to believe that this principle can, by itself, yield us the best motive for individual conduct, or, indeed, any true motive at all.

*The Greatest-happiness Principle gives us no Sufficient Motive, but it may put us on the Right Track.*

But there is one thing that it does : it helps us to feel certain that we have the right clue, the clue that will lead us to discover the right answer to our question, or rather to find out that such an answer is not obtainable by this method. For, on making trial of our knowledge, we find that our ignorance as to what will be the final results of a certain course of conduct is in most cases so profound that we are quite prevented by it from giving any but the most vague and useless answers to such questions as "What ought a man to do in order to cause the greatest amount of happiness to as many people as possible?" Really, about the most suitable answer that we in our present condition are able to give to the question is, "The best he can according to his judgment, provided that he does not interfere with other people's doing the best they can according to their judgment." And this answer gives for our purpose about the same amount of information as a man who wanted to know the size of a certain stone would derive from being told that it was as large as a lump of chalk. Our imperfect knowledge, therefore, or possibly our complete ignorance, about the ultimate results of certain kinds of conduct prevents our answering this question in any satisfactory manner.

*The Possession of Perfect Knowledge would probably make the Motives referred to effective; but we have no such Perfect Knowledge.*

There is, in fact, only one way by which man can hope ever to be able through the ordinary action of his faculties to get a satisfactory answer to our main question, and that is by increasing his *knowledge* and his powers of using it. By very careful observation of the sun, moon, and planets, and by equally careful study of what was observed, astronomers found out the law that binds the heavenly bodies together, and are now able to state it in very few words. It may be that similar careful observation of man and society will by-and-by enable men to give an equally brief and trustworthy answer to the question, "What ought a man to do, and why ought he to do it?" It is certain that this is the only way in which a really useful answer can come to man through his own unassisted work. It seems equally certain that man is at least as far from obtaining such an amount and kind of knowledge as a dog is from possessing a sound knowledge of algebra. But even if man's knowledge were *perfect* it is not certain that he would be guided by it, though it is probable that he would. If perfect knowledge does not lead to perfect action, the question, "Why should a man do what he knows to be best?" would still have to be answered.

*These Considerations lead to the Conclusion that the Best Motive
must come to us, if we can get it at all, from the Region that
lies beyond the Boundaries of our present Knowledge.*

Is it, then, quite impossible, from consideration of our own
nature, or of the circumstances by which we are surrounded,
to find the best motive on which to base a general rule of
conduct? Yes; at present it seems to be impossible to determine that motive by such means. For two thousand years
many of the ablest of men have been trying to find it. Scores
of motives have been suggested, but no one of these has been
proved to be the *best*, or has been received as such by even the
greater number of sensible men.*

*Though the Method considered will not yield the Answer to the
Question, "What ought a Man to do?" it does not at all
follow that one cannot be obtained by some other Method.*

But, although it appears to be impossible to find a proper
answer to the questions, "What ought a man to do?" and
"Why ought he to do it?" either by considering the nature
of man himself or that of the world in which he lives, it
does not in the least follow that no such answer can be
found anywhere. Millions of people are ready to declare
that they have got such an answer by an altogether different
method, and have found it thoroughly trustworthy through
life, and in hours when the dark shadow of death has come over
them; and it would be extremely unwise to assume, without
very careful enquiry, that these people have no ground for their
belief, especially when it is considered that some of those who
have held this belief have done much of the best work that the
world has ever seen. It does not come within the scope of this
book to refer to answers of this kind, or to the way in which it is
said that they can be obtained; but it is quite allowable to say
that time spent in the search for them will not be wasted, even
if the result of the search should prove to be that no answer

---

* If the reasoning in this chapter is correct it leads to the conclusion that
unless there is a Power outside of man that can and does tell him what he
ought to do, and why he ought to do it, he can have no rule of conduct but such
as may be based on expediency, depending on "pleasure and pain." This
expediency must be a very poor guide, because man's knowledge as to what
really is expedient is, as yet, so very imperfect.

can be found. Very few indeed altogether fail in getting some kind of answer—enough, at all events, to convince them that there *is* still a real region of mystery that cannot be brought into the domain of the senses and the reason; while any one that succeeded in finding a satisfactory answer to the question, "What ought a man to do, and why should he do it?"—one that would serve as a useful and trustworthy guide—would surely find that the time taken up in seeking it had been uncommonly well spent.

*Though no Answer to our main Question can be inferred from the Nature of Man himself, the Study of it yields many good practical Rules.*

It may be added that, though it seems to be impossible from a consideration of the nature of man himself or of the world around him to obtain the general answer required, it is quite possible by this means to frame useful though very imperfect sets of rules on the subject of conduct. This chapter, and the book itself, may fitly conclude with five selected rules that can be applied to a great number of the cases in daily life in which such rules are needed. These are,—

I. Conduct approved by all men at all times and in all places is good.

II. The conduct of an individual which would produce evil results if it were imitated by everybody is wrong.

III. The conduct of an individual which can give him pleasure only by causing corresponding pain to others is wrong.

IV. Conduct that is wrong when the individual is affected by it is also wrong when the State is affected by it.

V. The judgment of a man's *real* peers is his best available human standard of conduct in cases which seem doubtful and difficult to him, but are thoroughly understood by them.

Few, perhaps, could act in accordance with these rules under all circumstances, but it would be well for the State if all of us could be induced to try to do so.

# INDEX.

# INDEX.

By Authority: GEORGE DIDSBURY, Government Printer, Wellington.